"Tidy, swift entertainment. . . . [Rei Shimura] stands out as one of the most appealing characters in an ongoing series."
　　　　　　　　　　　　　　　　　—*Richmond Times-Dispatch*

"As usual, Massey is masterful at contrasting American and Japanese cultures and customs, but Rei remains the glue that holds this delightful series together."　　　　　　　—*Booklist*

"Massey is at her witty best in this latest caper, with surprising and charming takes on everyone from Asian culture to the high-stakes world of looted antiques. . . . Massey is truly a master of her craft."　　　　　　　　　　　　　　—*Asian Journal*

"Massey gleefully contrasts the young, bizarrely garbed generation, including Rei's own cousin, Chika, and Takeo's fiancée, Emi, with traditional Japanese society. Rei winds up with a badly bruised heart, but the ending hints at intriguing future possiblities."
　　　　　　　　　　　　　　　　　　—*Publishers Weekly*

"Most enjoyable."　　　　　　　　　　　　—*Baltimore Sun*

"Massey makes good use of the clash between American and Japanese cultures as a backdrop for an enjoyable story. . . . Entertaining."　　　　　　　　　　—*Chicago Sun-Times*

"Sujata Massey's latest whodunit has it all—great plot, exotic settings, and a mature protagonist."　　　—*India Abroad* magazine

"The Japanese-American antiques dealer who can't stay out of trouble has just celebrated her thirtieth birthday and is ready to raise some more hell."　　　　　　　　—*Chicago Tribune*

"A pleasure. Massey's skills as a writer give us palpable settings and deliver an intricate story. . . . Holds the reader captive from the first page."　　　　　　　　　　—*Crime Spree* magazine

Jim Burger

About the Author

SUJATA MASSEY was a reporter for the *Baltimore Evening Sun,* and spent several years in Japan teaching English and studying Japanese. She is the author of *The Salaryman's Wife, Zen Attitude, The Flower Master, The Floating Girl, The Bride's Kimono, The Samurai's Daughter,* and *The Pearl Diver.*

Also by Sujata Massey

The Pearl Diver
The Samurai's Daughter
The Bride's Kimono
The Floating Girl
The Flower Master
Zen Attitude
The Salaryman's Wife

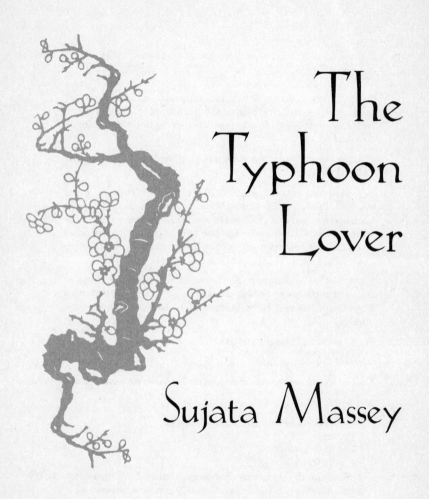

The Typhoon Lover

Sujata Massey

HARPER

NEW YORK • LONDON • TORONTO • SYDNEY

HARPER

A hardcover edition of this book was published in 2005 by Harper-Collins Publishers.

FIRST HARPER PAPERBACK PUBLISHED 2006.

Designed by Nancy B. Field

The Library of Congress has catalogued the hardcover edition as follows:

Massey, Sujata.

    The typhoon lover / Sujata Massey.—1st ed.
      p. cm.
    ISBN-10: 0-06-076512-7
    ISBN-13: 978-0-06-076512-5
    1. Shimura, Rei (Fictitious character)—Fiction. 2. Women detectives—Washington (D.C.)—Fiction. 3. Japanese Americans—Fiction. 4. Washington (D.C.)—Fiction. 5. Antique dealers—Fiction. 6. Tokyo (Japan)—Fiction. I. Title.
    PS3563.A79965T97 2005
    813'.54—dc22   2005046374

ISBN-10: 0-06-076513-5 (pbk.)
ISBN-13: 978-0-06-076513-2 (pbk.)

06 07 08 09 10 ❖/RRD 10 9 8 7 6 5 4 3

Acknowledgments

The Typhoon Lover owes its existence to many helpful people on both sides of the Pacific. The things that I've done right are because of them; all mistakes are my own.

I am indebted to my Sisters in Crime writers' group of nine years: Marcia Talley, John Mann, Karen Diegmuller, and Janice McLane. The staff at the Smithsonian Institution's Sackler Museum was amazing, especially the curators Louise Cort and Ann Gunter, its former public relations director Barbara Kramm, and Sarah Rodman of the Air and Space Museum. And with regard to the realities of modern espionage, I am grateful to the retired CIA analyst Rob Krespi for vetting the manuscript. I also salute the people who keep my spirits up with excellent coffee and conversation: Mike Sproge, Glen Breining, and the entire crew at the Evergreen coffeehouse, and the Baltimore intelligentsia who inhabit it (you know who you are).

In Japan, I give my deepest bows to Satoshi Mizushima, an English teacher at the Japanese Self Defense Forces School in Taura who carefully checked my Japanese; Chris Belton, an established Japan hand and great writer, for details of geography; Hidetomo Hirayama for the music; and my former neighbor Mihoko Morikawa, for the walk along the Hayama beach road. To William Morgan, Peter Vanburen, and Gentry Smith at the United States Embassy in Tokyo, thank you for welcoming me at a time of increased tension and for answering my many questions about how things are done to help Americans in trouble abroad. I also raise a glass to my dear friend and mentor, John Adair, Jr., owner of Kurofune Antiques in Roppongi, who continues to teach me about Japanese antiques. At the Grand Hyatt Tokyo, I thank Mark Kobayashi and Chisato Yagi for the tour. Yohei Omori, Waseda University alumnus, was a great tour guide to the campus and so helpful in many other ways.

This book was written during the year that my husband, Tony Massey, was mobilized by the Navy Reserve and left our home to serve with the Navy's Medical Corps. Despite the stress of his new job and cramped living quarters, Tony took charge of our children so I could return for a while to do research in Tokyo. I couldn't have done it without him—whether in uniform or not, Tony will always be my Navy hero.

Finally, there are the many good souls at HarperCollins who ferried this book from manuscript to print, and I thank you all. I remain in awe of my longtime editor and friend, Carolyn Marino; her able assistant, Jennifer Civiletto; and the publicity, art, and marketing departments. At Inkwell Management, the encouragement of my agent Kim Witherspoon and David Forrer made writing this book almost easy. *Arigato gozaimasu*, everyone!

Cast of Characters

REI SHIMURA: Japanese-American antiques dealer and woman-about-town.

HUGH GLENDINNING: a lawyer from Scotland currently working for a firm in Washington, D.C.

KENDALL HOWARD JOHNSON: Rei's socially and politically connected cousin.

GLASWEGIAN HANGOVER: a British band with buzz, featuring Hugh's brother, Angus Glendinning, and Angus's friends Sridhar, Keiffer, and Nate.

CHIKA SHIMURA: Rei's footloose first cousin, the daughter of Rei's aunt Norie and uncle Hiroshi Shimura, who live in Yokohama. Chika's older brother, Tom "Tsutomu" Shimura, works at St. Luke's Hospital in Tokyo.

MICHAEL HENDRICKS: rising star at the State Department's Japan desk.

YUKIO WATANABE, code name ITO: the consul of the Japanese embassy in Washington, D.C.

BRENDA MARTIN: colonel in the U.S. Army.

HARP SNOWDEN: a senator from California.

RICHARD RANDALL: Rei's former roommate, a Canadian teacher of English.

SIMONE: a friend of Rei's living in Tokyo who teaches French.

TAKEO KAYAMA, code name FLOWERS: Rei's former boyfriend, now head of the Kayama School of Ikebana.

EMI HARADA, code name THE BRIDE: eighteen-year-old daughter of Kenichi Harada, minister for the environment (alias Harmony), and his wife, Yasuko.

FUMIKO NAGASA: Emi's friend.

KAZU SAKURAI: celebrated potter; a Living National Treasure, who is married to Nobuko.

ALI and OSMAN BIRAND, code names BROTHER A and BROTHER B: brothers and partners in an antiques business based in Istanbul. Ali is single. Osman is the father of a son, Ramzi, code name Robert.

Plus a motley crew of students, fishmongers, cops, cabbies, club kids, and others who make a trip to Tokyo the ultimate experience.

The Typhoon Lover

1

I've never thought of myself as the blindfold type.

Not on planes, not in beds, and certainly not in restaurants. Especially not a place like DC Coast, where I was sitting on the evening of my thirtieth birthday, listening to my dinner companion trying his best to be persuasive.

"What happens next will be very special." Hugh said, picking up the small black mask that he'd placed next to our shared dessert. "You don't have to put the blindfold on inside here. Just a little later."

"You promised no party," I reminded him, but not sharply. My stomach was filled with a pleasant mélange of tuna tartare and crawfish risotto and crispy fried bass. It had been an orgy of seafood and good wine, just my kind of night.

"Hmm," Hugh said, studying the restaurant bill.

"If it's not a surprise party, where are you taking me?" I prodded.

"Let's just say I've got two tickets to paradise."

I rolled my eyes, thinking Hugh was showing his age, when I'd rather keep mine confidential. I didn't mind having a delicious, leisurely dinner, but he'd practically rushed me through cappuccino and crème brûlée. Hugh was frantic to leave, making me think he definitely had something planned.

As we waited for the car to be brought to us on the busy corner of Fourteenth and K streets, Hugh folded the tiny black blindfold into my hand. "It's never been used, if that makes you more comfortable. I saved it from my last trip to Zurich."

"I thought you didn't believe in regifting?" I asked lightly.

"Well, you didn't want a ring. What else can I offer you?" The undercurrent of irritation in Hugh's voice was clear. I'd worn his beautiful two-carat emerald for a short while, but ultimately returned it, because engagement rings scared me just as much as turning thirty did. Hugh was thirty-five; he'd been ready for the last three years. I wondered if I'd ever be.

The valet pulled up with the car and jumped out to open the passenger side for me. I got in, feeling a mixture of excitement and fear about what lay ahead. As we pulled off into traffic, I reclined my seat as far as it would go, hoping that this way, nobody would notice the woman with short black hair and a matching mask over her eyes. Anyone who caught a glimpse might think I'd just come out of plastic surgery or something like that—though most Washington women who went in for that flew to Latin America, where the plastic surgeons were good and there were no neighbors to bump into.

"Are we headed for the airport?" I asked, with a sudden rush of hope.

"No chance." Hugh sounded regretful. "It would have been fun to get away, but I can't risk any absences when the partner-track decisions are forthcoming."

Hugh was a lawyer at a high-pressure international firm a few blocks away. He'd been working for the last year on a class action suit that still wasn't ready to roll. His work involved frequent travel back to Japan, the country of my heritage, where we'd met a few years earlier. I would have loved to travel with him, but I couldn't, because I was banned from Japan. It was a complicated story that I didn't want to revisit on a night when I was supposed to be happy.

"Don't think about it," I muttered to myself. It was my habit to talk to myself sometimes, to try to shut out the bad thoughts that threatened what was a perfectly pleasant life.

"What don't you want to think about?"

"I'm getting nauseated from wearing a blindfold in a moving car," I said. "Not to mention that my nerves are shot because you won't tell me what's going to happen next."

"Oh, I'm sorry. Just hang on, I'll open the window." Hugh pressed the control that slid down the passenger-side window next to me. "We're just going around the corner to park. Will you survive another two minutes?"

I nodded, glad for a chance to listen to the sounds of the road. I could tell this wasn't our neighborhood, Adams-Morgan, with its mix of pulsating salsa music, honking horns, and shouting truck drivers. All I heard was a slow, steady purr of cars caught in traffic. After a while, the car moved again and turned a corner. Then it stopped. Hugh's window slid down.

"Paradise, sir?" A strange man's voice asked.

"That's right. We're staying till the wee morning hours," Hugh said. "Will this cover it?"

Before the parking valet could answer, I had a few words of my own. "Hugh, you *know* that I have a nine-thirty meeting at the Sackler Gallery tomorrow. You can very well stay until the wee hours, but I can't."

"Job interviews come and go. Thirtieth birthdays are only once!" He sounded positively gleeful.

My door was opened, and I unbuckled my seat belt. Then I felt a hand on my wrist, helping me out.

"You must be the girl getting the big birthday surprise." The valet's voice came from somewhere to the left.

I was busy working through the situation—was this a boutique hotel, maybe?—when Hugh tugged my hand. "There's going to be a downward flight of steps in a moment. Just take it slowly."

"What kind of a hotel has subterranean rooms?" I demanded.

"You'll know soon enough." Ten steps, and then a flat surface. "I'm going to hold the door open. Just step through."

I had no sight, but my other senses were bombarded. First, the sounds—"Japanese Girls," an Eels song pounding ominously, and lots of voices: talking, laughing, shrieking. Then there were the smells—smoke from cigarettes and sandalwood incense.

Someone took my other hand and pressed briefly down on the area over my knuckles. I guessed that I was getting a hand-stamp, the way bouncers did at bars.

"Hugh, this is so silly," I complained. "I want to see where I am.

If this is the S and M club we read about in *City Paper* I'm not going any farther."

Hugh sighed and said, "I'd hoped you'd stay blindfolded until the magic moment, but if you're that anxious, you may as well take it off. Go ahead."

Had I known of the series of events about to unfold—not this night, but in the crazy, dangerous days that rolled out, right after my birthday—I might have just kept the blindfold on. I would have remained in Hugh's thrall, powerless to make my own choices, but secure—still twenty-nine and safe as houses.

But I'm not the kind of girl who stays in one place for long, whether it's a city or a nightclub vestibule.

I slid off the blindfold, and opened my eyes.

2

The club was packed as tightly as Tokyo's Cube 326 on a good night—impressive for a live venue rather than a DJ club. I had never been inside a place in Washington this crowded and smoky. Wasn't there a no-smoking law in Washington clubs now? I wondered about it as I scanned the crowd, looking for familiar faces.

"Is that Kendall?" I asked Hugh, pointing to a slender redhead in a black leather jacket who looked like my married cousin from Potomac, but who was embracing a handsome younger man with a goatee.

"Yes, I gather she brought a toyboy from her office. But there's an even better spectacle right ahead." Hugh touched my shoulders and turned me so that I was facing the other side of the room. A stage was set up with a drum set and keyboards and microphones. Above it was a banner that said in glittering silver letters, HAPPY DIRTY THIRTY, REI!

I looked from it to Hugh. "You promised you wouldn't throw a surprise party."

He raised his eyebrows. "But I told you I was taking you to Paradise."

Suddenly I got it. This unfamiliar nightclub was probably a hot new music venue on U Street. I was amazed Hugh had been able to book it on a Friday night for something as inconsequential as my thirtieth birthday party.

I asked, "Is this Club Paradise?"

"Yes, isn't it brilliant?" He squeezed my hand back. "I had to keep the newspaper away from you all week so you wouldn't catch wind of what was going on." Hugh looked very pleased with himself.

"But I must know only a fraction of the people here."

"Andrea, Kendall, and I shared the invites. There are about a hundred fifty of our crowd here. The others, well, they've all paid to get in and that helps make up the cost of booking the space. I'm sure they'll be your friends by night's end—" As he spoke, he was putting a small glittering tiara on my head.

"People would pay to come to my birthday?" I was becoming even more confused as Andrea, a beautiful but moody restaurant hostess who'd become a good friend recently, came over to deliver some air kisses.

"Happy birthday, Rei," she said. "I'm going to handle the door and make sure nobody gets in on the guest list who should be paying."

Kendall bounced up and gave me a kiss on the lips that tasted like a Cosmopolitan. "Happy dirty thirty, dear. You know, I tried to talk Hugh into staving your thirtieth off for a few more years, but he wouldn't listen. Men!"

"What do you mean? She's thirty tomorrow." Andrea looked at Kendall as if she thought my cousin, who loved to brag about her M.B.A., couldn't count.

"A lot of girls don't publicly celebrate thirty until they're a little bit older, like thirty-five. Some of my friends from boarding school are going to do that, and I'm trying to decide whether I can carry it off. What do you think?" As Kendall spoke, she was twinkling at the young man she'd draped herself over before.

"It looks like some of your friends are here," I said, not wanting to answer her question. "You'll have to introduce me."

"Hugh let me bring about seventy-five of my nearest and dearest. They're so excited about the show, just thrilled once I explained about—"

"Watch it, Kendall," Hugh said warningly.

"Hugh, I never! George is just my intern, okay?"

"I'm sure he meant about the show, Kendall, not your toyboy—"

I bit my lip. The Viognier I'd had at the restaurant had made me too loose.

"Let's get some drinks," Hugh suggested. "Then I've got to dash up there, get the emcee thing started. We're half an hour behind schedule."

As Hugh brought each of us a drink and then wound his way through the crowd to the stage, I watched Kendall's pretty girl-friends in their preppy prints and Hugh's lawyer friends in suits begin to circle each other. Around them were many more young people in black leather and heavy metal, as well as fashionable young men with shaved heads and guayabera shirts, and girls with ironed hair and thigh-high boots. Now I understood why Hugh had been so obstinate about my clothes for the evening.

I was wearing a favorite pair of black shorts with a vintage Adolfo jacket in purple and black bouclé. Underneath the jacket was a purple camisole that barely grazed my navel, which glinted with a couple of pearls—a recent body alteration about which I had mixed feelings. Because I didn't want to be taken for a hooker, I'd insisted on mid-heel sandals rather than the Manolo Blahnik stilet-tos Hugh had given me that morning. Now I was sorry I hadn't worn the Blahniks, but overall, I was well dressed for the setting.

"Come on." Kendall took my hand in hers. "Let's get close to the stage so you'll be right there for everyone to see when Hugh makes a personal tribute."

"Kendall, I don't know anyone! I hardly want to be embarrassed in front of hundreds." I was being so Japanese, I thought while Kendall resolutely dragged me close to the stage. She was from my American side—my mother's old Maryland family. I couldn't be-lieve she was so enthusiastic about Club Paradise. She was no stranger to the bars at Zola or Zaytinya, but this place was consid-erably more downscale than her usual party haunts.

Hugh placed his whisky glass on a speaker and picked up a mi-crophone. The raggedy buzz of noise faded as he greeted everyone in the suave Edinburgh-goes-to-London-and-next-flies-to-America accent that made Americans swoon. What was it about the British accent that made everything sound smarter? It was similar to the effect of a Japanese accent, which made everything sound sweeter.

Hugh said how pleased he was at the turnout for the birthday celebration for someone known to readers of the *City Paper* as the current "Most Notorious Woman under Thirty."

"Rei's the first girl who's made the listing without sleeping with a politician, and for that, I'm enormously grateful," he said as a spotlight suddenly found me in the crowd. I waved reluctantly, because to hide behind Kendall would be pathetic. The people in the crowd were grinning at me now. A cocktail waitress with a nose ring pressed a *mojito* into my hand, and—ignoring all the warnings I'd heard about taking drinks from strangers—I sipped it, glad for something to do while the roasting continued.

"Now, when Rei and I met, she thought we had nothing in common until I lured her into my car to listen to my collection of eighties and nineties tunes. To make her birthday really special, I wanted to bring her that music she loves."

If a band was the focus, the spotlight would move from me. Great!

"Knowing Rei's taste, I aimed my sights at the European bands. I tried for Echo and the Bunnymen, but unfortunately, that lot are playing a show in London tonight." A chorus of groans. Apparently Echo wasn't a big favorite here. "Next I went for Bjork, but she's undergoing a crisis of fashion confidence and won't leave the house." There was some light laughter. "Massive Attack are recording the score for the next Lexus car commercial, and Garbage said they have to put out their recycling tonight."

There were more groans and a call from the back of the room, "Get on with it!" Hugh refused to be rushed. He took a sip of whisky and said, "I began to think there was some kind of bad star hanging over the night that Rei was born, but in the end, the answer was right before my nose. It's a mystery band, an up-and-coming British group that had its video premiere on VH1 last month, and made it into the British equivalent of Billboard's listings. They're touring the country, and this is their only stop in Washington. They turned down the bloody 9:30 Club to be here with us tonight!"

There was sharp applause at that, and I began to feel the hairs on my arm prickle. There was only one band that I knew Hugh was close to, and that was his brother Angus's group, Glaswegian Hangover, which was making a ragtag tour on the west coast at present.

"So, without further ado, let me introduce a band with true grit and originality. Yes, the band you've been waiting for . . . Angus Glendinning and the Glaswegian Hangover!"

The lights started flashing, and the band took the stage. I screamed with the others because I hadn't seen Hugh's younger, guitar-strumming brother in three years. The twenty-year-old who'd slouched around Tokyo with auburn dreadlocks had shaved them off so only a thin auburn halo edged his head. He wore a black T-shirt studded with rivets and tight blue jeans tucked into motorcycle boots.

The crowd howled as Angus picked up his guitar and lashed into an old Beatles song, "Happy Birthday," with a few new lyrics that made me blush. He followed it with a song that I'd heard him working on in Japan, all discordant clanging, but with new lyrics about being dragged into a war by an older brother he'd once loved but now hated with every ounce of his being. I would have liked Hugh's take on the lyrics, but he was back at the bar, grooving to the music while he waited for another drink.

I checked out the rest of the band. On bagpipes was a mournful-looking blond wearing a denim jacket and kilt with combat boots. An Indian-looking guy in a Manchester United football jersey was lost in the rhythms of the drums. There was a black bass player dressed in a battered leather jacket and jeans. All they needed was a Japanese to complete their United Nations, but I wasn't volunteering.

The band finished the song with a defiant upward-climbing riff and then Angus took a sip from a bottle that a fan thrust up at him. "Thanks, love. And thanks to Shug for organizing the venue and, what's that, a free round of McEwan's for all? Brilliant!"

Half the crowd surged toward the bar, wanting to take advantage of the beer. The die-hards who stayed at the stage started screaming names of songs they wanted to hear. "Methadone Morning!" "On the Train!" "Bleeding Heart Liberal!" I realized that the band's CD must have aired on more than a few college stations. The Glaswegian Hangover were semifamous.

"We'd love to get the jam going with a few songs off our new disc, *Liberal Elitist*. This song's called 'Pudding' 'cause it's unhealthy, which is the way we like it." Angus's accent was affected Glasgow working-class, which probably was crucial if your band was called Glaswegian Hangover. "We'll be playing our new songs mixed in with Rei's birthday track. Oh, and Shug—that's me brother, right?—wants me to let everybody know that our celebrity guest has arrived and will be appearing onstage shortly."

"Who is it?" I called out.

Angus shook his head. "Don't know exactly, but it's supposed to be a Japanese celeb. So don't go awaaayyy!" He launched into "Pudding" with a crash of guitar strings.

I wondered who the musician might be as I started dancing with Hugh, who had suddenly showed up and grabbed me around the waist. I had trouble keeping my balance, given the two *mojitos* I'd downed in the last half hour. Hugh moved behind me as the band slowly segued from its song about a Scottish school dinner gone wrong into the Grandmaster Flash classic, "White Lines." I was quickly wrapped up in the beat and the feeling of Hugh's body behind mine—finally, Hugh had to physically direct my attention to the stage, where I saw the Japanese guest: a young woman in a gold leather skirt, white go-go boots, and a white halter top. A curtain of perfectly streaked hair—gold and black—hung before her face, and when the hair flashed back, I saw my twenty-two-year-old cousin Chika's face.

"Chika!" I screamed in delight.

"I gave her my frequent-flier miles!" Hugh shouted in my ear. "She didn't want to miss your birthday!"

I turned and hugged him. "So she's staying with us!"

"Yes, she'll come back with us tonight. And I hope you don't mind, but the, ah, band will be with staying over, too."

"But where?" I knew I should be accommodating, but I felt a frisson of annoyance. Every week, it seemed, Hugh invited at least one or two overnight guests. Whether they were lawyers from his office having wife trouble, rugby players who'd been served eviction notices, or drinking buddies from Adams-Morgan who'd had one too many, Hugh unfailingly brought them home. He liked company. Hell, he'd been keeping me in his apartment, on and off, for years.

"Any free bit of floor," Hugh shouted again to make himself

heard over the din. "The lads are accustomed to bunking in bus stations and bathtubs. And they'll only be here a couple of days. It's not going to be like when Angus stayed for months in Tokyo."

"Hope not." I winked at Hugh, because I was actually fond of his hard-living brother. I turned back to the stage to admire my cousin Chika dancing in her high-heeled boots. Almost mechanically, she moved her arms and turned her hips, a robot-like contrast to the wild and woolly band, and the flailing bodies in the mosh pit in front of the stage.

"Chika's too cute," Kendall shouted in my ear as she danced by me. "Find out where she bought those boots."

"I'll ask!" I was overflowing with so much happiness that I wasn't shy anymore. My head felt light and my body full of rhythm as I jogged up onstage to join my cousin. We embraced, and before I knew it, Angus had grabbed us both in a pelvis-grinding hug. Chika pulled away, obviously startled by the bald white boy, and the audience roared.

Angus launched into my favorite 1980s classic, "Lips Like Sugar." As Chika and I started to dance together, I gazed over the mosh pit and into the crowd. All the way from the bar, I saw Hugh smile at me and raise a McEwan's in salute.

Kendall had commandeered some male friends to boost her from the mosh pit to the stage, and the next instant she was dancing alongside Chika and me. I wasn't surprised; Kendall was the most competitive woman I knew. She wasn't one to stay out of the limelight for long.

I danced between my cousins, thinking about my Japanese past on one side, and the American future on the other. I was shot through with joy, not caring that my Lycra top was inching upward, revealing the navel ring glinting in the spotlight. Chika was performing a careful series of steps, and Kendall was unzipping her black leather jacket and, now, pulling off her T-shirt.

Her T-shirt? I took a second look. Kendall, seemingly delighted by the catcalls of the audience, was wearing only a red lace bra and jeans. I glanced at Chika, who looked unimpressed, probably because girls in Japan had been disrobing on nightclub stages for years. Now I glanced back over the bobbing heads on the dance floor, looking for Hugh. He wasn't at the bar. He was probably close to the stage, getting a bird's-eye view of Kendall's cosmetic enhancements. That's what they had to be. We'd shared an outdoor shower during a beach vacation in college, and she'd been much smaller. Although maybe I was being unfair—could the breasts be a result of childbirth?

The crowd was screaming for me and Chika to take it off, too, and I felt a twinge of nervousness. I'd brought it on myself, I knew, but suddenly I felt that my navel ring was more than I wished anyone had seen.

"I'm stepping down!" I shouted to Chika as "Lips Like Sugar" drew to a close.

"Okay, I'll come along," she shouted back. "That girl is crazy!"

After we made it offstage, Chika asked me where we could get water. I was parched, too. I glanced back and saw that Kendall had started working on the top button of her jeans.

"Where's Hugh-san? I'd like to say hello to him—he was so kind to give me the ticket. Business class, even!" Chika's happy chatter brought me back to the reality that I was with her, and life wasn't as out of control as I'd feared.

"The last place I saw Hugh was the bar," I said, leading my cousin along. But he wasn't there. After Chika and I each bought a bottle of water, we threaded through the crowd to the back, where Andrea was standing at the door, checking names against a guest list. She was being very hard-hearted with a group of Georgetown students who were claiming they should be on the guest list.

"But I know Rei," one of them was saying. "She's, like, my best friend."

"Do you know this girl?" Andrea, her arms folded over a skintight "Power to the People" T-shirt, appeared ready to grind the girl under the her six-inch boot heels.

"Sure. Let them all in. Hey, have you seen Hugh?"

"Last time I saw him he was buying drinks for all his rugby friends. Are you loving your party?"

"Very much so," I said, and gave Andrea a quick hug before going back into the depths of the club.

"Is that Hugh-san?" Chika tugged my hand and I followed her

down a hall lit only by a sign for an emergency exit. There, one of the suits was vomiting over a trash can.

"Oh, no!" I said, because I recognized the suit. It was Hugh's.

"What did he eat for dinner?" Chika asked in a horrified voice.

"I don't think it was the dinner." I'd tried everything Hugh had eaten, and the restaurant had an impeccable reputation. Hugh must have been done in by the bottle of wine chased by whisky followed by the lager. It wasn't really his fault—he'd once been able to drink like that and hold his ground, but now he was thirty-two. Perhaps his metabolism had changed—as mine would, too.

I sent Chika into the ladies' room to bring back both wet and dry paper towels, while I helped Hugh through the end of his agony.

"Sorry," he said, sounding weaker than I'd ever heard.

"Don't be." I stroked back his hair, examining him. The charming Scot who'd toasted me with champagne a few hours earlier had been replaced by a red-eyed stand-in who had almost lost his accent. It was getting exhausting, living like this. Just two nights before that he'd gotten sick after a dinner party in Kalorama. I reminded myself that this was the same man who'd loved me enough to let me live in his apartment, who hauled antiques without complaint, who made a pot of tea for me every morning.

"I'm missing a great show, aren't I?" he asked, sounding pitiful.

"Angus and the band are amazing," I said. "But you'll hear them again."

"Yes. He's coming home with us." Hugh sat down on the floor, his back against the wall for support.

"That's right, but a little later on. I'll figure everything out. We'll have to take a taxi home, because I can't drive either."

"Don't take me home," he said. "You're having a—grand time— a birthday time—"

I shook my head. "Staying here doesn't matter. I'm as trashed as you are, practically. I'm beat."

It was true. Three years earlier, I would have stayed the whole night. But now I just felt exhausted.

My twenties were over. Thirty had already taken a very dirty toll.

3

The claim I'd made about a morning meeting had been all too true. I woke up at eight-fifteen with a pounding headache, knowing that I had to be at the Smithsonian within seventy-five minutes.

I dragged myself into the bathroom, where Hugh was sleeping in the tub. I pulled the shower curtain to give myself privacy while I used the facilities. I would have loved a shower, but it wasn't worth drowning Hugh.

I felt bad that he'd slept there. But he'd been sleepy enough to drop anywhere, and the spare bedroom and living room were filled not only with Angus's bandmates but with two roadies as well. In the bedroom I usually shared with Hugh, I'd placed Chika, who was still sleeping facedown in her tiny chemise. Before I'd gone into the bathroom, I pulled the sheet over her, just in case anyone stumbled into the room. I also wrote DO NOT DISTURB! on a Glaswegian Hangover flyer and taped it to the door.

How my head hurt! I would never drink like that again. I'd recklessly chased one glass of wine with another at dinner, then spent the rest of the night slamming down hard liquor. The evidence was all over the place—red pupils, triple creases under the eyes, and a greenish tint to my skin.

After gulping down two Aleve tablets and patting on a bit of makeup, I dressed in dark blue Donna Karan suit handed down from my mother, which I'd laid out the day before. I had a bit of panic when I couldn't find my panty hose, but they turned out to be on my dresser, coiled underneath a potted bonsai tree—yet another birthday gift that had appeared in the foyer the night before. I lifted the pot up and gingerly pulled out the stockings, praying they hadn't been torn. They were fine. I took this as a good omen—the only thing, maybe, that I had going for me on such a challenging morning.

I wasn't quite sure how the Sackler had located me, because I hadn't applied for any job there except for a college internship that never happened. Of course, I sent out résumés all the time, so when a brisk-sounding woman had called the week before, asking me to come to discuss a potential consulting job, I'd immediately said yes. Any offer of steady employment would be fantastic, given that I'd finished a big restaurant decorating project and was at loose ends.

I stepped into the Bally alligator pumps I'd gotten at the San Francisco Opera thrift shop the last time I'd been home, visiting my parents. Then I returned to the bathroom to bring Hugh clothes for his own workday.

"Who bashed in my head?" he muttered.

"You did it to yourself," I said, then relented. "You must feel awful. And I'm sorry we put you in the tub last night to sleep, but I needed a bed for Chika—she's sleeping in our room right now, so I brought you some clothes."

"Oh." He yawned. "Where are you going so early in the morning?"

"It's already eight-forty and I have that meeting at the Smithsonian in less than an hour."

"Sorry about last night." He sighed. "And I—lost it, didn't I? You saw me at my worst."

"You've seen me sick, too." But compared with him, I was the picture of blooming health. "It was a wild night. Parts of it were wonderful."

"I swear that I just had a whisky and a lager or two—"

"You also had a half-bottle of wine and a glass of champagne at the restaurant." I began brushing my teeth at the bathroom sink.

"Right. We drove from there— My car! Where is it?"

"I'm sure it's still wherever the valets put it yesterday evening. I can swing by after my meeting to retrieve it."

"No, no, I'll do it. I'll take care of it today. That shall be my penance," Hugh said darkly.

It was a twenty-minute walk to Dupont Circle, plenty of time to get the blood moving. I had a skim latte with four sugars in hand that I'd carried out from Urban Grounds. I'd have to finish drinking it before I entered the Metro, which had a strict prohibition against food and drink. As I sipped, I considered the situation ahead of me. I'd have to present myself to strangers, without knowing what they were after. But they had thought enough of me to seek me out. That was something I could cling to, with hope.

I regretfully tossed my half-full coffee and boarded the train. I held my bag closely against me, protecting it from the crush of people. Inside the bag were two different résumés. The first one presented my work as an antiques buyer; it focused on freelance work I'd done for a restaurant in Washington and private clients in Tokyo. The second résumé made me look more like a scholar—citing a sale that I'd made years ago to a folk craft museum and the writing I'd published about a historic collection of Japanese flower-arranging vessels. There were a few flamboyant successes on both résumés, but sadly, no evidence of a real job anywhere. The longest job that I'd had since getting my master's degree was working as an English teacher in Japan, and that, I sensed, was totally unrelated to anything the Smithsonian might want me for.

I hopped out at Gallery Place–Chinatown, but instead of turning toward the restaurant district as I did for my last job, I walked the few long blocks to the Mall. The sun had broken out at last. It was a day on which, if I hadn't had a headache, I might have jogged to the gym where Hugh and I shared a membership. I'd become addicted to gym classes, especially the ones that featured weight lifting, yoga, and ballet. It sounded like over-the-top fusion cooking, but I was happy with the new, sinewy muscles that had emerged in my arms and shoulders. Hugh said the best part of it was that I could now move heavy furniture without his help.

Well, today wasn't a weight-lifting day, but at least my posture was better than it used to be. I sucked in my abdominals a touch as

I passed the majestic, redbrick Gothic castle that housed the Smith-sonian's administrative offices, and kept them in place as I entered the circular glass atrium entrance of the Freer Museum's Ripley Center, which led in turn to the Sackler Gallery, a few flights down.

I'd sworn I wasn't going to look around, but I had to pause for a second glance at an impressive art installation right inside the en-trance. A modern Chinese artist had dredged up the hull of an old wooden Japanese fishing boat and perched it atop thousands of pieces of broken white porcelain cups and saucers. A boat afloat on china; I loved the metaphor, but cringed at the thought of all the pottery smashing that had gone on.

"Ma'am? The museum doesn't open until ten."

The security guard who'd been at the desk was suddenly at my side. I'd gotten too close to the artwork. I apologized and told the guard that I was a few minutes early for my appointment in the ad-ministrative offices with Michael Hendricks.

"We have nobody working in our museum with that name," she said, frowning at me again. "Are you sure he isn't a part-time volun-teer?"

"I don't think so." I scrambled through my bag for the paper where I'd written down the few details I'd been given. "A woman called me back as well. Her name is Elizabeth Cameron—"

"She's the ancient Near Eastern curator." The receptionist flipped through some papers. "She left a message about someone coming to a nine o'clock meeting."

"That might be me. My name is Rei Shimura." I felt uneasy, be-cause I didn't think ancient Near Eastern art was anything I could take a stab at. Also, the timing of the meeting was off. Michael Hen-dricks had said nine-thirty, or so I'd thought.

But it turned out that the security guard's message had my name on it, so she called another guard to escort me through the labyrinth of dimly lit galleries to the administrative section.

Not an auspicious start, I thought as we rode down the elevator to the second floor, where the administrative offices lay. I was stu-pid to have arrived late and without knowing more about why I was being interviewed. Perhaps they'd made a mistake calling me in. I knew about the art of the Far East, not the Near East or

Mesopotamia, as it used to be called. I would make that clear right away, I decided, and I'd be out the door fast—before nine-fifteen, probably. I would be able to make a ten o'clock Pilates class at the gym, if I hustled enough.

Huge double doors to the administrative section were locked, but the guard unlocked them for me. Right behind them there was someone waiting, a tall, slender African-American woman in her fifties. The green skirted uniform that she wore had silver oak leaves on the shoulders; her black name tag read simply "Martin."

"Are you Rei Shimura?" the woman officer asked.

I nodded, surprised that she not only knew my name but had pronounced it correctly. Rei rhymes with X-ray—which was what she seemed to be doing as she surveyed me all the way from my conservative pumps up to my bed-head hairstyle and bloodshot eyes. It seemed, from the tightness of her expression, that she could guess the kind of night I'd been through.

"You may come in, Miss Shimura. We're all here."

The guard departed and I followed the woman along a wide, carpeted hall and into a large room where a few people were sitting. The woman locked the door behind her, and I gulped.

I surveyed what lay before me: a windowless room decorated with a few framed posters from past exhibitions at the Sackler, and a huge film screen similar to the ones I remembered from college lecture halls. The room was filled with a long, teak table, a much larger table than was needed for the one woman and two men sitting at it. One of the men was a distinguished-looking, older Japanese; the other an athletically built man with hair cropped as closely as a soldier's. He was wearing what seemed to be the official D.C. uniform: a Brooks Brothers suit, the all-American label that Hugh, who wore only European designer suits, abhorred.

"Coffee?" The woman who had been seated at the table spoke to me gently, as if she realized I needed special handling. I nodded gratefully, even though I'd already had a huge dose of caffeine. As she moved to a coffeemaker set up on a side table, I checked her out—brunette pageboy hairstyle and a hip-length, hand-knit olive green sweater over a calf-length black skirt. Very artsy; perhaps she was the curator?

"Sugar? Cream? I'm Elizabeth Cameron, the one who called you." The woman confirmed my thoughts. "I'm so glad you could join us."

"I'll take both," I said. "And I'm glad to be here too." The last was a slight exaggeration, given the locked doors and serious faces. I knew that this was going to be like no interview I'd ever had before.

"I'm Michael Hendricks, from the Japan desk at State. Senator Snowden gave me your name." The guy in Brooks had taken the coffee from Elizabeth Cameron and handed it to me. He had an accent that I couldn't place, as clipped and correct as his military haircut. On second glance I realized that his hair, which I'd first thought was brown, was actually a salt-and-pepper mix of brown and silver. Men could gray prematurely and look fabulous, I thought sourly. At least, I thought it was premature graying. I couldn't guess his age at all, just as I couldn't make out the details of where he worked on the ID tag that hung from a chain around his neck. My eyes were simply too tired.

I turned from him to the Japanese-looking man, who was wearing a conservative dark blue suit. He was a guest here, too, I thought. I wasn't sure what to do until he bowed to me slightly; I bowed back more deeply. He smiled, and in that moment I knew I'd seen him somewhere. But my brain was too frazzled to make the connection.

I hesitated, holding my coffee, not wanting to be too presumptuous about my next movement—or any movement at all.

Michael Hendricks said, "We have a place set up for you on the other side." I tripped slightly in my awkwardness to get around the table.

"*Kiotsukute kudasai,*" the Japanese man said. *Be careful, please.*

"*Gomen nasai,*" I apologized back to him, then said in English to the others, "I'm a little uncoordinated," as I sat down gingerly on an unholstered chair.

"Oh, I don't think so. You danced pretty well last night." Michael Hendricks smiled easily. "I apologize for not introducing myself, but it was hard to get through the throng."

Could this be some game of Hugh's—a faux interview on the tail of a wild night? Was the military officer going to slide out of her uniform, any minute? Confusion washed over me. Carefully, I said, "I'm afraid I don't understand what this meeting's about."

"I'll start by introducing the remaining people. Now, you've spoken with Elizabeth on the phone already, I understand, and you just met Colonel Martin, who came in from Baghdad a few days ago to join us."

Brenda Martin nodded at me and sat down next to Hendricks as he continued his introductions.

"I'm grateful that Mr. Yukio Watanabe, the Japanese consul general, was able to take time away from his responsibilities at the embassy to join us." Michael paused. "Everything that we say must be kept confidential, Miss Shimura. Are you comfortable with that?"

Feeling flabbergasted by both the power of Mr. Watanabe and the demand being put on me, I said, "I could give you an answer if I knew what this was about."

"It's about considering you for a job," Michael Hendricks said.

"In that case, of course I'll maintain confidentiality. And I've brought my résumé." I extracted the résumé with the scholarly focus and slid it onto the table. Nobody picked it up. Feeling awkward again, I asked, "Does the job relate to Japanese art or antiques?"

"Not exactly." Michael Hendricks leaned back in his chair, studying me with eyes the color of a cold fall sky. "This mission involves ancient Near Eastern art. Even though this isn't an area you've worked in during the past, we believe you are qualified to handle this assignment."

"Dancing and all?" I thought I'd make a joke to relieve my nerves, but nobody smiled.

"I think we can all safely agree that dancing doesn't hurt anyone or anything. And now, we're running a few minutes late, so I'll get right to the presentation." As he spoke, I finally placed Michael's accent: eastern-educated—absent of slang and regional influences. He'd probably attended Andover, Exeter, or a similar northeastern boarding school.

The lights went out, and slowly the film screen at the end of the room lit up with the glow from a projector. REI SHIMURA BACK-

GROUND, the screen said. The words vanished and there was a photograph of me, a reproduced photo clipped from the Japanese newspaper *Asahi Shimbun*. I straightened up a little, because I'd always liked this shot, in which I appeared stunningly slender in an Azzedine Alaia dress a girlfriend had lent me to wear to a party at the Tokyo American Club. The Japanese paparazzi had snapped me because of a murder investigation I was peripherally involved in— something that had fortunately come out all right in the end.

"Rei Shimura lived in Japan from the age of twenty-four. Here she is outside the Tokyo American Club, a place where she once socialized with prominent expatriates like Joseph Roncolotta, who still runs a consulting business in Tokyo."

Next came a shot taken from the *Tokyo Weekender* party page: a picture of Joe Roncolotta lifting a beer at one of Tokyo's several German beer gardens, surrounded by Japanese businessmen. After that, the screen showed a picture of my antique-dealing mentor, Ishida-san, and then a picture of my Aunt Norie with a prizewinning flower arrangement that had appeared in the Kayama School of Ikebana newsletter. There was even a picture of me with Hugh, back in his days as a lawyer in Tokyo, leaving his old apartment building in Roppongi.

"May I say something?" I interjected. "My personal life really shouldn't be taken into account if this is about a job. It may even be illegal."

"Your personal life is what's *perfect*." Michael Hendricks's voice sounded almost reverent. "But don't worry, Hugh Glendinning is not of particular significance."

Hugh's image faded and was replaced by a new man's. It was another media snap, this one of Takeo Kayama emerging from the doorway of the Kayama School. Takeo, who had been my boyfriend a very long time ago, looked different. He still had the same knife-edge, elegant features, but the long, floppy, rock star hair was gone, cropped to a length perfect for business. He was wearing a long black trench coat open, flapping behind him, giving him the look of a bat. The coat, in fact, cut off half the face of the woman trailing behind him—a young woman, probably his sister.

"Now, here we have Takeo Kayama, the recently appointed

iemoto—that means headmaster, right, Mr. Watanabe?—of the Kayama School of Ikebana in Tokyo."

The outside details on the picture blurred as I focused on Takeo's expression, which seemed harder than I remembered. When I'd decided to return to Hugh, Takeo had been unpleasantly surprised—but I'd heard on the trans-Pacific grapevine that he'd quickly bounced back. Well, men always did, didn't they?

I listened as Mr. Watanabe, in careful English, described Takeo's life: the lonely childhood in a luxury apartment, his schooling at Tokyo University, and then the University of California at Davis, the building passion for environmentalism, and his brief passion for me. Or, as Mr. Watanabe put it politely, "the pleasant friendship with Shimura-san."

A shot of Takeo's country house flashed on the screen, and I felt a pang. I had spent a whole summer helping Takeo brighten old, stained walls to the colors of sea, sky, and garden. I loved that house, which had been built in the 1920s; it was one of the places I missed most in Japan. Takeo and I had been together at the house, ostensibly restoring it, but in truth spending almost as much time at the beach, or in bed. My friends had harangued me to invite them for a country weekend, but we'd never wanted company. Takeo and I had no need for anyone that summer.

"The friendship with Miss Shimura kindled Mr. Kayama's interest in antiques. Under her guidance, he began a study of Japanese antiques." As Mr. Watanabe spoke, the image on the screen changed to a photo that a paparazzo with a long lens had taken of us behind Takeo's beach house in Hayama. The two of us were lying close together, poring over a comic book. Now I looked at the image of my younger self and felt dismayed by how pin-thin my arms had been. Takeo hadn't minded, of course—one of his hands rested lightly on my Speedo bikini bottom. With a sudden rush, I remembered the things that Takeo and I had done, within the walls of that ancient, always empty house.

I tried to focus my attention back where it belonged. "That's a comic book we're reading, actually. I never taught him anything about antiques. He has no interest."

"Then why did he spend just over eighty thousand pounds on

Asian ceramics at Christies in London last year?" Michael Hendricks said, flipping to a photograph of a sales slip from Christies. "And just before that, ten million yen at Meiwashima Auction House in Tokyo."

"Really? I'd like to know what he bought." Ten million yen was about $100,000, and Meiwashima was a high-end auction house, a far cry from the country auctions I usually frequented. It had been a major effort for me to get a membership at Meiwashima, and once I was in, I realized I couldn't afford anything.

"Vessels," said Michael.

"Do you mean—like the boat upstairs in the atrium?" My eyes widened.

Michael shook his head, and looked as if he was trying not to laugh. "Containers. Mr. Kayama is after historic containers of all kinds—urns, bowls, vases, anything that could hold water and plant material."

"Oh, for *ikebana* purposes. Well, I'm glad he has a new hobby. Everyone should have a hobby." I felt embarrassed to have made the mistake. Of course I knew that ceramics with openings were called vessels—why hadn't I understood Michael the first time around?

"The problem is that the young headmaster's hobby may be illegal." Michael Hendricks cleared his throat. "Colonel, maybe it's time to give Rei the background on the situation with the National Museum in Iraq."

"I'm sure Miss Shimura has read accounts of the looting at the museum during the early stages of the war," Colonel Martin said. "Hundreds of civilians stormed the museum, grabbing whatever was nearby and looked valuable—mostly gold items from the closest open galleries. At the same time, many priceless treasures were actually hidden by the curators, who had anticipated the looting. But there was a third class of museum items that were probably taken by a few insiders who knew their worth. Within this category of missing items is a group of Mesopotamian vessels dating from approximately three thousand years ago." A grainy black-and-white slide flashed on the screen, showing a rustic pottery vessel shaped like a goat. Its long, curved horn made a handle, and there was room to pour something in at the tail, and then out at the goat's mouth.

"Our Iraqi colleagues at the museum called this the ibex ewer, because it's made in the form of an ibex—a wild goat native to the Mesopotamian area, which includes modern countries like Iraq, Iran, and Syria. The ewer vanished during the looting along with about three hundred other objects from the museum."

"What a shame," I said. For a country to lose its art was to lose its soul. Legend had it that the Americans had chosen not to bomb Kyoto during World War II because it was the center of Japan's high culture. But they'd bombed Tokyo plenty.

Next, a photo flashed on the screen of a round-faced man with thinning black hair. He was trudging toward an airplane with an oversize briefcase in one hand, looking every bit like a lawyer going to court.

"This is Osman Birand," Colonel Martin said. "A millionaire Turkish antiques dealer with a business in Istanbul. He's suspected to have dealt in antiquities stolen from mosques and museums throughout the Middle East. We believe that he may have been involved in brokering antiques stolen from the Royal Museum, but we have yet to find the evidence, and a buyer who'll testify, in order to charge him with anything."

The next picture: Osman Birand, without his briefcase and looking considerably more relaxed with a wineglass in hand, standing on a yacht with a taller, slimmer companion. The photo had been shot at dusk, so I couldn't see the details very well.

"Osman Birand had a party on his yacht in Hong Kong, just a few months ago. Takeo Kayama, pictured here, was one of his guests," Colonel Martin said.

I wasn't at all convinced that the fellow onboard was Takeo, and the situation didn't make sense. "Why was Takeo there?"

"Fund-raising for an organic flower-farming cooperative." The colonel raised her thin, arched brows. "He says he wants to apply the kibbutz prototype to help poor Arabs help themselves. Birand contributed the equivalent of twenty thousand dollars."

Organic flower farming did sound like Takeo, I admitted to myself as the image on the screen changed again, back to the country house. The headline over the magazine spread said "Seaside Beauty!" in the phonetic *katakana* script used for foreign words like these. It was true that the room was beautiful, and one could see the sea through the new, floor-to-ceiling glass windows that formed one wall of the old living room I remembered. When I'd last been in the house, it had been under renovation, so there was no furniture; now I saw it in its restored glory, filled with eclectic Japanese pieces from the early twentieth century, and other things that couldn't have come from Takeo's family: a carved dark wood Indian colonial *almirah* cabinet and a low, midnight blue couch that curved with a feeling of art deco. In front of the couch sat a gorgeous lacquered tea table decorated with an animal-shaped vessel with a sinewy hawthorn branch arching up from it.

"When this picture in the Japanese magazine *Lovely Home* was brought to our attention, we ran a computer-enhanced analysis of the ceramics in the cabinet," Colonel Martin said. "And then we brought it to Elizabeth, at the Sackler, for further analysis."

The next image was a split screen—a color shot of the vessel in Takeo's cabinet, and then the black-and-white image of the ibex ewer from the museum in Iraq.

"It's too bad that you don't know the color of the urn from Iraq," I said.

"It has that same distinctive reddish slip," Elizabeth Cameron said. "It's an ancient slip technique that not many use today."

"This vessel is believed to be one of the oldest original ceramics in Iraq," Colonel Martin added. "The ibex ewer has been visited by every schoolchild who ever went to the museum and ranks among the nation's most beloved treasures."

"So this is why you brought me in. It's not about my being so brilliant with ceramics, but about my connection to Takeo!"

Michael Hendricks cleared his throat and said, "Both ceramics and the knowledge of our suspect are items in your favor, but there are other factors as well. We know about your activities here and abroad. You've demonstrated an ability to think on your feet. You've always been remarkably successful—when you want to get something."

"But I don't want to get Takeo," I said. Takeo was toxic, I knew from my experience. I couldn't risk being around him, now that I was semisettled with Hugh, couldn't risk it for a second—

"Takeo Kayama may have bought this on the black market, but he is not the suspected thief," Colonel Martin said. "If we can get back this vessel and find out whether your old friend acquired it from Birand, we will finally have the piece of information we need to apply pressure."

I pressed my lips together, then spoke. "I still don't believe that I can do anything for you."

"As Colonel Martin has been explaining, the American forces are in a bind. We have, of course, military police and some investigators present in Japan, but the scope of their powers is extremely limited. Without permission from the Japanese government, they can't force a search of a Japanese citizen's home."

"I've told Mr. Hendricks that we can't do anything, either," Mr. Watanabe said in his soft voice. "There is not enough evidence for our national police agency to obtain a warrant."

"Why not just ask Takeo to submit his piece of pottery voluntarily to an inspection? Have you even tried to seek out a peaceful resolution?" I asked.

"We cannot risk creating a situation in which he might alert Osman Birand." Michael Hendricks pushed a thick manila envelope toward me. "In here, you'll find a new passport and an itinerary."

I didn't touch it. "What do you mean?"

"We'd like you to take a short trip back to Tokyo. You'll have a cover story—that you're buying antiques—and a new passport with an official visa that shows your affiliation with our embassy. During that time, we'll expect you to visit with your old friend Takeo Kayama at his family home. Without making it obvious, you'll find a way to examine the vessel closely and tell us if it's the item stolen from the museum."

"He'll never let me do that! After the way things ended, he won't ever want to see me, not in his beach house or anywhere that I can think of—"

The screen flashed another picture that had once run in a Japanese tabloid. It was taken on a gray afternoon in Roppongi, when Takeo and I were saying good-bye to each other as I was getting into a taxi. You could tell from the way our bodies leaned into each other that we had not wanted to part.

I felt something clutch deep inside me, and I began to sweat.

"He'll let you in," Michael Hendricks said, a hint of amusement in his voice. "Who wouldn't?"

4

Up-two-three-four.

Hold!

The eighteen-pound bar felt more like eighty during this third, most excruciating set of repetitions. I pressed upward, trying to keep the bar level, while at the same time gluing my lower back to the bench.

I had been insane to undertake a power-lifting class with a hangover, but after my ordeal at the Smithsonian, I couldn't imagine going home soon. I'd lightened the load I usually lifted, because this time I had a different kind of weight to bear.

It was my duty to go, each one of them had said. Colonel Martin said it was a chance to serve my country. Michael Hendricks argued that it was important to stand up against international art criminals who robbed the people of all nations. The Japanese consul believed that it was a special privilege to solve a serious international problem. But Takeo—I couldn't get near Takeo. If I did, I would wind up hurting him, hurting Hugh, hurting myself.

"Rei! Come on, don't forget the powerhouse!" Jane, the blond, outrageously muscular teacher, barked at me.

This powerhouse was not a sandwich, though I could have used one. Jane was referring to the abdominal muscles. I hardened my belly as I pushed up the bar, struggling to keep the left side in balance with the right.

I couldn't undertake a classified project that was actually governmental spying, though no one had used the word. When I'd suggested that this might be a job more appropriate for a CIA operative, everyone had reacted as if I'd passed wind. It was as if nobody in government used that acronym, just as nobody in Japan said the word *yakuza*. And Michael had asked me, completely straight-faced, to work for them for no pay. They'd give me my expenses, but that was it.

Not quite it, I thought, as I sat up and rubbed away the ache on the back of my arms, still brooding. At the end they'd revealed the carrot, the only reason that the mission really would appeal to me. If I went, I'd get to keep my new passport, with its clean pages and embassy stamp. I now had a legal method of entry back into the country that had ordered me deported because I'd once unlawfully entered a room to find evidence. I'd been caught by the Japanese police, and that was the end of me; greater good to society be damned.

Since that nightmare a year earlier, returning to Japan seemed akin to penetrating a high-security vault. Now I was being offered the passkey. The question was whether I could live with myself if I spied.

Hendricks and Martin had hammered into me the classified nature of the operation: nobody, not even Hugh, could know that I was working as an informant. Michael Hendricks had explained the story I'd give people: I'd been hired as a consultant to the Sackler, to shop for some antique Japanese ceramics at a major Tokyo auction taking place in two weeks' time. I'd spend a week or two in Japan, ostensibly visiting auction houses and catching up with old friends, among them Takeo Kayama, whom I was to refer to by the code name Flowers, Flowers-san, or Mr. Flowers. The code word for the ibex vessel that I was hunting down was Momoyama Period Vase, so it would sound to anyone listening as if I really were after seventeenth-century Japanese ceramics.

Feeling sick, I dragged myself into the locker room, stripped, and went to the showers. The water pounded down on my hurting head. I knew that my shoulders and arms would be throbbing with new pains the next morning. I didn't usually do straight weight lifting, just as I didn't usually go to espionage planning sessions or contemplate lying to Hugh.

Several women were waiting for showers now, women whose voices were slightly raised in irritation. I turned off the water and grabbed a towel, stepping out of the shower so fast that I slipped. Down I went on the ceramic tile floor, so fast that the women gasped but couldn't reach out in time to catch me.

The truth was that nobody could save me. As I struggled to my feet and wrapped the skimpy gym towel around myself, I knew that it was up to me, entirely, to save myself.

"Good timing," Angus Glendinning said when I walked back into the apartment an hour later. He was sprawled on Hugh's leather sofa, an unfolded map covering his chest like a blanket. Around him were scattered the remnants of breakfast: a five-liter bottle of Mountain Dew and some half-eaten bagels.

"What's doing?" I asked dully. I was too upset about my own situation to care about the mess.

"Do you know the way to Baltimore?" Angus sang in a dreamy voice. "We're supposed to be playing a live bit on a radio program in an hour and a half—"

"An hour and a half?" I repeated, looking at him, shirtless and shoeless and wearing trendy thigh-length gray underpants. "And you need to get through the DC traffic and out to the freeway and then to downtown Baltimore?"

"It's not downtown. The station's in an area called Tozen."

"What?" I took his creased itinerary and discovered that he was supposed to go to the campus radio station at Towson University. Towson was just north of the city, so the trip would be longer than he'd thought. "You're looking at a good hour and a quarter, if you hurry."

"Sridhar went out to pick up our van. The parking in this neighborhood's wretched. We had to park a bloody mile away last night."

Sridhar had to be the Indian tabla player, I guessed, because he was the only one of the band I couldn't physically place. The Caribbean bassist was at the dining table, smoking a cigarette and reading Hugh's copy of the *Wall Street Journal*. Through the open door to the powder room in the hallway, I could see the blond bagpiper working on his hairstyle. He was wearing a very nice terrycloth bathrobe—mine, I realized.

"You'll need to hurry to get there," I said sotto voce to the *Journal* reader, deciding he had to be the brains of the bunch. "I'm Rei Shimura, by the way. I hope you were comfortable. I'm sorry I wasn't here in the morning—"

"You're Hugh's chick. I recall from last night," he answered in a broad accent that Hugh had taught me was North London. "I'm Nate. And the digs are great, yah? Love the wooden chest over there—is it from Japan?"

As I answered Nate in the affirmative, Angus interrupted me. "We don't have to rush anywhere, Rei. People anticipate our arrival. They schedule around us."

I couldn't help smiling. "Is that so?"

"Yah. In fact, when we go to Japan next month, the promoters told us just to get ourselves there, and then they'd arrange the shows. They already arranged our visas—it's bloody brilliant."

"You'll be going to Japan?" It struck me as ironic that Angus had free access to the country, his visas arranged by Japanese music promoters, while I had to creep in through the back door.

"Of course! You know we've been signed to a label there, don't you?"

"I didn't!" This was major news. I wondered if Hugh had heard.

"We've got an Asian tour in the works," said Nate, who'd stood up and was starting to get dressed, pulling on black jeans. "Taiwan and also Singapore."

"Angus, I'm embarrassed I didn't know all this! You'll have to tell me more after you get back from Towson. I don't want you to be late."

"Right, well, we'll be talking about this on the radio show. Do you think you'll be able to hear and tape it?"

"It might be too far—"

"You can listen on the web," Keiffer said, emerging from the bathroom. I noticed that the blond drummer's hair, which he'd apparently been working on so hard, still looked as if he'd just rolled out of bed.

"Keiffer, if you'd like a private place to dress, try Hugh's and my room," I suggested quickly, when I saw him pick up a pair of red bikini briefs from the dining area. The boys' underwear styles appeared to be as diverse as their onstage attire.

"Shug's still there, in a rather bad way." Keiffer made a face.

"What?" I shot a glance at the bedroom door with the DO NOT DISTURB sign I'd tacked up when I'd left Chika there, sleeping, a few hours earlier.

"Relax, Rei, he's there by himself," Angus cackled, as if he'd read my mind. "Chika got up a while ago, woke us all with cups of green tea, actually. Totally gorgeous, that cousin of yours. Why didn't you introduce me when I was in Japan before?"

"Chika was away at school," I said, even though it had been summer when Angus was around. I had done everything to keep my Japanese relatives from learning about the decadent young troublemaker in my apartment. "So where is Chika, then?"

"She wanted to see the neighborhood, so she went with Sridhar to get the van. She's attending our gig as well."

"Sounds like a good time." The apartment would be empty for a few key hours, hours that I would use to broach the subject of my return to Japan with Hugh.

They left thirty minutes later, fully dressed and teeth brushed, after I gave out spare toothbrushes to the ones who'd forgotten. I should be a mother, I thought wistfully, as I watched out the window as they recklessly crossed Mintwood Place, oblivious of the delivery truck that had to brake for their passage. Who did they think they were, the Beatles crossing Abbey Road? They'd kill themselves before the end of the day.

Only Chika waited demurely in her pink pleather coat at the curb, and looked both ways as she crossed. I found myself hoping that she would be the driver.

I turned away from the living room window and cracked open the bedroom door to check on Hugh. The room was dark, the curtains were drawn, and a foul smell lingered in the air.

"Still feeling awful?" I asked as I came to sit down next to him.

"I've been sick all morning," Hugh said. "I set off for work, but had to return. It could be a virus, I suppose."

I looked at him. "I don't know. Binge drinking is pretty hard on the system."

"Oh, don't be so damn American," Hugh grumbled.

"What do you mean?"

"You go to a pub with Americans, and if you have more than two drinks, they think you're a lush."

"I didn't keep count of myself last night. That was the problem." Thank God that I was slowly and steadily feeling better. The exercise had done me good.

Hugh sighed heavily. "I'm just sorry the band's landed on us at this point. I'd expected that you'd give them breakfast, but since you were gone, I had to send them to the bagel shop. D'you think they minded?"

"They seemed to bear no resentment." Though I did, for his expectations. "Hugh, I had a job interview this morning! I told you last night, and every day for the last week. You knew I had to be out early in the morning."

"So, d'you get the job?" he said sarcastically. "And what's the salary, high five figures or did you push them to six?"

I shifted uncomfortably atop the duvet. The fact that I made about as much as a salesclerk—despite my education and ambitions—was something we didn't talk about. Nor did we address the fact that Hugh paid the rent, the car insurance, the grocery bills. I knew there were plenty of married women who lived this way without question or worry, but to me, unmarried and not even engaged, it was an embarrassment. And maybe that was why he expected me to be a short-order cook, at moment's notice.

"God, my head hurts," Hugh muttered.

"I'll bring you some Motrin," I said, picking up the bonsai plant, which wouldn't thrive in the closed-curtains gloom of the bedroom. I was not a doormat. I was just helping my boyfriend, who was not his usual self. "And then, I think I'll make some brunch for both of us. Would scrambled eggs suit you?"

"That's sweet, but I don't think I could bear it."

"At least try some toast fingers!" I implored.

"No, no. I could sip some tea, though."

Of course, tea healed all Asians and Brits. "Your favorite Darjeel-ing?"

"Too sweet; it'll make me sick again." He sounded woeful. "I'd better go with green. Chika made a large pot of it earlier, maybe there's some left to warm up."

No proper Japanese believes in warming over old tea, so I put on a fresh kettle of water to boil as I set about reorganizing the apartment. It was a wonder Nate had been able to notice the fine old pieces of Japanese furniture, buried as everything was by opened magazines and newspapers and discarded clothes. I picked up a can of Mountain Dew that had sweated a ring onto my hun-dred-year-old *tansu* and tried in vain to buff its finish back. Then I threw away more old newspapers and cans and put in their place the bonsai plant that I'd carried in from the bedroom. The gift-giver's card had been lost, so I'd have to guess who had sent the sweet little dwarf pomegranate tree with dark green leaves and reddish orange trumpet-shaped flowers. Whoever had sent it couldn't have known me too well, because I typically killed house plants through neglect.

Now I was thirty, I'd have to be more responsible. I pulled out the care instructions printed on a little plastic stick buried in the potting soil. The pomegranate bonsai needed occasional fertilizing, regular watering, and full sun. The card went on to promise orna-mental fruit in the fall. Hmm, it was already October. Where was the fruit? As I gently explored the plant's thick foliage, my fingers touched something inorganic. I drew back the glossy leaves to see a tiny black plastic disk. I'd seen enough spy movies to recognize it as a miniature microphone.

Happy birthday, indeed. I'd been bugged.

5

After I'd put the bonsai straight out of the apartment, I sank down on the sofa and considered the situation. Covert wiretapping had once been illegal, but probably wasn't anymore, because of the sweeping changes in civil liberties that had arrived with the new century. Someone had clipped the microphone to a plant that I'd brought in myself from the foyer of the apartment building. This was shrewd, a way to get the bug inside without physically entering the apartment. Now I wondered if there was a wiretap on the apartment telephone as well.

I shivered, because I'd almost persuaded myself to take the job. Despite the creepiness of the work, I was desperate to be in Japan. I could practically inhale the incense at the Yanaka Shrine, and my tongue curled at the memory of the smoky-sweet yams from the best potato-roasting cart. Autumn was the perfect time of year to visit Japan, when the persimmon trees along the train tracks hung heavy with red-orange fruit.

The thought of fruit returned me to my problem. The plant was outside the apartment now, but was that the right place for it?

I retrieved the bonsai tree and brought it into the study, where I found a place for it on a bookcase for the time being. This was the perfect act of revenge, I decided; the government team would now have the pleasure of listening to the Glaswegian Hangover for as long as they were in town. After that, I'd have to come up with something even more obnoxious.

The kettle whistled, reminding me of my original plan to make Hugh some tea. I poured the steaming water over the fragrant green tea leaves—tea leaves my aunt had brought on her last visit from Japan, a stash that was almost gone, but that I could replenish if I went on the mission.

I watched the tea brew to the right color, poured a cup, and took it to Hugh's bedside, but he was asleep again. I lay down next to him, intent on bringing up the potential trip to Japan the moment he woke up.

The afternoon stretched into evening, and still Hugh slept. Eventually, I did too. I was in the midst of a dream that I was climbing the moss-covered steps up to the fox shrine in my old neighborhood when I awoke suddenly. The little fox statue had been tumbling over and over, down toward me—I heard it shatter as it hit each step. No, what really was happening was that the telephone was ringing.

I grabbed the receiver and said a sleepy hello.

"Rei-chan, help me!" It was Chika.

"What's happened?" I asked, the panic in her voice spreading to me.

"It's a fight. I was just trying to park the van, you see—"

"Where are you?" If they were still in Maryland, I couldn't do much to help. The clock said that it was two in the morning.

"We're just around the corner in your neighborhood, on that street with the church. I didn't know the other car wanted to park in the same space. But some boys came out of their car and started shouting. Before I could do anything, Angus and his friends jumped from the van and started shouting back. Now they are hitting each other!"

"Does anyone have a gun?" I asked immediately. The content of my question finally roused Hugh on the other side of me.

Chika told me no. I shook my head at Hugh, who had staggered out of bed, and I continued talking with my cousin. "Chika, listen to me carefully. Can you get the band to return to the van?"

"No, no! I have tried. The boys told me just to lock myself in and keep safe."

Next idea. "Okay, I want you to roll down the window and tell everyone that the police are coming. That should slow down the fight. And we'll be there in a minute."

I put the cordless phone back in its cradle and explained the situation. Hugh nodded and began hunting around for his shoes.

"I don't know if you should go out."

"I won't let you go by yourself." Hugh grimaced as he spoke.

"I think we should call the police after all," I said, taking another look at Hugh. He appeared ill enough to be knocked over by the slightest blow. He'd be no asset to me on the street.

"The neighbors may have done that already," Hugh said. "We've got to get there first. If the police book them, my brother's tour is as good as over. Not to mention the threat of deportation."

I scrambled into my Asics. Hugh was having trouble of his own, coming up with only one running shoe and one Italian loafer—paired with his old University of London sweatshirt and flannel pajama bottoms, they looked pretty odd, but there was no time to be fashionable. I gave up on finding shoes and went out in my slippers, throwing a raincoat over my pajamas.

"How two exhausted people over thirty are going to break up a fight, I don't know," I muttered as we sped along the dark street. The old, bumpy sidewalks in Mintwood Place had charmed me at the beginning, but were a liability in the dark. Right around the corner, Chika had said. Oh, God, there they were. I could see a police car double-parked in the center of Octavia Street.

"We're too late," I said.

"Christ. I'll have to be their attorney," Hugh said grimly.

Something strange was happening. A Ford Explorer with an American University decal on its back window was reversing down the street toward us. The driver was a policeman, who pulled it into the no-parking spot in front of the church. He stepped out of the car and rejoined the police cruiser, which moved off slowly in the opposite direction.

Hugh had somehow gotten half a block ahead of me, so I hurried to catch up. The band's van was parked in a legal spot—I hadn't seen it before, but I recognized it by the "Scotland Forever" sticker on the back. Now Angus, Sridhar, Nate, and Keiffer were spilling out, their voices high and excited.

"They took 'em away, just like that!" Sridhar said.

"First time a bloody copper told me to take care. Great city!" Angus said admiringly.

Chika emerged from the driver's-side door and fell into my arms. She was trembling.

"What happened?" I asked.

"The cops came," Angus said. "They asked us if we wanted to press charges, but we said no, and they took those college prats off anyway, to issue some kind of citation for—what was it?"

"Disturbing the peace," Sridhar finished.

"That's right. The police dinna touch us at all, just told us to go home. Never got such gentle treatment before, not in the brawls we've been in!" Angus said, a note of wonder in his voice.

"They just let you go?" Hugh seemed as shocked as I was.

"Wait a minute." A suspicion was growing. "Angus, are you saying that the police specifically asked which ones were the college students?"

"That's right. It's like they could tell the whole story, that Chika was parking, and the others started the whole bloody mess. We dinna have to say a thing."

"What else did they say to you?" Now I knew for certain that our phone had been tapped. Angus and his friends were off the hook, and the others in trouble.

"Rei, let's not stand outside any longer," Hugh said in a low voice. "We'll get everyone home, that's the best thing."

But as we all made it through the apartment door, and it was locked behind us securely, I felt myself still spilling over with questions, which nobody but Michael Hendricks and his friends could answer. The government people listening in had to be behind the bugs, and thus behind this too-quick cleanup of a street brawl. Hugh seemed dazed by it all, and once inside, he turned down the boys' offer of an impromptu drinks party in favor of going back to bed.

"I'm very sleepy, too," Chika said, yawning. "But please, Hugh-san, don't give up your bed again to me. I really don't need it."

Now I had the bed problem all over again. "Maybe we can come up with some arrangement of pillows on the floor. But which room?"

"The study," Chika said. "Already, the boys have offered the futon."

"I'll bet," I said. "You saw how they"—I broke off, wishing I could come up with the Japanese translation for testosterone-driven—"how rude they could be on the street. I hate to think of what kind of misunderstanding might develop, if you slept in that room." At present, I knew, the boys were mixing drinks in the kitchen, just getting started on their party.

"Rei-chan, you are my cousin, not my aunt." There was a hint of annoyance in Chika's soft voice. "But please not to worry. I will share the futon with Sridhar, because his religion forbids him to touch women before marriage. It is the perfect arrangement, I think."

I bit back any further protests. She was twenty-two. But still, I couldn't help imagining her mother—my Aunt Norie—shaking her head in horror at the idea of Chika in bed with a tabla player, with the rest of the band crashed out around them, and the pomegranate recording whatever might be said—or sighed—during the night.

"It's up to you," I said at last. "But please remember, Chika, the walls are very thin. It's quite easy to hear things."

"Oh, yes," she said. "Mother mentioned that about the time she visited here."

That could mean Aunt Norie had overheard me with Hugh. I felt myself start to blush.

"Don't worry," Chika continued cheerily, "I shall tell the boys not to practice their songs tonight. We won't disturb you anymore."

6

Senator Harp Snowden had a weakness for good food—good Asian food, especially. His scheduler had said she could squeeze me in during the late morning, so I decided to bring him something to make up for any delays that I might cause. A new specialty bakery had opened near the zoo, and it sold quirky Japanese baked goods like puff pastry packets with curried vegetables inside, and croissants filled with chestnut puree. This seemed perfect for late morning, when the thought of lunch was on the horizon, but not yet a possibility.

Around eleven I carried the beribboned pastry box carefully into the Hart Senate Office Building. After a quick trip through a metal detector and a brisk walk past a huge, inscrutable Calder sculpture, I rode a crowded elevator up to the senator's office.

A new woman sat at the reception desk. She looked Asian but had features I couldn't quite place. She also had the same northern California accent as mine, but she mutilated the pronunciation of my name when she announced me over the phone to the senator. "It's like a ray of sun," I said to her after she'd hung up. "And Shimura sounds almost like Timor—"

"You can go back there now," she said, clearly not interested. "But Marianna said to remember he's got to get over to the Senate in half an hour."

I nodded and went through the door. Senator Snowden's office suite was huge, a charmless warren of cubicles and rooms where young people sat with their ears glued to phones and their fingers hovering over keyboards. Nobody looked up as I turned a corner and knocked on the half-open door that led to the senator's inner sanctum. He was at his antique partners desk, ankles up, with stacks of periodicals around him; he waved me in. I glanced around the room, seeing that a new artistic find—a Hmong quilt—had gone up between an old portrait of him with Bill Clinton and another with Nelson Mandela. Harp was a few years older now than the senator in the pictures, but he was still very handsome, with his patrician features and thick, silver hair. He was what every woman hoped her boyfriend would age into, I thought, as he swung his legs down from the desk and walked over to give me a quick embrace. He walked with a very slight limp that betrayed the loss of one of his feet, many years ago in Vietnam.

"How nice to hear from you, Rei. It's been too long!" Harp said, smiling at me.

"Well, you were really kind to see me on such short notice," I said.

"It's an important reason for us to talk. Michael told me you might be calling," he said, motioning for me to sit down on one of a pair of chintz-covered love seats near a large window overlooking Constitution Avenue.

"When he dropped your name, I had to follow up," I said.

"Of course. Actually, I've known Michael Hendricks for years. His father's Owen Hendricks," Harp said, settling down on the love seat across from me.

"Who's that?"

"A retired four-star admiral who was once in line to be secretary of the Navy. Shame it didn't work out. Anyway, our families each have camps on the same lake in Maine. Michael skippered my boat for years. I guess I could describe him as the son I never had."

"He's too old to be your son," I pointed out.

"You flatter me," Harp said. "He's in his late thirties, mature enough to have earned a Bronze Star in the first Gulf War, but restless enough to have left the Navy for civilian government service. It turned out to be a good fit for him, with his background in Asia and the Middle East. He's a rising star over there, Rei. I think you'll like working for him."

"How can you say that when you don't know what the work involves?"

Harp leaned forward and asked, "Has Michael asked you to perform an action that's illegal?"

"Not exactly," I admitted. "But it's—classified, so I'm not allowed to tell anyone about it. And since our meeting, my whole existence seems to have changed. My personal freedoms and even my living space aren't secure anymore."

"You mean that someone broke in?" Harp's eyebrows rose.

I shook my head.

"Aha. So you must mean . . . they're monitoring it for sound?"

I paused, not knowing whether I should answer. Maybe I'd said too much already. If he was so close to Michael Hendricks, he might pick up the phone and report that I was too talkative.

"Of course, while you're on a mission, that's par for the course. It's for your own protection, as well as theirs. I can assure you this room is secure, and so is any conversation that we have. We have some serious shared history, Rei. I won't betray that trust."

"I just don't know what I should do. Ever since the restaurant closed, I've barely worked. So this would be good, not to mention that it could improve another—situation—in my life." I was thinking about my visa status.

"How are things with Hugh?" Harp asked.

I sighed, thinking about Hugh's slow, tortured-looking exit from the apartment that morning. "Hugh's been under the weather since my thirtieth birthday party the other night."

"Really? If the party was too wild for him, it's probably a good thing I had to send my regrets." Despite his passionate liberalism, Harp was cautious about his image. I'd grown to respect this caution as a sign of real intelligence.

"Hmm. Well, you missed a few spectacular sights, but probably it's for the best." I thought about Kendall and her striptease. "But to get back to Hugh, despite his being a little ill, things between us are fine. His brother and the band are here for the moment, as is my cousin Chika from Japan—"

"A full house." He looked at me sympathetically. "Not that you could talk with him about it, anyway."

"That's something I wanted to ask you," I said. "When people undertake special jobs like the one Michael wants me to take on, why can't they tell a significant other?"

"Because they love the other person enough to want to spare him or her the worry, and in the long term, it's for the person's safety. When I was in Vietnam, things happened that I never told my wife. But now, the dangerous time has passed, and I can be open."

Maybe—when the ibex vessel was safely back in Iraq—I could tell Hugh. And he might actually be proud, rather than anxious or angry.

"By the way, Rei, I've been wondering what's in that box you brought. That is, if it isn't classified information."

"A few thousand calories worth of Japanese pastries from the new shop on Connecticut Avenue. I don't suppose you'd care to try one?" I pushed it toward him.

"Only if you join me. Delicious!" he said enthusiastically, after the first chew. "You have unerring taste."

"You're kind to say that." I reached for a curry puff.

"Well, my dear, I'm already anticipating the other delicacies you'll bring me after you get back."

Harp knew something, I decided as I said good-bye to him, left the building, and walked down Constitution Avenue. He knew that I was supposed to be going on a trip, or he wouldn't have mentioned delicacies. Michael had told him something, but probably not everything.

And I knew now that I was ready to go. I'd been running hot and cold on the issue for the last twenty-four hours, and there were some things I needed to sort out with Hugh first. But I was going. If I didn't go, I'd regret it forever.

I dragged myself over to the Washington Mall, past the tourists and joggers, and found a solitary bench. I was just getting out my cell phone to call Hugh, to arrange some sort of outdoor meeting where I could talk, in a limited way, about the situation that lay before me, when the phone itself rang. "Private caller" appeared in the display. I clicked "talk" and heard Michael Hendricks's voice.

"How did you get this number?" And how, I wondered, did he

anticipate that I was on the verge of arranging a meeting to break it to Hugh?

"The résumé you left with us yesterday included this telephone number. I gather that I've reached you on your cell?"

"Why even ask? I'm sure your colleagues could clarify the type of phone it is."

"Oh. So you're concerned about—privacy?" He sounded cautious.

"I should say so! The little thing that happened last night with the police and the guys in the band. And what about the bonsai you sent me with a strange plastic growth?"

"Oh, I see." He paused. "You discovered both bugs."

"I did."

"You're good," he said. "That is exactly the level of observation I expect you to use in Japan."

"But you're violating my civil rights! And Hugh's!"

"Rei, for operational security reasons, we need to know that we can trust you." He paused. "Come on, didn't it work out for the best last night? The police were alerted that Angus and his friends all were European citizens to be let go without incident. If that directive hadn't been issued, the band might have wound up in jail overnight with common DC criminals—a situation that would surely test their fake grit."

"I'm relieved that they weren't incarcerated," I said stiffly. "But let's return to my point. You bugged a place that isn't even my apartment. Hugh is the one you're going to have to answer to if and when he finds out."

"Once he gets up from his illness, that is," Hendricks said. "What the hell did he drink at your birthday party, anyway?"

"None of your business, and you're not presenting a winning case for my joining forces with you—"

"Let me try again, in person. Where are you?"

"Oh, come on now, I'm sure you know where I am," I answered tetchily.

"No, I really don't know. What's the location?"

"I'm on the Mall."

"Can you be more specific?"

I wondered if he was testing me again. "I'm on a bench near the National Gallery. Tell whoever has the binoculars to focus on the bench near the one with the wino stretched out."

"Rei, my office is not on the Mall, it's in Foggy Bottom. I'm going to go out and grab a taxi. I'll see you in ten minutes."

"That's ridiculous, I'm not staying here in the cold—" The temperature was fifty degrees, but weather was the first excuse that popped into my head.

"Then why don't you go inside the Freer? Let's meet by the coat-check area so that we don't miss each other."

It wasn't likely that we could miss each other, I thought, as I leaned against the entrance to the coat-check room, which was no longer operational—perhaps because of renovations, or maybe because of fears that a checked coat might hold a bomb. I didn't know.

Now I waited, sweating in my new fall coat, a pumpkin-colored wool melton, thinking about the good old days when a woman could hang a coat in a museum and not worry about the motives of the person she was meeting.

Michael Hendricks came through the door a few minutes later, dressed in a navy-and-black pinstripe suit, without a tie or an overcoat. He had taken a taxi, I guessed.

"You look irritated," Hendricks said. "Am I that late?"

"No. It's just that it's so hot in here, and the checkroom's closed."

"I'll take your coat. There's a place we'll leave it, deeper into the museum." He held out his hands for the coat, but just as I was about to hand it to him, I changed my mind and kept it draped over my arm. No chance that I'd allow him any opportunities to slide a bug into its lining.

The Sackler's galleries were subterranean, so we walked down a flight of stairs and were buzzed through the same locked doors to administration. Directly off the hall was a room with a buzzer, which Michael pressed.

"This is storage," Michael said while we waited. "They're paranoid about damage, so I'm sure they're going to ask me to leave my pen. Will you keep it at the bottom of your purse for me, and give it back when we leave?"

The pen looked like Mark Cross, but who knew what kind of pen it really was, I thought as I dropped it into the recesses of my bag and the door was opened to us by Elizabeth Cameron. Behind her stretched a series of tall steel cabinets, which I quickly figured out held all the goodies that weren't on display. I felt my interest rise, in spite of everything.

"Hello, you two. I can be with you in just a few minutes—I'm in the process of finishing assembling things for the lesson." Elizabeth inclined her head to the right, and I saw that there was a tall man with glasses doing something with one of the cabinets. Obviously, she didn't want to work with us in front of him.

"Sure. We wanted to look at the Islamic exhibit, anyway. May I leave Rei's coat somewhere around here?" Michael asked.

"No, that's all right. I'll carry it." Already, it seemed my im-promptu meeting with Michael and Elizabeth had been planned. I was determined not to take any more risks with my privacy.

Michael wanted to go straight to the show's masterwork, a 600-year-old ceramic platter painted with images of men carrying spears, but I cut him short. I'd been to the show a few months earlier, and it was a piece that I thought attracted more attention than was seemly.

"I've seen it," I said. "And what I find bizarre is that the museum label says that it was owned by a warlord. Warriors traveled a lot, so why would they carry such a huge ceramic item? Brass or gold or silver would be travel-worthy, but this just is unbelievable."

"Are you saying you think it's fake?" he said, drawing closer to the glass.

"Because of the cracks and the type of pigments used, I'm sure it's very old, though not being an expert in Islamic pottery, I can't tell you how old. In any case, the plate probably was crafted to look as if it had a noble, war-going heritage—as if those two words can be used in the same breath," I added.

"Given my years at Annapolis, I'd like to think so," Michael said easily.

"Oh, so you went to the Naval Academy." I was determined to give him a taste of having his own life on trial, just as he'd done to me the day before.

"Yes, I was there. Harp wrote the recommendation for my appli-cation. I believe it was the only time our infamous antiwar senator helped someone join the military." He smiled easily. "I graduated a few years before you started at Hopkins. It's a shame, because you certainly would have, ah, enlivened our mixers."

"Hopkins girls don't usually socialize with Annapolis boys," I said briskly. "But getting back to you, before the academy, you must have been at boarding school: Andover, Exeter, somewhere like that—"

"Exeter." He looked at me a bit more warily. "And I know about myself already, thank you very much. What else can you tell me about the ceramic?"

"I think it was used in a home. A wealthy private home, where the people who owned it liked to encourage an illusion of a link to the ruling class."

"Well, that's a good inference."

I turned to see that the speaker was Elizabeth Cameron herself.

"Rei, I'm glad you came back. It sounds as if you have a pretty good base of knowledge already."

I shrugged off her compliment. "It just doesn't seem plausible that traveling warriors would have carried breakable ceramics. If you think so, too, why does the label say what it does?"

"Its history is all information this museum's staff received from the Victoria and Albert." She paused. "Well, now that you're here, Rei, I was hoping you might like to look at some things that are usually in storage, that the staff's brought out for our study. My colleague has gone to lunch, so we'll be able to make ourselves comfortable there."

"All right," I said. "I always welcome the chance for a behind-the-scenes tour at a museum."

"I'm glad to hear that," Elizabeth said. "I reviewed your master's thesis on Japanese ceramics. I think you'll find this new arena of scholarship a natural fit."

"Rei, you're turning out to be a jack-of-all-trades," Michael said. "Kimono, pottery, furniture . . ."

"Conversant in many things, but fluent in none," I replied lightly.

"Now, that is unbelievable." Michael gave me one last speculative look with his icy blue eyes before saying good-bye.

7

I was glad to have eaten the curry puffs with Senator Snowden, because it turned out that I never ate lunch. I spent the whole afternoon with Elizabeth Cameron, examining a table laden with dozens of fabulous ancient ceramics. As I pondered a 2,000-year-old urn, marveling at the history between my hands, I asked her whether it had been exhibited before.

"Ten years ago," she said. "We have so many holdings that it is a challenge to give everything a chance at the spotlight. And the truth is that the public prefers colorful items to earthenware."

"I haven't seen anything like—what we saw on-screen yesterday," I finished carefully.

"The ibex ewer? Yes, that was a unique piece. This museum at least doesn't have anything in the same form. I think the important thing happening today is that you're getting used to the texture of these ceramics, the color of the clay—look at that distinct ashy whitish interior on the chip. It is very different from the red clay that's more common."

"So this particular, lighter clay . . . it's from a certain region?" I asked.

"It's from Babylon. Later on, pottery making took place in other areas, where the clay had a different mineral content."

"And where the aesthetic was more lavish," I added longingly. These pieces really weren't my taste at all.

"Later pieces are usually more highly valued by collectors, though I myself tend to appreciate the simple beginnings."

So that was one of the differences between someone like myself who sold antiques to people who wanted stunning home decorations—and someone like her who wanted to keep them safely behind glass for all to see, free of charge. As I left the museum late that afternoon, I felt I had mastered some basics, but I needed to keep learning. If I was going to look at Takeo's vessel with any confidence, I would have to examine many more examples from the period.

I rode the Metro back to Dupont Circle, and as I walked toward Adams-Morgan, I dialed Michael Hendricks at his office.

"You forgot your pen," I said after he picked up.

"Really? Hang on to it until I see you again, will you?"

"I left it at the security desk in a bag with your name on it." There was no way I would trust that pen anywhere in my household. It could be a camera or another bug or even a weapon.

"Well, then, thank you very much." Michael sounded almost amused. "By the way, Elizabeth told me you had a very productive time."

"It was productive, but not quite enough."

"What do you mean?"

I explained that I wanted to examine more ceramics from that time period, at other museums. In each place, I'd need hands-on access, and a curator to help me.

He paused after I'd told him what I wanted. Then he said, "Do you have a few museums in mind?"

I told him the Walters Art Museum in Baltimore, the Metropolitan in New York, and the Philadelphia Museum of Art. I'd done research at these museums before, and they were all within a few hours of Washington.

"All right," Michael said when I was done, "I'll fund your travel to those places. But first, let me contact each museum with a plausible story, and we'll have some business cards made up for you. But it's got to be done quickly, since our goal is to have you out to Tokyo by the end of next week."

"I still don't know if I can take the job," I said. "Aside from learning more about ceramics, I have to be sure that Hugh is comfortable with my going."

"What, you have to ask his permission?" Michael sounded impatient.

"I didn't say I needed permission. But he's never taken a job that I didn't want him to do—"

"What about Edinburgh?" Michael Hendricks said. "He went back there, supposedly to help draft the new Scottish constitution, and he wound up with Lady Fiona."

"It was a brief engagement, which he terminated," I finished. "So, it seems like you examined news clippings from the *Tatler* party page. Why didn't you include them in the slide show for everyone's amusement?"

"It wasn't pertinent, just as I think the exact nature of your work for your government isn't pertinent knowledge for Hugh. It's enough for him to know that the Smithsonian is sending you to look into buying some Japanese ceramics."

I hung up, thinking that Michael didn't know about Hugh's instinct for sensing trouble. Even though Hugh was sick, he was still sharp.

"What's the crisis?" Hugh asked when I called him at work—something I very rarely did.

"I wanted to see if you're feeling better," I said.

"I'm hanging in," Hugh said. "But I'm swamped with work. I don't think I'll make it home till late tonight. Sorry."

"Don't apologize to me," I said. "It's more of a shame for you, trying to recover, and your brother in town for just a few more days—"

"Angus and I already said our good-byes. He's heading off for Philadelphia today, remember?"

"Oh. I'd forgotten. Well, anyway, when you get home, maybe we can go out for a quick bite. There's something we need to talk about."

"Over food? Have you forgotten the state I'm in?" Hugh laughed weakly.

"No, it's just that . . . I would rather get out of the apartment to talk to you, that's all. It doesn't have to be a restaurant, it could be a coffee bar—"

"That place around the corner closes by six, and I doubt I'll be through till ten. I'd rather just see you at home."

"What are you doing for dinner, if you're staying so late at work?"

"I thought I'd pick up a takeaway soup, if I can find a delicatessen that's open after six. Downtown is pretty dead at that hour, so it might not be worth the walk."

"Let me bring you food," I said. "It'll save you time."

I must have worn Hugh down, because he reluctantly agreed. We made plans for my arrival bearing tom yum goong in three hours' time. In the meantime, I went home and told Chika that we were going out to eat at my favorite Thai restaurant and that afterward, while she packed her suitcase for her next stop at my parents' home in San Francisco, I would head to Hugh's office to take him something to eat.

"So, he has to go to work when he's still sick. It's a shame," Chika said gravely.

"That's right. And I don't know if he's going to be sick again, so I think it's probably better if I'm just there."

"Of course. I'd like to be home this evening, in case the boys call between sets. Sridhar promised."

I looked sideways at my cousin. "How was last night on the futon?"

She beamed radiantly. "Very fun. Liberating, really. I never spent so much time with foreign men before."

"All the men I know are foreigners," I mused. Hugh was so profoundly Celtic, and Takeo came from centuries of Japanese inbreeding. Come to think of it, the boyfriends I'd chosen in college had all been bilingual and of international ancestry. My roommate used to call the motley parade of beaux that crossed our doorway Rei's United Nations. I'd never dated anyone all-American like Michael Hendricks.

I shook myself. Why had that thought popped into my head? Probably, it was because I had turned thirty and felt a need to evaluate all the men I met, whether I liked them or not.

"Foreigners," Chika continued, interrupting my distressed thoughts. "They are more intense. The differences . . . it's exciting at first. But it cannot last for eternity, as my mother says."

"Oh, does she."

"She's not watching me that closely right now. She's working on an *o-miai* for my brother, though."

"Tsutomu-kun is going to have an arranged marriage?" I felt faint at the thought of her older brother, my beloved cousin Tom, so attractive, lively, and caring. Why did his mother think he needed help finding a partner?

Chika answered my unspoken question. "My brother is so old—thirty-three already. Japanese girls are becoming choosy. They won't want him in two more years. Now is the time he can still have any hope of selection."

"All he needs is some time off from work! Time to socialize, meet people on his own," I said. "How could a matchmaker find a better woman for him than we could?"

"I have no interest in fixing up my brother. But if you do . . ." She waved an elegant hand studded with heavy rings. "*Onegai-shimasu!*"

I request of you, she'd said in formal Japanese.

In a week's time, I would have the chance to see her brother and ask him how he felt about arranged marriages. But first, I had to get to Japan—and that meant working things out with Hugh.

8

"No!" Hugh said.

We were sitting on the carpet in his office with the Thai food spread out like a picnic between us. I had spent the last ten minutes explaining my situation: a onetime contract job for the government to bid for antique Japanese pottery, a special passport back to Japan. An opportunity to jump out of my diplomatic black hole—an opportunity that might never come again.

He'd listened carefully the whole time I'd spoken, not eating a bite. And now, the verdict was negative.

"You mean you don't think I should go?"

"No, no, no!"

"But why—"

"I mean no, as in no kidding! I can hardly believe it. What brilliant luck." Hugh's serious expression had turned into a radiant grin.

I could breathe again. "So you think I should take it? I haven't told them yet—"

"Of course you should bloody take it! Rei, thank God you came to Washington. Because of all that publicity you gathered in the last few months, someone high up must have twigged that you're the right person for the job. When you return here with whatever Momoyama vase you buy, I want to throw a party. Do you think, if you ask nicely, they'll let you have it at the Smithsonian?"

"I doubt it. Hugh, you must be on the way to recovery if you're thinking of parties again."

"Yes, watch me eat rice and soup without losing it." He did so, and when he spoke again, his voice was slightly hoarse from the chili-laden soup. "I'm not ready to open a bottle of champers yet, but if you'll do the honors of pouring us each a glass of water, we can toast to your legal reentry in Japan, which I'll be thrilled to witness."

I went to organize the lead crystal tumblers he kept in a cabinet, along with a bottle of mineral water, and various spirits. I asked, "Does this mean you'll actually drive me to Dulles Airport in rush hour? You don't have to, really. I can take the Metro."

"Better than that. I'll fly with you, babe. We can hunker down under the blankets and get into the kind of trouble that we used to on all those night flights."

"Hold on." I thought quickly. "You—you didn't even have time to fly anywhere for a three-day weekend for my birthday. How can you get the time off to go with me to Japan? And I'm in a situation where I have to go in a real rush—next week, in fact."

"Have you forgotten that I'm supposed to visit Tokyo every three or four months for trial preparation?" Hugh raised the glass that I'd handed him in a toasting gesture. "I haven't been in a while. It would be a cinch to convince the managing partner that it's high time for me to return and get the Tokyo office in high gear."

"Hugh, I'm sorry," I said. "This job for the federal government— you know that it's my first, and I don't think I would come off as a professional if I travel with my boyfriend in tow."

He studied my face for a moment. "Okay. We'll fly separately and meet up at my company flat. No one shall be the wiser."

I took a deep drink of water, then put my glass down. "I can't explain all the details, but believe me, they'll know. I must go alone."

"What do you mean, they'll know?" Hugh sounded impatient. "And who the hell cares, anyhow? Rei, I want to go to Japan with you. You're the one who made me fall in love with the country, and it's just not been the same going on business there without you. You know how to read street signs and order theater tickets and all the—" he stopped, as if he'd finally noticed how grave my expression had become.

"I must go alone," I repeated. "It will only be for a week, two weeks at the most. And if all goes well, I'll get my visa status changed so I can return again, as much as I like and with you. We're used to separations, sweetheart. I think we can manage."

"I wish you'd let me go with you, but if it means that much to you that you go alone . . . I understand. Yes," he said, his voice growing stronger, "I'll keep the home fires burning. I'll take a break from gadding about and put some extra energy into researching the case, which you know is greatly overdue."

I looked at him, blinking back the tears that I felt. He was really hurt. I said, "You're being very tolerant of the situation. Thank you."

He snorted and said, "Well, the bosses you've got sound just the opposite, if they've made you this agitated and uptight about the trip. I certainly hope they're paying you a living wage."

"They're sparing no expense, flying me over business class. You'll have to give me tips, so I can fully take advantage of the situation—"

Hugh frowned. "The government doesn't usually fly its employees business class."

"Well, this is a special branch of the government. I mean," I amended hastily, "because I'm a consultant from the outside, and not a federal employee, I get some perks."

"Ask them to put you on one of the planes that have the seats that recline back like beds. If there's fresh-squeezed orange juice, drink it. And don't forget to bring home the comfort kit."

The comfort kit. It would probably contain a little black eye mask like the one I'd been given on my birthday, a mask designed to help a person get some sleep—or to block out the truth about what she would have to do.

The next few days passed in a blur of travel and talk. I saw Chika off to visit my parents, and that very afternoon I took the Delta shuttle to New York, where I stayed overnight in the apartment of an old college friend before my big day at the Met.

There, I was able to look at and touch more Mesopotamian pottery, and I received an in-depth tutorial on the hand-shaping of vessels before I boarded the Metroliner to continue my journey. At the

Philadelphia Museum of Art, the curator turned out to know all about color, and we had a delightful two hours going through the museum's exquisite collections. By the time I showed up at the Walters Art Museum in Baltimore the next day, I was thrilled to examine an ibex pitcher that was a little bit younger than one missing from the museum in Iraq. Everywhere, people seemed surprised that they'd never heard of my being at the Sackler, but grudgingly came to accept that I was a new employee preparing to work on a forthcoming exhibition.

My time had gone so well that I was bolstered with enough confidence to spontaneously telephone my grandmother Howard, who lived in Baltimore, to say hello, and tell her I'd just been in town at the Walters. Grandmother Howard—Grand, as she wanted me to call her—was not easily impressed, but she was on the museum board, so I guessed that my visit there would please her. She was surprised but cordial when I called, and commanded me to meet her for lunch within the hour.

It was the first time I'd seen my grandmother in almost a year, I realized as I entered her favorite luncheon place, which was located in a pretty nineteenth-century town house just two blocks south of the museum on Charles Street. Grand looked just the same, with her fluffy white hair and a violet wool bouclé St. John suit. I hadn't known that we'd be dining together, so I'd worn pants—but very nice pants, part of a fawn-colored Jil Sander suit that my mother had passed on to me.

My sharp-eyed grandmother immediately recognized the pants as my mother's castoffs. After she had let me kiss her cool, powdered cheek she'd said, "I'd take you shopping for some new clothes, Rei, but the problem is that all the department stores have deserted downtown. Supposedly our new city government is putting on a renaissance, but how can you talk about renaissance when you can't buy a decent pair of shoes or a skirt in a city?"

I smiled, thinking how like my mother she was at that moment—and also, how like me. I'd been frustrated with the shopping in Washington until a branch of the European retailer H&M had opened downtown. Aside from a Thomas Pink boutique in the Mayflower Hotel, there wasn't much shopping for Hugh, either.

"Well, downtown Baltimore doesn't look too bad, aside from the streets being torn up. This restaurant, for example, seems greatly improved," I said, looking around at the restaurant, which still had its original black-and-white checkerboard floor, but repainted walls and an upgraded menu—a shift to mixed baby green salads with goat cheese from the molded chicken salad and tomato aspic platters that I recalled from childhood.

"I miss the aspic," my grandmother said. "At least we have some of the same waitresses who've been here since the late fifties, which is a comfort. Now, tell me about your browse through the Walters. I hope you caught the Renoir exhibition because it's only here another week."

"It was my first time there since they opened the Asian wing, so I spent all my time there," I said.

"The Asian wing. Yes, I suppose you would like that best." Grand sounded disappointed in me, as always.

"I'd love to hear about what you've been doing at the museum, and your other civic involvements." I wanted to change a loaded topic.

"Fund-raising and more fund-raising! It's supposed to be fun to give money away, but the situation's gotten bad in the last few years. Museums, theaters, all the places devoted to culture are falling by the wayside." She sighed. "So you said to me on the telephone your visit here was because of your new position at the Smithsonian?"

"Technically I'm a consultant," I said, "not a regular staffer. If this first assignment goes well, perhaps they'll ask me to do more."

"It's good for a woman to have a flexible kind of job, especially after marriage," Grand said. "And that wedding of yours, it was supposed to happen a few months ago, wasn't it? Your mother told me that something came up, but I'm afraid I never understood the real reason."

"We both got cold feet."

"So, has Hugh returned to his home in Scotland?" Grand raised the thin, silver shadows that were her eyebrows.

"No. Despite the canceled wedding, we're still together."

"Still together? But the engagement's broken, you said. I'm afraid that I don't understand." My grandmother pressed her thin, peach-glossed lips together.

"There's no more to understand than that. We choose to live together, in Washington, for the time being." I was trying to remain patient, but I had an urge to flee.

Grand shot me a look over the menu and said, "It's a question of morals, don't you think?"

"My morals are fine. In fact, I'm feeling so moral today that I think I'll start with the morel mushroom soup. What are you having, Grand?"

Later that evening, when I was telling Hugh about my experience over a quick supper of scrambled eggs, he was more charitable toward my grandmother than I'd been.

"Just think of the disappointments in life she's suffered, Rei. Her only daughter went on to move so far away, and now her granddaughter's showed up so terribly briefly—and cheated her of the fun of a wedding where half the gents would be wearing kilts."

"I haven't seen you in your kilt for a long time," I said, looking at him.

"Perhaps I'll break it out of the mothballs while you're away and go dancing," Hugh said, picking up our used plates and putting them in the sink.

"Sure. I'll get it for you when I'm in the storage closet hunting for my suitcase."

"A suitcase? Can't you do with a carry-on if the trip's just a week?"

"There's never enough room for shoes and clothes in a carry-on," I said. Actually, my carry-on would be jammed with all the important things related to the job—a tiny handheld computer capable of wirelessly connecting to the Internet, a miniature digital camera, an entire dossier of papers and pictures related to the ibex vessel, and the itinerary for my stay. I also was carrying reference books and the Meiwashima auction catalog, because I'd be attending the auction to evaluate Japanese antiques for sale as part of my cover.

"I'll lend you my new carry-on, then. I managed to cram it with three suits, a pair of wingtips, and my trainers on my last trip to Asia. I'm an expert at packing."

"Yes, you are," I answered, knowing that I could not let him anywhere near my luggage. Subterfuge was difficult, I decided as I brought over to the sink the last few dishes from the table. "Speaking of travel, have you heard from Angus?"

"Yes. He's added another week of shows before flying on to Asia," Hugh said. "All things considered, he's had a good experience in the states. Thank God he wasn't arrested that night. I still can't believe the cops let them off."

"Justice works oddly in our nation's capital." I yawned, thinking that I'd finally found the right place for the bugged bonsai: the fire escape, where it would have good sun and could pick up the sounds of burglars, not us. Michael had agreed to take the bug off Hugh's phone once I'd left for Japan. I was pleased at how readily he'd agreed to that until I realized there were almost certainly listening privileges attached to the cellular phone he'd given me.

"I'm worn out from my travels. I think I'm going to bed," I said.

"How tired, exactly? Shall I draw us a bath?" Hugh turned off the sink and put his arms around me. I lay with my head against his chest for a minute, enjoying the feeling of warmth and strength. It was nice to rest quietly for a minute, knowing nobody else was in the apartment. I could have easily just gone to sleep, but I had a sense Hugh had different plans.

Hugh slipped into the bath after me, and made it clear quickly that he intended to turn it into an outpost of a Japanese soapland. But it was easy to be seduced this way: pretty soon we'd tumbled out and had utterly soaked the sheets of the bed. I closed my eyes as his mouth began a familiar southward trek. In the span of a few minutes, all the city-to-city rushing and the long plane flight ahead of me were no longer things I was worrying about.

I twisted away from his mouth and climbed on top, the perfect position to take what I wanted. And Hugh loved it, too—I caught him watching me intently as I moved through the paces of pleasure.

"I'm memorizing you," he said, his hands tracing my breasts. "I don't ever want to forget this."

"Don't, then," I whispered just before I came, the pleasure radiating outward like a stone dropped from tremendous heights into a quiet lake. Afterward, I lay with one leg crooked over him, thinking about going to the bathroom to clean up, but feeling too weary and relaxed to move. "That was different."

"How so?" Hugh stroked my hair.

"You never talked about memorizing me before."

I felt his body stiffen against me, slightly, although his voice remained as warm as ever. "I'm sorry, darling. It's just that I have a rather melancholy feeling tonight."

"I'm sorry. I thought it was good for you, too." As I spoke, a chill settled across my skin, raising goose bumps. Could he have seen through my half-lies and figured out the truth about the creepy job I was going to perform?

Hugh took a deep breath and said, "I have a feeling that you might not—return to me."

"But of course I'm coming back! I have a round-trip ticket, open return, but you can imagine what the museum would do if I just went over there and blew them off."

"Right," Hugh said absently.

I hadn't understood his fear, obviously. "Do you mean—you have a fear that my plane's going to crash?"

"No, no, no! I'm sorry to be such a fool about it." Hugh slipped his hands over my buttocks, pressing me closer to him. "I suppose I'm anxious because this is new for me, being left behind. I don't want to stop you from going."

"I will come back to you," I said firmly. "And you'd better believe that this was not the last time for us in bed or I'll—have to put you through the drill again, right now."

"Heaven help me," Hugh said, sounding happier. "Give me a break, Rei. There are four more nights."

Four more nights.

We used them all.

9

The situation at Dulles Airport was chaotic, with my navel ring setting off the metal detector. This, in turn, inspired a pat-down body search and the unpacking of my luggage. I was very glad that I hadn't packed the Gorgonzola cheese that my aunt had wanted me to bring to her, because I could only imagine what the Japanese authorities would think when I arrived, eighteen hours later, smelling like it. Michael had cautioned me that an official passport was not a diplomatic passport; I was subject to search just like anyone else.

By the time I reached the departure gate, I found out that they'd given my business class seat to a salesman cashing in his frequent-flier upgrade. I started arguing with the flight attendant about the loss of my originally designated seat, not understanding that they'd put me in first class.

"Listen to me, Miss Shimura," the flight attendant said, as slowly as if she were talking to a child. "You go two rows up front, you get the ice cream sundae. You get the champagne. You get any damn thing you want, practically, but you do not have the right to yell at me."

I looked at her, a blond woman about ten years my senior, but made up to look twenty years younger. *Was this my future?* I thought bleakly as she waved dramatically at the first-class cabin where a few Japanese and American businessmen sat in solitary splendor. So, it was a perk; maybe because there was something special about my ticket, or maybe because I had come off like a cranky old lady.

As I settled in, the Japanese businessman who'd had a newspaper on the empty seat next to him looked disappointed to be losing the space.

How much did a seat like this cost? I wondered if there was some kind of State Department code in my passenger profile. The seat had been booked by an agency called S.A.T.O., which sounded Japanese, but turned out to have something to do with the government. Well, it was an agency I'd have to try to use again—if I had the chance.

I took a long, full sip of Veuve Cliquot and watched Virginia drop away below me. The sky was deep pink, darkening to purple. By the time we got to Tokyo, it would be eighteen hours later, and then, I was sure, the luxury would end—I would strap my suitcase onto the wheeled carry-on and hazard my way into Tokyo on a rush hour train. I'd be exhausted, but I'd be in the country I loved most. That was something to drink to any day.

I slept, surprising myself. When I awoke, the businessman was staring at me. He looked away quickly, then returned his gaze.

"Did you take a good rest?"

I nodded. I didn't usually talk to people on planes, given the trouble talking had caused me in the past. This man—round-faced; sleepy-eyed; wearing an expensive, conservative business suit—didn't seem like my cup of tea, especially since he reeked of whisky. I looked away, but still he persisted. "You sleep six hours, I think. We are only two hours from Tokyo, now."

"Isn't that nice," I said in Japanese and opened my Meiwashima catalog.

His eyelashes fluttered. "You speak Japanese?"

Welcome to the land of lost identity, I said to myself. In the United States, if people didn't think I was from Japan, it was because they knew for sure I was from China or Korea. To Americans, my identity was clearly Asian, never mind the half of me that was as WASP as Grand's favorite tomato aspic. It was the same in Japan; even after I'd spoken, I was always pegged a foreigner.

"A little," I replied, because I realized that now he really might not let me alone. I stuck my face back in the Meiwashima catalog, which of course was in Japanese, with only about ten percent of its written material comprehensible to me. My aim had been to study the catalog with a *kanji* dictionary at my side, decoding the information on the artworks that looked sufficiently superb to consider bidding on. But now I realized I'd have a helper hovering nearby who would wind up making me feel embarrassed about what I didn't know.

"Ara, Meiwashima. That's a fancy sale," he said. "But everything is—old! Do you like old Japanese things?"

"A little," I repeated, but this time in English—increasing my distance. "Excuse me, please. I would like to get up for a minute."

He got up with a creak and let me past, but when I came back from the spotless first-class lavatory, he made me step over his legs. I knew the trick—a chance to fully evaluate, and perhaps bump into, a woman's nether parts—so I made a point of going in face forward, and turning around in my seat.

"Can you read those *kanji*? Most foreigners cannot read," he said when I picked up the catalog again.

"The truth is, not very much. I may just put it away and sleep some more."

I slapped my CD player headphones on my ears and turned on my Rilo Kiley CD. Then I closed my eyes and listened to "Portions for Foxes" over and over until I fell asleep. When I finally opened my eyes again, the music was over and a bell was dinging overhead. The Japanese businessman and the nine other male passengers in first class were rising up into the aisle, collecting briefcases from overhead. I looked out the window into the grayness of Tokyo. It was late afternoon, the same time as when I'd left, but it was a new day.

Everywhere, the customs lines were long, except for the one that I was going to—an almost empty channel reserved for diplomats, or people like me who were lucky enough to have passports with a visa inside detailing an attachment to the American Embassy in Tokyo.

The man standing ahead of me in the diplomatic line was finishing up, so now my thoughts turned from global politics to anxiety. What if, somehow, the cover didn't work? I wasn't a diplomat. It was implausible that a museum employee would be in the line with a diplomatic passport. I'd be found out and humiliated by the customs officer, perhaps taken to a private room for interrogation by the National Police . . . my old friends, the ones who would remember my name.

I was thinking about the dark blue handcuffs I'd worn during my deportation a little over a year before, so I almost didn't notice the customs agent waving me forward. I tripped slightly and caught myself on the edge of the carry-on. Great. I looked like a diplomatic klutz.

The customs agent asked me in English for the passport. He opened the page to the picture, looked at it, then looked at me.

He turned the page. "American Embassy," he said, nodding to himself.

"*Hai,*" I said in Japanese. I figured that if I spoke simple Japanese badly, it might eliminate a more complicated discussion.

I smiled at him, hoping that this might be the end of it, but he turned to the computer and typed in something, and my stomach started churning.

The agent returned his gaze to me and asked where I'd be staying.

I glumly gave the name of the Grand Hyatt in Roppongi Hills. I'd argued for a Japanese *ryokan*, but Michael said the government insisted on using American businesses as much as possible.

My passport was stamped, and I was waved through. Free, in the land I loved, and the job was about to begin.

I'd expected to take a train, but it turned out that right outside the customs exit, there was an American with a shaved head and a sign with my entire name spelled correctly. I went to him reluctantly, thinking if they wanted me to travel incognito, having an American soldier meet me wasn't the way to go. The businessman who'd sat next to me, in fact, emerged just as the soldier-chauffeur was taking my carry-on, and looked at me reproachfully, as if he'd expected the two of us to share a limo into town together.

I fluttered my fingers at him and went off with my escort to a distinctly unglamorous van, which was already half-full with other government-sponsored arrivals: two military families with young children. I made funny faces at their babies as we rode away from Chiba prefecture and toward Kanto, where Tokyo waited. Outside, the sky was even grayer than I'd remembered; it looked as if rain clouds were hovering. Hugh had reminded me to check the weather reports before packing, but I'd forgotten. As a result I had no umbrella or raincoat, just a 1970s tweed coat that was hardly waterproof.

Shopping for waterproof gear would be easy, I decided as we pulled up to my hotel two hours later. The Grand Hyatt was a glass-and-steel tower located on the corner of a street of designer boutiques that never existed in my previous Tokyo life. This was Roppongi Hills, an area that city planners had experimented with greatly, as evidenced by a curvy pink chair set out on the street as an example of modern art. I gaped at teenagers in blue jeans lounging on it, and then, a moment later, a cluster of young women dressed in short, frilly gingham-check dresses, frilled bonnets, and black patent Mary Janes, taking photos of each other.

What was this, the land of Cabbage Patch dolls?

The Roppongi I remembered was the stomping ground of girls in eighteen-inch platform sandals. I used to feel like a baby because I couldn't handle those shoes—but now I realized that being a baby was cool. I jumped off the bus and tried to give the soldier a tip for hefting my luggage to the hotel door, but he politely refused.

"That's okay, ma'am. Have a good stay."

Once I'd entered the insulated, expensive world of the Grand Hyatt, I saw no more young women posing as children. Half the people in the ultramodern limestone lobby appeared to be stylish Japanese. The rest looked like foreign businesspeople on expense accounts. The desk clerks, all Japanese and gorgeous, spoke perfect English with the foreigners, so I was privately thrilled when I came up and was immediately addressed in Japanese. It had been so long since this had happened that I wanted to cry. And, I reminded myself, it was going to keep happening every day, as long as I was here to work on the mission.

I was eager to see my room, which, when the bellman took me up, proved as starkly modern as the lobby. The room had a king-size bed—a radical departure from the usual twin beds in Western-style hotel rooms in Japan. The bed was a low mahogany wood platform covered with a crisp white sheet. There was an asymmetrical desk of the same wood, topped by a small, flat-screen TV. The bathroom was luxurious marble, with everything you could want: electric toilet seat with built-in bidet and yet another flat-screen television. I peeled my eyes away from the tub to the bellman, who was still in the bedroom, demonstrating how to use a remote control by the bed to raise and lower two different screens over the huge windows.

I supposed Michael Hendricks would have wanted me to have both shades drawn down all the time, but at the moment I couldn't bring myself to block out Tokyo. I was so excited to be back in town. The moment I was alone, I dropped my coat and headed for the telephone with a blinking message light.

The voice mail was from Mr. Watanabe, who wanted me to call him immediately upon arrival. He'd left a number with a Tokyo area code. There was a second call from Hugh, asking me to let him know when I got in.

So Mr. Watanabe was in the city along with me. That was good, I decided as I started to dial. Of all the people I'd met at the meeting, he seemed the most palatable.

"Was Shimura-san's travel comfortable? Are you safely arrived?" he asked after I'd given my name. There had been no secretary answering the phone; this meant, probably, that he was at home. I heard the sound of someone, probably a child, playing "Chopsticks" in the background.

"Yes, thank you very much, Watanabe-sensei," I answered, using the extreme honorific rather than the more prosaic *san*. Mr. Watanabe wasn't technically a teacher, but he was such a senior diplomat that calling him *sensei* was in perfect order. I wanted to butter him up, because I expected to call on him for advice in the next week.

I continued, "I didn't expect you to be here in Tokyo, too."

"Well, my wife and daughters live here, so when I return here on government business, I enjoy a chance to see them." He paused. "Just as I'm sure you will enjoy the chance to see your relatives."

"Oh, yes." I hadn't thought of calling Aunt Norie and Uncle Hiroshi and my cousin Tom tonight because I'd been so eager to get in touch with my friends Richard and Simone, and whoever else they could dredge up after they were done with their evening shifts as English and French teachers.

"Have you seen the auction catalog yet?"

"I studied it on the plane." I paused, because I was unable to come up with more.

"*Ah, so desu ka*. I'm actually telephoning about the sale. My assistant stopped by the gallery yesterday and learned that Flowers-san already expressed interest."

I understood the code word for Takeo, but not the rest of what Mr. Watanabe was trying to say. "Has he registered as a buyer?"

"Yes, that's the case. He may not be there, though. I hear he sometimes bids by telephone."

That made sense. Takeo was such a hermit that he'd much rather lounge around his house in Hayama with a pizza than dress up and make pleasantries with the important buyers in the Tokyo art scene.

"I'll do my best to find out what he's interested in," I said. "One of the auction assistants is bound to know."

"I will be at the auction, although of course we must not acknowledge each other's presence. We can meet outside later on."

"Of course," I agreed.

"I do suggest that you arrive a little early to the auction, although of course you'll be very tired on your first full day here. Will you ask the hotel to book you a wake-up call that gives you plenty of time to get there by four?"

"I don't usually nap on the first day. I've made this transition many times, Watanabe-sensei. I'll show up early and do my best." The fact was that I had a lot of things planned for the next day— things like picking up the new Eastern Youth compact disc for Hugh, and shopping for bras for myself in the only country where A-cups ruled. But that was too much information for Mr. Watanabe.

After we'd wished each other a good evening, I hung up the phone and pondered my little telephone-address book. I thought I'd want to go out for drinks, but I was beat.

I telephoned Richard's cell phone and left a message that I

wanted to meet him the next day, after I'd rested. Then I swallowed a Melatonin along with two glasses of tap water. I ran a bath and sank into it with the antiques catalog held carefully aloft. I would use my last hour to try to guess what had caught Takeo's discerning eye—and how I could do the same kind of thing myself.

10

To sleep a full first night in Japan, followed by an awakening at a normal morning hour, is an impossible dream.

My normal wake-up hour, the day after I arrive, is three o'clock in the morning—or four, if I'm extremely tired the night before. Unfortunately, these hours are still too wee for Japanese hotel operators to consider turning on the hot water heater or serve breakfast.

But hot water wasn't an issue in this hotel, nor was heat or room service. I took a long, luxurious shower. I debated which telephone to use to call Hugh. Michael Hendricks had given me a sleek, high-tech cell that could receive and make international calls, take digital photographs, surf the web, and serve as a receptacle for ingoing and outgoing e-mail. Still, the frugal traveler inside me wondered whether I would get into trouble for using it for personal reasons.

I put off the decision and dressed in the yoga pants and sweatshirt at the top of my luggage and moved through a half hour of stretches. My back and hips were stiff after the long flight. I needed to get out of my room and get breakfast somewhere.

Tokyo's wholesale fish market lay six kilometers due east. As I jogged the route I knew so well, I found myself running directly toward the rising sun—or the place where the sun would have risen, if there hadn't been so many gray storm clouds. I didn't mind. I was elated to run through Roppongi Crossing, passing my old favorite dance haunts like Gas Panic, Wall Street, and MoTown House. In the evening, you could barely walk a straight line through the crowds, but now it was uncrowded, and the only things I needed to dodge were the disgusting asphalt flowers that drunken salarymen had spewed along the sidewalk the night before. From Gaien Higashi-Dori I passed the Lamborghini dealer where Hugh had spent many wistful hours, and then the International Clinic, where many foreigners went for discreet treatment of venereal diseases contracted at the nightclubs I'd passed a few kilometers back.

In my pleasant reverie, with U2 blaring into my ears from the Walkman I wore, I sped along the uncrowded sidewalks, giving the wide gray streets to the first delivery trucks, bicycles, and motorcycles, none of which speeded—this despite the open path, and the lack of police.

I was tiring by the time I passed Tokyo Tower, but I knew the best part of the run was coming: Shiba Park, where I slowed down as I passed the graveyard of the Tokugawa clan of shoguns, and took a brief stop to drink some water at Zojo-ji Temple. I resumed my run again and emerged under a giant *tori* gate into the Hibiya business district, then Shimbashi, with all its wonderful little eating and drinking places still closed. Finally I ran through Ginza, the luxury shopping district where people said that if you stacked ten ten-thousand-yen notes anywhere on the sidewalk, the tiny portion of land underneath the bills would still be worth more. Then it was a right on Harumi Dori past the grand old Kabuki Theater and straight into Tsukijii, where I was delighted to slow to a walk to avoid running into the huge, glistening fish laid out directly on concrete sidewalks. The fishmongers with their thigh-high rubber boots and shrewd expressions glanced at me, but didn't bother beckoning—it must have seemed obvious that a sweaty young woman in Asics was not a major restaurateur.

I was a glutton, I thought, as I ran my eyes over the glistening sea creatures lying so ingloriously on concrete. A sleek blue-gray fish that looked as if it weighed only about ten pounds—big enough for a feast with my friends, though the price scrawled on its side made that fantasy unaffordable—gave me pause.

"Excuse me, but what's that called?" I asked the bored-looking fellow standing in a wool sweater and rubber wader overalls behind the beauty. The fish had a number scrawled on it, but that was its only identifying feature.

"It's a kind of *shusseuo*."

"Really! What kind, exactly?" *Shusse* literally meant "career progress," and *uo* meant fish. Mothers gave children *shusseuo* before school examinations. It was interesting, and perhaps apt, that I'd gotten to see this fish this morning.

He glanced around, then lowered his voice as if he were going to tell me a secret. "*Wakashi*. It's very, very fresh."

"Oh, I bet it will make wonderful sushi." He was talking about young yellowtail. If yellowtail was good, a younger version had to be heavenly.

"Ah, yes, it will be gone within a half hour, I'm sure."

"Where was it caught, in Japanese waters or—"

"What about some service for a real customer?" a sharp voice barked behind me and I stepped aside.

I'd gone too far, asked too much. And the fact was, I couldn't take the fish. I bowed to the fishmonger and the man who had interrupted me and slipped off. It was six-thirty, so some breakfast spots around the market had to be open. I began searching for a little hole-in-the-wall place where Tom had taken me for an incredible seafood stew a few years earlier. After a minute's walk, I recognized its sign—a smiling octopus—but the door was locked. However, two doors down a long blue curtain fluttered in another doorway.

A red-faced man with a kerchief tied around his head bellowed out a welcome as I stepped inside the tiny restaurant. It couldn't have been more than ten feet long and five feet wide, with a blond wood counter and five stools. Every stool was filled, but the chef motioned for me to stand behind the chair of a fishmonger, who was finishing up a plate of squid roe sushi. I took the time to look around and decide what I'd order. The man next to him was eating *tai,* one of my favorite fishes. Soon, the fishmonger had departed and I took his spot. I asked for *tai* and *wakashi hammachi.*

The chef shook his finger at me. "We don't carry *wakashi* fish. It's because the little ones are caught too early that we have fish shortages, *neh?"*

"You're right. I'm sorry." My cheeks warmed with shame. Why hadn't I thought of this myself, when I'd been joking with the fishmonger outside? Ever since sushi had exploded in global popularity in the 1990s, Japan's once teaming tuna and yellowtail population had dwindled. Fishermen who caught baby fish like the one I'd seen, rather than waiting for the babies to mature and lay eggs for a future generation, were thinking of quick profits and disregarding the environment. But the whole reason they chose to be unscrupulous profiteers was the existence of greedy gourmets like myself.

The chef suggested *inada,* which was a slightly more mature form of *hammachi,* and I agreed readily. I sipped a tiny cup of hot green tea while I watched the chef deftly slice the fish and layer it on fresh sticky rice. Then, it was my turn. I swirled each piece of sushi through a mixture of soy and wasabi in a little blue bowl at my side. I was in a state of bliss. The only problem was that I knew another person was behind me, subtly but hostilely waiting for the seat. A few years ago, I would have turned around to acknowledge him and apologize, but today, I was bent on enjoying myself. I didn't turn. I kept eating steadily, at a pace that suited me.

"Okusama, another honorable customer is waiting," the chef said, scooping my plate away from me after I picked up the final piece of *tai* with my chopsticks.

I cringed. Why had the man addressed me as "honorable housewife," the kind of honorific men used only with female customers of a certain age? I'd gone through my previous life in Japan with restaurant and shop owners calling me *oneesan,* which meant "big sister."

The *tai* in my mouth suddenly tasted metallic, but I dutifully chewed and swallowed. Then I picked up the hand-scrawled bill and squeezed through the standing-room-only crowd to the cashier. The sumptuous sushi breakfast had cost about $8.50, a bargain compared with what breakfast would have cost in the hotel. I got a receipt for business purposes and tucked it safely away in my pocket, confident that so far, I was handling expenses in a way that my government would approve.

My worries about not knowing how to behave correctly continued when I reached the Meiwashima Auction House in late afternoon. The young woman behind Gucci sunglasses who was guarding the door didn't recognize me. In fact, she attempted to stop me from entering.

"I believe I am preregistered. Shimura Rei?"

"Oh, I'm sorry." The girl looked at her clipboard and nodded. "Yes, yes, I see your name is on the list. You may pick up paddle number fifty-three at the main office."

I remembered her from half a dozen sales past, but apparently she hadn't remembered me. Well, there were a lot of people, I thought to myself, as I joined the long queue standing at a desk behind which a crew of women were issuing pine paddles approximately the size of fans. I looked around covertly at the well-dressed shop owners and private buyers who were nodding and smiling at each other as they waited. I spotted a few familiar faces, those belonging to the owners of some big, fancy shops in Roppongi, Omote-Sando, and the like. The ones who recognized me gave the correct half-bow, to which I bowed back at the same forty-five-degree angle. There was no need to chat. This was a chichi auction—a place to which it had taken me a couple of years to gain admittance.

It took a good twenty minutes to get to the head of the line, and when I did so, I asked, as innocently as I could, if Takeo Kayama was bidding.

"He has a number, yes! And here is your paddle!" the clerk answered brightly.

"Sorry to bother you, but what is his number?" I said, slowly taking the paddle numbered 53.

"It's not a problem for Kayama-san; he already knows the number. He already registered," the clerk answered.

"We are old friends, and I do not want to bid against him. For that reason I would like to know whether he's placed any absentee bids on any of the items in today's sale."

"Yes, he has. But it's against the rules of our auction house to give direct information on a particular customer's interests."

"Oh, is that so? I apologize. Well, then, if you don't mind, I'll take my paddle."

"You already have it, Shimura-san. And why don't I give you this brochure, which explains our company rules in detail."

I turned away, not wanting them to see the blood that had rushed to my face. I'd screwed up in front of gossipy antiques people. I'd come in looking so proper, wearing the claret-color St. John suit Grand had sent from Neiman's right before the trip; the suit was so grown-up it made me look over thirty, which actually was my goal. But now—I'd lost my advantage by behaving like a kid.

The setup for the auction was a high stage with multiple televisions suspended from the ceiling over it, for close-up views of the items to be auctioned. There was a table where small items would be placed for viewing, and a podium on which the auctioneer would stand. In front of the stage, tight rows of small gilt chairs waited for the audience. Most of the seats were filled; I realized that because of the long time I'd spent in line, it was only twenty minutes until the auction started.

Mr. Watanabe walked along the side of the room, as if unaware of my presence, though I knew, from a cell phone call I'd gotten while waiting in line, that he'd seen me. I made a slow circle around the room's perimeter, seeking out the items that had the highest estimated values in the catalog. Takeo wouldn't bother with little things, and neither would someone who was supposedly buying for the Sackler.

One of the most confusing elements of the viewing—something I anticipated because of my past experience at Meiwashima—was that not all the items for sale were Japanese. For instance, there was a huge, fantastically carved four-poster bed—Chinese, I'd figured out from the catalog copy, although to me it looked like the stuff of fantasy in an Arabian Nights.

I moved on to ceramics. My interest was caught by a graceful

Momoyama period vase with a mottled gray finish. This was the kind of thing that I should be interested in.

I asked a young man wearing the severe black suit that was the auction house's uniform to open the case. He paused until I reminded him that the house rules stated that auction attendees were allowed close examinations of goods for sale before the actual event took place. Apparently not many of the shop owners bothered.

The young man's eyes were wary as he placed the vase on the examination table in front of the case. I sank into a deep squat, a posture of which my fitness instructor would have approved, and took out the tiny digital camera-phone, but before I could use it, the man stopped me. Apparently, I was breaking another one of the rules.

I put away the camera, feeling irritated and deciding that I wasn't certain the piece in front of me was as old as estimated. Although the Tokyo antiques-dealing community had an overall good reputation for honesty, some Japanese potters were so traditional in their approach to hand-shaping and firing that it would be quite possible to pass off something newer as older. Only very subtle clues could tell me whether the vase was likely to be as old as the catalog said.

I stared at the vase, and in my long moment of indecision someone brushed past, causing me to lose balance and pitch forward.

My life flashed before my eyes as I struggled to keep myself from knocking against the vase. But the young man had it in his hands. All was saved, though I looked undignified on my hands and knees on the carpet.

"My God!" I exclaimed, so discombobulated that I accidentally lapsed into English. Immediately, I switched to a Japanese apology.

"It's okay," the young man said, his voice shaky. "That other customer was hurrying by very quickly. It was not your fault."

I slowly came up to a standing position. My dodgy right knee was going to trouble me for the next few days, after the way I'd smashed onto the floor. No more runs through the city for a while, but that was a small price to pay in exchange for not being responsible to Meiwashima Auction Gallery for $50,000 worth of damage.

"Do you still want to examine it?" the man asked, as if he'd noticed that I was backing away from the vase.

"No, thank you," I said faintly. I'd had enough excitement, and I planned on taking a seat, one close to the back of the room, to watch the proceedings. But as I headed toward my seat, I shot a glance toward the young woman who'd almost caused the accident. Too young to be a buyer, she was probably somebody's clueless child, I thought with irritation. She was tiny—barely five feet tall, I thought, and absolutely adorable in one of the new Pucci print dresses that I'd seen in magazines—far too expensive for me to ever contemplate buying. She must have had it altered to fit her tiny frame. I watched her raise an arm as long and thin as a Pocky Stick pretzel to wave.

I followed the direction of her wave but couldn't figure out to whom she was beckoning. But then my attention was suddenly drawn away, because among the people seating themselves in the audience, I'd caught a glimpse of a familiar profile.

I had already seated myself in one of the few single seats left—this one between an elderly couple there to see the sale of a prized family heirloom, and a flinty dealer from Kawasaki. For this reason, I was hesitant to leave my seat, but I strained for a better view of the man in question. Not until he turned his head, so that I could see his face in full, did I recognize Takeo pointing to the seat next to him.

Suddenly, I felt very hot. My sweat glands had gone into overdrive. Why would Takeo be coaxing me over? Had he learned that I was asking after him, and actually been pleased?

"Meiwashima Auction Number Fifty-seven is about to commence," a voice droned over the speaker system. "Our staff respectfully requests that you make sure that you bring your paddle with you and that your financial details are registered with the office before you sit down."

Takeo's expression was almost affectionate, a surprise to me given the way we'd parted. The warmth made him look even more handsome than he'd appeared at first glance. My job was going to be difficult indeed, with Takeo still shooting me such a sexy come-hither look.

I had just gathered up my bag when I noticed that the girl who'd tripped me had entered Takeo's row. Mouthing obvious apologies, the girl slowly proceeded along the line of patrons, all of whom stood up for her in a massive show of Japanese courtesy. At one point, she stumbled slightly against an older lady. Perhaps her collision with me had been not a matter of carelessness but a lack of co-ordination. But then all my theories vanished, replaced by shock as the girl settled happily into the place that I'd mistakenly thought Takeo was saving for me.

11

Takeo had a girl.

Friend?

No, I decided as I saw his arm slip around her shoulders.

Girlfriend!

I thanked God for the second time in ten minutes, but this time silently. Thank God I hadn't embarrassed myself by trying to take her seat. From my spot, I watched the girl tilt her face up to Takeo and giggle about something, to which he gave a gentle, reproving shake of the head.

The auction was starting, so I tried to concentrate on the point of the evening—making an appearance as a serious potential buyer. It was advantageous that Takeo would see me in this light, especially if Takeo wanted the vase. My interest in it—perhaps bidding for it at the start, then gracefully giving up—would be at least a conversation opener for the two of us.

Three hundred items were listed for sale, and the wait for item 159 was long. The auctioneer's pace was considerably slower, and more genteel, than what I was accustomed to in the American auction houses that I frequented. Still, it was a good thing I was there for the whole auction, because just thirty items in, Takeo's girlfriend started whispering to him, and he put his hand up for the Chinese bed.

I sucked in my breath. What was Takeo, who always had been happy with a basic futon, doing buying a bed? Was he—buying it for her? Various confusing scenarios ran through my mind as Takeo kept his hand up while the bed's price rose from 200,000 yen to 1 million. He was the only one left at that price, plus the auction house premium of ten percent. As the auctioneer called out that the item was sold at 1 million yen plus ten percent commission, Takeo's girlfriend bounced excitedly in her chair.

I'd thought I'd been through enough surprises, but five minutes later, a regal, blue-and-gold export Imari dinner service for twenty set off more tugging and whispering. Takeo's hand rose again. He got it for 500,000 —a steal, but then, not many Japanese gave big dinner parties. I didn't understand why Takeo, always so private, would want to buy a restaurant's worth of matching china. It had to be for the girl, not for him.

An intermission after the first 100 items gave me a chance to make my move. Takeo and his young friend had risen, too. She was tugging at his hand, as if she wanted him to go back to the display cases, so I headed that way, too. As I walked, I tried to look as if I were immersed in the catalog, so it seemed natural for me to almost, but not quite, bump into them.

"Pardon me—oh, hello!" I exclaimed, feigning surprise. "It's been a long time."

Instead of answering me, Takeo walked past, dragging his girlfriend along with him.

Maybe he hadn't realized I was speaking to him. I hurried after the couple, and tried again. "Takeo-san, I don't know if you, ah, recognized me—"

My use of his first name couldn't be ignored. The girl's mouth hung open in a little violet O while Takeo answered.

"Shimura-san, of course I recognize you. I'm a little busy right now, though. Will you excuse me?" He pulled a cell phone from his pocket.

"No telephone use allowed in the auction house except for employees," one of the auction helpers said, miraculously materializing. For the first time that evening, I thanked the powers behind the Meiwashima Auction Gallery for the rules.

Takeo snapped his phone shut. He looked from me to the girl-friend, and then back at me, obviously unhappy.

"I'm back from the United States." I'd decided to play the part of an old friend to the hilt. "It's so good to see you! I'd love to catch up on old times—"

"Circumstances make that difficult," Takeo said coldly.

"Really? What's going on with you these days, besides taking over your father's flower-arranging school?"

"I'm getting married. My fiancée and I are just picking out a few items for the house."

I was aware that Takeo was watching me closely for a reaction. I was determined not to look as pained as I felt. I unclenched my jaw and offered congratulations.

"I'm surprised you were allowed back into Japan so quickly," Takeo said, his words cutting. He knew what had happened, even though he and I hadn't seen each other at all during that last time in the city.

I shrugged, trying to seem casual. "Well, my client has some clout—the Sackler Gallery. Do you remember? It's part of our group of national museums that you visited when you were in Washington—"

Takeo interrupted me swiftly. "Unfortunately, we must excuse ourselves, Shimura-san. Good luck."

"What do you mean? The sale isn't over yet—" Takeo's fiancée began in a baby-pitched voice.

"Dinner with your parents, remember? I was just about to call them to find out where they are. Let's go outside to make the call."

The princess was digging her long, lavender-glossed nails into Takeo's arm. "But I want to stay longer. We need a few more things."

"Your father wants to pick us up early. He's anticipating traffic problems because of the rain." Takeo smiled at her in a way that made it seem like the sun breaking out over Mount Fuji. I looked away from that smile, just as I had looked away from the great, glaring diamond on the girl's tiny hand.

"But we at least have to pay for the bed and the china," she pointed out.

"I'll do it by telephone. Oh, I see your parents already." I followed his gaze to a couple in the doorway. The woman was stout for a Japanese woman, but elegantly dressed in a tweed suit, with a frozen-in-place, slightly bouffant shoulder-length hairdo that I'd noticed diplomatic wives seemed to favor. She bowed slightly as she approached us. The man at her side was about the same height—about five-six, a standard height for Japanese men of the older generation, and thin. He wore thick glasses and a dark suit. He didn't look glamorous at all, but he was obviously well known to the Meiwashima staff because the people who had checked my name against a list were bowing deeply and ushering him in.

I could have stayed and forced Takeo to introduce me, but I could imagine how awkward things would get. And the fact was that Mr. Watanabe was heading toward the parents, smiling and nodding.

Remembering what Mr. Watanabe had said about keeping away from each other, I took this as my cue to leave. I made my bows to the betrothed couple and quickly passed by the parents and went out of the auction.

I'd gone so hastily and in such a state of confusion that it wasn't until half a block later, when I was soaked in pouring rain, that I realized I needed an umbrella.

12

Mr. Watanabe caught up with me a few minutes later in the alley where we had arranged, over the phone the previous evening, to meet after the sale. He appeared under a large black umbrella, which he held over me as we spoke. He was being so gallant that I was ashamed to even begin to tell him about my breach of etiquette, but I did, sparing no details. When I was done, Mr. Watanabe didn't immediately comment, but instead told me about the girl and her family.

Takeo's fiancée was Emi Harada, daughter of Kenichi Harada, the recently appointed minister for the environment. He was also a former diplomat, so the two men had crossed paths before and had exchanged greetings at the sale. Yasuko Harada, Kenichi's wife, was an active flower arranger and the patron of many social welfare causes. *As her daughter would soon be,* I thought to myself. Takeo, despite his radical tendencies, had chosen for his bride what Japanese for centuries had wanted: the youngest, purest woman with the most elite pedigree. But I should have known all this. I asked Mr. Watanabe why I hadn't been warned about Takeo's engagement.

"Unfortunately, her name never appeared in any information I received," Watanabe said, his eyes wide. "And, when I was speaking with her father just now, he said nothing about the engagement to me. Are you sure it's the truth?"

"She was wearing a huge diamond ring on her left hand," I said. "Surely there must have been an announcement of it somewhere, in the newspapers or something—"

"I don't think so. Can you read Japanese newspapers?"

Of course I couldn't. I stood there, the rain hammering my umbrella, hammering me with the realization that I'd forgotten how everything worked in Japan, from buying fish to auction rules and relationships.

"I suppose you'll have to make a meeting with him again," Mr. Watanabe said.

I would have thrown up my hands if they hadn't been engaged with the umbrella and my backpack. "It seems impossible. I explained to you already that he was very unfriendly."

"Oh, I'm sure that's not the case. This was just a first meeting. I'm sure the next one will be more harmonious."

"It won't work. He's moved on, and I'm just a reminder of old times he'd rather forget."

Mr. Watanabe looked grave. "Do you feel that you cannot do the job that you said you would?"

I looked down at the pavement. How fast would he fly me out of Japan—on the next day's flight? It was entirely possible. I breathed deeply and said, "I'm sorry I wasn't effective tonight. I'll try again."

"*Gambatte!*" he commanded, then tapped the end of his umbrella on the concrete, and walked on.

Later, as I sat at the Brazilian mahogany bar in Salsa Salsa watching my old friend Enrique muddle together lime and rum to make a welcome-home *mojito*, I thought about the significance of Mr. Watanabe's parting command: *gambatte*, the imperative form of a uniquely Japanese word, *gambarimasu*, which meant "give it your all." People said *Gambatte* to you before a test or a sporting event. *Gambatte* was about responsibility to someone else, your parents or your teammates or your school. And, in this case, both the U.S. and Japanese governments.

I sighed and pulled the tiny telephone camera out of my purse.

First, I entered the password I'd come up with—TAKE0, in honor of the mission. The zero I'd used at the end instead of the letter *O* escaped my mind on the first try; but then I remembered it and entered the password again, and the screen flashed "ready."

Time to practice. I aimed the instrument at Enrique and punched buttons until I saw his smiling image appear on the tiny screen. After I'd taken the picture, I admired it for a while. I'd gotten him dead center, and with his eyes open. For me, this was a very good first photo, with a machine that had seemed unfathomably complex during the hour that Michael Hendricks had attempted to explain its use. I remained confused by the many buttons on the tiny camera. In fact, I wasn't sure if I'd just saved Enrique's photo or deleted it when it abruptly disappeared from the screen.

"That's a cool phone. Or is it a camera?" A strange accent on my left made me jump, and I turned to see one of the backpackers from a group that had been sitting together. I'd noticed them when I'd come in and made the mistake of smiling a brief hello.

"Both," I said, looking at the speaker, who was somewhere around twenty-five, though it was hard to tell from his face, which was either really tanned or really dirty.

"May I see it? Where did you get it, Akibarra or—" He rolled his *r*'s like someone from Germany or a nearby country.

"The electronics district is called Akihabara, and sorry, but I can't let you play around with this camera. I'm not the greatest technophile, so I don't want to take the risk of changing any settings."

"Hmm, I reckon you and I could have more fun playing around at something else! I'm Jürgen." He grinned suavely, and I cursed myself for the expression I'd used.

"Acually, Jürgen, I'm not the best of company because I need to make a phone call at the moment—"

"Ach so! You must be some kind of spy girl with a Chames Bond camera not for sale in the shops—"

Damn it, but his voice was loud. I looked at him stonily and said, "It's a gift from my boyfriend, who I was just about to phone."

"Don't you mean your husband?"

"What?" I looked at him warily.

"A woman your age would ordinarily be married, right?" He swung off with laughter and returned to his friends.

I'd had about enough of unruly men, but I really did want to speak to Hugh. And now it was early morning in Washington, time to catch him before he left for the office.

"Good morning, my sweet," I said brightly after he finally picked up.

"Rei. So what's, what time is it?" He sounded disjointed.

"I thought it was about eight-thirty in Washington. I'm sorry, you were probably up late last night painting the dining room." I had made sure he had all the paint and supplies he needed before I'd left.

"Not quite. Damn, I have a meeting in half an hour." He groaned. "I feel like hell."

"Oh! I can get off the line if you need. I just wanted to let you know I was here and safe—"

"Don't go," Hugh said. "I'll call my assistant to tell her to reschedule. She's come up with more than a few excuses since my brother came back. And today's the end of it. They're flying out of Dulles for Singapore and then Tokyo."

"But that sounds illogical, I mean, shouldn't they have flown from California and gone to Tokyo first?"

"Nothing my brother does is logical. Including drinking. We closed the 9:30 Club last night, Rei. I'm knackered."

"Aren't you getting a little old for that?" He was never going to make partner if he kept coming to work late with a hangover.

He groaned. "I didn't mean to. And now I'm so hungover I could kick myself. I must say, if you'd been here it probably wouldn't have happened—"

"As if I have any impact at all," I said, with heavy sarcasm. "Remember, I was there at Club Paradise when you were sick enough to lose it in a wastebasket."

"So do you think I have a drinking problem?" Hugh's voice crackled with anger.

"Not exactly. It's just that—you seem to be losing count of your drinks, when you go out. You can't blame me for being a little worried." I eyed the *mojito* in front of me. I'd thought it was two-thirds empty, and was on the verge of ordering another. Now I decided it was actually one-third full, and I was going to slow down.

Hugh began to rail at me, and I saw no point in becoming involved in an argument that the rest of the bar would find amusing, so I simply hung up. Almost immediately the telephone rang again, and I switched it on, still exasperated, but determined to at least give Hugh a chance to apologize and redeem himself.

"Darling?" I said.

"What a nice greeting," Michael Hendricks answered in his cool New England voice. "When I was in Japan before, it was just *moshi-moshi*. Perhaps times have changed."

"Hello, Michael." I paused to compose myself. "I apologize. I was expecting a call from someone else. Which reminds me—may I use this phone for personal calls?"

"You're obviously doing so already, but don't worry. Just remember to avoid saying things into the phone such as my name, and the names of others involved in our situation."

"Sorry." I took a swig of *mojito*.

"Can you explain who the man is in the picture you just sent? You didn't include a text message."

"He's not of any significance to you! I was just practicing—" I paused. "How the hell did you get that picture?"

"You must have pressed 'send.' As I explained to you last week, the camera is wired to send files straight to my Blackberry. "

"Oh. I suppose you're also interested in the bad news from Mr. Watanabe?"

Michael spoke rapidly, his anger practically flashing across the phone. "What bad news? I haven't heard any news, and I don't expect to get progress reports from him! You are the one I expect to hear from, and I wonder about the fact that you've been on location for over twenty-four hours and I haven't heard a peep, just a photo of this Hispanic-looking guy holding a silver device that looks like a grenade—"

"It's a cocktail shaker," I said. "And Enrique's a bartender, not anyone you need to worry about."

"I see. So you're in a bar again?"

"What do you mean by 'again'?"

"Is it a situation where you can talk?"

I glanced around. At their table, the backpackers were giving a drink order to Enrique, so I told Michael about the auction, how I'd met Takeo but quickly learned about his engagement to the daughter of the minister of the environment.

"Aha. I know that name. He was in Japan's diplomatic corps before. I ran into him once in the UAE." Michael sounded as if his annoyance had ceased.

"UAE?" I asked.

"United Arab Emirates. It was during the first Gulf War," Michael said. "And regarding this engagement, I'll have our guys check it out. He might not really be engaged, but just trying to pull your chain."

I snorted and said, "He declared the news right in front of Emi, and she certainly didn't protest."

"He spoke to you in Japanese?" Michael asked.

"No, he was speaking English, perhaps because he noticed that my Japanese isn't as good as it was," I said glumly. "But she seemed to understand completely. I also saw her ring and the way he looked at her."

"And how did you feel about that?"

There was something in Michael's tone that made me shiver, so I said briskly, "I'm upset because it greatly compromises my chances at succeeding. You know that I came here to do something, which I'll still try to do, but with this gorgeous young girl around, the situation's going to be little dicey—"

"On the contrary. Engaged men are easy marks."

"Excuse me?"

"Men on the verge of losing their freedom do last-gasp, risky things. Why do you think bachelor nights are such an institution?"

Michael seemed as if he wanted to rattle on, but I noticed that Richard and Simone had entered the bar and were heading toward me. "Ah, I can't really talk anymore."

"Okay. Keep going, then, and make sure the next picture you send off into cyberspace is of something other than a frigging bartender."

Very cranky. I clicked off while Richard and Simone took off their raincoats glittering with water and came at me for a group hug that smelled of perfume and smoke, a strange kind of smoke I couldn't identify.

"Rei, it's been so looong," Simone moaned in her pretty French accent and came in close to peck both sides of my cheeks. Then Richard rushed at me like a small blond whirlwind and kissed me long and hard on the lips.

"What was that about?" I pulled away, stunned by the unusual show of affection.

"Just trying to pull Enrique's chain," Richard said, smiling at his boyfriend, who was grinning at the three of us. "You're a good kisser, Rei. We should do it again."

"I'll take a rain check," I said uneasily, because Jürgen and his friends were watching with considerable interest.

"It's the crystal," Enrique said, coming in close and setting down a dubious-looking pink drink in front of Richard.

"Cristal? That doesn't look like champagne." I was confused by Enrique's offering.

"Happy pills," Richard said. "Also known as *shabu* or *yaba* around here. Enrique says I get wild when I pop one. But, ooh, is it fun. Teacher's little helper!"

"It's not an everyday thing, *chérie*," said Simone, seeing the shock on my face. "But you know how it is. One of Richard's students, he passed a tough English qualification exam, so he brought his sweet teacher a little *presento*."

"I thought we could go dancing after this!" Richard bobbed his head back and forth. "Rei, I've missed you so much that I could almost jump your bones."

"You're gay, Richard," I reminded my friend. Looking at him so ebullient and silly made me feel wretched. I'd missed Richard and longed many times for a heart-to-heart chat like those we'd once had as roommates in a shabby, cold apartment in Minami-Senju. Now, he had shown up for our reunion flying as high as a Boys' Day kite. There would be no way to talk with him about the confusing situation I'd gotten into with Hugh, let alone anything else.

"Will you come dancing, Rei?" Simone purred. "Bar Isn't It has a really good ladies' night."

"I just came in last evening. I don't think I could make it, but you know, in a few days Angus Glendinning and his band will be here. Why don't we go dancing that night?"

"Hugh has you by a ball and chain, huh?" Richard said. "I knew you should never have moved in with him."

"Don't be ridiculous. It's just I'm still going through jet lag and had hoped for a cozy night catching up."

"Oh, of course! We don't have to go dancing," Simone said, shooting Richard a reproving look. "I have longed to talk with you, Rei, so many times. I don't even understand what has brought you from Washington—"

"A very serious job, which is another one of the reasons I can't paint the town red tonight—I'll never cope tomorrow," I said.

"But you can't work here. Your visa's revoked," Richard said a bit too loudly.

"Not anymore," I said, shooting him a warning glance, which he blithely ignored.

"How? It's impossible to get visas these days. Immigration to Japan has been cut, like, in half, after 9-11. How did you get back in?"

Trying to seem casual, I shrugged. "I'm doing some consulting for a government museum. They wanted me over, so they were able to pull a few strings."

"That's surprising. Your country's reputation is in the gutter, worldwide." Richard, proudly Canadian, sounded almost gleeful.

"Let's not talk politeeks," Simone said. "It's very dull, don't you think? Rei, is something wrong with your drink? Shall Enrique bring you wine instead?"

I shook my head. All I wanted was to escape the manic gaze of two people whom I'd once been comfortable with, but who now seemed like strangers.

13

Despite Richard and Simone's protests, I left Salsa Salsa soon afterward. Finding a taxi in the rain in a fashionable part of town proved impossible. My Bally pumps were waterlogged, and Grand's beautiful wool suit smelled like a wet dog when I finally arrived back at the Hyatt.

"Oh, dear," said the desk clerk, looking at me.

Oh dear, indeed. The rain became even harder during the night, and it was mixed with rough, gusting winds that startled me awake at three. And given my jet lag and the two drinks I'd had, I couldn't fall back into slumber. I tossed through idea after idea of how to get to Takeo. By five in the morning I thought I had a possibility.

Eight o'clock was about the right time to telephone Aunt Norie, who would have already given breakfast to her family. The Shimuras usually breakfasted together, no matter what. My aunt was the kind of cook who made *miso* soup and rice fresh every morning, and would present enough pickled vegetables and fish alongside it to make you think you wouldn't need another meal that day.

"I'm back," I said when my aunt picked up the telephone.

"Your father told us you would be coming. This news is wonderful, that you're back in Japan. How did you manage it?"

"It's a long story. Could you come into Tokyo today? I'd love to take you to lunch somewhere to catch up. I'm staying in Roppongi Hills, but I'd love to get someplace more traditional—"

"But Roppongi Hills is extraordinary! Mrs. Morioka and I ate at the French Kitchen in the Grand Hyatt last week after *ikebana* class. There are so many restaurants in Roppongi Hills that we could easily choose something. And perhaps Chika can join us, because her office isn't too far away."

I agreed, thinking that I might as well take her somewhere nice, since for once in my life I was on an expense account. We settled on a spot called Kitsune, which Norie said served Japanese nouvelle cuisine.

After the meeting time had been set, I asked Norie if she'd have time to take me to the Kayama Kaikan, the headquarters of Takeo's family's flower arranging school. Norie was a master teacher at the school, and she had always enjoyed a close relationship with the Kayamas. Norie credited herself with getting Takeo and me together, and had mourned when the relationship ended. Still, the situation remained warm enough between her and Takeo that every fall, he came to her garden to cut back her hydrangeas with his own special technique.

"Do you wish to study *ikebana* again, Rei-chan? I assumed you would be too busy with this wonderful new job!" My aunt's excitement fairly crackled over the line.

"I am interested in *ikebana*." I paused, knowing that with my aunt, it paid to be direct. "However, I'd like to talk with Takeo Kayama about it. I thought you might be able to be our go-between and establish a meeting."

To my surprise, my aunt paused. At last she said, "I don't know if a go-between is a good idea. He's actually engaged to be married."

"You knew?" How ironic that my own aunt had the facts, while American and Japanese intelligence were clueless.

"Yes, her name is Emi Harada. She is a lovely young girl whose father is a government minister. She's started studying flower arranging at the school, of course."

"I see. Well, you're right that she's lovely and young. I saw Takeo and Emi last night at the auction, and I think he was embarrassed to talk to me in front of her. It's unfortunate because—because I really want to spend a little time with him, and this business trip of mine is so short. Does it seem too much to expect—that he would be civil and give me a few hours' time?"

"Perhaps it is," my aunt said gently. "Maybe it's an American custom for the ex-boyfriend and ex-girlfriend to remain friendly, but it's not often done here in Japan."

That's right, I thought bitterly to myself. Because in Japan, women and men had such prescribed roles that they rarely had pure friendships, once they'd left childhood. I said, "I thought Takeo was different. And after what we all went through in Washington—Hugh and Takeo and I—it seems a shame that I can't continue a friendship with Takeo."

"Well, knowing Kayama-san's personality, I'm still a bit doubtful, but I'll try to smooth things. I think the only way, though, is if it seems like a coincidence that you see each other, not planned."

That's what had happened the previous night, and had failed. However, my aunt was privy to resources I didn't have. She told me she needed to think a bit more, but she'd have a plan in place by the time we met for lunch. I thanked her and hung up the telephone, feeling hopeful for the first time since I'd touched ground in Tokyo.

Two hours later, the streets were a quarter inch underwater when I set off for Kitsune. The restaurant was only a five-minute walk from my hotel, so I shouldn't have gotten as wet as I did. However, I'd decided to go shopping for a raincoat, umbrella, and the pièce de résistance I'd been missing in my wardrobe ever since I'd moved away: rain shoes, the ankle-high rubber shoes that were, as far as I knew, unique to the practical Japanese. I knew I wasn't going to find them at Christian LaCroix or Louis Vuitton or any other of the luxury boutiques in Roppongi Hills, so I shot over on the subway to the Ginza and ducked into one of my favorite department stores, Matsuya, where I found rain shoes on the eighth floor, along with a zebra-patterned umbrella and a shiny black trench coat in young fashion on the third floor. I also couldn't resist picking up a pair of slim-fitting trousers made of pleather, the plastic form of leather that had looked so good on Chika. I paid with my own credit card for the pants, figuring they weren't a work expense that Michael would want to cover—although the raincoat, umbrella, and shoes might pass muster, so I put them on the card he'd issued me to use for the hotel and incidentals.

As cool as I felt leaving the Ginza, I realized when I arrived at Kitsune that I had gotten the fashion code wrong.

"Rain shoes—in Roppongi Hills!" Norie muttered in my ear as we'd embraced.

"But Obasan, it is raining." I broke the embrace, sat down quickly, and picked up a menu, so as not to attract any further inspection.

"Yes, but . . ." Her voice faltered. "Those are more for . . . the suburbs or country. Gardening and so on."

"You can't mean to say you think that I should have worn my Bally pumps today?" I glanced at her low-heeled leather pumps, which appeared strangely dry. "How did you get here, in a plastic bubble or something?"

"I came by train, of course. I wore different shoes until I arrived at Shibuya Station, where I changed them. I placed my wet walking shoes are in a plastic bag, which is in the coat check area, where you may leave your coat and umbrella." She sighed and picked up her menu. "This typhoon is going to be a terrible one. It's a good thing we're meeting today, because the trains might stop tomorrow."

"Typhoon?" I'd been so caught up in worries about the auction that I hadn't turned on the television in my hotel room, or taken the time to read a newspaper.

"Yes, Rei-chan. A big one." My aunt told me about Typhoon Nigo, the second typhoon of the fall, one that had originated in the waters off Thailand and had gained strength as it advanced northward to Japan. Schools and offices were open today, but scores of airline flights had been canceled. Right in my aunt's neighborhood, shopkeepers were hammering plywood sheets over their windows. "I worry about your hotel, Rei-chan. All that glass."

"Tokyo's a big city! I'm sure that the high winds will be broken by the presence of all the skyscrapers and big buildings. And that glass in the hotel windows must be industrial strength."

"It's true the city won't be as hard hit as the seaside areas. But you never can predict the outcome. You should come home with me this afternoon, just to make sure you are safe."

"But Yokohama is closer to the water." As I pointed this out, the thought came to me that there was a location at even greater risk: Hayama, the small seaside town where Takeo's summer house was.

"Yes, but we'll be together, taking care of each other. This hotel is nice, but who here cares about you? Who would answer if you called for help?"

"But it's such a nice hotel. They have an attendant on every floor—"

"Ha! I doubt your hotel will have many employees coming to work tomorrow, if the train companies halt operations."

It was time to get down to business. We ordered lunch sets, because they wouldn't take too long to arrive: mine a lacy burdock root crepe filled with sweet *kabocha* squash; my aunt's the fish platter featuring *kinmedai*, a strong-tasting fish similar to porgy. I kept my voice low, even though the nearest table was occupied by young American and Australian financial traders who looked completely uninterested in us, and weren't likely to understand much Japanese.

"I have the Kayama Kaikan's class schedule here." After the waitress had cleared away the lunch dishes, my aunt pulled a paper from her purse. "The master class ends at noon today. It might last longer, though, because the teachers are planning their arrangements for a show in the gallery space at Isetan next week. I'm on the operations committee for it, in fact."

"That's wonderful. Do you think Takeo will be at the class today?" Every now and then, I recalled, he dropped in on classes.

Norie shook her head, making her huge *mabe* pearl earrings shake slightly. "I doubt it. He has less interest in these—what does he call them?—commercial ventures. However, I have learned that he has an appointment with the school's accounts manager at twelve-thirty, so that means he's in the building right now."

"Do you think we should stop by?"

Norie held up a warning finger. "I will visit the Kaikan alone after lunch, and ask the receptionist to send word that I must speak to Takeo-san about the show at Isetan. I'll think of something important, maybe a problem with the location."

"That's a clever idea," I said.

"Yes, I could make him very concerned if he knows that Mrs. Okayama is thinking about using PVC pipes as a lining material in her flower arrangement. He doesn't like us to use material that can't be recycled." Her eyes gleamed mischievously, and I laughed. How well my aunt knew the flower master.

14

Half an hour later, the two of us had waded over to the Kayama Kaikan, the impressive modern tower building where the Kayama family housed the administrative offices and classrooms for its *ikebana* school. The first floor was all glass, so I could see my aunt enter the dramatic sandstone lobby, shaking off her bright floral Hanae Mori umbrella. She caught sight of me and made a shooing gesture with her hand.

Where could I wait? The nearest building was the embassy of Canada. I was soon made aware of the fact that it wasn't a public waiting room, so I hurriedly asked for a visa form and began filling it out as slowly as I could. Americans didn't need visas for Canada, but I could always pretend later than I didn't know. And I might be a Japanese citizen, for all they knew.

If only my aunt would call. It was a long ten minutes until my mobile phone beeped. She told me that she was in the elevator, going up to the penthouse floor.

"Now remember, please ring my telephone in five minutes, because the fact is, once I get past the topic of the flower exhibition I won't have much to keep me in his presence."

I agreed, kept my eye on my watch, and dialed over to Norie at exactly the prescribed moment.

"*Moshi-moshi,*" she answered happily. "How nice to hear from

you! But the thing is, I'm sorry, I'm in a meeting at the school. . . .
Yes, I know you need to receive the key right away."

"May I get it from you now?" I asked, according to the script.

"The circumstances are a little bit difficult. I'm actually on the
ninth floor of the Kayama building, with the honorable headmaster . . . but if you come quickly, I think it would be all right."

"So, shall I do it?" I breathed into the receiver.

"Yes, yes, please come quickly." And she clicked off.

Phase two was under way, for better or worse. I left the Canadian embassy, sprinting the twenty or so yards to the Kayama
Kaikan. After I barged through the Kaikan's big glass doors, I had
to pause to have my backpack inspected by the doorman, who reminded me to put my umbrella in the stand. Once I was deemed
safe to enter, I walked past the jagged installation of sandstone
rocks—around which were placed flower arrangements that were
changed the minute a bloom started to wilt. It felt strange to enter
this dry, brightly lit facsimile of a garden, when the world outside
was so rough and stormy.

The receptionist, a beautiful young woman in a pink silk dress
who was raptly reading a magazine called *Gothic and Lolita Bible*,
didn't even look up when I told her I was going to the school's café,
which was open to the public.

"Third floor," she said dreamily.

"Thank you very much." I moved past, catching a glimpse of the
page she was studying, which showed a bonneted woman carrying
a teddy bear. The baby trend was driving me to distraction. I'd been
away, and gotten older, while everyone who stayed was getting
younger.

The elevator arrived and was disgorging a load of fifty-something women—who, because of their Japanese genes, appeared to
be somewhere in their thirties—carrying tall bundles of flowers.

I waited for them to pass, then got on by myself. Three, I pressed,
just in case anyone was watching. Then I hit nine, and all too soon,
the doors opened on the long, cinnabar-colored hallway that led to
the Kayama family's personal quarters. The first time I'd entered
the hallway, I'd been stunned by a Mark Rothko painting on the
wall. It wasn't there anymore. All the old, high-status paintings

were gone, in fact—replaced by framed photographs of wildflowers. A tiny penciled scrawl in the corner of each photograph told me that Takeo himself had been the photographer.

Takeo had taken over the reins of the flower school, and the details showed. He'd also moved offices. The old room, where Takeo had once lounged among decades' worth of *National Geographic* magazines, had its door slightly open, revealing not magazines but hanging racks of women's clothes. Natsumi, Takeo's twin sister, must have taken it for herself—unless the girlfriend had moved in, which wasn't likely. The next door over was the last in the hallway. It was the headmaster's study, once Takeo's father's room, and, I was guessing, now Takeo's own.

I knocked lightly, hoping that I'd guessed right. A few seconds later the door was opened by Takeo, wearing a gray cashmere sweatshirt and jeans. My gaze flickered from his tight expression to the welcoming room that lay behind him. Takeo had furnished his new office with what looked like Frank Lloyd Wright furniture from his Japanese period: elegant low chairs cushioned in persimmon velvet, with low tables between. There was a sofa in burnt orange laden with small, exquisite pillows made from old kimono silk. I breathed in happily at the sight of all my favorite colors, and my aunt seated in one of these chairs, her legs gracefully crossed at the ankle.

"What is this? You didn't tell me—" Takeo looked from me to my aunt with obvious shock.

"I'm sorry, I didn't want to interrupt the instruction you were giving me about the program by talking too much. But the fact is, Rei-chan has just come to town, and she has been so busy that today is the first time I've had a chance to see her! My dear, welcome home!" She rose to her feet, and beckoned for me to approach her for a hug.

"The key—I am—" I was forgetting how to construct a Japanese sentence, because Takeo was looking so irritated at my presence.

"Yes. Rei-chan came to receive our house key," my aunt said, taking it out and tucking it into my purse. "She will be leaving the Grand Hyatt to stay with us for safety during the typhoon."

"Isn't that a bit—overly careful?" Takeo looked out the window at the pouring gray sheet of water. "Even if a typhoon arose at sea, the likelihood that it would cause any trouble here in the Kanto area is very remote."

"But look at what happened in southeast Asia!" I decided to jump on my aunt's bandwagon. "Your country house in Hayama is quite vulnerable, to both typhoons and tsunamis—"

"It will be fine," he said stonily. "That building has gone through a war and more than a few typhoons. I'm not doing anything special."

"You must," I said. "At least pull out the shutters and make sure they're well latched. Do you still have that nice old retainer who can do that for you?" I'd forgotten the name of the Kayamas' manservant, who moved with them from home to home as the seasons changed.

My aunt interrupted before Takeo could answer the question. "I must rush off because I promised my son I would bring some food to him at the hospital—he'll never be released from duty, once the typhoon arrives. Anyway, Rei-chan, I hope that you can spare a few moments to say hello to Kayama-sensei. It has been a very long time," she added before stepping out into the hall.

"Well, she's right about that." I settled myself down in one of the chairs. "What beautiful furniture! It looks like Frank Lloyd Wright."

A flicker of something akin to pride passed across Takeo's face. He said, "I knew you'd recognize them."

"Wow." Did that mean he'd thought I'd pay him a call here? "I didn't know his furniture had gone into reproduction."

"It's not reproduction. They're originals," he said, sitting down across from me.

"Oh. So you really have become a serious collector," I said.

"Of course." He looked at me sternly. "Just as I'm serious about Emi. I won't jeopardize my engagement for any inappropriate interlude that you have in mind."

I willed myself not to blush, but it was impossible. "I can't believe you're saying that! I just sat down out of—courtesy—to finish the conversation we couldn't have last night."

"Well, this whole business of your aunt getting me alone, so you could arrive, was pretty obvious."

I looked out at the rain, steadying myself. Then I turned back to him. "Come on, let's be civil. We must talk, but you're right that this isn't the right place. I wish we could get away from it all, maybe drive out to Hayama and have lunch at the house."

"The weather's too bad for that," he said. "And Emi would hate it. She wouldn't stop asking me about you yesterday evening."

"Oh, really? What did you tell her?"

"I told a small lie. I said I knew you in college," Takeo said.

"Hmm. So she thought I was a classmate of yours at Keio?" I'd better get the cover right, in case I ran into her again.

"She believes you were, and still are, a professor. At UC Santa Cruz, where she knows I did my gardening certificate—"

"You mean—she thinks I'm old enough to be your professor?" I was horror-struck. I'd never wear that suit again.

"But you're American. She knows the rules are different there. She went to an American school when her family was in Turkey, you know."

"I didn't know. Another thing I'm wondering about is, how long have you been engaged?"

"Two months." Takeo smiled a bit unsteadily. "This is an *omiai*. There's no need for a long courtship."

"*Omiai*! Do you mean you're going to have an arranged marriage?"

He looked evenly back at me. "Why not?"

"But Takeo . . ." I paused, feeling helpless. "You're so . . . eligible. You don't need anyone to help you get married. And you're so . . . unconventional! From the looks of your fiancée, she's going to be more suited to attending fashion shows than Greenpeace rallies."

"I adore Emi," Takeo said softly. "She's beautiful and charming. We enjoy being together, and her father is most agreeable to hearing my ideas about wildlife preservation. Together, Emi and I can do quite a bit to help Japan."

So that was it. Takeo was marrying Emi because a close connection to the government minister would allow him to influence environmental policies. Feeling a chill run through me, I said, "You're awfully callous to marry someone just for her connections."

"Well, I've come to believe that we, the people who inhabit the earth, are not as important as the earth itself."

"But what about love?"

"With arranged marriages, we grow to love each other," Takeo said. "Whereas you Westerners, you love so passionately at first, and then there's nothing left for later on."

I was about to launch a counterargument when I realized that he might have a point. I'd been in love with Hugh for years, but we were nowhere near ready to get married. If only I were as certain about the future as Takeo seemed to be.

"I'd like to get to know her, too," I said stiffly.

"Why?"

"Well, I do still care about you as a friend. It's natural for me to want to become friends with my friend's wife, isn't it?" As I spoke, I looked out the window, because I felt too mortified to face him. "I don't know what Emi-san's work schedule is like, but maybe after the storm blows over, I could take her to lunch—"

"She doesn't have a job, because she just graduated this summer."

"Oh, which university?" I had already pegged her as the type who went to Gakushuin, the private university where the remnants of Japan's nobility still studied.

When Takeo mentioned Tokyo International Girls School, a private high school, I nearly choked. She wasn't even old enough to have started college. Talk about a Lolita complex; Takeo had it in spades.

"Well, Takeo, since Emi has some free time, perhaps we could all drive down to Hayama together," I suggested mildly.

"Rei, I'm tired of talking about this silly idea of a trip to the beach. It's not even summer."

"We could have lunch in the house, and then I'd really like to see what you've done with the rock garden. I'm thinking of doing something like that in Washington—" I cut myself off in mid-babble when I realized that Emi herself was standing in the doorway.

Emi was wearing a short, flared red dress that made me think of the baby-girl outfits I'd seen around town—but it looked about ten times more expensive. The front of the dress was obscured by an artwork she was holding, a colorful screen print of a Louis Vuitton handbag. Above it, her large eyes peered at me—really large, with big black pupils, like a girl character from anime.

She looked away from me and addressed Takeo in a soft, high, appropriately girlish voice. "Oh, excuse me! I didn't know you had an appointment with your *sensei*."

"Actually, I just dropped in. Takeo and I were talking about how his, ah, rock garden design could translate to one I am planning in the United States. Excuse me for not introducing myself last night! My name is Shimura Rei." I inverted my names, the proper way, and tried to elevate the pitch of my voice to sound like hers—girlish, proper, hopeful. What Takeo had said about her mistaking me for his teacher had gotten on my nerves.

Emi bowed back and gave her name in a bell-like tone. She smiled insincerely, then turned to her fiancé. "Takeo-kun, if it's not too much of an interruption, I would like you to consider this new painting. What do you think?"

"It's quite bright, isn't it?" Takeo said, after a moment's silence.

"It's Murakami Takashi," she said in a rush. "It will become even more valuable in another year, Father says."

Takashi Murakami's paintings of cartoonlike characters and status handbags were all the rage, but they seemed a little gimmicky to me, a materialistic new version of Andy Warhol, certainly not the kind of art an antimaterialist like Takeo would enjoy. But what did I know? He was now busy blowing thousands of dollars of the family fortune at auctions, on things like beds and china services.

"Sorry to be rude, but I shall be leaving now," I announced, wondering whether Emi's cheerful behavior was hiding the fact she'd overheard our bitter conversation. In any case, I didn't want to be suspected of trying to ruin their engagement, so I left, offering a second good-bye that neither of them acknowledged.

The door didn't close entirely behind me, and when I heard Emi's voice, I stepped into the doorway of the roomful of dresses. If she was going to rip into me, I wanted to hear exactly what she said.

"So . . . what about the painting? Do you like it or not? I only have it until Monday. The dealer wants to know."

"But I thought you bought it already?" Takeo sounded weary.

"I borrowed it. It's not sold until we decide we want it. I think it would really cheer up that musty old country house, don't you?"

"My house in Hayama?" Takeo sounded alarmed.

"Our house," Emi corrected him warmly. "You don't have many pretty things there, and I wanted to repaint anyway, to a nice bright yellow . . . kind of the Vuitton yellow, if you know what I mean."

I shut my eyes, trying to imagine a high school girl becoming chatelaine of that simple, elegant country villa. I couldn't fathom it.

"Perhaps we'd better see what it looks like there, first," Takeo said. "Actually, I was thinking about driving there tonight, because I should shutter the house."

So he'd taken my warning seriously—despite acting with me as if he weren't worried. This gave me a faint rush of pride.

"Why don't you get old Chiba-san to do it? That's his job, isn't it?" Emi's voice squeaked with irritation.

"Unfortunately, Chiba-san stays in Hayama only from spring to the end of summer. He's in Kyoto right now with my father and sister working on that installation at the Golden Pavilion."

"But you can't go to the country tonight. My parents expect us at the dinner for the French delegation."

"That's right. I'm sorry." Takeo sighed. "Well, then, you'll just have to tell the art dealer it's going to take a few more days to decide. He'll probably close up shop himself, because of the weather. If things are really so bad, I suppose we'll have to close the Kaikan."

"*Ah so desu ka.* With the Kaikan closed, will you be . . . less busy?" Emi sounded coquettish.

"Actually, I'll have lots of time. Now come here, Emi-chan. You haven't even kissed me hello yet." I heard a rustling and a laugh, and then the slow, unmistakable sound of someone's zipper going south.

Lolita in Humbert's lap. I tiptoed away, thoroughly disgusted with the two of them—and with myself, for the way I felt.

15

During the twenty minutes I'd been in the Kaikan, the rain seemed to have become harder. Torrents of water streamed out of the heavens, and when I stepped recklessly off a curb without looking, a swell of water rushed into the top of my rain shoes.

Miserably, I took shelter in the vestibule of an electronics shop to pull off the shoes and drain them. Through the store window, I caught a glimpse of television sets, small to large, all displaying the Japanese weather channel. After I'd gotten my shoes back on my feet, I went in to get a better view.

The screens displayed images of a swirling red circle moving across southwest Japan. The edge of the storm was now just seventy kilometers from Shikoku Island and predicted to arrive in full force by mid-evening. Several fishermen had been swept away and drowned in the swelling waves, and people living in small houses along the beach had been told to evacuate. Once the typhoon hit Shikoku, it might travel inland, wreaking havoc in Kobe and Osaka; or, if the wind changed, it might roll its way up the east coast, toward Yokohama and Tokyo. The government was urging that all possible safety precautions be taken in all towns along the coast.

The next shot showed Shikoku islanders preparing for the typhoon by boarding up windows and waiting in long lines for gasoline. There were film close-ups of grocery stores with bare shelves, and of housewives scrubbing their bathtubs with disinfectant before using them to store water.

Tokyo was inland, I reminded myself. No reason to panic. I returned to the rainy street, where I noticed, for the first time, how few people were around.

Well, it wasn't exactly a day for strolling. At mid-afternoon, the sky was as dark as if it were early evening; and the rain lashed relentlessly down. I wondered if my aunt's dire predictions about the storm would come true, since she'd been right about so much else.

Every taxi that passed had its "occupied" light on, and the unlucky pedestrians on the street all seemed to be running for shelter. My funky spotted umbrella blew inside out when I was still on Gaien-Higashi-Dori, a long five blocks from the Hyatt. I struggled in vain to fix it, but I was powerless against the wind. But at the end of the block, a lighted subway signpost showing six trees—the *kanji* symbol for Roppongi—had been knocked to the ground by the strong wind. But the signpost reminded me of another possible walking route. I could use the shelter of the subway to walk the rest of the way straight into Roppongi Hills.

The steep stairway leading down was slick with rain, so I had to tread carefully. A couple of times people bumped into me in their own haste to get out of the rain. I paid 160 yen to get down to the train platform, where I began my trek for exit 4, the way up to Roppongi Hills.

As I walked along, I listened to snatches of conversation. Two men were talking about how they were going to get to a business meeting, and then I overheard somebody else talking to a companion about hoping the line would be open again the next day. As I climbed the stairs up to the exit and passed through the turnstiles, I saw a hand-lettered sign in Japanese and English: HIBIYA LINE CLOSED EASTBOUND DUE TO FLOODING.

There was an attendant in the booth, so I stopped to ask him about it.

"Excuse me, but where's the flood?"

"Tsukijii. Twenty minutes ago, enough water rose to cause an electric short. The subway authority has closed the line until the storm passes."

He was talking about the fish market, where I'd gone the previous day. Of course, a station close to water would be vulnerable. How fortunate that Roppongi was farther inland.

I walked on and upward, out the Roppongi Hills exit. There were no teenagers congregating at the giant spider at the open-air Roku-Roku plaza; and while shops were open and glowing with light, nobody seemed to be inside. The escalators were turned off, for some reason, so I had to hustle up the stairs, then down a covered stretch until I'd made it to the Grand Hyatt.

At last, real shelter. As I kicked off the rain shoes just inside the entrance to my room, I saw that a folded note in a hotel envelope had been pushed under the door. I read the message that my aunt had left with reception. She hoped that I'd had a nice conversation with my friend, and she wanted me to remember to call her about when I'd be arriving in Yokohama. She'd decided to see her son at St. Luke's hospital first, but expected to be home by six.

Not likely, I thought, remembering what I'd learned about the flooding at Tsukijii, the stop closest to St. Luke's. I wondered if Norie had gotten there before the subway line closed down, or if she'd been trapped underground.

I kicked off the rain shoes, turned on the bath taps, and picked up the bathroom telephone receiver to dial my aunt's cell phone. A recording of a high-pitched woman's voice told me that all networks were busy; the call hadn't gone through.

It was rare for the Japanese phone system to have trouble, but at least I still had my American phone. I hadn't wanted to waste it on local calls, but this was a necessity.

I rummaged through all the wet clothes to get to my dripping black nylon backpack. Everything inside was damp: my hairbrush, my address book, my makeup case . . . I fished around for the phone, but it wasn't there.

No need to panic, I repeated for the second time in half an hour, as I began to work my way through every zippered pocket. When had I last used the phone? At the Canadian embassy, when I'd talked to

Norie. I'd placed it in the outside zippered pocket, so it would be handy in case my aunt called again. In that same space I found the visa application I'd started filling out to avoid suspicion. It was still there, along with my passport. But not the phone.

I used the hotel telephone to dial information, and I was quickly put through to the embassy. Nobody had found a cellular phone. Next, I tried the Kayama Kaikan. I recognized the voice of the fashion-loving receptionist and told her that I was missing a phone. She didn't have it either. I was too discreet to mention that I might have lost it in Takeo's office. I could only hope he'd contact me if he found it.

After I hung up, I looked out the window into the pouring rain, and wondered whether it was soaking my cell phone, somewhere or other. I could have lost the phone during my wild dash through the rain back to the hotel. Or maybe it had been taken out of my bag by someone. Now I thought about the people who'd seemed overly interested in me since the job had started. The man next to me on the plane, Jürgen in the bar, even the unseen person hovering behind me at the sushi bar. I'd just thought of them as annoyances, never imagining that they were a threat to my security. Any one of them could have been following me during the storm, when the rain had been so loud I couldn't possibly have heard someone run up behind me.

I leaned on the glass and shut my eyes against the avalanche of water outside. What a mess! I was stuck without my lifeline to Washington, Takeo was stuck with his ditzy fiancée, and my aunt was possibly stuck in a flooded subway tunnel. I'd almost forgotten the original reason I was looking for my cell phone.

I took out my little address book and dialed the Shimura family's number in Yokohama. Unlike my earlier attempt to reach Norie's cell phone, this call went through.

"I've been waiting to hear from you! Are you coming to us tonight?" my cousin Chika demanded.

"I don't think so, Chika. The train lines are flooded. That's why I'm calling, really, about Aunt—I mean, about your mother—"

"She's not here yet. She telephoned to say that she couldn't get back to Shibuya station, so she had to go a whole roundabout way using the Keikyu line. She's still traveling, I believe."

"I hope she gets home soon. You must let me know."

"Of course she will come home." Chika spoke with all the confidence of a Japanese child who was sure her mother would always be around to help. "But when are you coming to stay, Rei-chan? With this rain, I think you should travel tonight, before the floods tomorrow."

"I actually think it's safer to stay in place rather than travel." As I spoke, I flipped on the television, which was, unsurprisingly, showing a vista of heavy rain over rice paddies.

"Nobody's safe anywhere if there's flooding," Chika said darkly. "It's such a shame for you to be here now. And with this weather, I don't know when Angus-san and the band can arrive. They were supposed to fly in tomorrow, but I heard that all the airlines have stopped flying to Tokyo and Yokohama."

"When's the typhoon supposed to end?" I asked.

"Well, the worst of the winds and rain will be tomorrow, they think. Is the place you're staying safe?"

I looked around my room uneasily. I was so high up. I was sure the building was structurally sound and would not topple over, but I wasn't as sure about the safety of the windows as I'd made out to Aunt Norie. There was something spooky about being alone, in a tall hotel, with no one I knew nearby. And now I didn't even have a cell phone to use to call for help if the phone lines went dead.

I told Chika to please convey to Norie my gratitude for all her help, and to let her know that I'd lost my cell phone—so if she wanted to get in touch, the hotel line was best.

I hung up the telephone and crawled into bed. Then I remembered Hugh, and the bad way things had ended. This might be my last chance to talk to him, if, as it seemed, the phone connections would all go down. What time was it there, three or four in the morning? I always got confused about daylight saving time.

I dialed the apartment, and the phone rang eight times. Then the answering machine picked up in my voice. I left a message for Hugh apologizing for the hour of the call, but saying that I'd called early because of the typhoon—and if he didn't hear from me for days, not to worry.

It was a relief to have reached the answering machine, I thought after I'd hung up and settled down between the sheets. I could say exactly what I wanted and not worry about being interrupted and taken in other directions.

It was only when I was halfway to sleep that I thought about how strange it was that at three or four in the morning, Hugh hadn't been there to pick up the bedside phone.

I woke with a start while it was still dark and found that I'd soaked the thick cotton sheets with my sweat. In my dream, the moisture had been rain: I had been getting wetter and wetter, running through a downpour, with Michael Hendricks and Mr. Watanabe chasing after me. Ahead I could see a woman whose skin glowed gold; she had downturned eyes and a peaceful expression. Her right hand was lifted, with its palm toward me. In my dream, she seemed immensely comfortable, like someone I'd seen before, indeterminately Asian and of indefinable age.

I pulled myself up to a sitting position and turned on the television. The news showed smashed hotels and cottages throughout Shikoku. The electricity was gone, and hospitals were full of people who'd been hit with flying debris. The only blessing was that there hadn't been a tidal wave, because the storm had turned inland.

Inland. This meant it was heading up the Miura Peninsula toward Yokohama and Tokyo. What a time to be here, I thought, watching the footage of rain lashing the giant bronze Buddha in Kamakura. The newscaster droned on about how a storm of similar magnitude had swept the existing temple away from that Buddha some eight centuries earlier. I caught him saying something about how the electricity was gone in Kamakura and most of the Miura Peninsula, but then I stopped listening, because I'd clicked back to my dream.

Now I knew the identity of the golden woman: she was the goddess Kannon, the goddess of mercy revered by Buddhists. Kannon-sama was the savior of people in distress. Her image was a focal point in many Buddhist temples throughout Asia, but the Kannon I knew best was the thirty-foot-high gilded camphorwood image at the Hase Kannon temple in Kamakura, just a few miles from Takeo's summer house in Hayama.

She was calling me to go. And suddenly I realized that the typhoon itself would make the mission possible. Takeo was not going to be at the country house in Hayama, and his neighbors would be holed up in their tightly shuttered houses. Nobody would notice me borrowing the key that he kept under a potted hydrangea on the veranda or, if it was gone, gently lifting a window to get inside. I put my past conviction of breaking and entering firmly out of mind. Thanks to the power of the storm, and with Kannon-sama's protection, I'd be able to accomplish what needed to be done.

16

The 8:02 train out of Tokyo Station was still scheduled to run, although the government was urging people to stay inside. Only a few people boarded the train along with me in Tokyo, and it was easy to figure out who they were: workers who couldn't afford to upset their bosses. In short, people like myself.

I'd chosen Japan Railway's Yokosuka line, which was a slightly slower trip, because the JR rails were older and farther inland than its competitor, Keihin-Kyuko Railways. The only risky part of the trip was at the very end, the port of Yokosuka, but I'd be out six stops before that point. I was going to disembark at Kannon-sama's home—Kamakura—and take a taxi into Hayama, which didn't have its own station.

Japan Railway had upgraded the cars, which now had long inward-facing bench seats, rather than the cozy booth-style seating I remembered from my last time in Japan. You could pack more people into a train this way, but I hated sitting sideways on a train; not being able to look at the horizon made me nauseated. Sideways seats were another reason I had avoided the Keihin-Kyuko line. Now, I pulled out a little package of *sembei* crackers I had in my backpack and, despite the disapproving glances of people around me, began to munch. I couldn't afford to have an empty stomach in this situation. I also turned my head sharply to the left, intent on

seeing what I could of the horizon. It was impossible to see buildings or trees—just vague, hazy lights were visible. The route passed
apartment buildings I remembered, an amusement park, a string of
love hotels and small businesses. Everything looked so strange
without the usual bright lights.

I checked my watch. The trip from Tokyo to Kamakura was usually fifty-four minutes, but we'd already traveled ninety minutes
and were only at the halfway mark, Yokohama. I was feeling pre-
dictably queasy, so I took some deep breaths.

A new group of travelers had boarded in Yokohama: people who
were leaving work, unusually for nine-thirty in the morning. Usually, a commuter train was silent, but today, people were talking
about the storm. Someone said that large sections of Shizuoka prefecture were flooded. Shizuoka was a little more than an hour's
drive away. And at the pace at which the train was moving, it
seemed possible that the storm's brunt would arrive in Kamakura
before we did.

The train seemed to be moving more slowly, and it kept pausing,
inexplicably, for varying lengths of time—sometimes two minutes,
sometimes ten. I imagined that the conductor was getting information about flooded tracks ahead, and was waiting for the trains on
those tracks to be diverted to other tracks.

The train lurched on, and finally we were approaching Kita-
Kamakura: north Kamakura, the last station before Kamakura,
where I would get out. But as we approached, there was a sliding
sensation, as if the train were no longer connected to the track.
Then the train jerked hard and stopped.

I'd shut my eyes when I'd thought the train was hydroplaning,
but now I opened them and looked out the window. I could see
nothing but rain.

A disembodied voice spoke from the public address system. "We
have received word that there is flooding ahead at Kita-Kamakura
Station, which makes it unsafe for the train to proceed. After we are
granted permission, this train will return to Ofuna station, where
our honored passengers may kindly disembark. Alternative transportation to points north and south will be provided for you as it
becomes available. We apologize for any inconvenience."

I looked out the window again; through the rain I could see what looked like the Kita-Kamakura train station a short distance ahead. North Kamakura was almost within my reach, but the train wouldn't go there.

I stood up and turned to look at the bedraggled bunch of travelers in the car. I debated the danger of calling attention to myself, deciding it was a must in this situation, and waved a hand to get everyone's attention.

"Excuse me, but I was going to leave at this station. . . . Does anyone else live nearby and want to disembark as well? I think that perhaps we could . . . ask the conductor to open the door."

Nobody said yes. However, someone said, "But it's dangerous!" and another person, the man who'd given the weather report before, advised, "It's better to stay onboard for the return trip to Ofuna. There will surely be buses after a while."

After a while? That could be hours, maybe even the next day. I shook my head, gathered up my umbrella and backpack, and pushed on the door that opened down to the tracks.

As I'd anticipated, it didn't budge. I was going to have to get a conductor to let me out. I hurried out of the compartment and into the next one. I was in about the middle of the train, so I had quite a distance to travel to reach the engineer. As I ran through each compartment, heads turned in surprise at the sight of me. I tried more doors without luck. Two compartments later, I was met by a blue-uniformed conductor.

"Is there some trouble?" he asked.

"Yes, I'm sorry to bother you, but the thing is that I must get off this train now, rather than return to Ofuna. I noticed we're just a few feet from the Kita-Kamakura platform—"

The conductor pressed his lips together. "I'm sorry, but we can't go farther. We're waiting for another train to pass, and then we'll go backward."

"Would it be possible for you to release the control on the door and I'll just hop down?" It couldn't be more than four feet's distance to the ground.

"But there is no platform."

"I'll watch out."

The conductor looked distracted. "That is against rail policy—"

"This is an emergency!" I struggled to keep my voice controlled. "If the train were in danger, people would go out the windows to safety. Look, there are stickers demonstrating how to do it." I gestured to the window next to an elderly gentleman. "If I open a window, I'll get everyone wet. Please, if you just release the catch on the door for me, I'll be able to leave without causing anyone trouble."

The volume of my voice, and my growing histrionics, must have convinced him that I was more trouble onboard than off. Keeping his face grim, he lifted a handheld radio to his lips and spoke a jumble of quick commands and codes that I didn't understand, but that I gathered had something to do with alerting all other trains that a passenger was on the tracks. After he was finished, the conductor pressed a button that released the lock on the door.

Wetness rushed toward me as I carefully sat down on the edge of the train, letting my legs drop down into space. There were about three feet to the wooden railway ties below. The easiest thing to do was to slide down

"Please watch for danger!" he cried as I stepped carefully across the tracks, which were under six inches of water. When I reached the grassy bank on the western side, I turned and bowed my thanks. But the train had already started its backward course. Nobody was watching me anymore.

It was truly just a few minutes' slog to Kita-Kamakura station, which I found was in the process of closing when I walked in.

"No more trains," the ticket taker said. The usual courtesies— honorable customer and the like—seemed to be slipping away as the weather had worsened.

"I'm just going out to get a taxi," I said.

"Taxi? There are no taxis! No customer, no taxi!"

"Well, maybe I can call from the pay phone—" already I'd spotted a trusty lime-green NTT phone on the platform.

"Telephones don't work." The ticket taker seemed almost gleeful about the bad news. Maybe he had heard the "passenger on the tracks" signal my train's conductor had issued and was annoyed to have that passenger in his station. Or maybe things were just so bad outside that he was starting to crack.

"Are any buses running?" I ventured.

"Service suspended! Just as this station is closing, the bus system is closed, too."

I cleared my throat and attempted the girlish falsetto that Japanese women used to powerful effect. "I very badly need to go in the direction of Hayama. Is there any chance you will be driving home?"

"Not that way. And the beach road is already flooded in that section by the marina, I must warn you. The station manager is the one with a car here, and he's just about to drive to Zushi to gather some other employees who need transportation—"

"Please, could he let me out there, at Zushi station?" I asked quickly.

"But you are going to Hayama. Even from the turnoff, it's a four-kilometer walk. You cannot make it in this rain."

"I'm sure I can. I know it very well. I'm so close by," I said, running through the route in my mind. I'd taken it by bus before, past marine supply stores, antique shops, and restaurants. I was sure I would recognize these landmarks and know the turns.

He hesitated. "I can't let you stay in this station, because it's closing. Maybe I can ask."

"I'm willing to pay!" I cried again.

But it wasn't necessary. The station manager, a frazzled-looking man in his sixties, would not accept payment, even though he took me slightly past the station, to the main road that led into Hayama.

The roads didn't even look like roads anymore, I thought as we inched along. The rain lashed at a sideways angle because of the wind, a force so strong that it was making trees wave about. At some street corners, backed-up storm drains had created pools so deep that water stretched all the way up to the shop entrances. After we'd seen the second intersection like this, the station manager stopped his car.

"I'm sorry, but there's no point in going on," he said. "I will call the employees and tell them I can't continue on. I'm turning back. Perhaps you can take shelter at the nearest police box—"

The police were the last people I wanted to see. "Thanks, but I think I can get through on foot. I can get out here."

"But you can't! How will you cross the bridge ahead?"

"It's so short—I'm sure I'll make it," I said, sounding more confident than I felt. I knew the little half-moon-shaped bridge the station manager had mentioned. It was about twenty feet long. I could make it now, but there was no time to waste, if the flooding continued.

I said good-bye to the uneasy stationmaster and got out. The rain was being pushed hard by the wind, so hard that it seemed to be raining upward, over my rain shoes and onto my jeans, which within a few minutes were plastered to my legs. My breath came in gasps as I sloshed as quickly as I could through the water.

The bridge over the canal lay just past a deserted bus stop. It was a beautiful little upwardly curved bridge with short red handrailings—the kind immortalized in Japanese woodblock prints. I'd walked over this bridge before and taken photographs of the Zushi canal and the pretty antique shops and surf gear shops that lay along it.

I couldn't see the bridge today, because it was covered with water, but the handrails were still visible. I started across, clinging to the slippery wooden rail. Gusts of wind tore at me, and it felt as if the water was rising.

The water was up to my waist by the time I'd gotten over and was on land. I was shaking, but as I ran on, my pulse leveled out. I'd crossed the worst of Zushi's water, and now I was headed on the four-kilometer route into Hayama, running toward the mountain tunnels that would keep me dry for a few blessed minutes. I ran past restaurants, antique stores, and a post office and, finally, down to the beach road that led to Takeo's house.

From the left at the wall surrounding the emperor's palace, I still had two kilometers to go. I reminded myself about the seawall that would keep the sea from rushing inward, but in fact there was so much rain that the road was marked by deep pockets of water—flash floods like those I'd seen in Zushi.

As I ran, I held my head down because my eyes kept filling with rain. It was like crying in reverse. And the truth was that looking around was frightening. Things were clearly out of order everywhere; no cars drove along the road below me, although I did see some float by.

The back of my raincoat and jeans were as wet as if I'd been soaking in a bathtub. The front of me was a little less wet because I used my new umbrella like a shield, until it blew out about halfway down the hill that sloped down to what used to be the beach road. The road was now a fast-running river.

I stood at the edge of it, water up to my knees, wondering how deep it was in the middle. Merchandise from a beach souvenir shop—an array of life preservers, floating toys, and plastic buckets—bobbed past in the fast-flowing water. As a raft with the head of Doraemon, the magic cat from a popular children's television program, sailed by, I was hit by inspiration. I could travel the road on the raft.

Without giving myself a chance to change my mind, I reached out and grabbed for the rubber cat's head. I connected with the head, but found it harder than I'd expected to mount the small raft. My body swished through the water like a fish flailing on the end of a line, but I was able to keep hold of the raft with my arms. After a couple of failed lunges, I got my legs and the rest of me on top of the raft.

My weight was more than the child's raft was designed for, so it sank slightly in the water, but thankfully not all the way. We continued south past my old favorite restaurant, Chaya, then past the Morito Shrine, where I saw that the *tori* gateway was half-submerged. As we approached a big intersection, I realized that the stoplights were out, as in fact were lights everywhere. A power outage. Good thing there was no traffic at all.

Another two kilometers and I was drifting past the high wall of the emperor's summer palace. I wasn't sure of the palace's elevation—the grounds were landscaped in such a way that it was impossible to spy on the palace—but I had to imagine that it had been built, just like Takeo's family home, as high as possible. The gray police bus that always guarded the palace wall was gone. I imagined that the police had driven it somewhere safe for the duration of the storm. And surely none of the imperial family would be on the coast during this typhoon.

• • •

The street that led to Takeo's house was too small to have a name; it was really just a long, stone-covered driveway that led upward from a small group of cypress trees that marked the intersection. As the raft slowly sailed on, I saw the trees bent over like hunchbacked grandmothers—a situation caused by both the ruthless wind and the heavy wisteria vines on them, which were dragging in the water. Many people would have seen the vines as an overgrown weed, but Takeo had refused to let the city landscapers remove them. Now I was glad for it, because I reached out to the vines to help steer the raft to the trees. I grabbed hold and scrambled onto the bank. The raft sailed on.

As I scrambled up the path made of river stones, the water level dropped and my spirits rose. One kilometer to go. I scanned the few other old, great prewar villas on each side of the path. Heavy brown wooden shutters covered all their windows, and the luxury cars I remembered seeing in most of the carports were all shrouded in protective covers. I had made a fool of myself on the train and at Kita-Kamakura Station, but there was no chance that anyone in this area would notice me.

The long bamboo fence surrounding Takeo's house finally came into view. I could see rain cascading off its tiled roof, creating a small flood right outside the front doors. Some of the tiles were gone, smashed to bits on the ground amid dozens of knocked-over potted plants.

I unlatched the gate and hurried around to the back of the house. As I'd feared, there were plenty more smashed pots, and the potted hydrangea that was supposed to be on the veranda was nowhere in sight. It could have been blown away—or, I realized, it might have outgrown its pot and been planted somewhere. Takeo would have found another place for his spare key, or changed his habits and decided against leaving it outside.

The house key was nowhere on the veranda, but it could easily have been lost in the grass. I bent my head toward the grass and realized the impossibility of the situation. I really did not want to break and enter.

Was there an alarm system? There hadn't been in the old days, but given the value of what was in the house since Takeo's renovation, an alarm would seem like a smart thing to have. I pressed my face against the glass of the sliding windows that led to the living room. The paper *shoji* screens that normally would have shielded the room from the outside were not closed, so I could see into the darkened room, though not very well. It didn't look as if there were motion sensors.

Suddenly, I caught a blur of movement close to my face. To my shock, the sliding door was opening. As I tripped off the veranda in my haste to get away, the door was opened and a flashlight shone straight in my face.

Instinctively, I shut my eyes against the light. I knew I looked as gruesome and bedraggled as a mythical sea monster that had been thrown up out of the raging bay beyond the cliffs. And like a monster, I wanted to roar out my anguish at the trip I'd taken, only to be caught as a failure. But instead, all that came from me was a hoarse whimper.

The flashlight beam dropped, and I blinked my eyes to look at Takeo.

"Rei?" His voice was incredulous.

"Yes." I couldn't think of anything else to say.

Then Takeo said something I never expected to hear. "Come in."

17

Fifteen minutes later, I was in water again. But this time it was hot, surrounding me and still cascading out of a faucet. Takeo had sent me to his bathroom and had lit the candles, turned on the taps, thrown a towel and a robe at me, and left. I'd showered quickly, scrubbing off the dirt that had splashed over me outside, and entered the deep, hot bath. As I gazed at the candles on the bath's edge, illuminating the room like the Kannon's temple, I could admit to myself how foolhardy my journey had been. But I'd reached the end, I'd faced Takeo, and he'd let me inside.

I'd hoped to be alone, but if I played things carefully, I could still complete my mission. I was probably within a few rooms' distance of the vessel. Of course, the rooms all looked so different now, full of furniture and new things. Just like this bathroom, which had been redone with tiny tiles of amber, gold, and cream-colored glass that winked in the soft candlelight. There was a new sink that looked like a *raku* pottery bowl perched on a slate ledge. The bath's Grohe faucet was bronze and very modern, designed so that water tumbled out in a wide, flat sheet.

The sensual comfort of my bath made me feel guilty. The typhoon hadn't reached its apogee. The bathtub should be used as a collecting device for cold water, not for soaking myself.

After I'd toweled off and wrapped myself in the quilted winter *yukata* robe that Takeo had given me, I went out, following the banging noises to find Takeo outside on the thin ledge of veranda that ran around the house, pulling closed heavy wooden shutters. He waved at me, looking oddly happy, although he was now the bedraggled one, with wet clothes and leaves stuck in his hair.

"I'm almost done," he shouted, so I could hear him through the glass. "Just a few more rooms and all the shutters will be closed."

He came in a few minutes later, and I helped him get off his wet raincoat and boots in the flagstone entryway.

"You look like you need to warm up. I left the bath full," I said. It was Japanese custom to enter a bath clean, as I'd done, and reuse the same bathwater for the whole family. And if Takeo relaxed in a bath, I'd have the perfect opportunity for a quick look around the house.

"Okay, I'll go in. It could be the last hot bath for a while, if the town shuts off the gas supply," Takeo said, running a hand through his wet hair.

"I'd like to clean it out afterward and fill it with clean water," I said. "You'll want to have water stored, just in case."

"You're right. There was flooding here back in the seventies, when I was a child," Takeo said. "The house wasn't damaged, but we were without water and electricity for days. It was exciting for me then, but not so exciting for my father. I seem to remember we had houseguests who wound up stranded with us for a week."

"I don't want to do that to you," I said quickly. "But things are pretty bad outside—"

"You must stay overnight," Takeo said shortly. "You said the trains have stopped."

"Well, I'll do what I can to help you. I'm going to go through the rooms to make sure no delicate ceramics are near the windows, and so on. Would that be all right?"

Takeo smiled. "Thank you. You always remember the things I forget about."

"I hope Emi won't misinterpret my being here. Did she drive down with you?" My question was automatic, out of courtesy. I was certain that Emi wasn't around.

"No. She's back in Setagaya at her parents' house."

"Did she go there to stay during the storm?" I remembered how Norie had wanted me nearby.

"No, she's always there. It's her home until after the wedding, of course."

"Oh, of course." I was relieved to know she wouldn't be stumbling upon me in Takeo's robe. "But that's rough on the two of you, I suppose, all that parental control."

"We find our moments, here and there." Takeo winked at me and then went off to the bathroom.

After he left, I pondered what he'd said. This wasn't the way an arranged marriage was supposed to operate. But I'd caught a strong sexual current flowing between Emi and Takeo. It was a relief, really; I wouldn't have to worry about any unwelcome advances from him, though I hadn't understood why Takeo had winked at me. Was it because he now saw me as a buddy, an old friend with whom he'd share gossip about his girlfriend?

I reminded myself of what I really needed to be thinking about, and I got to work in the living room, going first to the sliding-door cabinet along an interior wall. I'd always admired this particular cabinet, which was covered in hand-painted paper that showed two girls, one in kimono and the other in a modish 1920s dress, sitting on a cliff overlooking water—a view similar to that of the east side of Takeo's garden. I thought, looking at it more carefully, it had to be the house's garden.

As I continued my flashlight tour of the various reception rooms, I found plenty of vases, small and large, but no ibex vessel. I was fortunate that I'd have the night hours to keep looking. If the vessel really were in the house, I'd definitely find it.

By the time I was done putting away the breakable items I'd mentioned to Takeo, the wind was at a nightmare pitch outside and there were frequent, ominous bangs against the closed shutters. Out of curiosity, I opened the front door a crack and felt myself stagger backward from the force of the sea wind.

There really was no chance of getting out tonight. After latching the door, I ventured into the kitchen to see what kind of provisions

Takeo had. He'd expected to be staying in his house alone, so I doubted he'd have stocked enough for two people to get through more than a day. I also knew he wasn't the kind who believed in canned and packaged foods. Not that he was someone who cooked from scratch; Takeo liked to order restaurant food at the last minute, but I doubted that the local pizza and ramen shops would be making deliveries.

I found uncooked rice and a few other basics in the cupboard, but the best prospect was the contents of a shopping bag from Matsuya's basement food arcade that I found sitting on the kitchen table.

It was better than I'd expected, and perfect for a vegetarian like myself: marinated tofu, pickled vegetables, roasted yams, spinach croquettes, and a petite apple tart. I put a saucepan of water on the stove to boil for the rice I'd make. Now there would be plenty for dinner and perhaps breakfast the next day.

I checked the refrigerator and found cans of energy drink and soy sauce, but nothing more. No bottled water. This was a new worry, so I went back to the crowded kitchen cabinet and took out the largest container, an old *miso* jar, and began filling it at the kitchen sink.

"I thought you were putting away the ceramics, not taking them out," Takeo said when he joined me a minute later.

"I didn't see any bottled water in your fridge, so I thought I should take a few preparations. And this was the largest container I could find."

"And one of the nicest," Takeo said. "You chose a two-hundred-year-old Kyushu piece."

"I didn't mean to use your oldest piece, but I didn't see anything more suitable. Sorry!"

"Oh, it's not the oldest ceramic in the house, but it has a great deal of sentimental value. It's been in our family a few generations, you know—"

"Do you want me to put it away?"

He shook his head. "Of course not. If it has held *miso* without accident for a couple of hundred years, it can hold water for a night or two. The fact is, I only have a half-case of bottled water in my car, which we'd better leave for emergencies. And I'll open sake tonight. Or would you prefer wine?" Takeo pried open the storage compartment that was built into the center of the kitchen floor. Where most Japanese would have stored root vegetables, he had squeezed in a wine rack and a wooden sake box.

"I—it doesn't really matter. I'll just have a glass of—whatever. Did you refill the bathtub with clean water?"

"Yes, indeed. And what do you mean, it doesn't matter? It's not like you to defer to anyone else about taste." Takeo's voice was teasing. Clearly, the bath had relaxed him.

"I'd say the same was true for you, too, except for your diplomatic reaction to the handbag painting." I smiled at him.

"The handbag painting—damn!" Takeo said. "After all of Emi's reminders, I still forgot to bring it. I was just thinking about the shutters."

"I hope Emi's not too upset." I didn't meet his eyes, but went instead to the stove, where I saw that the flame under the rice had gone out. "Hey, I can't get the burner back on."

Takeo went to the Tokyo Gas heater next to the kitchen counter and fiddled for a minute. "Well, I can tell you why. The gas has been turned off at the source."

"What does that mean?" Suddenly my thoughts were back to the storm outside. "Let's put the radio on."

There was no working radio in the house, so Takeo put a raincoat over himself and ran out to his car to listen to its radio. He came back ten minutes later with a report that the storm was at its peak, no great surprise to either of us.

"I wish there were better information than that," I fretted while Takeo shook off his wet coat for the second time in half an hour and laid it down in the entryway to dry.

"Well, if something really awful happens, we'll hear about it on the town loudspeaker. They broadcast from the police department, don't you remember?"

Any announcements of disaster would come after the fact, I thought grimly as I began arranging the takeout food on a blue-

and-white Imari platter. The Kayama villa, perched on a hill, would be a terrible place to be stranded or involved in a mudslide.

But I couldn't brood fatalistically, not when I'd been given such a succession of good luck: the miraculous passage to Hayama, unforced entry to Takeo's house, and food to sustain me. I was safe inside, and that was what counted.

18

Five minutes later, I had fixed the dinner tray and followed the sound of tinny, nostalgic music coming from the sitting room. Takeo had lit the room with hurricane lamps and candles. I set the food down on a low, lacquered art deco table and looked over at Takeo, who was hunched over a vintage windup gramophone I'd never seen opened before. Nearby there was a stack of old records, some of them just in paper sleeves and others in the original cardboard cases, their illustrations so faded that I could barely make them out.

"These are my grandfather's *enka* records," Takeo said, as if in answer to my inquiring glance.

I nodded, because I could have guessed as much. *Enka* was a kind of people's music, a songwriting tradition that combined current events with human feelings and flourished in Japan from the late nineteenth century into the early twentieth. I'd written a paper in college about the illustration of songbook covers, but I'd never actually heard a recorded *enka* song from this period. Listening to a wavering male voice barely audible against the wind outside, all the while standing in an almost dark house from the period, made me shiver.

I saw also that Takeo had filled a hibachi, a Japanese wooden table with a built-in brazier, with coal and lit it. A little screen sat above the glowing embers, and on it he'd placed a bowl of water, and within that, a flask of sake. I suggested that we finish cooking the rice on it. After I took the rice off to rest and finish its last ten minutes of steam-cooking, Takeo put the sake back on. It was time to eat.

The minute I'd sat down across from him and started to serve the food, a wrenching sound came from above.

"It sounds as if the roof's coming off!" I looked up in alarm.

"It's probably just some tiles. I remember, when I was having the roof replaced, you weren't pleased with the adhesive. Now I regret not following your advice," Takeo said.

"Well, I didn't push you very hard on it. You had a valid point about its toxicity, and whether it might get into the water supply." I couldn't put a finger on why Takeo was so mellow and gentle all of a sudden. I knew I should be grateful, but it made me a bit uneasy.

"Speaking of toxins, this is for you." Takeo handed me a brimming, gold-edged sake cup. "To what shall we toast?"

"How about to—just being here?" I offered. This was the way I felt. I'd thought getting into the villa was going to be impossible, and now I was in, having a cozy evening with an old friend. But now, of course, I found myself with a new problem. When I located the ibex vessel—as I was almost certain I'd do, tonight—what would happen to Takeo? I'd been angry at him the last two days, but now that our friendship had been restored, what I was going to do could turn out very badly for him.

"To being here. Together," Takeo added as an afterthought.

I joined him in clinking glasses. The sake burned my throat after the first sip, so I put down the glass. And while the carryout food was delicious, I found myself unable to eat more than a few bites.

"You've hardly eaten. Is there something wrong with the food?" Takeo said after a while.

"Not at all. I was just thinking I'd better—save it. I know there's not much for tomorrow, and what if—"

"What if we're here for days?" Takeo laughed. "There is a bag of rice in a kitchen cabinet, and we won't even have to go down to the beach to fish. The fish will be thrown up here—I remember that from the storm when I was a boy."

"And there's *daikon* growing in your garden, right? We'll be fine." Fine—except that the idea of playing house with a suspected international art thief made me feel queasy. Takeo's glass of sake was already empty, so I did what Japanese etiquette called for and filled it for him. Promptly, he refilled mine even though it was still two-thirds full.

"I saw a picture of this room in a magazine," I said. "It looks so different tonight, and I don't think it's just the lighting. Did you put a lot of the valuables away—I mean, things that were arranged in the room for the shoot?"

"I don't think we define valuable in the same way," Takeo said, instead of answering me directly. "To me, the first camellia I planted and raised as a boy is more valuable than any painting. Hey, why aren't you drinking?"

"I don't want to get a headache." It was interesting, but while I was away from Hugh, I was drinking about a quarter as much.

"I'm sure you won't," Takeo said. "Unless it's from that scream-ing wind outside. Shall I put on a new record?"

"All right," I said reluctantly. Maybe I'd gone too far with my questions.

This time, the recorded voice was that of a woman. As her sweet, high-pitched voice crackled from the old machine, I heard snatches of phrases about school, a school uniform, a lover. At the end of the song, the needle ran on, bumping again and again at the record's edge. Takeo seemed lost in thought and didn't move, so I got up and put the needle back on its rest.

"What did you think of the lyrics?" he asked when I returned to the table and sat down on the *zabuton* cushion.

"I caught something about a lover and pine needles and a school uniform, but that's about it," I confessed.

"The song is called 'Voice of the Pine.' It's the story of a young student who, after she lives away from her family for the first time, becomes corrupted."

Too close to home for me. I asked, "What about the rest of the lyrics?"

"She sings that she's forgotten all her teacher's lessons because of her nighttime lover. She wears a schoolgirl uniform wrapped around her shameless heart by day, but by night, she changes into

fancy clothes, and wonders to whom she'll show those colors."
Takeo paused. "It's a very sad ending, maybe not right for tonight."

"It sounds like a Japanese Lolita story," I mused aloud. "You've
got to tell me the ending!"

"After her family and lover desert her, she knows there is nothing left to live for, so she drowns herself in the Sumida River."

"People must have died along the coast today. Flash floods like
those I saw, flying tiles—"

"You're so pessimistic." Takeo leaned over and took my left
hand, which I'd been using to shred up the paper doily from under
the croquettes.

"You must be careful not to corrupt yourself," I said, finding myself unable to withdraw my hand from the caress. In a room this
dark, with the wind howling outside, the feeling of Takeo's touch
was electrifying.

"And what about you?" he asked. "When you started your perilous journey to this house, did you telephone your own fiancé in
Washington to tell him whom you were going to see?"

"He's not my fiancé," I said defensively, as thoughts began to
whirl through my head. Takeo thought I'd come to Hayama to see
him. "This evening is starting to feel strange. I apologize if I have
confused you."

"Wait a minute. Did you just say that you are not engaged?"
Takeo's voice sounded strange.

"I'm not. There's no ring. Didn't you see that?" I extracted my
left hand, the one he'd been holding, and waved it at him.

Takeo's expression, in the dim light, appeared almost dazed.
"After missing you for three years, your hand wasn't the first thing
I looked at. It was more—the rest of you—the whole person—"

"I'm sure I look older," I said drily.

"You look more sophisticated, actually. And the way you carry
yourself—your body, it's quite—muscular and more firm now, isn't
it?" Takeo finished his glass of sake and poured himself another, as
if he'd forgotten all the rules about drinking.

"Emi is absolutely exquisite," I protested, suddenly noticing that
my *yukata* was gaping open on one side, exposing a bit more than
my trapezius.

"I agree. And sometimes I feel quite ready to be married to her. Other times, not so ready." He looked at me again. "What would happen if I kissed you?"

"I guess I'd have to knock you through the shutters out into the storm. Although of course, it's your house, not mine, so that doesn't seem entirely fair—"

"You are the one who's not fair!" Takeo said, his voice rising with emotion. "I didn't know that you decided not to marry. And look at what's happened to my life, in the meantime."

"You never loved me, and I remind you that you willingly entered into your *omiai*." I couldn't figure out whether Takeo was drunk or just a bit tipsy. I had barely had more than a few sips because I knew I needed to stay very sober for my night's work—if I ever got around to it.

"Forget the *omiai*." Takeo's voice cracked, and then he kissed me.

Hugh. I absorbed the kiss, and began to respond to it. *Forgive me.* It was odd; the more I tried to think about Hugh, the less clear his image was. He was like the faded illustration on the record jackets. Everything that I had feared, back at the Smithsonian conference table, had come to pass.

Was it really wrong to do this? I wondered as the wind howled outside. Quickly, I'd moved from nervousness to something entirely different. We weren't sitting at the table anymore, but were stretched out on the floor, the hallowed ground where nobody ever wore shoes and we'd made love. And if I stopped Takeo, what would become of the night, the vessel, the whole reason I was there?

This was good, I said to myself as Takeo discovered the navel ring, laughing softly before he moved lower. I dug my fingers into Takeo's straight, thick hair and closed my eyes, giving in to my rising level of excitement. It was about time I relaxed, because ever since my arrival I'd been anxious about everything: the theft of my phone, my lack of progress in the mission, and the beautiful young girl who'd taken my place.

Well, now I was the one with Takeo, not Emi, and that in itself was arousing. Takeo, as corrupt as he might be about antiques and love, was also bizarrely safe—a man on the verge of marriage who would never come after me with messy, emotional demands.

So I did it: everything that he wanted, and then the things that I wanted, too, things I'd been afraid to ask Hugh, because they seemed too—foreign. Too Japanese. It was fate, I told myself, as Takeo sank into me so deeply that the tatami matting underneath me indented my skin. Then I didn't notice the scratchy mat anymore, didn't notice anything except the desire inside me gathering and intensifying, a typhoon that had come out of nowhere but seemed incapable of lessening.

Afterward, Takeo led me into the bedroom, where I was stunned to see the Chinese altar bed made up with fresh linens. It was only then, when he asked me to lie down again, that I really heard the sound of the wind outside the house, and I realized it sounded like someone crying.

19

Afterward, Takeo fell asleep almost immediately.

Just what I wanted—time to work. I waited twenty minutes to be sure he wasn't going to wake up, then tiptoed back to the living room, where I wrapped up in the discarded robe lying on the tatami. The sight of it shamed me deeply. But what would have happened, I thought, if I hadn't followed Takeo's lead? We'd still be up talking—arguing, probably. There would have been no chance at all to look for the ibex ewer.

I walked the edge of the room, thinking about where it must have gone. Takeo might have placed it in formal storage—a bank vault, or something like that. I shook myself. No, that couldn't be. Takeo didn't take care of valuable objects in the manner that I did. To Takeo, the ewer was like any other object he used to arrange flowers. After he was done with the magazine shoot, he would have taken the old flowers out to the compost heap, rinsed the vessel in the house's deepest sink—the one in the kitchen—and put it away. It wasn't the right way to treat an old piece of earthenware, but then, Takeo was even less of a curator than I.

The kitchen. I hadn't really looked through it yet. I carried the hurricane lamp with me into the kitchen. I saw a flash of movement, and realized that a mouse had run across the floor. Well, we'd been too caught up in things to put away the original food containers, which lay open on the kitchen table.

Where would Takeo put a vessel that he used for flower arranging? My eye was drawn to the massive old cherrywood *tansu* cupboard along one side of the wall. I gently opened the first sliding wood panel and held the hurricane light close as I peered inside. Sturdy blue-and-white teacups nestled alongside various earthenware bowls. The second compartment held square plates of different colors, some old and decorated with elegant hand-painted designs, as well as plainer modern ones.

I got to my knees and opened the lower sliding compartment doors. A prosaic watering can brushing the edge of a colorful Dale Chihuly glass vase that I remembered was one of Takeo's favorites. As I touched the glass vase to withdraw it, it made a scraping sound. Something was shoved in, tight behind. I wiggled out the vase, and there it was: the ibex vessel.

For a moment, I just stared. Then I lifted it gently to the kitchen table. It felt so light, lighter than I'd expected—it could break so easily. I found myself trembling, after I'd gotten it to the table. I hurried to the *genkan* to retrieve my backpack, where I had my reference photos and notes about the characteristics of Mesopotamian pottery stored in an inner compartment.

The papers were dry, thanks to the fact that I'd kept them in a plastic zip bag. I also pulled out my measuring tape, because size was the first thing to check.

Takeo's vessel stood eight-and-one-quarter inches high, as did the piece taken from the museum. *Good for the government; not good for Takeo*, I thought as I continued my survey. The ewer was reddish brown, as Elizabeth Cameron had said it would be; it also had a pleasing irregularity at the top edge, something that she hadn't mentioned but that seemed consistent for an old, hand-shaped piece. I closed my eyes and held the ewer, trying to memorize its texture. Too bad I didn't have the camera-phone: I could have had a digitally enhanced picture to compare with the slide from the museum—just as, if I'd had a chance to get to a professional laboratory, I could have had its age checked through thermoluminescence testing. All I had was my magnifying glass.

I used the glass to help me focus on the slight crackle of the ewer's surface, and then ran my fingers lightly over it. Strange that the piece had survived so long without a chip—but that was consistent with the museum's description. I held it to my nose and sniffed inside, catching the faintest odor of something organic. Takeo hadn't cleaned it the way many *ikebana* artists would have, with a mixture of water and bleach. That was good for the ewer, at least.

A natural thief, I reminded myself. I'd been sent across the Pacific to find out the truth about an object, and I'd found out the truth about a man. What had I expected? I'd felt so torn, wanting to succeed at the mission of finding the vessel; now I'd done that, but I was on the verge of destroying someone's life. No, three lives. I'd screwed up things for Takeo and for his fiancée, not to mention Hugh.

What was the next step? I stared through watery eyes at the vessel, losing focus. I was tired. A flash of movement at the periphery of the room startled me. I refocused and saw that Takeo was standing in the doorway.

"You're awake," I said, starting to put away the pictures. "I was restless, so I thought I'd clean up the kitchen."

He sat down across from me at the table, the hurricane light and ibex vessel between us. "This pottery certainly doesn't need to be cleaned."

"I—I—noticed it in the magazine photo. I wanted to look at it a bit. I don't know much about Mesopotamian ceramics, and I'm interested, you know, branching out a bit into Near Asia, as the scholars are calling the region now—"

"You have some papers with you."

I shoved them back into my backpack. "Sorry, it's confidential."

"What?" Takeo's expression turned from curious to hurt.

"Where did you get it, Takeo? Who sold it to you?"

Takeo shook his head at me. "Sorry, that's confidential."

I looked at him and sighed. "It was a mistake. I'm sorry."

Takeo gave me a long look. "Well, I'm not going to be able to sleep again. I'll make some tea."

"But the gas doesn't work—"

"The gas heater light came on again. That means Tokyo Gas and

Electric turned it on." Takeo filled a cast-iron teakettle at the kitchen tap. "And we never lost our water, either. This typhoon was a big deception."

The rain was much lighter now, it was true. But I knew he was referring to more than the storm. I would have to talk to him somehow, without giving things away.

"You were about to mention who sold this vessel to you?" I asked when Takeo brought the teakettle over to the table.

"Nobody sold it. It was given to me." He placed the kettle precisely on a rush mat, so the heat wouldn't hurt the table. Then he moved back to the *tansu* and selected two mottled green tea bowls for us to drink from.

I hadn't expected that, although it could be an excuse someone would use if he'd knowingly trafficked in stolen goods.

"So who was the generous giver?" I asked, when he sat down across from me again.

"I think I've told you enough," Takeo said lightly. "Now it's time for you to tell me what I want to know, things like whether you even wanted to make love with me in the first place!"

"Why won't you tell me who? As I mentioned before, I'm really interested in this type of ancient pottery—"

"It's out of your league, Rei. You couldn't afford it. It's a thousand years old."

The vessel was at least twice as old, I thought but did not say. "Who gave it to you? Takeo, it's very important that I know."

"None of your business." Takeo poured the tea, refusing to meet my gaze.

"Emi. You must have received it from her, or her father—" What Mr. Watanabe had mentioned about her father's previous government posting in Turkey came back to me.

He gave me a long look. "It was from her father, to celebrate the engagement. And now I've given you what you so desperately craved, tell me what I want to understand—why you pretended that you wanted me when all you really were after was one of my possessions!"

"I'm not going to take it." I put my hand over Takeo's. "I can only suggest one thing to you, that this vessel might be better off back with Emi's family—at least until the wedding. Believe me, Takeo, I'm suggesting this for your own well-being."

"I can't."

"Why not?" I couldn't even begin to sip the tea Takeo had made. It was too hot.

"Because—because I had seen it in their home, and admired it, so he gave it to me. It was part of the *omiai* process. I don't think you can possibly understand—"

"Oh, but I do." I looked at Takeo steadily. "Mr. Harada gave you something very precious because he wanted you to ensure that you married his daughter."

"I didn't agree to marry her because of a piece of pottery!"

"Of course you didn't. You decided to marry because of her father and what he could do to advance your environmental causes."

Takeo's skin flushed with anger, but he didn't deny it. He just sat silently.

I thought again. "Okay, I understand now why you can't return it to the house. But maybe you should keep it somewhere safer for the time being, like a bank vault. I could assist you with setting something up."

"If you think I should put everything over three hundred years of age in a vault, this house would be half-empty."

"Takeo, I'll do it for you, if you like. Please, just believe me this once—"

"I'm afraid I've been too believing," Takeo said. "Our last evening—it was all a show, wasn't it?"

"It wasn't," I said, not wanting to think about the fact that I'd come twice, two betrayals of Hugh within seventy-two hours of my arrival in Japan. I shouldn't have felt this kind of pleasure with someone who was so bad for me.

When things were awkward, the best solution was escape. I stood up and said that I was going to pack up.

"But it's still raining," Takeo said. "Your clothes are wet and the floodwaters still must be high—"

"I've really overstayed my time here," I said. "I'm sorry. I wonder if you would be kind enough to lend me jeans and a T-shirt or something like that. I'll mail them back."

It was almost nine in the morning by the time I'd taken my shower and gotten Takeo to lend me a shrunken pair of drawstring farmer's pants, one of his many Greenpeace T-shirts, and thick wool socks that would protect my feet from the wet insides of the rain shoes.

"You forgot something," Takeo called after me as I unlocked and slid open the front door. There was no more rain, but everything, from the top of the bamboo fence to the leaves and grasses, glittered with teardrops of water. Along the driveway, there were large puddles, but I knew I could make my way out—even if I had to cross people's property to stay on high ground.

"I don't think so," I muttered, continuing down the stone driveway.

"Take it! I want you to have it as a memento, since this was what you were really after."

I turned and saw he was holding the vessel carelessly, a couple of fingers in the handle.

"Don't drop it!" I shouted, unable to hide my fear.

"You've always cared for things more than people, haven't you?" Takeo shook his head.

It was more than that. Maybe the anger was a face-saving move, I thought suddenly. Takeo could have finally understood that there was something amiss with his engagement gift and wanted out of the whole corrupt deal.

"All right, I'll take it, thank you very much." I strode up to him, thinking, this will settle it for all. It's not the way the people in Washington expected things to go, but I wouldn't look a gift ibex in the mouth.

Takeo placed the vessel in my hands. "I'm sorry, Rei."

"You don't have to say it—"

"You're right that what we did doesn't—work—anymore." He shook his head mournfully. "And I can never undo what I've done to Emi."

"It may sound unbelievable, but I do wish the two of you well. I wasn't trying to take you away—" I tried to blink away the tears that were forming.

"I understand," Takeo said shortly. "Well, we won't do it again. We've learned."

"I guess this will be good-bye, then," I said. We looked at each other for a long moment.

"I probably shouldn't see you again. In Japan, it's just—"

"I know. My aunt explained how things have to be." I paused. "Well, if I'm going off with your vessel, I want to travel safely. Could I trouble you for a good, strong box and lots of packing paper?"

We walked into the house again, and I set the vessel down on the tea table in the living room, while Takeo came up with a box and tissue paper. The sound of the unlocked front door sliding open startled both of us. We exchanged glances.

"Your father?" I asked nervously.

"He's in Kyoto. I don't know who it could be."

I had a sudden flash of fear, as if someone had come for the vessel, just as I'd finally gotten my hands on it.

Takeo gave me a last look and walked out of the room toward the entryway. After a moment's hesitation, I followed, reasoning that it would be better to present a united front against a burglar, if that's what we were up against. I took the precaution of picking up a telephone receiver, because even though it didn't work, the burglar wouldn't know.

I stopped short in the hallway when I saw the small, slim girl in a pink raincoat holding a Hermès print Kitty umbrella.

Emi had arrived.

20

"Emi-chan, how wonderful to see you. You came all by yourself? What a surprise!" Takeo, never good at pretending, didn't sound happy at all.

Instead of answering him, Emi stared at me, her eyes, if anything, larger than before.

"It was just a quick visit," I stammered. "I—I am just now leaving—"

"But you are wearing his clothes." She gestured at the Greenpeace T-shirt and baggy farmer's pants that I had rolled up a few inches over my ankles.

I thought quickly. "Yes, I was caught in the rain. My clothes were soaked through. He kindly lent these things to me so I could walk out to catch a train back to the city. In fact, I was just leaving—"

"You always say you're leaving."

I stopped, remembering what I'd said to her the last time.

"The rain stopped last night," Emi continued. "So you must have come yesterday."

"It was a surprise visit," Takeo said before I could muster up another faltering excuse.

"Oh, I see. Just as the auction was a surprise, and going to the Kaikan was a—coincidence!"

"I'm sorry," I said.

"Sorry!" Emi's voice cracked. "And to think I was so silly to ask my father's driver to go to the trouble of bringing me here. Everyone advised against it, so why did I come?"

"Are you saying that the floods have subsided, then?" Takeo said. I could have shaken him for his insensitivity.

"Not all of them. I was scared we wouldn't make it, but I really wanted to see you. I brought the painting that you forgot."

The handbag painting. She'd risked driving sixty kilometers in a typhoon-struck region to make sure Takeo saw the handbag painting in the house. Or maybe she'd done it because she'd had a sense that we'd meet in Hayama and things would happen.

"I'll bring in the painting. We'll all look at it," I offered, sliding into my shoes and starting out the *genkan* to the garden. I saw a long black car idling, and a blue-uniformed man standing in the garden, his hands crossed before him. When he saw me, he made a quick bow.

"Excuse me, but could there be . . . an honorable hand-washing place . . ."

I could imagine how long the car trip had been. I took the painting out of the trunk of the idling car and led the driver into the house and to the powder room off the hallway. After that, I thought I'd see if I could discreetly get the ewer out of the living room and into my backpack.

When I ducked my head into the room, I found that Takeo and Emi had gotten there first. Takeo had put his hands on Emi's shoulders, but she was twisting away. In doing so, she caught sight of me and gasped.

"Do you want him? Well, you can have him!"

"Please calm down, darling. Nothing has changed. Rei will assure you of the same thing." His eyes pleaded with me.

"I have no interest in Takeo," I said softly. "All he is to me is an old friend—"

"Oh, that story. Old friends, old times. Just because I'm young doesn't mean that I'm stupid. I know when it's time to go, and I'm leaving—" She broke away from Takeo. Passing the *tansu*, she grabbed up the vessel. She paused for a minute, then swiveled toward me.

"I'm sorry you're upset," I said. "I wish you all the best for your marriage, I was just telling Takeo."

"Everything's changed, since you've come. It's because of you—" and before I could realize it, the ewer was hurtling through the air, right at me.

I screamed and reached out my hands for it, but I was distracted by the sight of Takeo, in my peripheral vision, diving in front. We bumped into each other just as the ibex ewer hit the tatami.

"Oh, no!" I screamed, feeling my own world crash along with it. Emi dashed from the room. Takeo ran after her. A car door slammed and an engine started.

As if on cue, the chauffeur emerged from the powder room, drying his hands. At the sound of squealing tires, his head turned toward the open door. "What's that?"

"It sounds like someone went," I said, stepping clumsily into my shoes and hurrying out, just to see the limousine slaloming down the hilly driveway. Takeo and Emi were nowhere in sight—obviously, they'd gone off together.

"She's not driving, is she?" he asked, his face crumpling into an expression of panic.

"I don't know who's behind the wheel," I said.

"She must be driving. And if anything happens, I shall be held responsible. I should never have left the car to tend to my selfish personal needs—" The chauffeur gave me a little wave and started running down the driveway.

"You're not going to catch them!" I called after him. "They were going—really fast!"

"I must try!" His voice floated back to me faintly as he disappeared down the hill.

I wasn't going to join the chase. I had my own disaster to clean up. I stepped out of my shoes and dejectedly dragged myself back to the living room, where the vessel lay in pieces.

I sank to my knees, examining the fragments. It was terrible how easily the vessel had broken. Heavy clay usually broke in larger chunks, and perhaps might have even survived a fall onto a mat-covered floor. The only reason could be the force with which Emi had thrown it.

I took a tissue from my pocket and began to lay the pieces of pottery on it. I couldn't imagine how I was going to explain to Michael Hendricks what had happened to the priceless vessel. Suddenly, the loss of my visa to Japan seemed like nothing in comparison with my knowledge I'd caused the destruction of one of the oldest, greatest antiquities of the Middle East—no, of the world.

Ouch. A rough bit that I'd picked up broke through the skin of my forefinger, and I watched idly as a tiny drop of blood slowly formed through the open skin. Earthenware wasn't usually hard enough to cause damage when it broke, but it somehow seemed appropriate for me to have blood on my hands, mixed with the dust of one of civilization's ruined treasures. I left the ruins on the floor to get up to find some toilet paper to stanch the bleeding. In the process, I stepped on more broken pottery. Damn it. I crouched down to pick the piece out of my thick sock, and then I saw it—the interesting texture I'd felt in the night, patterned with light, rightward-swirling whorls from its time on the potter's wheel.

I stood there, my bleeding finger forgotten, feeling my heart hammer as I looked, shard by shard, to make certain about my conclusion. Yes, the ewer had been formed on a potter's wheel, an invention that wasn't part of ancient Mesopotamian pottery making. I examined it further, making mental notes.

Takeo's vessel was a fake. And for once, a fraudulent antique was a very good bit of news. No world treasure had been smashed. Takeo wasn't guilty of harboring stolen art; neither for that matter were Emi's parents. Everyone was off the hook, and I could shoot out of this hellhole of Japanese embarrassment back to Washington fast—tomorrow, maybe. I'd make a few calls to see if I needed to take the shards all the way back to Washington or whether Mr. Watanabe could accept them.

I used the box Takeo had found for me but had hastily abandoned upon Emi's arrival. Every sizable piece went in, and then I used a damp cloth to wipe clean the place on the tatami where the vessel had fallen. As I packed up the shards, I thought about whether I should leave Takeo a message telling him not to worry about the loss.

I couldn't, I realized: any note that Emi found might set her off in another rage. I would have to go incommunicado, permanently. But the important thing I could hold to myself was that their engagement present was innocent, even if their relationship wasn't, anymore.

21

The train system was running again, but slowly. While I was waiting at Zushi station, I picked up the pay phone and was happy to hear a dial tone. Guilt made me call Hugh first, but I was still cowardly enough to use his number at work, where I could assume—from the time of night—he would be absent. I left a voice message saying that I'd been cut off from communication because of the typhoon, and added that I'd lost my cell phone, so if he wanted to reach me, it would have to be by phoning the Grand Hyatt.

Next, I called Michael Hendricks; yes, it was two in the morning Washington time, but I figured he would rather hear something from me, after two days of silence, than nothing at all. He picked up his cell phone halfway through the first ring. Either he was already awake or he was as jumpy a sleeper as I.

"Well, what a dramatic surprise. I thought you'd gone AWOL," he grumbled after I'd identified myself.

"I have a really good explanation."

"I'm glad. I was beginning to wonder if I needed to send the JSDF after you."

"JSDF?" I asked, thinking Michael trafficked in far too many acronyms.

"Japanese Self-Defense Forces. Our friends in uniform."

"Michael, first I lost the cell phone. Then with the typhoon, I couldn't find a working phone, not until five minutes ago."

"And where is this phone?" his voice was clipped.

"At a station platform in Zushi. I know it's nonsecure, but I'm sorry. It was all I could get, and you were saying you wanted to hear from me—I've got good news."

"You made contact with Mr. Flowers?"

"Better than that." In a few sentences, I told him that I'd found the vessel and ascertained that it couldn't possibly be 3,000 years old. But Michael wasn't as pleased as I'd expected. He expressed horror at the breakage, and he seemed doubtful that I was right about its age. Also, he wanted to know more about the circumstances of the accident—chiefly, why Emi had been around and angry enough to throw it.

"It was all a misunderstanding. She drove up unexpectedly and discovered me talking with Mr. Flowers." There. I kept it short and simple.

"Hold on. You said you were at the house, but I didn't know Flowers was involved. Did you—tell him that you were interested in the Momoyama vase?"

"Of course not! He thought I was just there to get out of the rain. We closed up the house, had dinner, and afterward, I took advantage of the time he was sleeping to find the vessel." The hell if I was going to tell him what I'd had to do to get Takeo to fall asleep. "Unfortunately, he discovered me examining it, but I think he believes that I'm interested in Near Eastern art. And it was good that I talked to him, because he explained the thing was actually an engagement present from her parents."

"I see." Michael was quiet for a moment. "So when did they become engaged?"

"I believe it was last June."

"The photo spread came out in May," said Michael. "So he actually had the vessel well before this engagement."

"I don't know why," I said. "Maybe they gave it to him a little bit earlier, when they were hoping he would follow through with asking her to marry him."

"It strikes me as odd," Michael said. "There's too much mystery about the ownership, and we don't know the piece's age until the lab experts examine the fragments."

"I thought you hired me because I am an expert," I said. "But that's okay, I can hand over the shards to Mr. Watanabe to take wherever you like."

"No names, please. Have you told him that you have the vase?" Michael's voice was tense. When I replied in the negative, he said, "Good. Let's keep the situation between the two of us, for now. I'd like you to package up everything and send it by the fastest air service possible. I'll use the lab at the Sackler, of course."

"What's going on? I thought you and our—Japanese colleague—were partners in this project."

"His role was to make the phone calls to let you back into the country legally, and to assist you, should you have found yourself on the wrong side of the police, which fortunately has not happened yet."

"All right, boss. Or may I call you captain?"

"I retired as a lieutenant, okay? And I don't mean to snap at you. It's just I've been a little—worried, because of the botched call earlier."

"Which call?"

"You called me yesterday around two in the morning. I assumed because of the weather situation, the signal was lost."

"But I didn't call you," I said.

"You did. I saw the number of your government phone flash up on my phone's caller ID feature."

"Like I said a few minutes ago, I lost the cell phone. If a call was placed using it to you, it must have been made by whoever has the phone." Now I told him in detail about how the cell phone had disappeared from my backpack.

"Whoever had it must have broken your password," Michael said. "What the hell did you choose—your birthday or your first name, something that anyone could think of?"

"Why does it matter what I chose?" I answered, thinking sorrowfully that Take0 had been far too simple.

"When did you last use the phone? Think about whether anyone was watching you or listening."

"That night I called you from the bar—there was a guy, this an-noying Austrian, who came up to me wanting to see the phone. I said no, of course, and he wandered off, but he might have been listening when I was talking with my friends later on—not that I said anything about the mission or Flowers, but still—"

"Have you seen this guy again?"

"No. I remember him introducing himself to me as Jürgen. I could probably find out where he's staying—I'm sure it's one of those backpacker flophouses."

"Don't bother," Michael said. "You need to stay focused. I'll send you a new cell phone, but not to the hotel where you were. Can you find yourself a safer location?"

"My aunt and uncle's house in Yokohama is pretty far off the radar screen. But what's the point? I finished the job. I was hoping to call a travel agent today to get on a flight home."

"But the job's not over," Michael said.

"I found the vessel—"

"You found a Momoyama vase," Michael corrected. "It's not necessarily the right one, as you said. There could be two vases: a real one and a reproduction."

I sighed. "What if it was a fake all the time in the National Museum, and nobody knew it?"

"If that's the case, whoever bought it from the looters is still guilty of a felony. And as it stands, things definitely sound suspicious. Someone may have stolen your government phone to ascertain who your contacts are."

I didn't want to concede that Michael was right, but what he was saying fit into the troubled thoughts I'd had while walking to the Zushi train station.

"I don't want you calling this cell number or my office number anymore. I'll get a new cell for myself and give you that number the next time we speak at your aunt's house. Can you move there today?"

"I guess so. I was getting to like that hotel, though." Oh, for a hot shower there, and room service.

"You're being watched, Rei. Your current location is unsafe. Pack up, pay the bill with your government credit card, and discreetly make your way to Yokohama."

"But can't I find another place? I could maybe rent a room some-where."

"A rented room is not as secure as a family home."

But a family home meant protection, meaning I'd get nothing done. I said a depressed good-bye as the train pulled slowly into the station.

In Tokyo there was standing water at some street corners, and a lot of trash blown about, but none of the kind of devastation I'd seen on the Miura peninsula. I picked up both the *Japan Times* and the *Asahi* to read while I rode the last stretch, a bit of subway, over to Roppongi. The newspapers said that Japan's southeastern edge had been hit very hard, with billions of yen lost in property damage, and twenty people dead. At least five people had been swept over bridges similar to the one I'd crossed in Zushi—the account from eyewitnesses of how these people had been lost made me cringe at my misplaced bravery.

The Hyatt's desk clerk had noticed my absence the previous night and expressed relief that I hadn't been a casualty of the storm. I apologized for causing her worry, then asked her to please pre-pare my bill and call a private car to take me to the airport, as I'd be checking out shortly.

"Have you shortened your business trip?" the clerk asked.

Why did she care? And how did she know I was on business? Suddenly paranoid, I said, "It was always going to be a quick trip, but now at least the planes are able to fly, so I can get out."

When I made it up to the hotel room, it took a moment to re-member which switches operated the curtains and lights. While I stripped off Takeo's clothes and stuffed them into the plastic bag meant for laundry, I turned on the television to see what the ty-phoon had wrought.

After that I took the shower I'd been long awaiting, and dressed in Grand's suit, perfectly cleaned by the hotel's dry cleaner. Then it was time to pack. I was beginning to regret my various shopping sprees, because even tiny things like bras take up space, if you've bought six of them. Packing the underwear, so lacy and cheerful, made me think about Hugh. I toyed with the idea of calling him to tell him I was going to be at Norie's, then reminded myself that he was still sleeping. I'd check in with him later when things weren't so hectic. And I still needed time to figure out what I would say. The Japanese had a don't ask, don't tell policy toward infidelity. And Hugh might be happier knowing nothing—especially since this had been an infidelity that would never be repeated.

Emi Harada. Takeo Kayama. The names floated back into my consciousness, and I realized that it wasn't because I was thinking aloud. The television announcer was saying something about Emi and Takeo.

I turned back to the television, where the story had changed to the cost of typhoon damage. I began channel surfing and stopped on TBS, the sensational channel, which was showing a snapshot of Emi at her high school graduation.

Emi Harada, daughter of the current minister for environmental affairs, was in critical condition at Saint Luke's Hospital in Tokyo following an automobile accident in Hayama. The car in which she was traveling, witnesses said, had run through a traffic light, hitting one car, then crashing through a souvenir shop and out to the beach. Her companion had also been in the car but escaped injury and reportedly pulled Harada from the car. I saw a shot of Takeo from behind, following police officers into a sedan.

Emi was injured, and it was my fault. So what if she'd been at the wheel—her mind had been somewhere else, back at the house, where she'd seen me and instantly understood the horrible thing I'd done. It had been so upsetting that she'd had to flee, had no time to wait for the driver. She'd been a novice steering a huge sedan, and her mind had been crazed with rage and perhaps fatigue. And the crash must have been shattering. I suppose it was a miracle that Takeo hadn't been hurt; I'd clearly seen him walking away. But why away? He should have gone with his fiancée to the hospital. The police could have asked any questions they had there. Unless . . .

Unless, I finished thinking, Emi had been trying to kill them both.

Now my sorrow for Emi began to mix with panic for myself. If the police were investigating the accident as an attempted murder-suicide, the whole business about motive would come up. And how long could Takeo stave them off without telling what he'd done the previous evening . . . and with whom?

Everything had changed. I was out of my room fifteen minutes later, my hair still wet from the bath. Now I knew that I had to break all contact with Takeo. Sending back the clothing I'd borrowed was too much of a risk, so I balled up the shirt and pants in a plastic bag and threw it into the trash collection bag hanging on an unattended maid's cart in my hallway. The clothes were gone in an instant. Too bad the rest of my problems couldn't have gone there, too.

I sailed downstairs on the noiseless elevator, paid my bill, and slid into the backseat of the Mercedes the front desk clerk had summoned. I told the driver to take me to the nearest DHL office, where I went in and mailed the shards of the vessel—except for one piece that I'd wrapped in tissue and kept in the outer pocket of my cell phone holder. I had made a snap decision about the piece; I could be wrong. I wanted to hold on to something until I knew for certain.

After I'd paid, not flinching at the high overnight charge, I jumped back into the car and asked the driver to take me to Shibuya Station. Even though I could have paid him to take me all the way to Yokohama, I didn't want a record of the address where I was headed. Instead, I'd take my chances on the train, watching carefully when I disembarked at Minami-Makigahara Station to see if anyone was following me.

It turned out that I was the only one to get out at my aunt's neighborhood station. I walked slowly uphill, trailing my suitcase behind me. A major storm might have swept the region, tearing limbs from trees, but in the Shimura family's tidy neighborhood, the streets had already been swept clean of organic litter by the housewives. Aunt Norie even had taken advantage of a few particularly graceful pomegranate boughs and arranged them in a large Satsuma urn outside her front door. I studied the tranquil, undeniably practical arrangement as I waited for someone to answer the doorbell. After five minutes, I realized the bell might not be working, so I rapped lightly on the door.

Chika answered promptly. She looked from me to my suitcase, then back again. "What's this?"

"You're supposed to welcome me." I leaned forward to peck her cheek. My cousin smelled like baby powder and looked fresh as ever in a starched white T-shirt and low-waisted Burberry plaid pants.

"But you had a room in a great hotel! Why in the world would you come here? We have no electricity or gas, probably for another day."

"You're my relatives and I'd rather be with you, helping in any way that I can," I said piously, exchanging my rain shoes for a cheery pair of tartan slippers my aunt kept on hand for guests. "Why would I prefer to stay in some impersonal box of a hotel room?"

"A box with room service and privacy," Chika said. "If you don't want your hotel room, I do. With the band coming in, I want to be staying nearby, and have, you know, freedom of movement."

"Freedom?" Aunt Norie, carrying a pail of broken camellia branches, appeared in the entryway, a frown etched between her eyebrows. "What kind of freedom is that, can you explain to your mother?"

22

Chika looked down at the fuzzy balls on her house slippers, then at me, as if for help.

I cleared my throat and ad-libbed, "It's just what I was explaining to her, that I once believed freedom of movement was so important, but now that I'm older I know it is family that counts. I wish I'd followed your advice and stayed here during the typhoon."

"*Ah so desu ka!* Yes, you do understand." Norie turned her gaze toward me, fondly. "What a good surprise to see you today. I'm sorry that we don't have hot water for you, or any electricity at all—we are using the old things you like, though, lanterns and hibachis and such—"

"Does your telephone work?" I asked.

Chika answered for her mother. "Not yet, but our neighbor heard that it may be restored by evening. I'm so worried that, you know, the band will arrive and not be able to reach me."

"But Rei-san probably needs the telephone for work purposes, which is more serious. Especially since the cell networks are down." Norie frowned at me. "I hope that our conditions don't last so long they cause an imposition."

I assured my aunt that they wouldn't, and then, after I'd moved my suitcase into the downstairs tatami room and laid out the futon for myself, I started cleanup duty. For an hour I picked up branches in the garden, and then I ruthlessly cleaned out all the spoiled food in the fridge. Aunt Norie sent Chika and me on foot to the grocery store, because she wanted to conserve what gas was in the tank of the family car. Pumps wouldn't be operable at gas stations until the power came back.

Chika and I came back with less than we'd hoped to get. All the bread was sold out, and the grocery store had the same issues of spoiled cold foods that we had in the house. We wound up with packages of Japanese curry sauce, a few vegetables and fruits, and canned soup, coffee, and beans—all things I reasoned that we could put in a pan and heat over the hibachi.

To my surprise, Norie already had a pot of rice and hot soup made when we returned—she'd grated the dried bonito fish she kept in a wooden box, and mixed in the homemade *miso* she fermented herself and stored under the kitchen floor. She garnished this perfect soup with some *shiso* leaf she'd grown in the garden.

While Chika set to making a curry from the vegetables and a packet of sauce, I complimented my aunt on her ability to run a calm household during a crisis. She shook off the praise. "Being here is easy," she said, as she deftly peeled a potato she was holding in one hand. "Your uncle was stranded at his office for two days! I am looking forward to greeting him tonight after two days away. And Tsutomu, well, he should have come today, but he's stayed on. The hospitals in Yokohama and the smaller places without power are sending the medical emergencies to Tokyo, so it's quite a lot of work for St. Luke's and all the other hospitals. I plan to go tomorrow morning to volunteer."

"I'll go with you," I said, picking up the potato peels out of the sink and putting them in the trash.

"But what about your work?" Norie asked. "I don't want to interfere with it. What do you still need to do, exactly?"

"Nothing, really," I said. "I'm just hanging tight for a few days."

"Will you see Takeo-kun again?" my aunt asked. It was the first time my aunt had mentioned him since the afternoon at the Kaikan.

"I—I don't think I need to," I said. "That meeting took care of all our unfinished business. Thank you for your help."

"He didn't seem so—pleased at the surprise. I've been worrying about what I should do the next time I am faced with him at a flower event."

"There is no need to worry," I said. "Really. I think you were right, it's just about impossible for a man and woman in Japan to be friends. Especially after an engagement," I added.

"Well, so now you know."

Dealing with the electrical shortage had kept me from thinking about Takeo and Emi, but Norie's questioning had brought back all the horror of the infidelity, the discovery, and the car crash. I didn't have much to say during dinner, even though Uncle Hiroshi and Tom arrived home around eight, in time to eat with everyone around the hibachi. Now I watched the family eating the ready-made curry, proclaiming it as good as any from a restaurant downtown. To me, the sauce was too thick and overspiced, but I never liked Japanese versions of Indian food.

My cousin Tom glanced over, raising his eyebrows at my lack of appetite, but I didn't react, and he retreated back into his own distracted state. He'd been that way ever since he'd returned. The hospital was overflowing. People with chronic conditions who needed electricity to operate their ventilators and IVs had come in, along with those who had become dehydrated from lack of water, were cut by broken glass, or who had injured themselves falling over things in their dark houses. Tomorrow, he predicted grimly, there would be a new group with food poisoning. And to top it all, the victim of a bad car accident had been flown in by helicopter. The operating room had been completely full, so she'd had to be transferred by ambulance to a hospital on the east side.

The lights came back on midway through the meal, and everyone cheered. Norie rushed to turn on the television that usually formed the soundtrack to all household meals, and Chika excused herself to use the phone. Uncle Hiroshi was talking about floods at his favorite golf course, and while I nodded to show that I was listening, my thoughts remained focused on what Tom had said. The accident victim he'd mentioned sounded as if it could be Emi. I wanted to ask him about her, but not in front of anyone.

It took a long time to clean up, since the water was still off and we had to do things with a store of rainwater in the backyard. But finally, the dishes were as clean as they'd get, and I settled down with my relatives to watch the TV news at eleven.

There was news about Emi Harada. It wasn't good. Norie, who of course hadn't heard the earlier TV report, turned to me and gasped, but I kept my eyes on the screen, where a reporter was soberly telling the world that after three emergency surgeries and the efforts of eight doctors from two of Tokyo's leading hospitals, eighteen-year-old Emi Harada had died.

23

I had a premonition of bad media, so I expected to find a flotilla of TV vehicles outside Norie's house the next morning. But at six in the morning, I was still blessedly anonymous, albeit depressed. I'd do anything to undo my trip to Hayama; if I hadn't been there with Takeo, Emi would still be alive.

I tiptoed downstairs to make tea for myself but discovered that Tom had beaten me to the task. He was at the dining table, a steaming cup at his side and the morning paper in front of him. He'd been reading an article about Emi Harada, I deduced from the photo that I spotted on the lower half of the folded paper.

"Is she—the patient you couldn't admit?" I said, picking up the Imari teapot and pouring a cup of green tea for myself.

"How did you know?" Tom looked up at me, and I saw the pain on his face.

"I knew about her being airlifted to your hospital," I said. "So it was a guess."

"Well, you guessed right. But the fact was, we didn't admit her." Tom explained that the emergency airlift to St. Luke's had been disastrous. He, the ER chief, hadn't known she was coming in until the helicopter was ten minutes away. And both of the hospital's operating rooms were in use. There was no space to treat her, so he'd had the hospital radio back to take the patient elsewhere. The helicopter wound up landing, anyway, and Emi had been transferred by one of St. Luke's ambulances to Hiroo Hospital.

"What was it, actually, that caused her death? Bleeding or—"

"The article doesn't mention the specific cause." Tom shook his head. "Instead, there's lots of detail about how she was going to marry Takeo Kayama next month. No wonder Mother was so upset yesterday evening, because of that connection."

"Will you read the article to me?" I asked. Tom was one of the few people who knew that I had the reading level of only a Japanese third-grader.

"Certainly. But it doesn't say much." Tom read aloud the short article, which reported that Kenichi Harada had apologized for his daughter's accident to the owners of the souvenir shop and the chief of police in Hayama.

"I know that people here apologize about as often as they breathe, but this is ridiculous!" I fumed, thinking of how futile being sorry was. I'd said it to Emi, and it had just sent her rushing off to the car. "He's a man who's lost a child. Why should he be organizing apologies right now?"

"Rei-chan, her death caused a huge use of police and fire vehicles when they were needed for storm relief. Think about how the families of suicide victims pay if someone jumps the tracks and causes a commuting delay. Frankly, if anyone else needs to offer an apology, it's probably me," he said glumly.

"You? But why?"

Tom folded the paper up, as if he could store away the trouble, before he spoke. "I did not stabilize her before sending her on, and she was clearly in shock, from the paramedics' description." He took a deep breath. "The hour that follows a trauma is what we call the golden hour. A patient has the very best chance for survival, if treatment comes during that hour."

"But you had no available operating room, you said."

"I could have stabilized her for transit. Made sure she had adequate IV fluids, at least." He looked down at the folded paper, then back at me. "Why are you so interested in this, anyway? It is my problem, not yours."

"Actually, the problem is kind of—ours."

"How so?" Tom looked at me warily.

"I was introduced to her through Takeo."

"Really! Was she a nice person? Did you like her?"

I nodded slowly, because the truth was that I'd thought she was shallow, until the end when I'd realized that she actually loved Takeo. And now—she was gone. There was no chance for her to rebuild her relationship with Takeo, or to reconsider her life and wait to get married to somebody who was really right for her. I felt terrible.

"You're crying." Tom grabbed a paper napkin out of the holder in the table's center.

"I don't mean to, I'm sorry."

"You must explain more, because this is not a normal reaction," Tom said.

"Emi thought I wanted to take him away from her. That's why she died."

"That makes no sense," Tom said. "How do you know what she was thinking, anyway? You just met her briefly at the auction house, right?"

"When she saw us—socializing—at Takeo's house, she became so upset that she jumped into her father's car and drove off." I spoke in a monotone, trying to keep from crying again. "She was so distraught, Tom, I wonder if she willfully crashed the car—"

"Just because you were socializing with an old friend?" Tom looked at me hard. "What form, exactly, did this socializing take?"

"We were just there, together." I couldn't bring myself to explain the full story. "But she mistakenly thought we'd become a serious romantic couple. Of course she didn't know about Hugh."

"Do you mean to say that—during the typhoon—you were in Hayama?" Tom interrupted, his voice incredulous. "You must have been. That's where the accident happened."

I nodded glumly. "Please don't tell anyone. I am still in a panic that the whole story will get out, somehow."

"Why? Do you think that she mentioned you to her parents? Or anyone else in her family?"

"She's an only child, and she couldn't have talked to her parents that fast. She literally saw me, put things together in her mind about what happened, started yelling at Takeo, threw—threw—a piece of china—and ran out of the house into the car." I paused. "But there was the driver of the car, who arrived at the house. He saw me."

There was a sound of movement upstairs. Aunt Norie was getting ready to come down.

"That's a shame," Tom said. "I'd say that we need to arm ourselves with a bit of knowledge about the causes of her death." Tom paused. "I have a colleague at Hiroo Hospital who may have some information."

"But that—that action could cause more attention," I said. "And why do we need to know the minutiae? She's dead, that's enough for me. I feel bad enough already."

Tom shook his head. "Emi's father is very powerful. We need to know who's at fault in the death, because he could ask for an investigation into the emergency transport for her medical care. And in any case, I'm going to make my own apology to him."

"Do you mean—you'll write a letter?" I cringed at this idea of Tom declaring himself at fault on paper. And given the mood he was in, he'd probably expose me, too.

"I'll see him at the funeral services at their home in Setagaya. It makes sense, because last night, after you went to bed, Mother was on the telephone with her flower arranging friends getting information about the memorial. I know she's going. I'll go, too, if I can find someone to cover for me at work."

The Japanese mourn quickly. Emi's cremation, which was attended by close family members, was set for the very next evening. And to my dismay, Aunt Norie was insistent that I also attend.

"It doesn't seem right that I go, Obasan," I said to her, when she first raised the issue with me. We were doing the laundry, for her a daily ritual that had been postponed during the time of the typhoon. Norie was ironing, and I was folding the ironed things.

"But you must. Already I've determined that Hiroshi and Chika cannot go because of his office schedule. For me to go alone, without family, is embarrassing."

"But your son Tsutomu's going to be there." Absently, I matched one of my cousin's black socks with a brown one, then caught myself.

"Yes, but he's a bundle of nerves. He won't do much good at my side, whereas you are like the elder daughter I never had. You will be a good reflection on us and the Kayama School." Aunt Norie kept her eyes on me as she ironed, completely in control.

"I don't want to go." But as I said it, I was thinking of what Michael wanted me to do, to find out more about the art and antiques holdings of the Haradas. This would be a way to get that done, all at once. But it felt like preying on Emi's family at a rough time—a time that had come about because of the injection of me into Emi and Takeo's romance. Emi's death was my fault.

"You look sickly, Rei-chan," my aunt said, expertly flipping over a pair of my underpants to iron its other side. I always fought against her ironing my underwear, but she always won.

"It's—it's the smell of that spray starch," I said.

"Well, you've not left this house—except once, to go to the store—since your arrival. I need you beside me. I can hardly believe that you would refuse to pay your respects to the young woman who was going to be the *iemoto*'s wife, the future of our flower arranging school."

And so it came to be that a few hours later, I was squeezed next to my aunt on the Toyoko Line train bound for Setagaya. Tom, who had gone into work hours earlier, would meet us on the platform promptly at 5:02.

"So, is everyone from the flower arranging school coming?" I hoped so, because if there was a large crowd I was less likely to be noticed by the people I was loath to see: Emi's family, their chauffeur, and Takeo.

"Oh, no," my aunt said. "Apparently, Takeo-san asked only the top administrators to be there—and of course, the few teachers who had been involved in Emi-san's training."

"Did you teach Emi?" I asked, startled by this revelation.

My aunt dropped her gaze to her lap and smoothed the black

wool crepe skirt she was wearing. I was in black, too—a business suit taken out of Chika's closet that was almost perfect, except that the skirt was a few inches too short. My aunt had given me a silk handkerchief she'd ironed that morning to spread over my knees to protect my modesty.

"Well, I was supposed to teach her."

"Aha," I said. "So it didn't actually happen?"

My aunt glanced around, as if she feared she might be overheard. The seats we'd taken together actually had some empty spaces around them, because although it was rush hour, we were headed into the city instead of out. "Emi-san was scheduled to take a private morning workshop with me twice a week, but actually, she didn't come after the first time. Maybe it was because she had so much trouble."

I felt a flash of sympathy for Emi. "She couldn't be worse than I was. Don't you remember all those embarrassing times for me at the school?"

My aunt shook her head. "It's true, Rei-chan, you do not have a natural gift for flower arrangement, but you can concentrate and follow directions. I don't like to speak ill of the dead, but Emi seemed—distracted. Not quite there. I imagine she was thinking exciting thoughts about her engagement, needed to shop for clothes and china—that kind of thing."

It was true that Emi loved to buy things. Maybe my aunt was right. I nodded and said, "Well, anyway, it will be good to go with you. I'm not the greatest at knowing what to do at funerals. I'll just follow your lead."

"Oh, I'm a very poor example to follow," Norie said. "I failed to involve her enough in *ikebana*. I just couldn't understand her." Norie put her hand in her purse and touched the *kouden*, a small envelope containing cash that she was bringing to the funeral. I'd contributed 5,000 yen of my own to the envelope, bringing the total to 15,000. I doubted that her family needed financial help with funeral expenses, but bringing *kouden* was important as a show of respect.

"You're an excellent teacher. It's a shame she didn't come back for a second lesson."

Norie sighed. "I just couldn't understand her, in the same way that I can't understand the situation with Takeo-san."

"Really," I said cagily.

"I find it strange that there has been so little mentioned in the media about Takeo-san. He was shown briefly on television last night; I recognized him. And surely, she was visiting him in Hayama, though why so soon after the storm, when the roads are bad, I don't understand. Unless . . ." My aunt's voice trailed off.

"Unless what?" I asked dutifully, wondering if she had guessed anything about my role. Tom wouldn't rat on me, I was sure of that.

"Unless Emi spent the night of the storm with him, in his house. Yes, that must be it!" Norie's voice was low, but strong with conviction. "No parent would ever want the news to be known that his daughter spent her last hours at an overnight visit with a boyfriend."

"I suppose not," I said, relieved that the heat was off. "But surely Takeo will be at the funeral?"

"I'm sure that he will. And he will need kindness from all of us, and who knows, perhaps in a year or so he will be ready to think about marriage again. Although it will be harder for him, with this scandal on his record."

24

My aunt had no idea of what scandal was, I thought as we got off the train, located Tom looking grim in a black suit, and took a taxi driven by a white-gloved septugenarian to the Haradas' house in Setagaya. As we rode along, Norie talked about the old Shimura family compound about a mile away, the house my grandparents had to give up after the war to American troops, and then never were able to afford to regain. Houses in the calm residential neighborhood filled with tall ginkgo trees were very expensive now—too expensive even for someone like Tom, a successful physician, to buy.

"Who lives here, then?" I asked, and to my surprise our gray-haired driver answered.

"Rich people! Television producers, senior government officials, actors. Do you know the actor in the Samurai Soap commercial? Yes? He lives the next street over. I have driven him once or twice."

Aunt Norie, Tom, and I all exchanged a quick, amused glance, and the man kept up a pleasant patter until we came to a long white wall with a paper lantern outside marked with the *kanji* character for mourning.

"Oh, a funeral. I'm very sorry," the driver said somberly.

"It's actually a memorial service. And thank you," Norie said, fumbling in her purse her reading glasses.

"Eight hundred yen only. And please tell me, when I shall return?"

"I'm not sure," my aunt said. "I thought we would just tele-phone for taxi service in a while—"

"Very few available this evening. And you won't want to incon-venience the mourning family by asking to use their telephone. Re-member, not all the telephone lines are restored in this area."

My hackles went up immediately; it didn't make sense that this man wanted to take us back. But Norie exclaimed that it would be very kind if he came for us in an hour's time.

After we'd gotten out and Tom had buzzed the entry button next to the gate, I whispered to my aunt that I thought we should use Tom's cell phone to call for another taxi to pick us up.

"But why, Rei-chan? It makes sense to have a car waiting, espe-cially in the evening hours. And that nice driver-san will be coming back. If we don't come out for him, he'll ring the bell and that will create a lot of trouble, you know, call attention to us."

"It's odd. I think he's too interested in us. You never know who he might be," I said as the gate swung open silently for us. A long walkway stretched ahead, with a few other black-clad mourners entering through a huge carved door that looked as if it had come from an Indian temple. It was unusual for a Japanese house, but then, so was the house itself—a newly built two-story cream stucco building with stained-glass windows. It looked like a cross between a church and a mosque, I thought, surveying the domed ceiling. No doubt the Haradas had chosen to re-create, in Japan, some of the things they'd admired most during their years abroad.

Inside, the memorial service was different too, chiefly because half the guests appeared to be twenty and under. Young women clutched each other and cried, too young to hide their emotions be-hind handkerchiefs. It seemed like a group, and I imagined most of them had gone to Tokyo International Girls School with Emi. One girl caught my eye, because she wasn't as painfully thin as the oth-ers; she was plump, in fact, and the loose black dress she wore, which reached to mid-calf, only made her look larger. She sat alone on a carved rosewood chair, her reddened eyes darting toward the living room door as each person entered—as if, I thought, Emi might suddenly show up and change everything.

The grown-ups in attendance were, of course, colleagues of Emi's parents. I recognized the chairman of one of Japan's automobile manufacturers, as well as various politicians. Mr. Harada was at the center of them all, grave-faced, wearing a black suit and his old-fashioned black-rimmed spectacles. He was a blur of motion, nodding and bowing to the callers. It hit me that the same kind of mob scene would have taken place a few months later, for the wedding. But then, everyone would have been smiling.

Feeling sick, I turned away and focused my attention on the Haradas' house. Like many upper-class Japanese homes, it had a number of square rooms that could be transformed into larger spaces by opening sliding wood-and-paper screens. But in this house, unlike the other Japanese homes I'd visited, the tatami flooring was covered with Oriental rugs—antique rugs, I realized, as I stooped down to pick up a card that I'd dropped on purpose, in order to get a close look. I couldn't tell a Tabriz from a Kerman, but I could guess that these rugs cost a lot.

The rugs also provided a buffer layer so that the Haradas could use non-Japanese furniture, like the great walnut dining table stacked with *kouden* envelopes and overseen by two unsmiling men in black suits, one of whom I instantly recognized as the chauffeur. I turned away quickly and studied the framed photos of the family with notables. I identified Japan's last prime minister and the host of the most conservative television news program. I thought about what was missing—regular family pictures. But maybe the Haradas didn't think it was right to place casual family snapshots on the same level as their most honored contacts.

I squeezed my way into the kitchen, where half a dozen women wearing aprons and head scarves were arranging trays of food. Everything was rose marble; the appliances were stainless steel, typical in the West but unusual in Japan. Someone had gone to a great deal of trouble to affix photographs to the fridge, which I knew from experience was resistant to magnets. But here, in tiny frames, were the kind of family pictures I'd been looking for: a young father holding a chubby toddler girl on his shoulders. A round-faced schoolgirl in a black uniform standing by the Great Buddha of Kamakura. A plump teenager making rabbit ears over a friend's head, as the two posed in front of the Sphinx.

I could see Emi's big eyes and smile in each girl, but I was stunned by how chubby she'd once been. It was hard to believe, given the Pocky Stick frame she'd shrunk into. Had she developed an eating disorder—and if so, when? Surely it had happened before she'd met Takeo, I thought, remembering the recent school photograph of Emi that had appeared on the television news. She'd been thin then.

One of the caterers asked me what I needed, and I answered vaguely—too vaguely, because I was instructed in no uncertain terms that if I wanted something to eat, it was available in the dining room.

I went out, trying to steer clear of the chauffeur, yet somehow inspect the quality of the Haradas' art and antiques. The problem was that there was almost too much to take note of: a ceramics collection that contained Korean celadon, Chinese blue-and-white and Japanese modern and antique pottery. I was drawn to a simple tea bowl made of a reddish clay that reminded me of the ibex vessel, and I gently lifted it to examine the bottom. Decoding pottery was, for me, much easier than decoding a newspaper; after about ten seconds' study, I had figured out that the bowl had been shaped by Kazu Sakurai, a famous Kyushu artist whom the government had recently named a living national treasure. I put the bowl down carefully, and after I was sure it was settled back into its place, I turned to go into the next room.

Yasuko Harada—Emi's mother—was regarding me with an uncertain expression. I hesitated, not knowing whether I should make some kind of explanation. But before I could do anything, two women descended on Mrs. Harada, bowing and murmuring. My opportunity was lost, but maybe that was a good thing. What could I possibly have said?

I walked purposefully into the next reception room, where a white brocade-covered coffin rested at the foot of a dais constructed in front of the *tokonoma,* the ceremonial alcove that was the focal point of the room. A type of altar had been made around a three- by three-foot framed photograph of Emi. Around it stood a sea of floral wreaths that all had identifying tags showing which company had given them.

I gazed at the portrait of Emi in a stiff brocade floral kimono, a kimono that I knew was typically given on a girl's eighteenth birthday. This "coming-of-age day" kimono was expensive—usually costing between 5 and 15 million yen. In Emi's case, I guessed it had been even more.

The young, sad girl I'd noticed when I'd entered the house was standing near me, looking at the picture of Emi. Then she knelt next to the coffin, folded her hands in prayer, and whispered something. In the end, she peered into the little window through which Emi's face showed. She got up rapidly, and backed off.

I had been avoiding looking at the corpse, but I did look now. Emi's eyes were closed, her long lashes lying neatly against her fair skin. She looked like a beautiful young girl asleep. I found myself having the same reaction as the other girl, leaving quickly. It was too sad to linger over this sleeping beauty who could never wake up.

"Did you know her from high school?" I asked the girl, when I caught up with her in the next room over the hors d'oeuvres table.

"Not really. I just started at Waseda, and she is—was not—in college." The girl had been aiming her chopsticks toward a piece of deep-fried tofu, but suddenly changed direction to a piece of sashimi. Was it guilt, because I was standing near her?

"That tofu looks good," I said mildly.

"Yes, but too oily."

Just as I'd thought. "So, how did you know Emi-san?"

"My family lives nearby. We attended primary school and junior high together. Then she went away to Turkey, and came back last year. Her parents sent her to Tokyo International Girls School. That's where those other girls are from." She tilted her head toward the other room.

Often, when Japanese families took their children with them to live abroad for a while, they felt that they could never again enroll the children in a traditional Japanese school. At such a school, discrimination against a child who spoke English too well, and had gotten used to certain freedoms, was too likely. I imagined that the Haradas might have thought this way—but it didn't quite jibe with what I'd expect from a family conservative enough to arrange a marriage for an eighteen-year-old daughter.

"How interesting," I said. "Well, you must be a true friend to have stayed in touch. My name's Rei Shimura. What's yours?"

"Nagasa Fumiko." She bobbed her head. "I would like to think she remained my friend, but I don't know."

"How so?" I asked gently.

"Well, Emi-san used to look more like I do. She became so—slim—in Turkey. And I think she was a little embarrassed to be seen with me."

"Oh, no, you're a lovely person—I envy your skin." I'd had to think fast.

Fumiko shook her head. "Everything had to be perfect for her. Not just the face, but fashion, slimness, manners. Even before she became engaged to that *ikebana* headmaster."

I noted the way she spoke about Takeo—rather flatly, with no special enthusiasm. Maybe she thought the arranged marriage was a bad idea. I wanted to ask her about it, but suddenly there was a swelling of noise in the next room, a raising of voices and the sound of someone male, shouting in poor Japanese. "Please. Just to see—"

The hubbub rose, and Fumiko and I exchanged glances. There was a sound of something breaking in the next room. I waved at her to follow me. If something was happening between people, maybe she could provide an explanation.

In one corner I saw a caterer bent over a smashed cocktail glass, and a huddle of women around her, trying to help. But all the action was heading out of the room toward the entryway. A beautiful foreign boy with dark curly hair, wearing a black shirt and black jeans, was being hustled out of the house by three smaller Japanese men, including the chauffeur. The boy's full lips were twisted in a grimace and his eyes blazed with wetness—tears? I was stunned. The sight of such naked emotion made me want to draw back, as if I'd intruded.

"He's here," Fumiko murmured.

"Is that one of Emi's old friends?"

She shook her head.

"Then who is he?" I persisted.

"I'm sorry." She looked at me, and I saw a mixture of sorrow and panic on her face. "I have to leave."

"I didn't mean to—" I started to say, but Fumiko had pushed her way through the crowd as if she couldn't get away quickly enough.

"Do you understand anything about what happened?" I asked Tom, when I'd squeezed my way through the throng to where he was standing.

"I don't exactly know. I saw that foreigner talking to the other young people. Then those men asked him to leave, and he tried to resist."

"Those were the men who guarded the *kouden* envelopes," Norie interjected. "Maybe he was trying to take some money. Now, Rei-chan, tell me, are you enjoying yourself? The house is so beautiful!"

I looked at her. "It's hard to have a nice time at a funeral."

"True, true, it's terribly sad, but the food is lovely. And I've gotten the chance to meet some nice young friends of Emi-san's, a few of whom are thinking of enrolling to study *ikebana* in one of our holiday mini-courses."

"Really." My thoughts about the boy who'd been thrown out vanished.

I was making my way back to the mourning room when I spotted Takeo Kayama, looking right at me as he wove his way through the crowd.

I gave him a warning look and shook my head slightly, but he continued in my direction. I'd known he would be at the memorial, but I'd assumed he would use good sense and stay away from me. Well, I had some choices of my own, and my choice was not to talk to him.

I made it through the doorway before he did and, spying hall stairs carpeted with an Oriental runner, hurried up them. Nobody would think of going into private living quarters during a memorial. I crouched against the wall under a painting by the French artist Balthus of an Asian nude, despite the barking dog behind a nearby closed door.

A Balthus painting, come to think of it, was a very significant personal asset. I turned around in my crouch and tilted my head back so that I could study the oil painting of the Japanese-looking woman who was standing at a mirror, her robe open, with a malevolent-looking dwarf peeking through an opened door at her. It looked like the cousin to a very famous Balthus painting, which showed a half-dressed Japanese woman reclining in a bathroom with Turkish tiles, gazing at herself in a hand mirror.

How could a civil servant afford an original painting by Balthus? I tried to memorize the details of the painting to check against the Art Loss Register, a website devoted to tracing stolen art. It had to be a real Balthus, didn't it, if there was a motion sensor above the frame?

My examination was suddenly interrupted by the soft waterfall sound of a flushing toilet. Before I could change my position, a door opened halfway down the hall from me. Mr. Harada came out. As he headed toward the stairs, he caught sight of me and stopped.

25

I bowed, but Mr. Harada was staring intensely. I wondered whether he remembered me from the auction house, and if he had even heard anything about me from Emi.

"There are dogs up here. You must not go inside," he said firmly.

"I was actually looking for a bathroom—"

"There is a facility downstairs," he said stiffly. "Any of the caterers can show you."

I was lucky that he believed that I only wanted to go to the bathroom. Quickly, I bowed my head again and apologized. Then I went into a short recitation of the words people used, at funerals, to convey sympathy for a terrible loss. At the end, I said, "I'm so sorry about your daughter's passing. She was much too young."

"She was our greatest treasure," he said, keeping a wary eye on me.

"Yes, there are many beautiful things in art and nature, but nothing as lovely as a child." After I said it, I felt a rush of pain. My private pain, the one I tried not to think about.

He nodded. "That's right. I'm sorry, I didn't hear your name."

He was trying to place me. I hesitated, remembering Tom's worries about liability, but also his desire to apologize. "I'm Shimura Rei. I'm here with my family, who are connected to the *ikebana* school—"

I didn't finish, because Mr. Harada had raised his hand to someone in the hall downstairs and moved on as if I didn't exist.

I spent the next fifteen minutes glued to my aunt, ducking behind her every time Takeo entered the room. I noticed that Mr. Harada motioned to Takeo several times, bringing him into one circle of men after another. The two of them had a strong relationship, it was clear. I noticed the way Takeo held Mr. Harada's arm, almost supporting him at times. Mr. Harada hadn't been exactly warm to me, but why should he be, under the circumstances? I saw now how shaky he was, and I was glad Takeo had moved on from pursuit of me to concentrate instead on his intended father-in-law.

It turned out that I was wrong about Takeo. When it was time for my aunt, Tom, and me to locate our shoes among the dozens visitors had left stacked in the shoe cabinet, Takeo descended on me again.

"Help." I heard his voice in my ear as I was bending to put on my shoes. As I turned to see him we bumped foreheads. It hurt, but that wasn't half as bad as my realization that Aunt Norie was right behind us, witnessing the encounter.

"Help me, Rei," Takeo repeated softly in English, as if to make his words less likely to be understood.

I could imagine the kind of help he wanted. Well, I wasn't delivering it again. I jammed my feet into my shoes and launched myself out the front door. Our taxi was waiting. I planned to get into it, lock the doors, and wait for the rest of my party to assemble.

But Takeo ran out after me, not even bothering to find his own shoes. He closed the distance between us, and once we were outside the house's gate, he grabbed my arms and faced me in the warm orange light of the funeral lanterns.

"Use some sense." I shook off his hold. "Your fiancée is lying in a box inside the house and you're trying to chase me down."

"Because I need to talk to you about—what happened with Emi."

The taxi driver had seen me, and had swung the black door open automatically for me; I bounded in, but unfortunately Takeo followed. I jumped out on the other side, so I was standing on the street, and he followed me out again.

"If you don't want to talk here, give me your cell phone number. I'll contact you later."

"I don't have one. My phone was stolen."

"Stolen! So you're having strange problems too."

"I may have my own problems, Takeo, but let me tell you, they're nothing compared with what *could* happen. We mustn't attract attention."

"Nobody can see with the taxi blocking us like this." Takeo ran a hand through his hair. "It's about Emi. I'm facing legal troubles because of the way she died, and I don't know what to do."

"You are?" I felt a twinge of worry mixed with guilt. I knew that the whole nightmarish scene inside had been caused by my own rash actions.

As if sensing he'd hit on something that affected me, Takeo spoke again. "We have to talk. You're the only one who can help me, at this point."

"All right, I'll talk to you," I said quickly. "But I don't know where we could possibly meet. I can never go back to your house in Hayama, and please don't suggest my aunt's house, because she really wouldn't approve—"

"If you are with your aunt in Yokohama, let's meet at Sankei-en. Behind the big teahouse, there's a forest trail. I will be waiting there tomorrow at eleven."

"Good-bye for now," I whispered and climbed back into the taxi just as its door swung open for my relatives.

Norie immediately wanted to know what Takeo had wanted. I told her that I was too upset to talk. The driver muttered as if to himself about the crazy younger generation.

We caught our train, and an hour later we were home. It was nine o'clock. Uncle Hiroshi had come in the door a few minutes earlier and was impatient for his supper. Norie started cooking, and I used the time to ask Tom about what had happened with Mr. Harada. We were downstairs in the corner of the dining room, where I had busied myself setting the table. Tom was leafing through a fax that had come in on the telephone-fax set up on a side table.

"So, how did the apology go?" I asked.

"It was fine," he said shortly. "He seemed more jumpy and distracted than angry. I suppose that's natural, given the situation."

"Did you actually admit that you were the one who said St. Luke's couldn't take her?"

"I told him I was in charge of emergency services that day, and the rooms were full. I said that we organized the taxi that took her to Hiroo Hospital." Tom picked up the second paper. "Looking at this medical note, it made sense that we sent her to Hiroo. It's one of the few hospitals in Tokyo with a unit for treating drug overdoses."

"A drug overdose?" I caught my breath.

"Technically, she died because her heart stopped. In fact, she lost consciousness before she crashed the car."

"Do you think it was an attempted suicide?"

"Not at all." He swallowed hard, then went on. "There were high levels of amphetamine in her blood."

"What kind of amphetamines?" I asked, thinking about a lot of things, all at once: how casual Simone had acted about the pills that she and Richard had shared. They hadn't made it seem much more dangerous than a few drinks. But Emi had taken amphetamines, and they'd stopped her heart.

"An autopsy will determine exactly what it was," Tom said. "Though chances are it will never be publicized. My guess is that it's just a kind of diet pill that's very popular with young women. Ephedrine, speed, maybe even Ecstasy, though that's still more popular with foreigners."

"I assume she was an occasional user?" I asked, thinking of Richard's laid-back attitude.

"No," Tom said shortly. "Her body was cachetic—the muscle mass and fat were wasting away. She'd been using for many months, if not years. And the pathology reports showed high deposits of lead—one of the by-products of synthetically made drugs like speed."

"Lead poisoning makes it hard for people to concentrate," I said, remembering how Emi hadn't been able to follow a flower arranging class.

"You're right about lead doing that, and the amphetamine itself makes people paranoid," Tom explained. "Ironically, the effects of amphetamines, at first, make the users feel that they can perform better at work, or on tests, or even with their sex partners. Many different versions of amphetamines are popular with gay men—"

"I know," I said glumly, thinking of Richard. I couldn't believe he had fallen into drugs, and so had Emi—a young girl gone, the result of paranoid rage that had sent her hurtling off in the driver's seat of a limousine, causing all manner of havoc before her heart finally gave up.

"What's going on in this country?" I moaned. "I leave for a little while and come back and find that everyone's gone crazy, being self-destructive—"

"It's true that Japanese behavior has become more similar to that in your country. Amphetamines are our most abused drug. This used to be more a problem limited to the military and businessmen, but now you can buy speed pills in almost any Tokyo nightclub, and if you're a girl, well, you often don't have to buy for yourself."

I nodded, thinking that this was a variation of the free drinks on ladies' nights at bars; young women didn't have to pay, because men wanted them to be eager sexual partners.

"Emi went to Tokyo International Girls School," I said. "Maybe she was able to get the drug there. Although from the photos I saw of her at the house, it looked as if she'd already started to slim down while she was living in Turkey. Of course," I said, remembering what Takeo had told me, "she went to the American school there."

"Is that so?" Tom sounded pensive. "Yes, we have had troubles here with Americans and drugs—but you know that." He turned his gaze on me. "You are from San Francisco, the historic center of recreational drug culture. It must have been hard for you to resist cultural influences."

"Oh, come on. Every other person in San Francisco is an ascetic who does nothing, whether it's drugs or meat or sugar." I hated it when my cousin pulled a *sempai* act on me, taking on the role of boss just because he was two years older.

"Well, in any case, it is doubtful that Harada-san is going to reveal publicly the cause of his daughter's death. On the other hand, it's a shame that justice can't be served," Tom grumbled. "I wouldn't be surprised if that foreign boy we saw at the party was a dealer of amphetamines."

"Don't be xenophobic," I chided him, but not too roughly, because I had a burning question. "Tom, is there a way to find out whether the amphetamine was contaminated?"

"What do you mean?"

"I mean, what if it was cut with something lethal?"

"Well, she took it in a tablet form, so that seems unlikely." Tom rifled through the papers. "No, no sign of anything but amphetamine. But as I told you, that in itself can kill."

I nodded, but my thoughts were elsewhere. There was still a chance that Emi's death wasn't accidental. I remembered Takeo's rushed words about the trouble he was in. Was he under suspicion for giving her the drug that had ended her life?

"You seem a bit tense," Tom said. "Now I worry that I shouldn't have told you what I know. And I want you to try to lift your mood. The bad weather must have kept you from running, but perhaps you can start again tomorrow."

"Now that's good therapeutic advice." I smiled at my cousin, who was looking at me anxiously. "All right, I think I will go to Sankei-en tomorrow and run through the gardens."

"Please telephone first to see if it is open," Tom advised. "If there was a lot of storm damage, the place might be closed."

"Of course," I answered, my thoughts still on Emi, the drug, and what Takeo might know.

26

My departure for Sankei-en was complicated by a special delivery of a new cell phone, which came with a padded black case that, in turn, had a steel clasp attached to it. As I hooked the holder into the front right-side pocket of my hooded cashmere sweatshirt, I was reminded of a child having to wear mittens on a string.

The return address on the box was the American embassy in Tokyo. This raised all kinds of questions from Aunt Norie, so I had to embroider yet more details about my job for the Smithsonian. The phone was, if anything, more complicated than the last one I'd had, and I spent twenty minutes figuring it out while I lounged in a quiet section of Minami-Makigahara Station—not a difficult spot to find, since rush hour was over. I was all alone as I finally got the numbers pressed in correctly and heard the sound of a phone ringing in Washington.

"I've been going through a report on the death of the bride," Michael said after we'd exchanged terse greetings.

"And what have you found?"

"The cause of death was never released by the hospital. Typical."

"Actually," I said, feeling a rush of pride, "if you'd like, I can give you some details from the medical record."

"What?" Michael's voice was sharp.

"You can't tell anyone because it could get my source in trouble.

But she died because of heart failure triggered by an amphetamine overdose." I told him about what the medical notes had revealed—and what I'd figured out about her unhealthy weight loss through my conversations with Fumiko and Takeo.

"That's good work," Michael said grudgingly. "I don't suppose—there's anything else?"

Using a minimum of words, I filled him in on what I'd noticed at the Harada house—from the mysterious young man who was thrown out to the expensive Japanese pottery to the Kazu Sakurai bowl and the painting that I thought was a Balthus. I didn't go into the business of Takeo chasing me down.

"I don't suppose you know what paintings by Balthus sell for at auction?" Michael asked when I was through.

I'd checked out all the sales statistics that I could find on the Internet the previous evening, after Tom had gone upstairs and I'd sneaked onto his desktop computer. "One Balthus painting sold in Paris a few years ago for over two million dollars, but that was an isolated case. Since then, the paintings of his that have come on the market went in the range of six hundred thousand to seven hundred thousand dollars. The Kazu Sakurai piece is in a lower range, but still very expensive—I imagine the bowl I examined would sell in the middle four figures, at least. Sakurai doesn't have a website, but I might be able to find out more about the prices directly from his business in Kyushu."

"I see." Michael paused, and I heard the sound of turning pages. "The bride's father—let's call him Mr. Harmony—his annual salary is probably about half of what one of those Balthus paintings you mentioned cost. Do you think he'd blow two years' salary on a painting?"

I'd once blown a year's earnings on a *tansu* chest, but I'd resold it at profit. Maybe Mr. Harada operated in a similar way. "Mr. Harmony could buy for several reasons."

"Such as?"

"Well, he might have inherited money, or he might have made successful investments or earned extra money from another job like consulting. I first saw him at the Meiwashima auction house, and he appeared to be known by the staff. Maybe he sells there as well as buys. He's definitely an art connoisseur. That's why his giving a reproduction historic piece as a gift to his future son-in-law makes no sense to me."

"Speaking of the vessel," Michael said, "I'm surprised you haven't yet asked what our contacts have to say about its provenance."

"It's been evaluated already?" I calculated backward, realizing that the broken ewer couldn't have arrived more than forty-eight hours earlier.

"They're still working on it in the lab, but I've already heard that your theory will likely prove correct."

"Well, thank you very much." This was an understatement. I was relieved to know that I was right, and that I hadn't caused a major loss to international art history.

"You've done fine so far," Michael said. "It must be around nine in the morning there. What's on your agenda today?"

"Tak—Mr. Flowers—wants to meet to talk about something. Legal troubles, he said."

"Well, hold his hand if you must, but don't lose track of the final objective. And don't get embroiled with the Japanese police, okay?"

"I won't even ask a cop for directions. And what's this about the final objective? I believe that I've delivered what you wanted. I should be on my way home now."

"I'd like to keep you around for a while. It seems to me there's something going on with the late bride's family and all their art. I want to know more about the painting, so I can check it against international police records."

I had written a full page of notes about the Balthus, as well as some of the other paintings and artwork. I relayed all the information in detail, then told Michael good-bye as the train rolled in. While using a cell phone was not illegal on trains, it was strongly discouraged—this meant I'd probably be the only person talking in the car, providing an earful of entertainment for whoever could pick up whatever language I was speaking. Until Michael and I developed a new version of pig latin, I was staying off the phone on trains.

• • •

It was this Japanese understanding of the importance of peace and quiet that had led to the establishment of Sankei-en, a lush walled garden in north Yokohama. Tomitaro Hara, a nouveau riche businessman who'd made his fortune in the early nineteenth century, had given his estate grounds so that the public could admire acres of purple iris each spring, followed in turn by cherry blossoms and azaleas. These flowers were out of season now, and the garden had suffered damage in the typhoon. Whole trees had been ripped out of the ground, and at the teahouse Takeo mentioned, the windows had been blown out. A crew of workmen wearing split-toe rubber boots were putting in new windows as I passed by. They called out a warning to me about the trail beyond being blocked. I pretended I didn't hear and continued on.

I'd expected Takeo to be waiting for me, but he wasn't there. I waited a full fifteen minutes before he showed up, looking unlike himself in a Tokyo Giants baseball jersey, oversize cargo pants, and a backward-turned baseball cap. He'd added sunglasses for good measure.

"Did those workmen talk to you?" he asked, shooting a look over his shoulder.

"They told me the trail was blocked," I said.

"Apparently it is. So why don't you proceed out by yourself over to—the pond where the irises bloom? I'll join you there a few minutes later."

I wasn't used to Takeo being as nervous about observation as I was, but these were hard times. I walked back toward the workers and held open the park map, consulting it as if I didn't know the gardens well. I strolled on to the pond. The iris had already bloomed and were just neatly tied bundles of dull green, but the pond was full of geese, which immediately left the water to surround me.

"I have nothing," I told them in both Japanese and English, but they remained around me, stubbornly calling, until I remembered a piece of cookie wrapped in a napkin at the bottom of the backpack and distributed it. But that only set off more excitement, keeping me busy until Takeo arrived.

"These geese are driving me crazy, and I'm tight on time, Takeo. Let's get to the point, okay?" I spoke while making useless shooing gestures with my hands.

"So, what's your next thing, a jogging date?" Takeo looked skeptically at my black yoga pants and tank top, over which I'd layered a hooded zip-front gray cashmere sweater, then sighed. "If only my life was simple."

"No, jogging was my cover to get away from my family. Though you look like you're off to a baseball game, not very smart because I don't believe the Giants ever play this early on a weekday morning."

"There are people who dress like this," Takeo grumbled. "In any case, I don't want to look like myself. The police might be following me."

"Why are the police concerned about you?" I was almost afraid of the answer. Takeo had slept with me because he hadn't been in love with Emi. Her death would have freed him. The facts laid out baldly looked bad for him.

Takeo swallowed hard, looked down, then looked up at me again. "Drugs. Emi actually died from a drug overdose. The police think that because I was the man with her, I gave her the drugs."

"Well, you knew what she was doing, didn't you?"

He looked at me warily. "What do you mean?"

"Did you see her take the pills?"

He shuddered, then nodded. "It happened very fast. She swallowed three pills in the house without even taking water. I tried to stop her, but it was impossible."

I remembered Takeo's arms around Emi. What I'd thought was his effort to comfort her might have really been an attempt to stop her from taking the drugs—if he was really telling me the truth.

"So you knew she was using drugs. The obvious thing would be to tell the police."

"As I told you, they think I was her supplier. Of course you know I'm not."

"Okay, I believe you. Then who could it be?"

"No idea." He shook his head. "Maybe one of her high school friends. There were always a lot of friends stopping by to visit her, or she'd drag me to those ridiculous clubs in Roppongi. I didn't realize she was taking anything until after the *omiai* was set. Then it was too late."

"What do you mean, too late? Better to break an engagement than a marriage."

"Well, I didn't realize it was—serious. A lot of girls take these pills as a diet thing and for energy. I thought that after the wedding, either she'd stop taking them on her own or I could convince her to do so."

He was in a dreamworld. I said, "Let's get back to the accident. She was high—"

"Well, yes. She drove like someone who was crazy, I guess because of the drugs and also not really knowing what she was doing—I'd been trying to steer myself, but I wasn't able to change our course toward the shop, and we hit." He bowed his head. "It was actually my fault."

"But not the death," I said, trying to console him.

"Oh, but it was." Takeo's expression was anguished. "I didn't mention the drugs to the paramedics. And I asked them to send her to St. Luke's because your cousin's in the emergency room there, and I thought that when it came out about the drugs, he'd be sympathetic and figure out a way to help without getting us into trouble."

"Oh, my God. You were behind that decision to go to St. Luke's?" I was stunned.

"Yes. I made a mistake." Takeo's voice was bitter.

"Why didn't you go along in the helicopter? I saw you going off with the police instead, when I was watching the news broadcast."

"They demanded that I go. They wanted all the details of the accident, who was driving and so on. And the reason I'm late is—just this morning, new police officers came to my apartment. They'd found out from the doctors at the hospital that she'd been on amphetamines, and they wanted to search both my apartment in Tokyo and the house in Hayama."

"Did they find anything?"

"In her handbag, she had a lipstick case containing some tablets. I immediately took a drug test." Takeo looked at me steadily. "I tested negative, which should have been enough, but they've been questioning me about my friends in the environmental protest movement, insinuating that I run around with criminals."

"Have you gotten your family lawyer involved?" I asked. The way things worked in Japan, connections and backroom talk were everything.

Takeo's voice was deadly quiet. "If I talk to that lawyer, it means he goes to my father. If my father catches a breath of scandal, he'll take away my right to run the Kayama School. I'm thirty-one, Rei. I've worked all my life to run this school, and I—I was going to be able to do so much more for Japan—"

"That's right. You were about to become the son-in-law of the minister for the environment, and you were going to influence government policies on land and pollution." I remembered how ambitious it had all seemed, a few days ago. Now it just seemed sad. "And speaking of Emi's father, I think—I think you must still have an ally. Certainly, Kenichi Harada would want the fact that his daughter died from amphetamines to remain quiet."

"I went to the house early yesterday, before the memorial, and we talked. He wanted to know if I'd known, because he hadn't. I told him how I thought it was a phase, and how very sorry I was not to have been more—active—about stopping things." Takeo put his head in his hands.

"Was he angry with you?"

"He was upset, but he told me, in quiet strong language, that he wants nothing to be known about what happened. While I was there he telephoned the detective in charge of the case to reiterate the point."

"Well, that should take care of the problem—"

"It won't. The detective in charge said he wouldn't expose the cause of Emi's death, but he is trying to identify whoever provided the drugs, as part of a larger crackdown."

"Do you know anything about the young man who was thrown out of the funeral?" I asked.

"The foreigner with the curly hair?" Takeo sounded pensive. "I know I've seen him before. I didn't make the connection that he knew Emi until the funeral. Who is he?"

"I have no idea. We should find out. Perhaps that's the drug connection."

Takeo shook his head. "You, not me. I don't want to implicate anyone falsely. I mean, if you knew what I've had to say already to protect you—"

A light flashed, startling the geese, who rose up in a mass flurry. Caught off balance, Takeo pitched forward. I reached out my arm to catch him, but his weight caught me off balance and we both tripped into the pond.

The water was only about knee-high, but cold.

"It looks like I'm the one who needs protection," he said. I laughed, because I couldn't help myself. The situation was so ludicrous.

"Yes. I once had a much better time with you underwater in Hayama. Remember?" Takeo asked as we stepped back up onto dry land.

"Yes, I remember." I paused. "But you know, it can never happen again. I don't want it to."

"You're right." Takeo looked at me for a long moment, then dropped his gaze. "We can never go back to being lovers. But at least we can help each other."

"All right, then," I said, taking off my Asics sneakers one by one, pouring out the water, and putting them back on. "You were saying you had protected me from the police. Why did my name even come up?"

"It wasn't your name. Emi's father's chauffeur told the police that a woman dressed in man's clothing had been at the house, and her presence had agitated Emi. When the police asked me about it, I told them a woman had come by to ask for some assistance after the storm. I said I didn't know her."

So he'd lied. I should have been relieved, but this news set off a new storm of worries. "I hope that lie doesn't come back to haunt you."

"Well, now you know how deep I'm in. By the way, there's something I want to ask you about," Takeo said. "You mentioned that you had a cellular phone stolen. When?"

"The day I went to talk to you at the school. I think someone may have grabbed it when I was going home after the storm, because I know I didn't leave it downstairs at the baggage checkpoint. I called to ask."

"What did it look like?"

"It was one of those camera phones. It was dark blue and there was a brand name on it, Linxar."

"Emi had a dark blue telephone that I didn't recognize. I saw it in her purse when she was taking out the pills."

"Oh! So maybe I left the phone by mistake when I was talking to you in the headmaster's study." I thought about the password that had been broken—Take0 would have been an easy guess for Emi, and my choice of it as a password would have made her believe I was obsessed with her boyfriend.

"Now the police have it, because they have her purse."

So the Japanese police would find, in the phone's memory, the list of numbers I'd called, including Michael and Hugh in Washington, my aunt in Yokohama, and Mr. Watanabe in Tokyo. The numbers wouldn't lead them to drugs, but would lead to everything I'd been bound to keep quiet. I looked at Takeo, then away. I had to get out. I was so panicky, suddenly, that I couldn't stay in the park another moment.

Across the pond, a group of schoolchildren, mothers, and teachers were walking; someone in this group had probably flashed a camera, startled the geese, and caused us to fall into the pond. Now I needed them. I was still a little younger than the casually dressed mothers, but I'd make myself blend in.

"I'm going to try to slip out with that school group," I said to Takeo. "I think it'll attract less notice, just in case someone did follow you and is waiting on the outskirts of the park."

"What if I need to talk to you again? I'm really worried."

"I have a new phone." Grudgingly, I gave him the new number but instructed him to purge it from his phone's memory, once he'd completed a call. Then I said, "Can you try to do something for me?"

Takeo shot me an exasperated glance and did not answer.

"When you go back to the Haradas' house, I want you to keep your eyes open for another piece of pottery that looks like the ibex ewer you had in your house. Don't say anything, just be aware."

"Why?" Takeo asked fiercely. "Why is that vessel so important?"

"I could tell you, but then I'd have to kill you." I said it lightly, as a joke, but he didn't laugh.

"I'll do what I can. I'm expected to pay a call there anyway in the early afternoon. We're all going to the cremation."

The cremation. I'd been to the cremation of my Japanese grandfather. I'd seen the coffin slide into the oven, seen the big metal doors latch closed, and then heard the sound of the flames. I'd been so terrified that I'd run outside, but there I saw a plume of gray smoke rising from the chimney. I couldn't escape the horror of the death, no matter where I went.

"I'm so sorry," I said now to Takeo. "I haven't gotten a chance to tell you yet how sorry I am for everything that happened, and that you lost her."

"It was a short engagement," Takeo said. "But I did care for her. I understand now that it would have been a terrible marriage. But I did care."

After I took my leave of Takeo, I sent an e-mail to Michael giving him a brief message about the Japanese police having custody of the telephone. Then I closed up my phone and clipped it into the lining of my sweater pocket, deciding this was safer than my backpack.

I caught a bus to Yokohama Station, and as I stared at the bustling traffic around me, I thought more about what Takeo had said about caring. It was a word he'd always used a lot: he cared about social justice, endangered butterflies, and so on. He'd even continued to care about me, since he'd decided to keep my name from the police, or was it more that he cared about losing his flower arranging empire?

He might have cared about me, but he never loved me.

A familiar face with dark green eyes swam before me, but I closed myself to that image, and tried to think happier thoughts until we reached the train station.

27

Waseda! I'd spent a junior year abroad here, so I felt a small explosion of nostalgia to be back in this paradise for smart, unconventional young Japanese. Waseda University was one of a kind in the city; it was tough to get into, and its graduates went not only into business but into advertising, media, and other creative fields. It also boasted the highest population of foreign students at any Japanese institute of higher education—that was why I'd gotten in.

From Waseda Station, I took a narrow curving road toward the campus, where I was quickly surrounded by a mix of prewar and modern academic buildings. I had to pause at the Okuma auditorium, a golden brick building topped by a medieval-looking tower. I used to meet my friends from Waseda's art study club in the peaceful garden next to the tower, because we thought art could flow only from tranquillity—and student life in Tokyo was not, on the whole, tranquil. As I walked closer to look at the tower, it made me think about how the European castle style remained popular for love hotels. At the Haradas' house as well, with its stained-glass windows and fancy furniture, Old World European aesthetics prevailed. Given Kenichi Harada's worldly views, it seemed strange that he hadn't wanted Emi to study at a university before marrying.

I was annoyed to learn that the international students' center was no longer in the center of campus, but in a section of off-campus buildings; I made the trek over, then discovered the administrator was at lunch. I had to shift to plan B and visit the registrar's office, where I found an exhausted-looking woman sunk behind a computer terminal with a stack of folders at her side.

The woman listened warily to my story: that I was urgently trying to get in touch with a student I was currently mentoring.

"Her cell phone must be off, because she's not answering," I said, taking out my new phone and waving it about, as if it contained the proof of my efforts. "My best thought is to meet her outside the classroom. I thought you could tell me where she is, geographically, at this moment."

"I'm so sorry," the woman said in a standard apology that brooked no rejoinders. "We cannot allow anyone to enter the classroom and disrupt the schedule."

"I won't go into the class, I swear. If I could just wait outside the door, I could catch her in time so she doesn't miss her interview."

"Interview?" the girl repeated dully.

"Yes, at the Diet. For an internship there."

She blinked, because I was talking about Japan's parliament. It was the most important place I could think of, offhand, and not a place I could ever remember a Waseda student interning.

"It's very important for her to have this interview. Her future depends on it." I spoke earnestly, hoping the jogging clothes I was wearing wouldn't dissuade her from thinking that I was an important person.

"I'll check for you now. But please don't disturb the professor." The administrative assistant closed the screen she was working on, and replaced one sea of *kanji* characters with another. With lightning speed, she pressed keys and flipped through web pages. At the end, she printed out a sheet for me.

"Here you are."

"I'm so grateful. Thank you very much. You've been very kind." I bowed a thousand times and backed out of the office, running into a stocky sixty-something professor, whom I recognized at the last minute as the person who'd given me a C in linguistics.

"*Gomen nasai,*" I apologized, turning to bow. My mistake.

"Shimura?" Professor Morito didn't use an honorific with me, as was typical for older professors toward students. "Well, I never thought I'd see you again. The last thing I heard was that you'd become a salesperson of old things—"

"She's a mentor," said the secretary. "She's arranged for one of our students to have an interview at the Diet."

"Yes, yes, I'm hurrying to meet a student. Excuse me for being rude, but I really must run!" I said over my shoulder despite Professor Morito's continued grumbling commentary on students who squandered lost opportunities. The truth was that Professor Morito was right. I hadn't worked hard enough at linguistics or learning *kanji*, and as I walked down the boulevard, studying Fumiko's class schedule, I wished desperately that I was fluent in written Japanese. Here was the time, 13:00; the name of the topic she was studying was unintelligible. The only thing I could tell was that she was studying at the Information Technology Center, a place where I wished now I'd spent more time during my year overseas.

There was a little glass window in the door of Fumiko's classroom, so I peeped through it a few times, looking for her in the class of about fifty, before I realized that I was attracting the attention of several students. I slunk back to the opposite side of the hallway. Nobody was around, so I made a phone call to the Meiwashima Auction Gallery to find out whether Kenichi Harada ever brought things to auction. No, he hadn't sold anything, but he had been a longtime customer. I thought about calling Kazu Sakurai's studio in Kyushu to ask him whether Kenichi Harada had been a customer, but I didn't know the name of the town the studio was in. I'd have to research it later.

I looked again through the classroom window. All the students had their laptop computers open, hindering my inspection of their faces. I was a bit shocked to see students using laptops in the classroom, but I guessed that was a reflection of my age. It would have been nice to have had a laptop during Professor Morito's class, so that I would have missed his myriad cranky expressions.

I hoped Fumiko wouldn't be a dead end, because I needed information. I didn't have time to follow false leads, when the Japanese police were probably close to figuring out I was a player in Emi Harada's death. To derail them, I had to get Takeo the information he needed about the drug supplier.

Finally, I heard the snap of all the laptops closing. There was much scraping of chairs and a babble of voices, and then the students streamed out. Fumiko was wearing a generous sweatshirt and jeans. She did a double take when she saw me, letting me know that I didn't need to worry about reintroducing myself.

"*Ohisashi buri desu,*" I greeted her. *Long time no see.* It had been less than twenty-four hours, but so what?

"Do you teach here?" she looked at my clothing with seeming confusion.

"Please tell me I don't look that old," I said, falling into step with her. We passed out of the building and started our way down the campus's main pedestrian boulevard.

"I didn't mean a professor. I thought you might be a teaching assistant. I mean, why else would you be here? You told me you'd finished your studies."

"I came today because I need to talk to you about Emi. It's starting to get out about the amphetamines—"

"Don't say that word!" she whispered, panic in her voice. To think a college student was this paranoid about drugs! It reminded me that I was in another country.

"Sorry. Let's talk about it in a quieter place. May I take you to lunch?" I was starving, despite the stress.

"I only have about thirty minutes." She looked at me anxiously.

"I know a great, quick *okonomiyaki* shop nearby." I knew that *okonomiyaki*, the delicious Japanese savory pancake, was as essential to the survival of Waseda's students as pizza was to American undergraduates.

"Omori-san's shop? Is it even open for lunch?"

"Yes. I know most students go in the evening. It won't be crowded and we'll have the privacy we need."

• • •

Feeling as if I'd been away from Waseda for only a semester, I walked into the restaurant and I led Fumiko straight to the old table of the art study club, close to the restrooms—a good location because of the amount of Kirin we drank in those days. The lacquered pine table was well worn from many student elbows. The center of it had been cut out and had a round electric cooktop, which was quickly turned on by the cook-owner, an old grandma type who greeted me with a smile of recognition. Omori-san asked us a few questions, then carefully poured a mixture of egg, soy, scallions, and octopus onto the hot surface. It was up to us to poke at the pancake, from time to time, to see if it had set.

I liked the pancake fully done, but I deferred to Fumiko when she decided to start cutting it up for eating a scant five minutes after it had started to cook. She was obviously in a rush.

"So, you seemed to understand what I said about the—substance." I opened the interview, keeping my voice low and calm.

"Did her parents find out?" She watched me anxiously.

"Yes. They need to know who the supplier was."

"It wasn't me! I never—"

"I believe you. But I think you might know something. When that boy ran out of the funeral yesterday, some people were wondering if he had something to do with the drugs. It seemed as if you recognized him."

"I do," she said in a low voice. "He's a student in the foreign exchange program. His name is Ramzi Birand."

"Birand?" I sat up straight. Birand was the name of the Turkish art dealer Michael Hendricks had mentioned during the slide show about Takeo. "How do you spell it?"

"If you want to see the spelling—" she touched her backpack—"I have our student list with me. He's auditing a history class."

Fumiko rummaged through a folder and handed me a piece of paper. The list was typed in English, signaling that this was a cross-cultural class with a high number of foreign students. Birand's name was spelled right, and his nationality was listed as Turkish. There was also an address, with a telephone number.

"You mentioned to me that Emi never studied at Waseda—or any other college. So why did Ramzi attend her memorial?"

Fumiko pressed her lips together and shook her head.

"Please," I said. "If you're keeping a secret for Emi, there's no point anymore."

"He—he was her boyfriend at the American school in Istanbul. This past summer, he came to Japan and enrolled at Waseda to be near her."

Another man. Something I hadn't expected from the innocent-looking Emi. Trying to readjust my thinking, I asked, "What was their relationship like?"

Fumiko closed her eyes, then opened them. They were slightly wet with tears. "She—she sent me a lot of e-mail from Istanbul about him. He was two years older, and they met at a school party. She was always talking about how smart and handsome and funny he was. She was crazy about him! Then, her parents found out."

"I gather they were nervous about it?" What parent wouldn't be nervous about a teenager embarking on a serious relationship?

"Not nervous—furious. Her father was angry that she'd gotten so seriously involved—and he moved their whole family back to Japan. He put her in a girls' school and told her that she could go only to a women's college after she was done. But she kept writing to Ramzi, and he found a way to gain admission to Waseda."

"Oh! So they carried on their romance here—"

"Only for a little while. When the parents found out Ramzi was here, Emi was forbidden to see him again." Fumiko pressed her lips together. "Emi's father couldn't force the university dean to make him leave, so he and his wife decided to make Emi completely un-available to Ramzi. They made her have an *omiai.*"

"In your opinion, was the arranged marriage to Takeo an at-tempt at—punishment?" I was skeptical, remembering how posses-sive and passionate Emi had seemed toward Takeo.

"Not punishment, but control. They just thought that it was time to get her safely married. They said she'd gone too far."

"Are you sure about all this? I saw Emi together with her fiancé. She seemed really excited to be with him, happy to be furnishing their house." I didn't add how I'd overheard the sounds of her and Takeo settling into each other for a serious snog, just a few days ear-lier at the flower arranging school.

"She kind of liked him, I guess. There were many advantages he could offer her."

"What kind of advantages?" I asked, wondering if she'd been as calculating as Takeo.

"Well, she did have choice about the man she married. She thought Takeo was the best of the men she met because he was so successful. He was so busy with the *ikebana* school that he told her he'd spend a lot of time away on business but he'd provide her a generous allowance, and she could stay at the apartment in Tokyo or the house in Hayama, whatever she wanted."

"But—but what about the physical nature of marriage to a man so much older?" I tried to express it delicately. "Wasn't that frightening to her?"

"Oh, she'd done it lots of times, with Ramzi and then—with Takeo. She told me all about it. She said it was quite nice, actually. She also said that one day my time would come. But look at me— who's going to want to sleep with such a big fatty?"

"Please, don't talk about yourself that way!" I said gently, but my mind was racing. Takeo and Emi had embarked on their traditional marriage plan with complex and mercenary agendas. But being typical modern, young Japanese, they'd had sex along the way—and that had changed everything, at least for Emi. Takeo's charisma had led to her undoing, to the start of her falling in love. And perhaps the drugs she took made the decision easier.

"Did she start taking drugs in Istanbul?" I was beginning to think that Emi had changed from a good Japanese girl into a teenage libertine while she was abroad—just as Japanese people were wont to say about "foreign-returned girls."

"I think so, but it got a lot worse here," Fumiko said. "She was already slim enough when she arrived. I told her she shouldn't keep taking pills, but she insisted it was the only way to keep the pounds off. And after her parents found out about Ramzi, I think the pills made her feel better, emotionally."

"So," I said, studying the list of students in the class that Fumiko had showed me at the beginning of our conversation, "I don't recognize this address where Ramzi lives, and it's not right here in Takadanobaba. Did you ever go there with Emi?"

"No, and she didn't go there either. He lives with his uncle over their shop in Omote-sando. Actually, if that's all you need, I should go now. I must not be late for my next class." Fumiko held out her hand for the paper.

Thanking Fumiko profusely, I copied the information onto a napkin and snuggled it in the cell phone holder. I gave her back the student roster and declined her attempt to help pay the lunch check.

"Please, it's on me. You've been very, very helpful," I said.

"Why? What are you going to do?" Fumiko looked at me anxiously.

"I'm not sure exactly. But I'd like to talk to Ramzi."

"If I'd known you were going to talk to him, I would never have told you anything—"

"Why? Are you scared of him?"

She shook her head. "Of course not! But he was always hanging around, trying to spy on her during the times she was with Takeo. He's a little bit strange. He will be upset if he knows I was talking about him."

"Thanks for the warning. I'll be quite careful," I said as we parted. And I would be, because a new theory was forming in my mind. Ramzi and Emi had a plan for the future, but it had been dashed by Emi's growing attraction to her betrothed. Who would want to stand by while a beloved girlfriend prepared to marry— and then have all hopes of seeing her again forever dashed by her death? Ramzi had probably stormed the memorial because he wanted to say something to her parents, make them pay for what they'd done.

28

Omote-sando had always been my aunt Norie's idea of shopping heaven. There wasn't much I could afford on the long boulevard lined with tall zelkova trees. It had become a satellite Paris; the street was home of the highest-grossing Louis Vuitton store worldwide, and there were also lavish boutiques devoted to Chanel, Yves St. Laurent, and Christian Dior, very close to an older, Japanese-owned tourist haunt, the Oriental Bazaar—which obviously had been named in less politically correct times.

Normally, I would have passed the Oriental Bazaar by, but today I paused between the huge porcelain lion-dogs that guarded its entrance. There were a few things inside that might be of use to me, and the prices would definitely be the best on the block.

I hurried past the furniture sections crowded with Korean-made replicas of old Japanese chests and into the books section, where almost everything was published in English. I skimmed the new edition of *Born to Shop Tokyo* and came up with the town, Umeda, where the Japanese sculptor Kazu Sakurai was based. The author recommended that foreigners visit his shop by making an appointment ahead of time and bringing plenty of cash—a minimum of $3,000 for the smallest piece. Well, that was the value of being a Living National Treasure, I thought wryly, scribbling down the phone number on a shopping circular and sliding it into the cell phone case. Maybe I could live without a backpack after all, I thought, leaving the books section in search of toys for my niece and nephew in Washington. Having mixed-sex twins to shop for was a challenge, but I ultimately settled on a pair of Japanese police officer dolls—one a man and one a woman, a sign of political progress. And the dolls weren't just for play—they would teach fine motor skills. Win especially would have fun taking off the dolls' black lace-up shoes, though he'd need his mother's help to put them on again.

How soon would it be until I saw Kendall and the twins again? I wondered as I tucked the package containing the dolls into my backpack and continued on my trail to Ramzi Birand's address. I had to come up with something here. I didn't know what I was looking for, but if I didn't find it, I didn't know when I'd ever get home.

For now, my business was the Birand family. The address was easy to find, because it was in a pretty lane that ran behind a small street containing my favorite coffee shop, Appetito, right across from the Hanae Mori building. Right now, stretched across the street's entrance, there was a huge banner stretched bearing the cryptic acronym FCUK. It wasn't till I got to the other side that I learned that this stood for French Connection United Kingdom.

I'd try to get Ramzi to come out to Appetito with me for a quick private talk. If he lived nearby, it was probably his favorite place. While Japanese students lived and died for *okonomiyaki*, foreign students were addicted to coffee and pastry.

When I reached 17-11-2A Kawashima, a couple of turns past Appetito, it didn't look like the apartment I expected. The address was that of an antiques shop named Treasures of Tabriz, according to the curly gold letters on the door. Ali Birand, proprietor, was the name listed underneath. Ali, not Osman.

I peered through the plate glass window at a ceiling dripping with baroque-style light fixtures. Under the soft electric candlelight I caught sight of a tasteful grouping of Ottoman and French regency furniture. The floor was covered by an Oriental rug with a minute hand-knotted pattern of flowers in delicate creams and blues.

My mother would have gone mad for this shop. It was her decorating taste exactly. I didn't believe in lusting after things too rich for my budget—I'd gotten into trouble that way before. Still, it wouldn't be hard to feign enthusiasm for what was in stock at Treasures of Tabriz.

A soft chime announced my arrival as I opened the door and stepped inside. I hadn't seen anyone through the window, but once I'd made myself known, a slender woman who looked like a Japanese equivalent of my mother—expensive fur-trimmed sweater, stylish boot-cut pants, and socialite pageboy—popped up from behind a large cardboard box. With her long manicured fingers, she'd been uncrating an ancient-looking terra-cotta horse from a wooden box. Wood shavings spilled over its edge, marring the perfection of the shop. It even smelled expensive here, I thought, taking a whiff. It smelled like Russian tea, a blend of orange and cloves and black tea that had been all the rage in San Francisco when I was younger. I remembered my mother and her book club in the living room with a pot of Russian tea on a Chippendale table, discussing Toni Morrison's novels. I looked around Treasures of Tabriz for a teapot, but saw none except for a gorgeous blue-and-gold Sèvres piece set on a high shelf amid an entire tea service for twelve.

"Welcome," the woman said, her voice politely modulated but a bit curious, perhaps because of my appearance. The only kind of woman my age who would walk into an elegant antiques shop wearing Asics running shoes, a cashmere hoodie, and yoga pants would be a confused backpacker or a wealthy expat wife who didn't yet understand how women were supposed to dress for shopping in Tokyo.

"I came from Waseda." A semitruthful statement. "Is this—is this the place where Ramzi Birand lives?"

"He lives upstairs with his uncle—the owner of this shop." She inclined her head gracefully, revealing sparkling diamond studs. "I am so glad that you came to visit. Ramzi's been very sad, and we are worried that he has no friends. Would you care for some tea while I call him?"

"I don't want to put you to the trouble," I said. But, of course, I did. A cup of tea would hit the long-lost Russian tea receptor in my brain, and it would also busy her for a minute so that I could inspect the shop more thoroughly.

"It's no trouble at all. Please, wait just a minute." She disappeared behind a hanging tapestry.

I strolled around the room. There were plenty of nineteenth-century European antiques of the sort that used to be sold in Baltimore's Howard Street shops where Grand took me, every now and again during my childhood visits, to educate my eye. In the Birand shop, these pieces of furniture were nicely offset by Middle Eastern serving pieces of filigreed silver and brass, which bore hefty price tags that signified either valuable metal or age.

I walked back to look at the Chinese terra-cotta horse that was standing on the counter. It had a stick-on price tag on it that said 6,000Y. Was that yen or yuan? I didn't know the current value of Chinese currency, and the box was stamped as coming from Shanghai. As I bent to look at it, I saw the ears of another horse sticking up through wood shavings. Without looking any further, I knew the horses were reproduction pieces, because real Tang dynasty horses sold for about $500,000 a piece.

"May I help you?" A man's voice this time, in what I would call newcomer's Japanese—slow, measured, accented with the sounds of another land. I straightened my posture and turned to regard the speaker: an olive-skinned man with closely cropped hair, a hooked nose, and piercing hazel eyes. Fifty-something and foreign, I decided, looking at the fine business shirt he wore tucked into wool gabardine slacks.

"Hello, sir. May I ask if you are Mr. Ali Birand?" I asked in excessively courteous English, trying to make up for the way I looked.

"Yes, I am. And you, who are you?" He beamed, as if the English I'd used had been a welcome surprise. As he spoke, he picked up the box of horses and moved it back behind the counter.

"My name is Rei Shimura. I was in the States before, but I'm at Waseda right now." Again, very close to the truth.

"Ah, that explains your so beautiful English." His smile deepened. "So you came to see Ramzi?"

"Yes, we've all been quite worried about him. I've brought some papers for him from class."

"Really?" The thick brows pulled together. "I wasn't aware he had many friends. In Istanbul, he was so popular, but here—he just hasn't tried enough, I think."

The danger would be if Ramzi emerged and looked at me without recognition. I had to prepare myself. "Actually, he doesn't know me very well at all. I'm an older student, you know—"

"And he only had eyes for one girl, didn't he?" Ali Birand sounded rueful. "With age there is wisdom—something my nephew certainly lacks, in his own character and those of the friends he's chosen."

Ali Birand's allusion to Emi made me want to jump right into some questions, but the saleswoman interrupted us. She was carrying a tray containing two tall Middle Eastern tea glasses, each resting in an engraved brass holder. Mr. Birand took the tray in his own hands and settled it down on a marble-top table in front of a pale blue velvet sofa. He indicated that I should sit down.

"That's for sale, isn't it? I don't want to make it dirty." The bottom half of my pants were still damp with dirty pond water.

"Please, please! You are an honored guest. You must enjoy Miss Iwada's tea. It is something I have taught her."

I'd never thought anyone could out-Japanese the Japanese at courtesy. Giving up, I took the glass and settled down, making sure to stretch my legs out so they didn't rub against the sofa.

The tea had been brewed at least ten minutes earlier, I judged by the rich taste of orange and cinnamon and the drinkable temperature. It seemed almost as if they'd been expecting a visitor.

"I hope it's not too hot," Miss Iwada, the salesclerk, said to me in Japanese. I could tell from her face that she was figuring out which side of the Pacific I really belonged to.

"It's delicious. I must say that I didn't expect this beautiful shop, and to have tea as well. Thank you so much." I spoke in Japanese to her, wondering how much Mr. Birand understood.

"Oh, no, I am so glad you are here. Ramzi-san has missed all his classes since the—accident," Miss Iwada said. "His uncle told him to go, but he just refuses. He would stay in his room all the time if he could."

"It's so convenient to have the apartment over the shop. What a beautiful space it is—for how long have you been here?" I switched back to English, so I could better include Ali Birand.

"We've had the building for a year, but it took a lot of renovations to make a place for the shop—which opened last month. But it's not our only place; my brother and I have other antique stores in Istanbul and Cairo and, once upon a time, in Baghdad." He smiled wryly. "I'm afraid your army put a dent in that business."

"I can certainly understand why you would want to be here, in Tokyo. And I'm intrigued by the store name. Isn't Tabriz a city in Iran?"

"It was the cultural center of old Persia. The rug near the window was made in Tabriz one hundred years ago. It took eight artists two years to create it."

I sighed in appropriate admiration, then said, "But are you Turkish?"

"We are. But you know, everyone in Japan thinks of Turkey just for rugs, not for high-class antiques. So we chose the name Tabriz, and we offer treasures from all over the Middle East, including Turkey. Not just the Middle East, but Italy and France and England—that is an Italian marble table, where you just put your glass."

"Ooh, sorry!" I picked it right up. "I hope I didn't damage anything. It looks so antique!"

"That table will be fine." He smiled graciously. "My brother acquired it from the Italian ambassador, whose family had owned it for two hundred years. Other objects—like the tea glasses and rugs—were made recently but by skilled artists carrying out a generations-old tradition."

"And the terra-cotta horses you were unpacking?" I couldn't resist asking.

"I was just opening them when you arrived," Miss Iwada said, turning to look at Mr. Birand, as if for guidance.

"A Chinese museum has fallen into some financial difficulty, so we were able to purchase these Qin dynasty horses. They are quite valuable, so I thought I would bring them to this market first. But if they don't sell here, I'm sure they will be of interest to our clientele abroad." Ali Birand spoke so confidently that for a minute I almost believed him. But if these were real warrior tomb horses, they would have been hand-carried by Mr. Birand himself from China instead of shipped by crate with the price tags still affixed, and he'd know their real value. He obviously thought I knew nothing about Asian antiques.

"Oh, dear. I fear that I could never afford anything here, except maybe a tea glass." I ran a finger along the glass, and it made the light singing sound of fine crystal.

"You chose a nice reproduction set. We have a special price. Ten thousand yen for a set of five," Ali Birand said.

One hundred dollars for five gorgeous tea glasses. Aunt Norie would like them, and none of the other housewives in the neighborhood would have anything comparable. Tea glasses would be the perfect present for me to bring after my mysterious day away from her home; hopefully they would distract my aunt from asking what else I'd done in Tokyo.

"I'll take the set," I said, fishing into my backpack for my wallet.

"For a student, you have exceptional taste. Now, I fear, I have an appointment across town. It was lovely to meet you, Miss Shimura."

Mr. Birand pulled on an inky black cashmere coat and disappeared out the front door and down the street. I watched him set off, thinking about the charming, poised way he'd presented himself. And what of Ramzi? He had the Birand looks, with the advantage of youth. But last night, when he'd been thrown out of the Haradas' house, he had been awkward, unsophisticated, emotional—the very opposite of his uncle.

The salesclerk was dexterously wrapping up the package in gold paper when Ramzi finally slouched into the room. He wore a stained rugby shirt and Levi's that hung low at the waist, exposing a flash of boxers with an American flag pattern. He looked around expectantly, then settled his lazy, long-lashed eyes on me.

"Ramzi-san! How are you doing?" I asked, looking him over. He was lean, but not too thin. He didn't look at all like my idea of a drug user.

"Iwada-san, didn't you say a friend was here?" He looked blankly from me toward the saleswoman.

The Japanese Ramzi had spoken was broken—understandably, because it was still a very new language for him. I switched to English.

"My first name is Rei," I said. "I was at Waseda today, and I bring you some papers and a message from Kashima-san."

"Kashima-san? You mean that nerd in my Internet class?" he said in quick, perfect English, but with a slight accent that seemed to curl upward like the steam from my cup of tea. The English had worked. He had become interested in me, as I could tell from the way he'd turned his lanky body toward me.

I couldn't comment any more on Kashima-san, having never met the person whose name had been smack in the middle of the roster Fumiko had shown me, so I tried to move on. "I've got the information with me. Why don't we go to Appetito just around the corner? We can eat while we talk."

"I'm not hungry," Ramzi said.

"You must eat! You haven't had anything in five days!" Miss Iwada said.

Ramzi scowled at her, and the tension was broken only when a Japanese man started to come into the shop, but backed out, as if the sight of the two of us in our jeans and sweats had made him decide that this shop was not a proper one after all. I hadn't gotten much of a look at the man, but he must have looked like a good customer, because Miss Iwada hustled out to the street to entreat him to return.

"Did she put you up to this?" Ramzi said to me as we watched, through the window, while Miss Iwada bowed to the man and implored him to return.

"Iwada-san? Absolutely not. How could she, when I've never met her before?"

"Just as I've never met you. You're not in any of my classes. I don't understand why you're here—"

"I saw you at the memorial gathering." I took a deep breath. "You're right, it's not about schoolwork. It's about Emi."

29

"Emi?" He turned to me with eyes filled with pain. "What business is she of yours?"

"As I said, I was there and I saw those men make you leave. It was terribly unfair, I thought."

"Yes, it was." His voice was bitter. "I was thrown out while her murderer stayed sipping whisky, the bastard—"

"Who's a murderer?" I asked, picking up the box of glasses I'd paid for.

"Her fiancé. The one who crashed the car that she died in." As he spoke, I saw Miss Iwada coming back.

"Let's talk about this outside," I said, taking Ramzi by the arm, figuring that gentle force would work better than words.

"I don't understand who you are! Why do you care about this?" Ramzi practically exploded when we were out of the shop. I remembered that Fumiko had said he was strange, so I answered as calmly as I could.

"It's complicated. I knew her, but I knew Takeo Kayama, the person you think murdered her, first. He was the one who introduced us."

"Oh! I suppose he sent you here to plead his case. Frankly, I don't know why he even bothers." Ramzi's voice rose sharply, startling a German shepherd, who barked mercilessly, almost dragging his owner, a small woman, forward.

"Stupid dog. Reminds me of the ones Emi's parents have," Ramzi said as we passed along.

"Keep your voice down. More people understand English than you might think," I cautioned as we turned another corner and the yellow-and-red awning of Appetito appeared. "I suppose you come here all the time, living as close by as you do—"

"I don't know the area at all. And I'm not eating," Ramzi said stonily.

He was firm. I couldn't even get him to agree to coffee, because he said the substance served in Japan was nothing like what he was used to in Turkey. I could see his point, so I got myself a cup of steaming milk tea, even though I'd had half a cup of Russian tea just minutes earlier, so I would be buzzing for hours. I also put two chocolate croissants on two plates, just in case.

I carried the tray over to a table at the window, where Ramzi was staring out at a boy wearing a stovepipe hat and polka-dot pants who was locking a bicycle. At second glance, I realized that the person was a girl.

"Crazies," Ramzi said, but his tone was almost warm. "I'm going to miss seeing Japanese crazies."

"At least she isn't a Lolita," I said, watching the whimsical person disappear into the Shu Uemura makeup boutique. "What do you mean by missing them, though?"

"I'm going back to Turkey. There's nothing more for me here."

"I can understand why you feel that way." I had an urge to put my hand over his, but instead, I put a plate with a croissant in front of him. "Chocolate helps."

"So, who are you really, Chocolate-Tea-and-Shopping Lady?" He used the words lightly; clearly he thought I was a phony.

I had to make an impact, and get him to feel allied with me. "I'm Takeo's ex-girlfriend. From some years ago."

He sat bolt upright. "So you came to see me because you were jilted, too?"

Jilted. Interesting choice of word, but I couldn't ask him about that yet. "I came because I'm confused and concerned about a lot of things that happened, starting with the fact that you were forcibly removed from Emi's house by those men. Why did that happen?"

"Those men told me I was upsetting her parents. Apparently, I always did. But for them not to let me even see her one last time—" He passed a hand over his eyes and turned away from me.

"Why were they so hard on the relationship? Didn't your parents meet at some point while you were both in Istanbul?"

"Our fathers did business," Ramzi said. "Lots of business. A Japanese will do business with foreigners. But not personal relationships. Not even my father's money made me good enough for Emi."

"The Haradas are very traditional," I said, choosing my words carefully. "It's not the way most Japanese are. The arranged marriage for Emi, right after high school graduation, seemed—almost medieval to me."

"Yes, the Haradas like the old world." He sank into silence.

"I gather your father sold antiques to the Haradas?" I ventured.

"Yeah. There are plenty of my father's wares in his house—so ironic, when he throws me out!"

"Your uncle mentioned to me that he and your father sell more than just Middle Eastern pieces."

"Yes. They carry everything—lots of French and Italian, which sells to the Turkish buyers; and of course Turkish and Middle Eastern, for the Europeans who want something ancient and exotic." He made quotation marks with his fingers to emphasize the seeming silliness of those adjectives. "The mix of pieces that you saw in the shop just now is pretty much like our shop in Istanbul. Only the shop in Istanbul takes up half a city block. It's huge."

"How does your father obtain the French and Italian pieces?"

Ramzi shrugged. "He does a few scouting trips a year. But more often people bring things to him to sell. He runs in diplomatic circles, and those people sometimes want to sell or exchange their pieces for something my dad had in the shop."

"I saw a Balthus painting in the Haradas' house. Did that come from your father's store?"

"Who?" Ramzi looked at me blankly.

"Balthus was a recently deceased French painter who did most of his work in the mid-twentieth century. Upstairs at the Haradas' house, I saw a portrait of a young Japanese woman, with a kind of dwarf in the corner. It looked like a Balthus, but I wasn't certain."

"I went upstairs in that house just once. I'm afraid that I didn't spend the time looking at anything on the walls." Ramzi gave me a tight, mirthless smile.

I tried a different approach. "Did you know Emi when she was chubby?"

He cocked his head to one side. "She told me she'd been heavier, but I could never imagine it. She came to our school in her sophomore year when I was already a senior. By the time I met her at a party, she was perfect. Like a doll."

"I agree," I said. "She was very beautiful."

"Oh, but you didn't see her at her peak. When she came here, and all that crap went down with the engagement, she got thinner. Too thin, I think."

"Do you know why she became so thin?"

"The way everyone does: by not eating. She was unhappy, just like me."

"Did you ever see her take any tablets?"

He started to shake his head, then paused. "Well, there were always vitamins. She sometimes took them in front of me."

I looked at him hard. How could a college boy not know about drugs? He hardly struck me as the sheltered type.

"Those vitamins," I said. "Where did she buy them?"

"I don't know. Maybe her mother bought them for her. Who cares?" Ramzi paused. "What do you know that you're not saying?"

"I think she may have been taking amphetamine tablets. They're popular with young women who want to lose weight."

"Oh." He sat for a minute, the shock registering on his face. "Who said Emi was taking that? How do you know?"

"It's apparently what the police think. They asked Takeo all about it. Haven't they asked you about it yet?"

Ramzi's voice grew cold. "I know the stereotypes about—my country. But people in my social class—we have better things to do than buy and sell drugs. My uncle isn't smuggling them in his furniture crates, and I'm not selling them on the campus at school, okay? And what you're talking about—amphetamines—it isn't a Turkish thing. People take hash and opium in Turkey, but not people in our class."

"You mean—your class in school or your social class?"

"Social class. The American kids, well, there was a segment that loved drugs. I knew those kids and I went to their parties, but it was just for the girls. Nothing else."

"Thanks for explaining," I said. "I meant no offense to you. It's just that—it would be safe for everyone concerned if we could figure out who sold the amphetamines to Emi. Like I told you, the police are asking around."

Ramzi shook his head. "This is so—new to me. I just can't believe she would do a thing like buy drugs. Buy handbags and pretty clothes—yes. But not drugs! What if Takeo provided them?"

I shook my head. "He didn't provide them, I'm certain, but he did know something was going on, and he was worried. He'd hoped he could get her to quit after the wedding."

"After the wedding," Ramzi said, his voice soft. "Emi said things would be better after the wedding. He'd be working, so we'd have time to relax together at the country house. We could even travel together, if the situation was cool."

"That sounds like a plan," I said. A plan I would have hated, if I were the cuckolded one.

"Well, that plan went to hell when he killed her! I can't help thinking—" Ramzi's voice broke off.

"What did you think?" I asked gently.

"Maybe he found out about me, and he was so angry that he—he just—"

"He never knew about you," I said, meaning to reassure him, but instead seeing tears form in his eyes. Well, of course. Ramzi was in the process of learning that he'd been even less visible and less important than the Haradas had made him feel.

"When was the last time you spoke to Emi?" I asked.

"Three weeks ago. I knew from—from a friend who helped us— that she had an appointment at the bridal salon at Matsuya. I was waiting by the escalators when she came out, but her mother was there. I had to walk away. It wasn't until an hour later that Emi phoned and asked me to stop following her."

"That must have hurt terribly."

"I couldn't understand it. We've had arguments before, but this was—this was unexpected. She said she wanted to concentrate on the wedding and get on with life. I know she really didn't mean it. She was probably confused." He paused. "Maybe because of those pills that I thought were vitamins. How stupid can a person be, not to have known?"

"Well, it sounds like she'd started on the path much earlier. How could you have suspected anything, if her baseline of normality was actually a drugged state?"

Ramzi seemed to struggle with an answer. "I really don't know if what you're saying is true. I just know that I loved her, and if her family had stayed in Turkey like they should have, we'd still be together."

"Do you think her parents brought her back here because—because they were so upset about the relationship?"

"That's what they said to Emi, and she told me. My father didn't care about me seeing her—just that I really told him where I was going at night, came back when I said, that kind of thing."

It sounded reasonable to me. "So your father was pretty supportive. Is that why he let you come to Japan to study?"

"He wasn't excited about it. He thought, after the Haradas left, that it would be better to leave things alone. But I knew my uncle had gotten the visa and had rented a building here. It was the perfect situation for me, and my father had to let me go. I was nineteen, and I'd come into my trust fund the year before."

"Must be nice," I said automatically.

"No, it's not nice," Ramzi said stonily. "The reason I have that money is because my mother died five years ago."

So he'd lost a mother. No wonder he'd clung to his girlfriend so desperately. Feeling as though I'd really put my foot in things, I said, "Ramzi, I'm so sorry about all that you've suffered. Of course the trust fund is something you never wanted—"

"My mother's death is nobody's fault."

His choice of words was interesting, I thought as we parted a few minutes later and I began my damp-footed trek home. Whether he was conscious of it or not, he hadn't absolved me of Emi's death—something I wasn't ready to do, either.

30

My journey back to Yokohama seemed to take forever. Outside the grimy train windows, the late afternoon sun illuminated mud-stained roads, toppled signs, and sagging power lines. How odd it was to see my beloved, immaculate Japan looking like an unmade bed! But Typhoon Nigo's damage would take time to clean up. I supposed the scenery along the route would eventually, perhaps within a few weeks, be almost the same as it had been before the floods and winds. Still, for the people who knew and loved Emi, life would always be divided into "before the typhoon" and after it.

Ramzi had complained about the injustice of Yasuko and Kenichi Harada's attitude toward him. He had a point, but I pondered what it might feel like to see one's daughter plunge headlong into sex at sixteen. I remembered how furious my father had been when I'd told him, as an eighth-grader, that I wanted to go with some girl-friends and a group of much older boys to a midnight screening of *The Rocky Horror Picture Show*. He'd been outraged that I'd even asked. I dated covertly, and with considerable fear of discovery, until I'd left home at age eighteen for college.

Covert dating. Spying and sexual infidelity. My terrible behavior of recent days probably had its origins in my own family history, but I had no time for self-analysis. I needed to remember what

Ramzi had said about the art, and his father's relationship with Kenichi Harada.

Emi's father must have done business with Osman Birand more than once, because Ramzi had recognized several pieces in the house. There was a relationship. The ibex ewer could certainly have gone from the Birands to the Haradas. I knew that a fake vessel lay in its fragmented state in Washington. Did a genuine ancient vessel even exist?

A recorded female voice sweetly reminded me to take all my personal belongings with me as I disembarked at Minami-Makigahara Station. I was glad of the reminder, given my distracted state. The train was so crowded that I'd had to stand the whole way, and endure the slightly disapproving looks of people who saw how much space my backpack, stuffed with the gifts, was taking up on the overhead luggage rack. Now I took it out, opening room for someone else to stow a carry-on suitcase.

I squeezed through the bodies and made it out to the platform at Minami-Makigahara Station. It was ten minutes by foot to my relatives' house, and during that time I would be blessedly free of people crowding around me. I checked behind me for company—no, nobody was following me up the quiet hilly street that led to my aunt's home—and took out my cell phone.

"I received your e-mail," Michael Hendricks said, after I'd greeted him.

"I didn't think you'd have read it already. It's what, six in the morning?"

"That's right. What I want to know is whether you wrote rather than calling because you thought I'd yell at you."

"Actually, I thought I'd avoid being overheard. You can't imagine what it's like always being surrounded by people."

"I can't," Michael said. "It's pretty quiet on the Japan desk."

"I suppose if worse comes to worst, we can bring in Mr. Watan—"

"No names please," Michael said crisply. "The colleague you wanted to mention—let's call him Mr. Ito—is one of Mr. Harmony's colleagues. Because of that relationship, Ito is no longer an asset to this operation. And now, let's talk about something else."

Watanabe was Ito, Harada was Harmony, Emi was "the bride," and I was—what? A bungler, at the very best. Feeling rather subdued, I said, "Did you know that the antique dealer's brother recently opened an antiques shop in Tokyo?"

A long pause. "No, I didn't. When?"

"A month ago."

"So what's the place like?"

In short order, I described Treasures of Tabriz, and the reproduction Chinese horses I'd seen. And mindful of Michael's new insistence on aliases, I called the dealers "Brother A" and "Brother B," and Ramzi "Robert."

At the end of all this, Michael said, "Rei, as we know now, the vase Flowers had wasn't genuine. But that doesn't mean it passed from the brothers to Mr. Harmony. Why would a successful dealer sell a fake to a connoisseur?"

"It happens all the time. A connoisseur can't be an expert in everything. There was a significant Japanese bowl that I noticed in the Harmony household, and really, that's the only thing I'm positive is authentic. It makes sense that Harmony would be more aware of fine modern Japanese ceramics than ancient Middle Eastern work—just as I am."

"What you're saying, though, is only half of it. You're telling me why Harmony might have taken the piece. But what would the motivation be for the dealer to scam a well-connected diplomat? Brother B would risk losing his entire international clientele if word got out that he was a cheat."

"It could have been a matter of anger."

"Why? Did the son say there was an argument?"

"There was no fight between B and Harmony that Robert mentioned, but the fact is that the bride's parents refused to let her see Robert. They even shipped her back to Japan. This could have wounded Robert's father's pride enough for him to give Harmony a fake in exchange for payment."

"Hmm," Michael said. "It's an interesting theory, but it puts a lot of importance on a high school relationship. How likely is that? I mean," he said, "maybe you remember your first boyfriend, but were your parents vested in how that relationship turned out?"

"They were vested in destroying my relationships," I said, remembering.

Michael laughed, the first time I could remember him doing so. "And now that you're over thirty, it's probably the reverse."

"You're right, but don't let me lose my train of thought. I can make sense of Emi's parents' actions more than I can understand Brother B's laissez-faire parenting. Apparently Brother B wasn't thrilled that his son wanted to study in Japan, but because Brother A had already moved to Tokyo to open a shop, and Robert was of legal age and had his own trust fund, B didn't try to stop him."

"Ah, the trust fund left to him by his late mother?"

"Oh. You know about the mother?"

"I have done some research," Michael said. "What I've learned is that she was Iranian, was wealthy, and fled Iran with her parents for Paris during the revolution. She met her husband when he was taking a course there in arts and antiques. They married, and Robert was actually born in Paris. He holds two passports: E.U. and Turkish."

"I bet he used the E.U. passport for his student visa," I said. For a Turk to get a student visa would be much harder. "What about the mother? Do you know when and why she died? Robert was shaken when we talked about her."

"There was a car accident four years ago," he said. "The Mercedes she was driving was hit by a speeding bus on a mountain road near a resort. Not only did she die, but five people on the bus did, too."

"Oh, my God. And the bride was lost in a car accident, too." I was silent for a moment, thinking about how painful this coincidence must have been for Robert.

"You still there?" Michael's voice had a hint of anxiety.

"Yes. The main reason I called—I want more background on why the Harmonys left Japan. As you were saying, a high school romance is hardly reason to jump ship from an important ambassadorship. I wonder why he came back and took that other post. I think Mr. Ito would be our best source here—"

"You can't talk to him. I told you that already." Michael's voice was impatient.

"But why?" I challenged. "If you trusted him enough to bring him into the conference room at the Smithsonian and to arrange for my reentry into the country—why can't I ask him what I really need to know?"

"The father of the bride is a colleague of similar rank in the government. If we ask Ito about Harmony, there's a good chance he'll feel that the loyal thing to do is call the guy and warn him of our interest."

"I don't know about that. I liked Mr. Ito."

"Yes. You liked Mr. Flowers, too."

I bit my lip. "What are you insinuating?"

"Nobody said that you had to sleep with our suspect."

A slow flush spread through my body as the words registered. At last I said, "I'm trying to decide whether to hang up on you."

"Please don't. I'm sorry if you're embarrassed, but I have suspected this for a while, and I have to know. There aren't supposed to be secrets between us."

When embarrassed, go for sarcasm. "Actually, I'd think you would be delighted about what I did. The sacrifice of my virtue, or whatever you want to call it, meant that I was able to remain in the house overnight and locate the vessel. In fact, I answered the question you sent me out to answer, yet I still haven't been released from active duty—"

"I haven't called you home because you're doing so well," Michael said. "By all means, Rei, find out what you can by using the underground channels you seem so good at working. And I know you came onboard pro bono, but—this job has turned out to be more difficult than we all thought. I've put in a request already to arrange for some financial compensation."

Yes, I was a real whore.

I hung up, knowing that I should feel good about both the money and the praise, but I was only more depressed. How would I know the job was finished when the job description seemed to be changing daily? And I was disturbed that Michael knew about Takeo. Somehow, it gave him more power over me, and I didn't like that feeling at all.

I put the phone back into my sweater and rounded the corner, entering the residential neighborhood where Norie and Hiroshi lived. A Japanese policeman was standing alone in the center of the street. I continued on, but the policeman stepped directly in my path.

"This is an identification check," he said, in a voice that was all business. "May I see your foreigner registration, please?"

So the police had found me.

31

Identification check. The only thing I had going for me was that I didn't have my card with my name—although that in itself was a violation of the law. Foreigners were supposed to carry foreigner registration cards. Nobody really did in the old days, because the police didn't run around hassling people. But that was then. This was now.

"I'm just visiting on a tourist visa. I'm not a resident, so I don't carry a card," I said, eyeing the street for signs of life. A block ahead, a salaryman was turning into his walled garden. There was nobody else around, just a big black car purring gently in a no-parking zone. Maybe that was what had brought the cop here—a chance to ticket the car, which some trusting Japanese person had left with the keys in the ignition. And now it was time to ticket the foreigner.

"When did you arrive?" the officer demanded.

"October fifth."

"And when is your departure date?"

Why had I bought Jackie and Win police dolls? This man was the farthest possible thing from cuddly. "I'm not sure. The next week or two."

The officer shook his head. "You must show me your passport and embarkation card."

Now I was in trouble. The fact was, fine print on the embarkation card said I was required to carry it with me at all times while in Japan. In the old days, nobody ever did that either.

I looked up at the tall officer, trying to establish a human bond. He looked so stern. He hadn't even demanded my name; I guessed that was because he knew it. The whole thing was a setup.

Damn, damn. I lowered my head and began, very slowly, to unzip my backpack. I certainly wasn't carrying my passport—after my bad luck with the first cell phone, I had stashed it in my suitcase in Aunt Norie's house.

I couldn't decide whether to admit to him that I didn't have the passport with me or to feign surprise about its absence. This man would show no mercy, and under Japanese law he had the right to take me into police custody and postpone telling the American embassy about my whereabouts for as long as suited police purposes. I was screwed.

I crouched down as if to grope in my backpack. All I wanted was for the ground to open up and swallow me, I thought as I looked at the policeman's large feet, in black suede running shoes. I blinked and looked again. Yes, he was wearing Nikes, not black leather lace-up boots like the police dolls in my backpack.

Why would a Japanese policeman wear the wrong shoes to work? A policeman would never do that. But an imposter might.

Trying to seem unsure, I rose up slowly and then hurled the backpack as hard as I could at the man's groin. He doubled over, swearing, as I sprinted up the street toward Norie's house. But before I knew it, I heard the big black car start up. He'd recovered enough to get himself into it. I now realized that it was his.

As I pounded the asphalt, I thought about the cell phone in my pocket, and the impossibility of pausing to make a call to 119. The man was probably a gangster, and he might even have a gun. In the land of gun control, gangsters seemed to be the only ones with guns.

I heard the car creeping around the corner I'd just turned. My only hope was to go where the car couldn't, over the walls and into the private gardens that surrounded the houses. But where was an entry point? I ran past one house with a six-foot stucco wall, knowing that it was too high and had nothing for me to grasp. The next one was bordered by a shorter bamboo fence, though, and hand over hand I pulled myself up, using the muscles that had previously been tested only in gym classes.

He'd seen me go over that garden fence; but now he couldn't see me anymore, and I had two other garden walls to choose from: one garden on the left, and one on the right. I ran for the higher one, which I knew bordered a house catty-corner from my relatives' house. It was high, though—about seven feet. I stood in front of it, breathing hard, trying to assess whether I'd make it. Fear made me feel as though I'd been running for an hour, but no more than a couple of minutes had passed. If only I had the power to get to the house.

Powerhouse. I remembered the pet phrase of my trainer at the gym in Washington. Women's strength was always in the belly. I just had to concentrate and pull my belly to my back. Feeling long, straight, and strong, I moved quickly upward, using the ivy that covered the garden wall for footholds. The top was in sight. The narrow, powerful wedge that I'd shaped myself into pulled over the top and then dropped down easily on the other side.

I was running through a garden, feeling the crunch of flowers under my feet. Sorry! I apologized between breaths as a woman peered at me out of her brightly lit dining room.

Another wall at the back of the garden, a little bit higher; I struggled more, scraping my hands as I climbed this one and half fell into the next garden. This was Aunt Norie's neighbor's garden, three houses away; I recognized the neighbor as she peered out at the intruder running through her bed of chrysanthemums.

I hoped she would call the police. Maybe the presence of real cops would scare away the impersonator. I had no inclination to make the call myself, right now—it was such a quiet night that I was sure my ragged voice would carry. I couldn't give myself away.

I couldn't run much more, but I was almost home, I thought as I faced the stone wall where, on the other side, I knew Aunt Norie's few remaining camellia bushes were planted. I took a deep breath, preparing to climb, then paused.

He'd know I was going home, I thought with a feeling of awful certainty. If he'd lain in wait for me in the Shimuras' neighborhood, he certainly knew my address. I imagined myself inside, and him knocking on the door—or, even worse, him presenting himself to Aunt Norie and getting in by pretense or force. I could make out headlights on the road, outside the other garden wall—the one that fronted the street. He was probably already there, waiting.

Norie's street was a cul-de-sac, so I could make my way out of the neighborhood by running through all the walled and fenced gardens, and back down to the main road where he'd found me. That was about the best I could do. I still had my train pass zipped into the cell phone holder, so I could board a train and get out of the neighborhood. Maybe Richard would take me in for the night, because all my cash and credit cards were in the backpack. I wondered what my pursuer would make of all that, and the police dolls and the boxed tea glasses, which I'd heard smash after the backpack bounced off his body.

I escaped the residential section, but I still felt vulnerable on the main road. I took a parallel path, down a smaller street crowded with little restaurants, to reach the train station. Then I jumped onto the first train heading back to Tokyo. It was rush hour, but I was too frazzled to observe any etiquette. My phone had switched itself into e-mail mode, and I had to press the "enter" button over and over again to get back to a telephone menu. At last I was able to dial my aunt's home number. Norie picked up. Her tone was impatient.

"Where are you? I've been so worried. A policeman was here just a few minutes ago. He wanted to return your backpack, which you apparently lost and a kind person turned in at the police station."

"Obasan, listen carefully. That man is not who he says he is. Tell me if he's still there—yes or no."

"No. He's not here. But as I was saying, Rei-chan, he would like to bring you your backpack when you return—which will be when? You're an hour late already."

"Obasan, if he really was a cop, why wouldn't he have just left the backpack with you to give to me?"

She paused. "He was a little strange, I suppose. His shoes—"

"Yes, they were the wrong ones, because it was the only part of his costume he overlooked." I gulped, because my throat was so dry. "His coming to you proves that he won't give up looking for me."

"Ara!" Aunt Norie exclaimed, the reality finally dawning on her. "I should call the police."

"Tell them there's an impersonator lurking in the neighborhood," I said. "Give them a physical description, including the shoes. If he's lingering around, they might find him. Oh, and tell them he's got a big black car. I couldn't identify the model, but it was a large sedan."

"Rei-chan, you are the one who noticed the most. You must be the one to give the description—"

"I'm sorry." I dropped my voice. "I'm in a situation where I just can't talk to them right now. I can only promise that I'll be careful and call you when I reach safety."

"Where are you going?" Aunt Norie's voice broke. " Not back to America. I know that place is not safe. Chika told me about the men who tried to beat up Angus-chan in your neighborhood—"

"My passport's at your house, remember?" I tried to sound reassuring. "I'm not going anywhere. I'm just looking for a quiet place where I can figure out the next step."

"A police station. That's where you should go!"

"I will call you later. Good-bye. And you must take care, too."

After I clicked off the phone and tucked it back into my pocket, I sat, gazing out the window and thinking. My retreat would have to come tomorrow, after I'd gotten more money. In the meantime, I'd need to find somewhere to spend the night, with no more than a fifty-yen piece in my pocket.

In actuality, there were several old friends and colleagues I could ask, but none of them had a spare room to put me in—and I was ashamed to ask for a favor when I hadn't bothered to pay them a social call on this visit. No, the only people I'd already visited, whom I could ask straight out with no worrying, were those paragons of responsibility, Richard and Simone.

I disembarked at Shibuya amid the evening bustle. As gray-haired salarymen in gray suits swarmed toward the trains, they were nearly knocked over by a reverse migration of young partyers. Twenty-something boys with hair the shade of Marilyn Monroe's and hot pink sneakers on their feet, teenage girls who'd worked their school uniform skirts to breezy new heights, fashionistas of both sexes in cowboy boots and shearling—they seemed to curve around me and lift me into their current. We were like a flock of birds, flying westward to where the best stores, restaurants, and nightclubs lay.

I remembered meeting friends at the statue of Hachiko the dog right outside the west exit; and a bit farther on, I remembered once feeling almost paralyzed with pain as I glimpsed Hugh sitting at a trendy wine bar with another woman. The bar was still there. I had an urge to stop in for a glass of something to calm my nerves, but then I remembered that I had exactly fifty yen to get me through the night.

I pressed on toward Language House, the school where Richard and Simone had set up a partnership. They'd chosen the location well, on a small side street loaded with comic book shops, bars, clothing boutiques, and record stores.

An animated billboard advertisement for Panasonic's new camera featured the singer Ayumi Hamasaki smiling down like an angel of the Tokyo night. Keep me safe, Ayumi, I thought to myself. And don't you dare take a picture of me in these clothes.

I was just going into the language school when the cell phone vibrated in my sweater pocket. I answered and heard Michael Hendricks's voice.

"Hold on a sec." I was relieved to hear from him, but I needed to find a really private place, so I headed for the ladies' room, which I knew had a door that locked. An English conversation school was not a place I wanted to be overheard having an English conversation.

"What's going on? What's happening to you?" Michael said.

"How—how did you know something happened?"

"It looked like you were trying to send e-mails. Lots of short messages came over with nothing on—"

"Oh. All I can think is that I accidentally bumped the phone when I was climbing!"

"Climbing?"

I explained about the man who'd been waiting for me, and my narrow escape.

"I'm concerned about what happened to you," Michael said slowly. "Still, I can't help wondering if, in this case, he might be the genuine item. It's fully within a policeman's rights to pursue an un-cooperative person. And perhaps there's more flexibility about shoe style than you think."

"His sneakers aside, no Japanese cop would lie in wait like that. If he was on a mission to bust illegal foreigners, he would be in cer-tain Tokyo neighborhoods, not middle-class suburban Yokohama. And how would he know to show up at my aunt's house when there was no information in my backpack containing that address?"

"What if he was a real cop sent on a private job by someone higher up?" Michael asked, not pausing for an answer. "We know the police have custody of your old cell phone. I'm sure they've gone through it. Maybe you've become a person of interest to them, which is just what I was hoping would not happen."

"It's true, but . . . who would that someone higher up be? Mr. Harmony?"

"I'm thinking of Ito."

"Poor Mr. Ito. You're so untrusting of him—"

"He left a lot of gaping holes in the information he was suppos-edly providing us. Things like the engagement and the shop open-ing. For that reason, I can't trust him anymore."

"But you were so proud of your investigative skills. Now you're putting the onus of investigation on him, and I don't think that's fair."

"My business was to investigate you," Michael said bluntly. "He was responsible for the Japanese intelligence—and as you have pointed out, we had precious little, which compromised your work. Tell me, when's the last time Mr. Ito had contact with you?"

"After the auction. And he did explain exactly who Emi was, when I asked him afterward." But, come to think of it, he hadn't re-turned the calls that I'd made after Emi's accident. Why not?

Michael broke into my thoughts. "I bet he's headed back to Washington. I'll check on it. In the meantime, what can I do to help you?"

"To help?" I was incredulous. "Right now, I'm alone in the city with fifty yen in my pocket, and I'm not sure whether I should run to or from the next cop I see. What the hell can you do about that?"

Michael's voice remained cool. "I'll arrange for you to pick up some cash at the embassy tomorrow morning, when it opens at eight-thirty. Now, what about your passport? Was it in your backpack, too?"

"Nope. It's still safe and sound in my suitcase at Aunt Norie's."

"Great. We can send a courier to pick up the suitcase and bring it to you at the airport. You'll get your ticket there, too. Now, the question is where you're going to sleep tonight."

I'd caught a whiff of something that made me uneasy. "What ticket are you talking about?"

"Your airplane ticket home. As you've reminded me ad nauseam, I've kept you on active duty too long. You'll come home tomorrow."

"No! I know I sounded—stressed—a minute ago, but that doesn't mean I want to run away."

"Why wait? As you pointed out, you're in serious danger."

"But—" I broke off. It was hard to explain, but the incident with the cop had changed everything. All my old feelings of humiliation at being at the mercy of the Japanese law had come back. But this time, I had the possibility of revenge. If it was true that some government bureaucrat had ordered my abduction, I wanted him exposed and brought down. I wouldn't be chased out until I knew the answer.

"Rei, can you hear me?"

"Yes, I can. And I'm sorry I snapped at you. I'm not ready to go, not when I'm so close to finding out what happened." I leaned against the tiled wall for support, because it felt stronger than I did.

"Come on, Rei. There's a time to exit gracefully. And don't worry about the mission. We can work on getting a warrant to get into Birand's shop, Harada's house, wherever the damn vessel might be. But it's too high a risk for you to stay in Tokyo."

"I agree it's a bit dicey at the moment," I said, seeking to mollify him. "After I get the money from the embassy, I'll jump on the first train out. Don't send a courier for my suitcase. I can get it myself."

"Out to where?"

"I'm thinking of Kyushu. It's quiet, and I want to visit a pottery studio. After that, I'll think seriously about whether I should come home."

"Kyushu," Michael said, sounding mystified. "I suppose you want to make the most of your trip and bring home some pottery?"

"Not exactly." Men could be so dense. "Don't you remember that I said the Harmonys own a bowl from a Kyushu artist?"

"Yes, but I don't understand its significance in light of what's going on." He paused. "Go there if you want. Get the hell out of the city. I'd say go tonight, but I can't get the financial arrangements together quickly enough. What I'm going to do is have money wired to you through the State Department. I'll call the duty officer at the embassy in Tokyo right after I'm done. Where will you sleep tonight, if not at your relatives' house?"

"I'm going to ask Richard if I can sleep on his spare futon. Right now, I'm at his language school, waiting for them to finish teaching."

"Your gay ex-roommate?" Michael said.

"Right. There's no danger that I'll do anything stupid with him."

Michael sighed. "If that arrangement falls through for any reason, call me back. I'll come up with a safe house for you."

Safe house. Powerhouse. Language House. It all ran together in my head as I clicked off and went back into the reception area, looking for my friends.

32

While I was talking, classes had ended. Richard and Simone had taken the students on a field trip to Smoke Hose, I heard from one straggler who was still putting on a coat.

A language discussion group in a nightclub? I shook my head at the seemingly unlimited creativity of my friends. What did they really think the students would gain by struggling to hear foreigners shout casual English at each other in a loud setting?

"The goal is to be able to understand lyrics!" Richard shouted in my ear when I arrived at the club twenty minutes later. Smoke Hose was on the fifth floor of one of Roppongi's quintessential nightclub towers. There was a different club on each of the nine floors. Club Isn't It had been the hottest dance club in this particular tower three years earlier, but now hardly anyone had gotten out of the elevator on its floor. Richard and Simone had picked the noisiest, most crowded place, the new bar called Smoke Hose. The name was not a misspelling but a reference to the exposed ductwork on the ceiling and walls, and of course to the haze of cigarettes.

The students in the language class were seated at two round tables right at the front. Everyone had the same kind of ruled notebook, a sharp pencil, and a cocktail. Even the cocktails appeared to be the same—cosmopolitans, which by now I'd figured out were the city's drink of the moment. The goal, Richard explained, was for the students to attempt to transcribe what they were hearing. I couldn't catch more than the singer's refrain, "pounding rain and I love you again," but maybe that was the point. For anybody, this show was a critical test of language comprehension.

"She's Canadian," Richard informed me after the interminable performance finally terminated. "It's perfect for Simone's students doing French, and mine as well. Though it turns out she's mostly singing in English, which is pissing off the French students. And then it's Angus and company, just like you told me."

"The Glaswegian Hangover?" I caught my breath, trying to remember when Chika had told me the band was going to arrive.

"Of course. You told me they were coming in, and I checked the schedule, and it was delayed a couple of nights because of Nigo. Remember, you wanted to go out and see them?"

"It's just that I'm—I'm somewhat embarrassed to see Angus after—after Hugh and I haven't spoken for a while." I spoke fast and low, because a couple of the students were leaning in to listen, with pencils poised to write down my words.

"What's going on?" Richard scrutinized me.

"The fact is, I don't know if I have the stamina to make it through the whole performance. Like I told you and Simone, I need somewhere to crash tonight and I'll be forever grateful for your spare futon."

"I can understand you not wanting the news getting around about how you look tonight." Richard paused, then delivered the bad news. "Like a soccer mom who was left out in the rain—but this business about not talking to Hugh? Please explain."

I sighed and said, "It all started with a stupid little argument we had on the phone the night you met me at Salsa Salsa . . . and it kind of continued. I shifted places where I was staying, so, well, . . . we haven't been in touch for a while."

Richard pursed his lips and said, almost primly, "How would you feel if he did this to you?"

"I'd be angry, unless there was a good reason."

"Precisely. And whether or not you have a good excuse for what you did, you can think one up now. Where's your cell phone?"

"Did you smoke something tonight? You seem awfully forceful," I said in a low voice.

"No, I'm not. It's a casual, every-now-and-then thing. And don't distract me from the topic of this conversation. You've got a phone call to make."

Richard was right. The time had come to make the call, and there actually was a lull in the noise because the Canadian singer was gone and the roadies were redoing the stage layout for the Glaswegian Hangover to come on. Chika came in, though, and sat down next to me.

"I'm so glad to see you," I said, giving her a hug.

"Yes, I—I'm surprised to see you. Mother said you were in trouble. She called me about it. And it turns out all you wanted to do was get to the show!" Chika giggled, putting her hand over her mouth.

"That's not it at all," I said. "Chika-chan, I am mainly here because I'm hoping to stay with Richard afterward. I can't stay at your house any longer because someone's looking for me there."

"Who?" Chika looked alarmed.

"I don't know. That's the problem."

We'd been speaking in English, and I realized now that the students at the table were listening with interest, some taking notes. Christ. How could I call Hugh in this environment?

When Chika went to the stage, answering Sridhar's call for help moving a speaker, I made my own move to the edge of the room to escape the eavesdropping students. I punched in the number for Hugh's office.

When I asked to speak to Hugh, Rhiannon, his personal assistant, sounded surprised. "Rei, it's such a relief to hear from you! Hugh's been a real pain for the last week, let me tell you, worried out of his mind. Neither of the phone numbers you gave him worked, and I triple-checked as well, with no luck. What happened?"

Feeling deeply guilty, I mumbled something about the typhoon and moving around.

"Now, if only I can get him. He's in conference with a gentleman from the Treasury Department, but I know he wouldn't want to miss you—"

"I could call back in an hour."

"No, no, he'll have my head on a platter if he misses this. And I know he's off to New York for something later on. This is the only time to catch him. Hold on, love, I'll ring his private line."

Half a minute later, Hugh was on, his voice sounding as if he were in a tunnel.

"Hi, Hugh! Is your telephone okay? Can you really talk?" I asked by way of greeting.

"I put you on the speakerphone because I have to go through some e-mail while we talk. So what's doing?"

"Ah, won't the speakerphone disrupt you and your client?"

"He just left. It's okay."

Hugh's words were reasonable, but his manner put me on edge. He hadn't called me darling, as he usually did, or given any inkling of the reaction that Rhiannon had led me to expect. He was reviewing e-mail while talking to me, for God's sake.

"What's doing, Rei?" he repeated.

"Well, I'm in a new nightclub called Smoke Hose, and your brother is about to take the stage. Right now he's tuning up his guitar, and my cousin Chika's helping move a speaker on the stage—"

Hugh interrupted me sharply. "What are you trying to do, establish the fact that you're in an actual location with witnesses?"

"Not at all. I was just answering your question. Why the interrogation?"

"You're no longer registered at the hotel where you said you'd be. The cell phone number you gave me was answered by another woman the first time around, and now is disconnected. You were at your aunt's fleetingly, but not anymore. If this is your idea of a business trip, I can only hope that your client has better access to you than I do."

Did his words have a subtext, or was that idea just my paranoia? "Hugh, I apologize. I did call you several times, including once in the night when I thought you'd be in bed, close to the phone. But all I ever seemed to get was your voice mail. Didn't you hear those messages?"

"Of course I did, but you left no information that allowed me to contact you. Anything could have happened, and you'd never know. We had a bomb scare in the building last week, for instance—"

"The apartment building?" I asked, struggling to hear. Angus and the boys were onstage, tuning their instruments.

"No, at my office. Andrews and Cheyne. You didn't read about it in the papers?"

"Hugh, I've been so busy I've barely had time to look at the papers."

"I'm busy, too, but I check the papers every day. The *Post* and the *Times* and also the Japanese papers I can find online, just so I have an inkling of situations that might affect your safety—"

"If you're reading the Japanese papers, you must realize that the typhoon we had last week affected everything. I never had a phone that worked to call you. I'm just trying to make amends—"

Hugh sighed audibly. "For that to happen, I need you to stop all this evasion. Tell me the truth about why you went."

"You know it was for the Smithsonian Institution."

"I was so frantic about you that I called over to the Smithsonian to find a contact. Nobody there knows your name."

"That must be because the Smithsonian is so large. They can't keep tabs on every museum's activities, and the Sackler is one of the smallest."

"You're lying to me. Because when I called the Sackler, nobody there knew of you either—"

With an ear-shattering bar of electric guitar, The Glaswegian Hangover were on.

"Hugh," I shouted, "your brother's started playing. I can't hear you."

"Well, bloody well step outside the club for a minute."

"If I do that, they might not let me in again, and I have no money." And if I lost contact with Richard, I'd lose my bed for the night.

"Priorities . . . mine . . . wrong place . . ." I could make out only a few of Hugh's words. It was like trying to understand the Canadian singer all over again.

"I'll call you later, Hugh!" I called into the receiver. "I love you!"

"Go to hell," Hugh shouted in return.

33

The saving grace, as the night rolled on, was that the music was so loud. I didn't need to speak; I could just sit there and nod every now and then. I could not smile, though I mustered up an approximation of something like a smile when Angus raised his bottle of Kirin to me from the stage. Even when Chika and part of the language class took to the front of the club to execute a line dance to the song "Loved You Last Night, Hate You Today," I couldn't laugh and cheer the way the rest of our group did.

I'd lost Hugh, just as I'd lost him time and time before. We fought as much as we loved each other—if you looked at it objectively, our union had really been one long disagreement broken by spells of remarkable sex. I remembered the last four passionate nights before I'd left. Maybe we'd both been so eager because it was a way of suppressing the lie that lay underneath us. Hugh must have sensed that something was up, but he had not dared to pursue it until I was gone.

Angus and his friends performed two forty-five-minute sets. I went with everyone to Café Almond afterward, and we walked back to Shibuya amid a throng of excited students, drunken musicians, and my two old friends. Chika slipped in beside me and we linked arms, like Japanese schoolgirls.

"Do you want to stay with us?" asked Chika, who was bunking

with the band at their hotel, the Roppongi Lily. She'd already called her mother to report that she had found me safe and sound, and the two of us were staying at a girlfriend's apartment.

"Thanks, but I really do want to stay with Richard."

Chika cocked her head. Her long, striated black-and-gold hair fell across her eyes, and she pushed it back impatiently. "You're so lucky you don't have to make excuses. You can do just what you like."

"Well," I said carefully, "I've actually found that lying's worse. I don't recommend it at all."

Chika's pretty face flushed. "My parents don't want to know the truth. This is easier on everyone."

We paused, momentarily, because there was an obstacle in our path. A Japanese girl in her late teens, eyes closed, was lying on the damp sidewalk in front of us with her legs and clothes askew. Behind her was the doorway of a nightclub; the bouncers standing there seemed to be jeering at her.

"Drunk. The poor thing!" Chika said, stepping around her.

"Wait a minute. Who's taking care of her?" I called out so the bouncers would hear. They looked away from me, so I called it out again.

One of the bouncers said, "Who knows? She had too much drink. She just fell down." He didn't look at me as he spoke.

"How do you know? It could be an overdose, something really dangerous!" I said, crouching down and adjusting her clothes. Seeing my action, the last remaining students in the group formed a knot around the girl and me and began murmuring expressions of concern.

"Excuse me, but who brought her here? Where are her friends?" One of the female students spoke up.

"She stepped out with a man. He went off to get a cab, I think—"

"Maybe he won't come back," someone else in the crowd said in a knowing voice. The others murmured in agreement.

"It's the way things are," the bouncer said, throwing up his thick hands helplessly. "This thing happens every night."

"We could call her parents." I opened the small Kate Spade bag at her side to look for a piece of identification. There was nothing;

just a pack of tissues issued by a loan shark, a Shiseido lipstick, ten thousand yen and change, and a small red pill.

"This! Look at this!" I held it up for everyone to see. "She could have OD'd. She needs to be seen at a hospital—"

"Rei, put that thing away," Richard interrupted. "You don't want the cops to take you in."

It was true that I didn't want any face time with the police. I let my group carry me along, but not before I'd made certain that the bouncer had called an ambulance.

The sight of the collapsed girl haunted me as I lay on Richard's mildewed guest futon, trying to get to sleep. I'd been to the bathroom, looking for a sleeping aid but finding nothing on the bathroom shelf except Richard's amphetamine tablets. I flushed the tablets down the toilet, and left a tiny note inside the foil where they'd been wrapped: *Sorry. But it's because I love you.*

In the dim glow of his clock radio, I stared at the Marky Mark poster on the wall across from me, the famous Bruce Weber shot of him in Calvin Klein underwear, leaning against a pillar, shading his eyes. It was almost as if he didn't want to be identified, though of course he did; the picture had made his career.

Nobody had known who the girl on the sidewalk was. Nobody had cared. I would have been the same, dead, without a passport to even identify me, if I hadn't gotten away from the man near my relatives' house. I really had no safe haven. I had to leave.

The band had a car and driver, so one of the last things I'd asked for, before we parted, was that the driver pick me up at Richard's address at ten minutes to eight. He was too early to be of use to the boys, but he would be able to offer me a safe passage to the embassy, and then on to Tokyo Station.

The boys had been so giddy the previous night that I wasn't sure if my request would really make it to the driver, but sure enough, just before eight the next morning the same Lincoln Continental was waiting for me with the same man who'd ferried Chika and the boys off after Café Almond. I told the driver where I wanted to go, and he sped me there quietly. We didn't break our silence till we reached the huge, boxy gold building that was the U.S. Embassy. When I'd tried to get the cab to wait for me alongside the chancery's long black fence, a Japanese police guard had come up and refused to let him even stop. It was because of security, they said. As a compromise, I told the driver I'd look for him at Hotel Okura across the street.

Michael had told me to be there at eight-thirty, but a line of about 100 people—Japanese and others—were already waiting for admission. Feeling depressed, I joined the end of the line. When a blond woman backpacker walked straight to the guard post at the front of the line and was instantly waved through, I turned to the Brazilian-Japanese man waiting behind me.

"Did you see how she went ahead of everyone?"

"Americans can go ahead. Even if they don't have their passports."

Feeling guilty, I thanked the man for the information and went straight to the front. There, things didn't go as smoothly as I hoped. For one, because I didn't have my passport, I had to convince the guard that I was actually American, not Japanese. Of all the times to fit into Japanese society, this was not the time I wanted. I persisted and remembered something Michael had said about a so-called duty officer knowing my name. At last, the guard gave me a long look, then went into his booth and made a phone call. I heard him speaking into it, saying that my English was almost perfect, but my name was Japanese, so he didn't know. He listened for a minute, then hung up and nodded at me.

"Miss Shimura, you may step through the metal detector."

I did that and practically sprinted along the short path to the next security checkpoint, which was yet another metal detector at the embassy door. Once I passed through it, my gaze turned from a room packed with visa applicants to a small, intense Caucasian man with his shirtsleeves rolled up, who held out his right hand to me.

"Miss Shimura. I've been expecting you. I'm Jim Renseleer, the vice consul. I'm going to walk you through the passport replacement process, and then I'll bring you on to your next meeting."

Shaking his hand, I said, "I don't actually need a new passport. I'm really here about—money."

"But you didn't have your passport at the gate."

"I couldn't bring it with me this morning." I wished I could say more, pour out my nightmarish last twenty-four hours to this concerned-looking man, but I knew that I should not.

"All right, then. There's an army officer here on temporary duty who wants to see you. I believe she'll be handling whatever transaction the State Department has decided is appropriate."

He was suspicious of me, I thought, as he led me down a gray-carpeted hallway. I knew that I was a contradiction in terms: the American citizen who looked Japanese, the person without a passport who didn't want a new one but simply wanted money.

"Here you go. Good luck." He opened the door to a conference room crowded with desks and computers. I stopped at the threshold and gaped at the officer who was sitting at the conference table.

The woman at the table had tawny skin, hazel eyes, and a commanding manner. This time, she was out of uniform and in a plain blue suit, but I would have known Brenda Martin anywhere.

The colonel inclined her head at me. "Good morning, Ms. Shimura. I see our receptionist hasn't gotten you coffee yet. How do you like it?"

I remembered our first meeting, when I'd arrived dressed well enough, but wrecked from my night at Club Paradise—I'd sensed she could tell. Today I'd again had a hard night, and I was wearing wretched, filthy clothing. Did I need coffee? Incredibly. But I was not about to admit I was collapsing.

"Oh, that's okay. I don't need any coffee."

"Here, sit down." She motioned to a chair pulled up on the other side of her desk. "You look exhausted. Michael said you've been through a lot in the last few days."

I wanted to change the subject. "Do you work in Tokyo now, Colonel Martin?"

"Not exactly." She sipped from her own cup of coffee. "I'm in Army intelligence, though, so I travel quite a bit. I arrived a few days ago, after I'd reviewed the evidence you sent. I'm still getting adjusted to the time—which is why I was glad you wanted to come in first thing this morning."

"I see." I shifted uneasily in my chair, knowing I should feel reassured, but feeling only more nervous.

"I have the money for you right here. Do you wish to check the amount before you go? I need you to sign a receipt for me." She slid an envelope across the polished desk, along with a thin paper slip and a pen.

"Intelligence," I said, thinking it over. "I had thought this was just—State Department stuff. Does that mean Michael's in Army intelligence, too?"

"Michael is ex-Navy, remember? And I'd rather have him discuss the specifics of his organization. But he's a good man to work with, I'll tell you that much." She smiled at me.

"Really." A chill settled over my skin, despite the warm, even heat of the building. If she wouldn't tell me, that probably meant Michael was part of the CIA. Now I thought about all the things— the monitoring that had been done for me, the ease with which an official passport had been issued, Michael's insistence on code names, the spontaneity with which he offered me a bonus.

"I love my work." Brenda looked at me intently. "I've been able to combine an interest in foreign relations with justice. And believe it or not—I got where I am starting out in a capacity similar to what you're doing now, though it was less dangerous."

"That's right. My job wasn't supposed to be dangerous at all."

Brenda lowered her voice. "I understand there has been a casualty. Michael offered you the option to go home, but said you wouldn't. We can still get you a ticket, any time you say the word."

A casualty. She made Emi's death sound like a small event in a big war. But I wasn't giving up on that war. Resolutely, I said, "I'm not going until I've accomplished what I promised."

"What if it's not here, after all? The interviews you've done so far have added to the case that the brothers are selling fraudulent merchandise, but not the original we were worried about."

"Yes, they are selling some new pieces that they're pretending are old, but why would they sell copies of stolen artworks? That would be utter insanity for their business. It would draw the police straight to them—"

"That's why our plan is to pass on what you've found out to organizations that can better investigate the complexities of suspected art theft. And as I just mentioned, you could return to the United States as early as this afternoon."

"But what about Emi's father?" I didn't mean to interrupt, but I couldn't help myself. "What did he do during his time in Turkey that got him bounced back here? And how did he get the funds for the world-class art collection in his house?"

"Even if some of his art was obtained through shady connections, it seems clear that he didn't steal any. Remember the original mission, Rei: it was to locate a stolen work of art that was taken out of Iraq. The mission was not to embarrass the Japanese government, our longtime friends who actually agreed to give you, a persona non grata, a chance to resume life on Japanese soil."

I listened to Brenda Martin's words, and I had to admit that she had a valid argument about not wanting to cause unnecessary trouble with the Japanese. But the fact remained that a Japanese man had been lying in wait for me the previous evening. I told the colonel what had happened, and my suspicions about who was behind it.

"I think I know why that incident happened," she said when I'd finished.

"Why?" I sat up straighter in my chair.

"Your experience last night came about because you blew your cover." Brenda Martin's voice was suddenly cold. "You flew to Japan in the guise of a museum consultant, but instead you turned yourself into a one-woman, legal task force asking people too many questions about drugs and their sex lives. Obviously, you teed someone off, and that individual sent an enforcer to find out who you're working for."

"I've told no one," I said.

"Good," Brenda answered. "Now, in accordance with Michael's wishes, I'm not going to try to force you to leave the country. I do think it's a good thing that you're at least going away from Tokyo for a while."

We looked at each other. I'd won the skirmish, but barely.

"Thank you," I said.

"Absolutely. That's why I'm here. Now, I understand that you have a new cellular phone?"

"I do." I patted my pocket. "One of the few things I didn't lose yesterday."

"You're lucky you got into the building; it's against the regs," she said crisply. "Let me give you a few phone numbers where you can reach me, although you should feel free to continue to call Michael. How long do you expect to be away?"

"Just a day or two." Long enough to see the potter, and have the questions answered that had been at the back of my mind.

"And during this time, may I have your word that you won't try to speak with anyone in the Japanese government, whether it's someone as lowly as a cop or as high up as a government minister?"

I nodded glumly and signed the receipt. I wanted to get out of there.

"This is the best number to call, if you want to discuss something personally with me." A long, French-manicured fingernail tapped the first number on the card. "The other ones will allow you to leave a message with a human being."

"Okay. Well, I'm actually hoping to be out of town within the next few hours—that is, if I can get a ticket—so I'd better go."

"*Gambatte*, Rei." She held out the envelope, which was still lying on the desk. "And don't forget to take the money."

It wasn't until I was in the limousine ten minutes later that I opened it and saw how much there was. A million yen—the equivalent of $10,000. And an unsigned note inside: *Michael said for you to keep the change.*

34

I'd been planning to travel to Kyushu on the bullet train, taking the whole day, but I was now rich enough to take an hour-and-a-half flight direct from Haneda Airport to Fukuoka. First, thought, I'd need my passport, and that would involve retrieving it from Yokohama. I weighed the risks of taking the train to my aunt's station and then walking to her house, but I decided that would be foolhardy.

I asked the driver to give me the name of a trusted colleague, and by the time we'd reached Angus's hotel, I'd booked my own car and driver and reserved a seat on the one o'clock flight to Fukuoka. Feeling supremely organized, I used the house phone and called from the lobby to Angus Glendinning's room.

"Hi, I'm calling up from downstairs. I just wanted to say I'm done with borrowing your driver. He's in the hotel drive, awaiting your next command."

"Command? What the hell time is it?" Angus croaked, sounding exactly like his brother first thing in the morning.

"Nine-thirty. Too early, huh?"

"Christ, I'm exhausted. Your cousin's a madwoman. Kept me up all night."

"Really?" I'd thought Chika was interested in Sridhar. Had she leapfrogged to Angus?

"Yeah." Angus laughed richly. "She just, like, wanted to give us all Japanese lessons all night to make a good impression on TV today."

"That's right, your chauffeur said that you need to be at TBS at eleven for an interview," I said, vastly relieved that all he was talking about were language lessons.

"There's still time. Come up for a coffee or something. Chika made it already."

My second offer of coffee this morning—and this one was worth taking up, I decided. I hadn't had any time to catch up with Angus, and now he was fully available and sober. I thanked him for the invitation and rode the elevator up to the tenth floor. Outside Angus's room, the *Japan Times,* the *Asahi Shimbun,* and a Japanese tabloid popular with male readers, *Tokyo Supootsu,* lay waiting. I picked them up to bring in before I knocked.

Angus answered, half-dressed in a hotel towel and with wet red hair standing on end.

"You must have just gotten out of the shower," I said, feeling shy in the presence of all that Glendinning skin. "I'm sorry to have come this early. Shall I leave and give you time to dress?"

"Why so formal?" Angus said, imitating Hugh's upper-crust Edinburgh drawl. "Come in, darling. You look like you could use wee kip on the sofa."

I put the paper down on the coffee table in front of a cheerful striped sofa. The Roppongi Lily was a decent hotel, not as luxurious as the Grand Hyatt, but with Western amenities like the sofa, a desk with cables for a laptop, and a double bed. I looked for evidence that two pillows had been used by two people, but there was no way to tell. All the pillows were on the floor.

I looked around for Chika. "Where's my cousin?"

Angus yawned. "Off to work, Sridhar said. But she was good enough to spirit herself around and make everyone's coffee."

As I poured cream in my own cup of coffee, I pondered the meaning of Angus's statement, which seemed to suggest that Chika had slept in Sridhar's room. Well, I liked the prospect of Chika with Sridhar more than the thought of her with Angus.

"I'll take another cup, Rei. Make mine black as your beautiful hair," Angus called. He'd slipped on his jeans while I'd been fixing my cup, and he was now lounging on the sofa, leafing through the newspaper.

I took him the black coffee, figuring it was the least I could do after borrowing his car. And I wanted to use his bathroom, too. "Do you mind if I spend a few minutes freshening up?"

In the bathroom mirror, I evaluated myself. Not pretty at all, even after I'd washed my face. I was still wearing the same bedraggled clothes as the day before—and my hair was so awful. I was an ugly, easy mark for the cop who'd stalked me. And where was the policeman from hell today—still looking for me?

I scrutinized Angus's many grooming aids tossed across the vanity table. There was a surprising amount of makeup to play with, and a bottle of temporary hair coloring. The shade was flame red.

I stuck my head out of the door and called, "Angus, do you mind if I try out your hair color?"

Angus was on the phone, talking with someone. "Yeah, yeah, tonight's great," he said, not noticing me.

I waved and held up the bottle questioningly. Angus smiled. I decided to take this as a yes. Besides, it was an economy-size bottle; there'd be plenty left over for him.

I read the instructions quickly. The redness achieved would vary, depending on one's original hair color and the amount of time the dye was left on. Black hair, I figured, would fall at the longer end of the waiting time. I washed my hair in the sink with Angus's Aveda shampoo, and then applied the color, using the provided plastic comb to distribute it evenly. Then, I donned a little shower cap—it amused me to imagine the macho Angus wearing this item—and waved a blow-dryer around my head. This wasn't part of the instructions, but I remembered my mother sitting under a giant bubble dryer when she had her blonding treatments. Heat could only help speed the process or intensify the color.

I thought about asking Angus—after all, he was the expert at this—so I turned off the dryer, adjusted the towel I was wearing around my shoulders to protect my sweater, and went back into the bedroom.

Sridhar, dressed in drawstring pants and a striped turtleneck, had joined Angus and had his own copy of *Tokyo Supootsu* in hand. When he saw me peep out, his eyes widened.

"Excuse the shower cap, I'm just working on restyling my look." I winked at him.

"Is it—because of the picture?"

"What picture?" Angus asked from his lazy perch on the couch.

"Chika saw it while she was riding the train. She called to warn us," Sridhar told Angus in a low, angry voice.

"So someone snapped a picture of us behaving badly last night?" Angus laughed lazily. "Well done. The timing's great, with the TV bit about to happen—"

"That's right," I chimed in. "People say that there's no such thing as bad publicity. How much trouble did you boys get into, after we parted last night?"

"We weren't the problem," Sridhar said, staring at me in a way that seemed almost reproachful. "You were."

"Oh," I said, starting to feel worried. If my face was in the paper, it would probably fan the flame of the man who was chasing me, and any of his colleagues as well. But who would have photographed me? "Did somebody take a picture of us standing around that poor girl who was passed out on the street?"

"I can't believe you haven't guessed." Sridhar's tone had turned from cool to frigid.

"I don't want to guess. Let me see!" Suddenly, I was frantic.

"Yeah, where's the infamous snap?" Angus was rummaging through his own copy, a perplexed look on his face. Apparently he hadn't known that in Japan, the back page of the paper is the front.

"Page three," I said, feeling dead. "That's usually where the scandal stories and photos are placed."

"Bingo," Angus said as I leaned in to inspect the close-up black-and-white photo of a man and woman.

It was bad. The couple in the picture were Takeo Kayama and my-self, at the very moment at which Takeo had tripped toward the duck pond and I'd attempted to stop him and wound up in the water, too. The photographer had captured the two of us in each other's arms, laughing, and improbably surrounded by fluttering ducks. I didn't have enough time to decipher all the writing underneath, but I did make out my name and Takeo's, both spelled correctly.

"Who's the arsehole?" Angus finally said.

"His name is Takeo Kayama. He's an old friend."

"A boyfriend, according to the papers," Sridhar chimed in. "Son of the eighth richest man in Japan, who only the day before was mourning the death of his fiancée."

"I didn't know you could read Japanese," I said.

"I can't!" Sridhar retorted. "Chika translated the story for me over the phone."

"I had no idea someone was watching us with a camera," I said. "If only they'd come up and asked for an interview, I could have easily explained. We weren't hugging. It was actually an accident— he, we, fell into the pond. The ducks took off because of a light— damn it, that probably was the first camera flash! I remember more light going off when we were in the water, but I just didn't make the connection."

"Why were you having a walkie-walk by a duck pond with a guy who just lost his fiancée?" Angus demanded. "You're making a bloody fool of my brother, not to mention yourself."

"Takeo needed help, Angus. I'd just gone there to help him. And this picture—well, it will be even worse for him than me, if you can believe it." I put my face in my hands, wishing everything would go away.

"Go on, hide your face!" said Sridhar. "I would too if I committed such a devious deception!"

"The way Hugh talked about you to us . . ." Angus drifted off, sounding heartbroken. "He loved you more than life itself, and I know he thought you were going to Japan to work, not to become a total slapper!"

I looked at both of them, knowing the worst part was that I couldn't protest. There had been a one-night stand, and that was essentially the same thing as an affair. I stood up and attempted a wry half smile. "I never thought I'd get a moral lecture from two guys in a rock band. *Sumimasen*. I'll just get this crap out of my hair and I'll leave."

"So, where are you going?" Angus asked. "To this Takeo dude?"

I wiped away a bit of the foamy substance that had dripped underneath the shower cap onto my forehead. "No, I'm actually leaving town for a while. This kind of—misunderstanding—and the snap judgments of people I considered my friends make me realize I'd rather not stay around. I'll—I'll just go into the bathroom and rinse this stuff out—I'm supposed to rinse it out, right?"

"Yeah," Angus answered, not even looking at me.

"So that's why you're changing your hair color." Sridhar snapped his fingers. "New bloke, new look, eh?"

"It's not because of him."

"Like I said before, I liked your hair the way it was," Angus said.

When I came out of the bathroom again, they were gone: to Sridhar's room, maybe; or to one of the other guys, I wasn't masochistic enough to hunt them down to say good-bye.

Aunt Norie silently answered the door when I rang. I'd said "*Tadaima,*" the phrase that meant, "I've returned home," but she had not answered with the corresponding "*Okaeri nasai.*" I was not welcome. My suitcase had been packed and was standing next to the front door.

"You changed your hair color," my aunt said dully. It figured that even if she didn't want to talk to me, she couldn't resist criticizing my appearance.

"I did it because of the man who followed me last night. It's supposed to wash out after a week or two." I hadn't left the color in long enough, or combed it through right, because the end result was a horrible hodgepodge of black and red chunks.

"Oh? You mean you didn't do it because of what's in the papers and on television?"

"Obasan, please understand that Takeo and I are not in a relationship," I said, choosing my words carefully. "We had met at the park to chat and didn't know we were being followed by a paparazzo. I was trying to help Takeo when he tripped into a pond, and that's all the picture shows."

"On the TV news this morning, they called you the ducky lovers,"

Norie said, her distaste clear. "A reporter even interviewed the taxi driver who took us to Emi's memorial service. He said you and Takeo had a passionate discussion right outside the family house!"

"I didn't want to keep that driver waiting around. I knew he was a gossip—"

"Oh, don't blame him. It would come out anyway that you were the girl who was banned from Japan, the girl whose return resulted in the death of a young bride-to-be—"

"I didn't kill Emi," I said, my heart pounding. "Is that what they're saying?"

"No, but it's just a matter of time before someone asks. That policeman yesterday evening was probably genuinely looking for you to question."

"Maybe so, but I doubt it. And the truth is, through this all I was only trying to help—"

"To think that I let you convince me to arrange a meeting with Takeo-san at his office, which started all the trouble!" Aunt Norie's voice rose into hysteria. "I've already spoken with your uncle and cousin about this. I fear we'll never be received socially again, and it could affect their jobs—"

The sad thing was that she was right. "Well, there's one way Japanese people have always survived socially, when a family member misbehaves."

"I'm not going to kill myself over your—your ridiculous actions."

"Of course you won't," I said. "But you can cut me off. Disown me. Not have me as a niece anymore."

Norie blinked, and I could see tears in her eyes. "I would never do that."

"I think you should if things are as bad for you as you've just said."

"Rei-chan." My aunt took a shuddering breath and seemed to calm down slightly. "I didn't intend to speak so sharply. You are one who makes mistakes. But you weren't brought up here. There's so much we should have taught you, that we haven't done."

"It's not your fault. And I'm sorry I dragged you into the matter with Takeo." I picked up my suitcase. "Do you know if my passport's in here?"

"I double-checked that it's in the front pocket. But where are you going? Not back into Tokyo, I hope, because that's where the press is crawling, looking for another chance to catch you doing something silly."

"I'll be miles away, where nobody expects to see me," I assured her. "And when I come back, I promise that I'll figure out a way to make things right."

35

When I first visited the island of Kyushu, I was on a holiday with my parents, buying pottery. The part of the daylong train ride I remembered best was passing Mount Fuji—how the faraway snow-capped mountain grew in size as I badgered my parents about getting out to climb it. But the train raced by, Fuji was gone, and I was heartbroken. So all the time we'd been in Kyushu, wandering through tiny, one-restaurant villages that did not serve the Italian pasta I craved, I'd griped to my parents about not stopping at Fuji-san to climb it. With the typical hubris of a seven-year-old, I was certain that I could make it to the top—and I wanted the walking stick, stamped with the milestones, that each successful climber brought home.

As the All Nippon Airways jet passed near Japan's most revered landmark, the pilot encouraged us to look for it through the windows on the left side of the cabin. I strained my eyes but couldn't see Fuji. The season was cold enough for snow to have covered the mountain, making it difficult to spot against the thick white clouds that enveloped it.

I was looking for something that, just like Fuji and its cloudy cloak, was masked by cloud cover. But I was highly doubtful that my trip to Kyushu would result in a revelation. I'd meet the potter, if I was lucky, and perhaps he could tell me something about how

Mr. Harada had paid for his artwork. That's all I might gain: a little more information on how the sophisticated collector did business, a tiny glimpse through the clouds.

The touchdown in Fukuoka was smooth, and my passage through the airport was just as uneventful. Nobody was on the lookout for me here, I realized with relief as I made my connection at Hakata station to a limited express train bound for Karatsu, the famous pottery region. A train attendant hawked copies of all the national papers, including *Tokyo Supootsu*, along with little cans of coffee, beer, and *bento* box lunches, but nobody who bought a paper glanced accusingly at me.

When the attendant came to me, I bought a lunch. Quickly, I demolished the picture-book arrangement of rice, sake-glazed salmon, and pickled bamboo shoots. I'd eaten nothing until now, and so I had been dangerously nauseated on the plane. I'd survived that flight, but barely, and now I was determined to arrive in Umeda in good condition. I'd taken the time, back at the airport, to change my clothes; now I was wearing Grand's smart St. John suit, which seemed a little incongruous with my hair but was the best thing I had in my suitcase. I also had a large box of Belgian Leonidas chocolates, which I'd bought for the equivalent of $100. That's what my expense account was for: I had to present Kazu Sakurai with a valuable gift that he couldn't possibly find locally. Judging from the tourist materials I'd picked up in Fukuoka, there wasn't much shopping near Umeda. Sakurai's pottery studio was the entire shopping scene.

My phone vibrated. I picked it up reluctantly and, remembering what I knew about phone etiquette on trains, answered in a low voice.

"Rei-san! What's wrong with you?"

It was Chika.

"It's not the way it looks," I said. "And I wish you hadn't gotten the boys all upset for nothing—"

"Hugh's wonderful. How can you do such a thing to him?" Chika was crying.

"It was a picture taken out of context—"

"Lie to him, but not to me." Chika's voice was hard.

"You're as tough as your mother," I said.

"And you—you're just—American!" Chika hung up after that.

Trying to calm myself, I read the artist's brochure, which was il-lustrated with color photos and had text in English, German, and Japanese. Kazu Sakurai was the ranking descendant in a family of pottery artisans—pre-Christian potters, if one was to believe the claims in the brochure.

I was skeptical about some of what I was reading, but not all. The history of Japanese pottery, I knew from my studies, originated in Kyushu as early as 10,000 BC. Kyushu potters made cooking ves-sels and female figurines that were different from the pottery found by archaeologists in other parts of Asia. This pottery style most probably came from Mongolia; thus, the early Kyushu pottery had more in common with Middle Eastern work than with what was commonly regarded as Japanese. Sakurai, the brochure told me, had spent twenty years studying the archaeological fragments of these pots, and had experimented with firing methods. When he felt he could produce pots that were almost identical to the earliest, lost works, he produced a collection of urns that won the grand prize in Japan's foremost pottery competition. After that, he turned away from the sophisticated glazes of his father and grandfather in favor of rustic historic forms. His fame grew, and within a few years he was designated a Living National Treasure, recieving an annual stipend to pay his apprentices' salaries.

There was nothing as tacky—or helpful—as a price list in the slick brochure. I figured that if you had to ask what it cost, you clearly couldn't afford it. The brochure explained that visitors would be granted access only to the studio shop. Should someone wish an audience with the master, he or she was advised to secure an appointment.

So I needed an appointment, I thought with a sinking feeling. At least I had the benefit of a little more than $9,000 in my backpack. I hoped that I wouldn't have to blow it all. I took out my cell phone, studiously bypassing the announcement of accumulated voice mail messages from Chika, Hugh, and Michael Hendricks. They were all probably calling to criticize me for my photographed embrace with Takeo. It was the last thing I wanted to discuss in a quiet train com-partment.

A woman who sounded a good deal older than me answered the

phone. I pitched my voice into the high, polite register, saying that I was in from Tokyo and needed to see the master for guidance on choosing a piece of pottery.

"I'm very sorry, but my master is not available on short notice. However, I am happy to offer you personal assistance while you visit us. Is it a wedding gift that you seek?"

Why had she asked about a wedding? The thought of Emi and Takeo made me press my lips together. Then I remembered that I'd pitched my voice to resemble a Tokyo office lady's. She'd probably assumed that I was unmarried and had pooled resources with my colleagues to be able to afford something from a Living National Treasure.

"I'm not sure if it's going to be a present or not. But I do want to shop."

"*Ah so desu ka,*" she said gently. "Well, perhaps I can give you some ideas about what we have in your particular price range."

"Thanks. Is there anything for about fifty thousand yen?" That was just a bit less than $500, and seemed a generous starting point.

"I'm so sorry, but at that price there is only one item we have: a *hashi-oki* service for five. And it would be made by an apprentice in our workshop who is under my master's direction, but not, you understand, custom-made . . ."

I winced. She was talking about chopstick rests, little pieces of porcelain used to hold the business end of chopsticks during a meal. "Did I say fifty thousand? I meant to say five hundred thousand."

"Oh." She laughed lightly. "In that case, you have another choice. We have at the moment a set of teacups made in the ancient style. And if you have a bit more flexibility in price, you will have the chance to commission something specially, though you said you needed to buy quickly."

"I don't know," I confessed. "What I really would like is to see what is in the studio, and humbly request your master's advice."

"Yes, I understand your wish. My master would like to meet with everyone who comes through the studio, but regrettably, in order to meet customers' deadlines he cannot do that. And since the typhoon, we have been very busy repairing the property."

"It's such a shame. I heard lovely things about the esteemed master from Harada-san, and that's why I was interested in a commission."

"Harada Kenichi-sama? The minister for the environment?" Her voice warmed.

"Yes."

"Ah, he is a very special friend to the studio. I think—my master may want to send his greetings to him. Your name is . . ."

"Matsuda Reiko," I said sweetly, taking the name from a real estate ad pasted near the train's ceiling. Matsuda was a very common name; if word of my visit reached Mr. Harada, he would probably scratch his head and remember a Matsuda from somewhere.

"Matsuda-san, we are delighted to hear from a friend of our honorable customer. I am Sakurai Nobuko. I apologize for not introducing myself earlier."

The potter's wife? I sucked in my breath because all through the conversation, I'd thought she was some kind of employee. Nobuko Sakurai had consistently referred to her husband with the feudal term *danna-sama*, which literally meant "master," and that could have been a term used by an employee instead of a wife. I understand now what people had told me about southern Japan—it was more antiquated than anywhere else in the country. In fact, as the train had passed the gardens of small houses, I'd seen men's and women's clothes hung on separate lines, something I'd heard was done so that the male garments would avoid contagion from the inferior female clothing.

"Well, I must prepare something for you to bring to Harada-san," Mrs. Sakurai said. "At what time would you like to visit the studio?"

I looked at my watch. "I'm about two hours away. Would a four o'clock visit be inconvenient, though?"

"Oh, no. Four is usually the time for our tea break, anyway. You must join us."

After hanging up, I tried to put my worries aside for a few minutes and take in Kyushu, one of Japan's most famously beautiful islands. It had been devastated by the typhoon, even in the inland area where we were traveling. Citrus groves were littered with fallen *mikan* tangerines, and the rice paddies were brimming with muddy brown water. Almost every tiled roof had large blocks missing, and downed power lines were everywhere. The damage here, while similar to what I'd seen in Tokyo and Hayama, was worse for the local residents because so many of them were farmers. Mrs. Sakurai had said the pottery studio had suffered damage, too. No wonder she had warmed up when I'd talked about spending half a million yen. Visitors to Kyushu would be fewer, and times harder, in the winter ahead.

The stationmaster at the closest town to Umeda advised me to take the number 8 bus, which was just about to depart, so I did. Once aboard, I thought about whether I should have taken a taxi; I had the funds. No, I thought, taxi drivers talked. Taking the bus would make me less memorable. I'd already begun to regret dyeing my hair, because while the streaky look was common in Tokyo, it wasn't in the village of Kyushu.

"This is the stop for Umeda. Please don't forget your things," a recorded female voice said from the bus's loudspeaker. I decided I'd better get out, because it looked as if the town was essentially a single road, spanned by a few shops. I stepped off the bus with my suitcase, and my feet crunched into something. I looked down. Pots. Everywhere, the earth was mixed with the shards of *kuromon*, as black pottery was called in this community. It wasn't new pots that had been lost in the typhoon, I realized; those shattered urns were close to the houses, where I could see they'd held things like farm tools, umbrellas, or plants. What lay underneath me, I thought with a thrill, was the town's centuries of life as a pottery village.

I raised my eyes a bit higher and started scanning the houses for something that looked like the studio. From the brochure, I knew it was located on this road, about an eighth of a mile away. Vacant, overgrown fields stood on either side of the houses; here, undeveloped space—which was a luxury in most of Japan—was running rampant with weeds. I'd seen very few people as I'd walked, just an old grandmother in baggy *monpe* work trousers pushing a wheelbarrow packed with freshly pulled *daikon*. She'd offered me a bag to take back to the city as a souvenir, and I'd been caught un-prepared. People didn't usually solicit that way in Tokyo, and I was unsure what the right, unmemorable response should be. In the end, I agreed to take a 500-yen portion, which I hoped would make her think favorably of me, though I had no intention of taking them back to the city.

"Are you going to see Sakurai-san's studio?" the woman said while tucking the coin I'd given her into her blouse. I'd nodded, and left it at that. It made sense; the only reason anyone from far away would come to this one-street town would be for a glimpse of the Living National Treasure.

Sakurai's studio was marked only by the *kanji* characters making up his name, placed on the wall surrounding the house, which looked to me like a typical middle-class tiled-roof house—except that many tiles were missing. They lay haphazardly scattered around the gar-den. As I approached the door, I realized that a thick black snake was lying in front of the steps. I halted, wondering how in the world I could bring myself to step over it.

As I stood deliberating, a young man with a rakish hairstyle, baggy jeans, and a black sweater turned the corner with a wheel-barrow of his own; it was filled with broken tiles and debris. The apprentice, I guessed.

"Good day. Excuse me, but are you Miss Matsuda?" he asked. His accent was different from the Kyushu dialect I'd heard spoken in the train station and aboard the bus. He was probably a trans-plant like myself.

When I nodded, he bowed. "The master is expecting you. How was your journey? You must be very tired."

"Yes. I mean, no. It's just—" I gestured toward the snake.

"Oh, I'm sorry! In Kyushu, these snakes are everywhere. So an-noying." He rolled his wheelbarrow toward the snake, and I caught my breath. Was he going to run over it?

That turned out not to be the case; the snake raised its head and slithered off into the bushes.

I gave a sigh. "Thank you."

"There's a peaceful way to do everything, the master says."

I smiled and said, "This is turning out to be a very exciting day."

"It is also an excitement for us. When one of Harada-san's friends comes to call, it is a special opportunity indeed," the apprentice said effusively.

"Oh, please don't say that, I'm getting embarrassed." I paused, thinking about the meaning of his statement. "Actually, have many of his friends come before?"

"Yes, he's sent us several friends from around the world who became customers."

The young man opened the front door, ceremoniously standing back so that I could be the first one in. A slender woman in her sixties dressed in a simple wool sweater and skirt appeared and sank to her knees, pressing her forehead to the polished pine floor.

"Welcome to our humble studio. I am Sakurai Nobuko." Mrs. Sakurai was smiling, causing her wrinkles to stand out in deep relief. Despite her fine clothes, I could see evidence of the years, and the environment, in her face. She looked like someone who had worked, and lived, hard.

I knew I wasn't supposed to reciprocate as dramatically, so I just gave the deepest possible standing bow, such as a disgraced executive would make at a press conference, and murmured my name and my apologies for disturbing her. When I stood up, I saw that she'd been staring at my hair.

I pretended not to notice. "I'm sorry to have disturbed you so much. I don't suppose that it is still possible for me to see the master?"

"Yes, yes, he's just finishing up at the wheel. I apologize for his lateness."

This was all very confusing to me, the fact that a Living National Treasure and his wife would be so obsequious to a stranger with some, but not much, money to spend. Maybe in Kyushu, the strong Japanese tradition of hospitality was even stronger. Or, I realized, it could boil down to simple Japanese reasoning: if the Sakurais gave excessively to me, I would have to outdo them. As I followed her into the studio, I wondered how much Mr. Harada's other international friends—perhaps even the Birand brothers—had spent.

36

I'd been expecting a luxuriously appointed shop, but the studio was more akin to a Japanese home. An idealized Japanese home, of course—a room large enough for fourteen tatami mats, its expanse of grass-covered flooring broken only by a low *kotatsu* table and three *zabuton* cushions covered in Kyushu indigo cotton. The only way you could tell it was not a typical tidy reception room was that the *tokonoma* alcove held a statuesque greenish brown *ikebana* vase that in turn was holding a branch of *mikan*, to which a few tangerines elegantly clung. The shoji doors were open to the garden, which was the only source of light in the semidarkened room.

Mrs. Sakurai followed the direction of my interest. "We lost our tree in the storm."

"I'm sorry to hear that, but you've made a lovely, spare arrangement. Have you studied *ikebana*?" I asked.

She laughed, putting a hand over her mouth. "No, I never had that kind of time. I've spent my life helping the master. There has never been time for flower studies." She paused. "Harada-san's daughter, she will marry a flower master soon, *neh*?"

Her words confirmed my thought that the Sakurais must not have learned about Emi's death. The remoteness of Kyushu from Tokyo—not to mention the loss of television during the electric outages—made that likely. Certainly national newspapers were available at the next town over, but there hadn't even been a convenience store in Umeda—and who had the time to sit and read newspapers when there were pots to be shaped, a roof to be retiled, and a destroyed orange tree to be disposed of?

I fretted inwardly about how I could break it to Mrs. Sakurai about the Haradas' tragedy. Then a sliding door in the back of the room moved and the gray-haired master entered, his shoulders slightly stooped under a thin burgundy sweater. He wore loose *gumue* trousers like those Takeo favored for gardening, and thick green socks with a split toe.

The simplicity of the potter should not mislead me, I reminded myself as I decided to go for broke and bow, on the floor, the way his wife had bowed to me. He was a Living National Treasure, so if I wasn't humble enough, he might be offended.

"Please, there is no need," he said gently, urging me up.

I gave my introductory greetings and offered my shopping bag, which contained the expensive chocolates.

"No, no, we cannot accept it. Please, this is too much." This time Mrs. Sakurai spoke, but as the courteous protest sprang forward, so did her slim hands. She took the bag and laid it gently to the side.

"It's just a few handmade chocolates from Belgium," I said apologetically. "Really a very small thing. I'm not sure if you like sweets."

"Oh, Belgian chocolate is very delicious. Thank you. Tell me, you must be very tired from your travel. The train takes all day, *neh*! How about some tea to restore you?"

"I flew," I said. "I took the train only from Fukuoka. I'm not tired at all. On the contrary, I'm so excited to see your great works."

"I'm terribly sorry, but there is not much here at the present moment," Mr. Sakurai said, sliding open the doors of a long cabinet set against a wall. I remembered doing the same thing at Takeo's country house, where the cabinet was neatly organized with boxed-up pottery. In the Sakurais' cabinet, extra shelves had been set in, to hold a copious amount of ceramics, all unboxed and arranged for display. Overhead were spotlights illuminating the ceramic treasures in gentle hues of green, brown, and black. Now I knew why Mrs. Sakurai had kept the room dark—to give the pottery, which itself was on the dark side, an almost magical glow, once the cupboard was opened.

No price tags, I thought, as my gaze ran over the breathtakingly simple plates, teacups, bowls, and vases. I saw the snake from the garden reincarnated in a *choka* or spouted sake ewer, which had an applied clay pattern of a snake curling up the side that formed a handle. It was too big for me to take home, let alone afford, but I thought I'd ask him about it.

"That we call *haritsuke*," he said. "It's an old method that had almost vanished from use among today's potters."

I knew from my own studies that *haritsuke* was a technique popular from the 1700s through the mid-nineteenth century, but I asked a question about its age so that I could lead into my next query. "So, what do you think about this controversy that the earliest potters in Kyushu were not Japanese at all?"

"Well, of course the Koreans were brought here from the 1600s onward," he said. "But there are some of us who were here much earlier. It's not a legend, but reality."

"That makes sense. I heard there is more in common with Middle Eastern pottery than Asian," I said. "That *haritsuke* technique—I feel as if I've seen examples of similar work in ancient Near Eastern pottery."

He nodded, smiling. "You're right. And I recently had the opportunity to explore more ways to work with *haritsuke*. If you're interested, I can show you some smaller examples for sale."

He disappeared from the room and came back with a box, which he set on the table. I sat down across from him and watched him open it. There, against a padded backing of brown silk, were the chopstick rests—five little brownish gray eels upon which one could set down dining implements. I found myself looking away from them immediately, and forced myself to concentrate. What was my problem? I realized that because these eels were so small, they were closer to looking like worms. Five hundred dollars for wormy chopstick rests; I tried not to recoil.

"How charming," I said, then wanted to bite my tongue for using a word they might find patronizing. It felt so odd to me to play the role of a dressed-up person with money; I was always on the other side. "I would like to buy something a bit larger, if it's possible. Your wife had mentioned teacups."

"Yes, I think we still have the set of cups. I'm slow." He gave a slight, self-deprecating smile. "You know, it takes about a full week for me to make a set. That's why there isn't much for sale. But I do have these."

The next box he opened held five cups, all of the lovely, brownish green color that came from skipping the bisque stage before the pot was fired in a wood-burning kiln. It was another historic method come back to life in Sakurai-san's weathered, skilled palms.

"Please hold them, if you like," he urged, and I put a hand out toward the box, silently praying that I wouldn't do anything as stupid as dropping a thousand-dollar teacup on the polished *keyaki* wood table. The feeling, in my hand, was good—oddly familiar, though. I studied the almost invisible whorls on the piece, thinking. Then I turned the cup over and saw the little indentation I'd seen on his bowl at the Haradas' home, and on the ibex ewer.

"You must hold them all. See what you think, please."

He wanted me to buy them, I thought as I put the first cup down and picked up the second. Now I knew he was complicit in Mr. Harada's deception. What to do?

I glanced away from the cups and saw that Mrs. Sakurai had come back holding an earthenware teapot and teacups similar to the one I was holding.

"I'm sorry. Shall I wait to serve the tea?" Her voice was apologetic.

"Please, I wish you hadn't gone to the trouble for me," I said. Secretly, I was glad to see her. I needed a break before I committed myself to spending thousands of dollars, and I also thought it would be advantageous to ask my questions before the deal was closed.

"She's very tired from travel. Of course she will drink tea," the master said. "Why did you take so long to prepare the tea?"

"So, please tell us the news of Harada-san and his family," Mrs. Sakurai said.

I couldn't keep going any longer. In a low voice, I said, "I apologize for the sad news I must bring you. Last week, his daughter passed away."

"Oh, dear," Mr. Sakurai said softly. He dropped his head for a minute, as if praying. Then he looked up at me again. "I'm so sorry. I didn't know. Please tell us about the situation."

"It seems impossible. She was such a young girl, about to become a bride—" Mrs. Sakurai choked and set down, on the tray, the cup of tea she'd been pouring for her husband.

"So you met her, then?" I asked.

"Oh, yes. Her whole family came last spring to see about having the groom's gift made," Mrs. Sakurai said. "Emi-san was such a lovely young girl, so slim and with so much energy, yet complete refinement—just what you'd expect from an ambassador's daughter. If I may be so bold to ask . . . what happened?"

"She was in a car accident," I said. "The street signals were out because of the typhoon."

"A car accident," Sakurai said, his voice heavy. "Life can be taken away, just like that. Having children ourselves, we can imagine her parents' grief."

"They drove to see us that last time, remember?" Mrs. Sakurai said. "Emi-san was their only child. I remember Harada-san's wife saying that she wasn't sure she was ready to let her daughter go. I told her that she would be young enough to enjoy her grandchildren. I shouldn't have tempted fate with my words."

"I'm sure you didn't do that. I am truly sorry to have brought you such bad news," I said.

"No, please don't worry. You came here for other reasons, happier reasons, and we asked you about Harada-san. We are distracting you with our grief! I apologize." Mrs. Sakurai bowed her head.

No, I thought with a mixture of chagrin and hardness, they were not distracting me. They were clearing the way for me to ask what I needed to ask. "You mentioned that they commissioned a groom's gift. Was it a set of cups similar to these?" Ever since I'd seen the cups, I'd had a suspicion they were an order for someone that hadn't come to fruition.

"No, it was something not so Japanese," Mr. Sakurai said. "A kind of *choka* using the *haritsuke* technique I mentioned."

"A *choka*?" I repeated. He had used a word for a spouted vessel for liquid, such as a ewer.

"Yes, a *choka*." Mr. Sakurai shook his head sorrowfully. "I completed it in the spring, in time for the engagement ceremony."

"I wonder if I've seen it," I said carefully. "Does it resemble a goat, by any chance?"

"Why, yes." Mr. Sakurai looked surprised, but nodded. "I didn't know anyone would recognize it as my work, because Harada-san was quite specific about my following the model of an existing ancient piece. I don't usually do that kind of thing, but, well, he is a very special customer."

"I think I saw it in a magazine," I said. *Special customer* might mean that Mr. Sakurai would call Mr. Harada after I left, raising his suspicions. "So, ah, do you still have the original model here?"

"No. Mr. Harada took it with him when he picked up his *choka*." Mr. Sakurai cocked his head at me, the grief he'd shown earlier replaced by a wary interest. "I wish I could show you a photograph . . . but Harada-san requested that I not photograph it for my artist's record. I agreed because the piece was not an original design."

"Speaking of original designs, I am quite enthralled by the set of cups you showed me. Are they really available for sale?" I decided to swing back into consumer mode, to allay any suspicions that might be forming.

"Of course. I mentioned them to you on the telephone."

"I would like to buy them." It was part of my cover—and now I had hard evidence of where Takeo's ibex ewer had come from.

"I am honored by your choice." Mr. Sakurai bowed his head, and so did his wife.

Feeling completely awkward when they faced me again, I said, "Will it be possible to arrange the details this afternoon?"

"Of course. Matsuda-san, are you returning home this evening?" Mrs. Sakurai inquired.

"I hadn't anticipated finding a perfect set of cups like this, so I didn't book a flight. And it's quite far back to Fukuoka—I don't think I could make a connection, even if I left now."

"Flying is convenient," Mrs. Sakurai said. "Harada-san usually flew to see us, but the last two visits he drove."

He drove. Had he been worried that airport luggage inspectors would come across the ibex vessel as he brought it to Kyushu and then carried it back? Why didn't he take the train instead? Driving seemed hard—but it might have been the method for someone who didn't want to be noticed.

"In case I can't catch my flight this evening, can you recommend a nice place to stay?" I asked, changing the topic.

"Oh, please stay with us. It's very humble here, but we would be honored . . ."

Ordinarily, I'd have delighted in the opportunity to spend a night under the same roof as a master potter and his wife, but not tonight. "Oh, I wouldn't dream of inconveniencing you. I wonder if you know where Harada-san liked to stay, while he was in the area . . ."

"I really don't know. The last time he was headed for his country house, wasn't he?" Mrs. Sakurai turned to her husband with a questioning look.

His country house. Something Ramzi had said came back to me. Emi had promised him that they'd have time together at the country house after her marriage. I'd thought it was Takeo's place, but maybe it was somewhere completely different.

Mr. Sakurai broke into my thoughts. "So, how did you say you knew Harada-san? Is it because of your husband, or . . ."

Husband? I wore no ring. Was it the fact that they thought no woman my age would still be single? I would have to go for something vague. I just said, "That's right."

"Ah, another diplomatic couple. I noticed your accent was different, and you have that special hairstyle. You must have been to so many interesting countries!" Mrs. Sakurai smiled at me.

"Matsuda-san, forgive me, but I must return to the wheel in my pottery." Mr. Sakurai stood up. "My wife can help you with the necessary details for the teacups. I hope you enjoy the efforts of my poor labor."

I bowed and murmured my thanks, wondering how the payment process should go. As Mrs. Sakurai carefully wrapped the box containing the cups in three layers of handmade *washi* paper, I realized that the rectangular plate next to the wrapping table was where I should lay my payment. I laid down the equivalent of

$6,000, allowing for the tax. After she finished the wrapping, she excused herself, taking the tray into the next room. She came back with some change and a receipt, which I slid into my wallet with some relief. A thousand dollars for a teacup—I almost felt that I was getting a bargain.

37

There really was no chance of leaving Kyushu that night. My suspicions about the length of the trip were confirmed when the local bus finally got me to the nearest train station, and I realized there was an hour's wait for the next limited express train to Fukuoka. The agent for All Nippon Airways said that the final plane to Tokyo left Fukuoka around seven. Given that I'd be getting to Fukuoka around nine, the agent offered to make a reservation for me at the ANA hotel. I told her I'd decide on hotels when I arrived and make the reservation myself. Actually, I planned to use a different name and stay at a different hotel, paying cash to protect my anonymity.

I checked my watch again and bought a can of hot Georgia Coffee from the station's vending machine. As I sipped, I congratulated myself for seeking out the Sakurais. What I'd learned about Kenichi Harada commissioning a reproduction of the ibex vessel had been fascinating. But it still left a question—why had he done it? Takeo had said that he'd been given the vessel—the fake one, though he didn't know it—after he'd admired Mr. Harada's possession. But why hadn't Mr. Harada given him the real thing—especially if the piece was going to stay in the family?

I drank more coffee, and as the caffeine shot through me, so did a new idea. Mr. Harada might have felt that he should not burden his future son-in-law with an illegal piece. On the other hand, he obviously knew he was in possession of a priceless artwork, and he simply might not have wanted to give it up. Famous artworks that were stolen had to remain under wraps; they were too well known to be sold, and they usually remained in the original thief's hands or were traded to another underworld figure.

And as far as the underworld went, I'd always assumed that Mr. Harada was a customer—but maybe he had played a more active role. He was a diplomat who'd traveled freely through the Middle East before the war, and because of his status, he was probably exempted from luggage screening more rigorous than the basic security X-ray.

I looked around the station and spotted a deserted row of seats. I sat down, took my cell phone out of my backpack, and punched in Takeo's private number.

"It's me. Can you talk?" I asked when he picked up.

"Yes, if I can fit you in between TBS and NHK and the other news organizations I never knew existed! Have you been busy, too?"

"Not that way. Nobody knows where I am."

"Well, where are you?" He sounded impatient.

"In southwestern Kyushu."

"Oh! So you've run away. I wish I could do that."

"Takeo, I need to ask you something. Did you ever go to Emi's family's summer house?"

"Twice. Why?"

"Do you remember the address?"

"Certainly. If you went all the way to Kyushu to find it, you're in the wrong place. The house is on the Izu Peninsula, about an hour and a half from Tokyo."

If Mr. Harada had driven all the way from Kyushu to Izu, perhaps it was because he didn't want the vessel to be noticed by the airport security staff—since now that he was a government minister, he wouldn't have the blessing of diplomatic clearances anymore. Why he hadn't used the train seemed mysterious, though. Maybe he just didn't want to be noticed, especially if the country house was where the vessel wound up. I asked Takeo if this was the place where he'd first laid eyes on the vessel.

"Yes, but—Rei, you're not thinking of breaking in, are you?"

"Of course not. But I would greatly appreciate learning the address from you."

"I don't believe it! You're up to the same business as when you came to my house during the storm."

"I'm sorry, Takeo. But if you let me know about this place, I might be able to do something that—shifts attention from you, and the whole horrible misunderstanding may resolve."

"How will it shift attention from me if you get caught as a burglar again? There's high security at the place—it's not like my country house."

High security, because there had to be priceless treasures within. Things were coming together in my mind. Knowing what Takeo had told me, I wouldn't go inside, but I'd feel I'd done all I could if I could give the address to Brenda and Michael quickly and let them get a search warrant. Now there was enough information to get a warrant, I was almost certain. But I couldn't tell Takeo about my plan.

"Takeo, please. Just tell me the name of the town. You won't be implicated for helping me in any way, if you just tell me that—I can do the rest."

"No, I won't."

"You just care about yourself, don't you?" I said, utterly frustrated.

"No." His voice cracked. "It's because I still care about you that I won't tell. Can't you understand?"

Takeo hung up, and I sat there with the phone in my hand, watching the crowd of people across the room board the train. The train. It was finally here.

I grabbed my carry-on suitcase and made it onboard just before the conductor blew the whistle.

By the time I got into Fukuoka, the moon was high. I was starving, so I stopped at a little ramen shop for a bowl of steaming noodles topped with a raw egg. Moon-viewing noodles, they were called. The egg cooked slowly atop the noodles, and I ate slowly, savoring the rich taste of the noodles, the broth, everything. Then I felt fortified enough to search for a hotel. I wanted a place where I would be totally anonymous, where no desk clerk would look at me or ask for identification or a credit card. The obvious answer was to stay at a love hotel, where check-in was self-service, in a curtained booth.

I'd stayed in a love hotel once with Hugh, but never with Takeo. Takeo was far too dignified for pop-culture sleaze. Tonight, I chose Love Palace, a hotel in the form of a Gothic castle. I knew that there was still a vacancy because not all the twinkling exterior lights were turned on. I walked quickly into the lonely lobby and then into the check-in booth, drawing the curtain. I realized that I was embarrassed, not just because I might be recognized, but because it was a sorry situation to be checking into a love hotel all by oneself. Still, once I had followed the blinking lights that lit up on the carpet and directed me to my room, I decided that I'd made a very good choice. The room was almost as large as my space at the Hyatt, and the bed was huge and had fresh linens. As I was unpacking my bags, the cell phone rang and I snatched it up.

"Rei." The voice was husky, full of pain, and maybe slurred with alcohol. Hugh's voice.

"Oh!" I dropped the phone in surprise, but it just landed softly on the bed.

"Where are you?" he asked.

"A love hotel," I blurted, before realizing the implication. "I was just looking for a cheap, quiet place to spend the night. I'm actually alone—"

"I'm sure not for long," Hugh said darkly.

"You must have heard from Angus?"

"Yes. But I already knew the worst. I read the Japanese news on-line, Rei, and when I Googled your name it led me to a site with scandal pictures—and I saw it there."

"You would Google the woman you love, rather than just ask her what's going on?"

"Well, that's why I called you, actually. To ask." Hugh's voice dripped with politeness. "Did you shag him?"

I sucked in my breath, shocked at the hardness of his language. But I couldn't lie, not for another moment. "Just once. And I'm sorry."

"Christ." Hugh was silent for a minute. "I don't—I can't believe it. You betrayed me."

"You must understand that I didn't go to Japan for that purpose—it was a terrible mistake—"

"You're asking me to *understand*?"

"It was a mistake!" I repeated. "That picture doesn't express any kind of intimacy that continued after—the incident, which was really just a one-night stand. In the picture at the pond, it was an accident, I was just trying to help him out—"

"I'm sure you helped him very nicely. And now, Rei, I'm off to work, where I'll be sitting down with people who actually need my help, and whom I can count on to behave like decent human beings."

For the second time that day, a man hung up on me.

After I was done crying, I splashed my face with water and looked at myself in the bathroom's tiny mirror, which had illuminated cherub light fixtures.

There was one last person I could call, someone whom I was reasonably sure would not hang up on me when he heard what I wanted from him.

I dialed Ramzi Birand.

38

It was noon when I'd transferred from Haneda Airport to Tokyo Station, where I'd promised to meet Ramzi outside the Japan Railway ticket office. However, I found him in a different spot, leaning against a pole plastered with ads for a loan shark agency. It was a wonder I located him. I'd just left my carry-on and the teacups in a storage locker, then paused to scrutinize the tomato and carrot sandwiches at Vegetaria, and it was there, when I was peering into the distance, that I saw him. Despite the crowding at the station, there was space around him, the usual arm's length Japanese commuters gave a foreign man, even a good-looking one with dark curly hair, a modish peacoat, and flared jeans.

"Let me buy your ticket," I said after I'd greeted him and thanked him for meeting me. After the way we'd left things, I wasn't even sure he'd be willing to give me the address of the country house. It turned out that Emi had taken him by train, and while he thought he could retrace their steps, he couldn't give me an exact address. Ramzi knew nothing of *kanji* or even the easy *hiragana* alphabet; it was a wonder to me that he'd made it through a semester at Waseda. But then again, he was planning to drop out.

"How do you know which platform is correct, when there are so many?" Ramzi asked in frustration as I led him two platforms over to the place from which the Odoriko limited express trains departed.

"I studied the big map by the ticket machines. You know, the map that looks like a lot of colored spaghetti?"

"Your hair looks like spaghetti," he said, looking me over.

"It's a change of pace," I said. My whole look was different. Back in Fukuoka, I'd had an hour to search the teen boutiques and put together my own version of the Lolita look. I bought a short red pleated skirt, blue-and-yellow striped tights, a yellow sweater with a Doraemon appliqué, and Minnie Mouse barrettes that I'd used to randomly clip strands of my multicolored hair. The salesgirl loved the look. If this was what twenty was supposed to look like, I thought as I surveyed myself in the dressing room mirror, I was actually glad to be ten years older.

The change of costume had been inspired by my conversation at six in the morning with Brenda Martin, whom I'd phoned out of a sense of duty.

"Why go all the way to Izu? You could just give me the address," she'd said immediately.

"My contact doesn't know an exact address, but he thinks he can show me the way. Then I'll share the address with you." I tried to sound more confident than I felt.

"And who is this contact?"

"It's nobody in the government, okay?"

"Who is it?" she repeated.

I hesitated before answering. "Ramzi Birand."

"Do you mean Emi's ex-boyfriend, with whom you made contact two days ago?"

"Yes. He went there a few times with her, and he's willing to show me the place. As I mentioned earlier, all things are pointing toward the original ewer being there."

"I'm concerned that this is too high a risk," Brenda said. "Especially since your face has been in the newspaper and on TV. How can you expect to do anything anonymously?"

"I already changed my hair—I'll change more. And Michael didn't think it was a bad idea." The fact was that he hadn't said it was a good idea, either. He'd just told me not to go into the house, and I'd agreed.

"I'm going to call over to him now to get his take on it, because it sounds risky to me. Can you wait until I get back to you?"

"It's too late. I already made my plan with Ramzi. I can't let him go out there alone."

"God help you if you're not being straight with me," she grumbled. "In any case, keep your cell phone handy."

"Come on, I'm at the end of the journey. I'm just getting the address. Then I'm out of here."

Out of here, I thought, as Ramzi and I waited for the train. In a way, I wanted out—but another side of me wanted to stay. I had wanted to visit a particular temple with Aunt Norie, and to spend hours at a Sunday morning flea market. I wouldn't get the chance to do any of this on my visit—or perhaps ever again.

"Why did you do that to yourself with those stupid clothes?" Ramzi's disapproval of my Lolita look interrupted my brief, self-pitying wallow.

"I wanted to look more your age, so people wouldn't be surprised at our traveling together." I paused.

"Emi never dressed like that."

"Well, she may have had better taste than I do. She definitely had more money." I changed the topic. "Do you see that train coming in? It's the Odoriko line. Does it look familiar to you?" I was hoping so, because there were a couple of railway lines that went to Izu, and if I got the wrong one, we would never locate the right town.

"I'm not sure—wait. Dark blue seats. Yes, I remember blue seats," he said, looking through the windows of the empty train as it rolled up to the platform.

It figured that he would remember a sensory detail and nothing else. After we settled ourselves into two velour seats in the very back—I wanted to be able to see everyone who was sitting around us—I asked him if he remembered the station where he'd disembarked in Izu. Quietly, I told him the names of the stops we had ahead.

During his time with Emi, he explained, he'd always let her be the guide. But he did have an important piece of evidence: a snapshot in his wallet of the two of them grinning, with a historic black ship in the bay behind them.

The black ship made me think of Shimoda, where the U.S. Navy commodore Matthew Perry arrived in 1853 in a black ship and demanded entry to a country that had shut out foreigners for the previous 220 years. Shimoda was the place, Ramzi said, where they'd spent an hour looking around before catching a bus for a thirty-minute ride out to the town where Emi's parents' place was. I bit my lip, thinking about how many small towns and villages there might be within half an hour of Shimoda. And who knew if he was even right about the timing of the bus ride?

Fortunately, he had correctly remembered the bus platform, near the Lawson's store next to the station. He pointed to a bus that showed its destination, Dogashima, in English.

It was ironic, I thought as we rode quietly along, both of us gazing outward, that I'd made it all the way to Shimoda, a place of historical intrigue. An American diplomat, Townsend Harris, had arrived here in 1856 to start the United States' first consulate in Japan, completely against the wishes of the Japanese. Much diplomatic wrangling followed, but what most Japanese remembered with great distaste was that Consul Harris had asked for the services of a young local woman called Okichi, who reluctantly obeyed the shogunate's request for her to become his personal maid for several years. Okichi served Harris faithfully as a nurse—and perhaps a mistress—until he retired from duty and returned to the United States, leaving her unprotected from the community's scorn. Okichi then tried to run a number of businesses, but by the time she was in her fifties, she had become an alcoholic. She finally committed suicide by drowning herself.

Shimoda had numerous memorials to Okichi in its temples and shrines, to remind everyone of the sad sacrifice made by the Japanese people to the future of international relations. I'd read the literature and thought that the real villains had been the community people who'd called Okichi a barbarian, but my sentiment wasn't shared by many. Everyone thought the tragedy was Harris's fault, for conscripting her to his service and tainting her reputation.

Foreigner's cruelty kills Japanese beauty. That was the way the story had played out 160 years ago in the Japanese popular press. Come to think of it, that headline could have been used in yesterday's tabloid.

"This is it. I remember getting a bottle of water at that machine." Ramzi pointed out the window at a Dydo soft drink machine set next to a bench.

The tape recording on the bus had announced this place as Osawa Onsen, where there was a hot spring.

"Did she ever speak to you of the town being called Osawa?" I pushed the stop signal as I spoke.

"I'm not sure." He frowned. "I'm sorry. I think I heard that word somewhere. Is that this town's name?" He squinted at the station sign, which was written in *hiragana*.

"Let's jump off. We can always catch another bus, if we're wrong." I was already standing up and following a couple of backpackers who were getting off.

We paid our fares—$11 apiece for just a thirty-minute bus ride—and disembarked. The backpackers walked off, clearly following signs for a hot spring resort.

"Did you take a taxi from this point?" I asked Ramzi.

"No, we walked this way," Ramzi said, sounding confident. As we walked alongside a rice paddy and then cut through an orange grove, Ramzi explained that Emi had led him on a circuitous route so that people wouldn't talk. It was a summer house, and the Haradas weren't there very often, but still, the risk that someone would notice Emi with a boy was too great to bear.

After passing through the fields, we reached a wall at the back of a house. The wall, covered with black tiles fixed in a diamond pattern with thick white plaster, was a fortified style particular to Shimoda, to fortify its houses against strong sea winds. Over this beautiful wall a succulent vine trailed, making it picture-postcard perfect.

"This is the back of the house, I think. I'll know for certain in a minute," Ramzi said, leading me along.

"I heard there's a security system in the house," I said, eyeing the wall with some nervousness.

"Yes, there's an alarm system, but I've got the code."

"Really? I wouldn't want to chance anything," I said. After he'd revealed his trouble remembering directions, I couldn't imagine that he'd know any code.

"No, I have it. Here, in my calendar." He patted his pocket.

"Why did you write down the code?" I asked suspiciously.

"I told you that we had plans to meet here again. It made sense for me to know."

I shook my head. "We mustn't go in. If two foreigners like us are caught—well, it could mean jail or deportation. Believe me, I have experience in these things."

"Why did you ask me to bring you here, if you didn't want to go in?" He sounded impatient.

"As I said to you on the phone, I just wanted to see the place from the outside."

"Well, I came because I plan to go inside." He scowled at me.

I hesitated. I supposed my only option was to abandon ship and not go a step farther. If Ramzi stormed the house and something went wrong, the police would come and we would both be in the soup.

"Ramzi, if you go in, it's your decision. But I'm not going to stay on the premises if you do that. I'm not willing to take the risk."

He pressed his lips together. "Then why don't you just go?"

He'd called my bluff. He knew I had to see the house. "Please, Ramzi. Let's just walk there, and I'll give you time to mourn, I really will, and then we'll go back."

"It's a left turn ahead, I think. This looks familiar."

I took the turn with him, and then he stopped. Ahead of us was an especially high wall of diamond tile, with *kanji* characters making up the name Harada on a mailbox, followed by the numbers 2-17-1 and the *kanji* for Isobe. I copied down both the *kanji* characters and my translation to call in to Brenda Martin as soon as I had some privacy, away from Ramzi.

"What are you writing?" Ramzi asked. He'd walked over to a pair of tall, iron gates that barred entrance to a long driveway disappearing into what looked like a small forest. The property was huge; I'd thought only Japanese aristocrats lived that way.

"Two-seventeen-one Isobe Street, in Osawa. That's the full address," I said, walking over to join him. "It looks like a beautiful place."

"Ten hectares of forest. Emi took me around. It's great," Ramzi muttered. Then he stepped to the right and flipped open a small box, revealing a keypad. He punched in a code, and slowly, the gates opened.

"You can't go in," I said quickly.

Ramzi turned to me. "I told you what I was going to do. Why else did you think I came here?"

As I stared at him, a sense of foreboding started to grow inside me. "Ramzi, what are you planning to do inside the house?"

"It's not your concern."

I could hardly choke out the words. "Are you thinking of . . . ending your life?"

"Suicide? I've thought of it before, yes, but not now." His manner was brisk. "I'm here to take back something that belongs to me."

"Okay, but let's—let's just wait a moment, maybe go around the corner to talk. We shouldn't just hang around right in front—" I had been thinking that the way we looked was fine for the train, but I was worried that in this exclusive neighborhood, we might attract suspicion.

"Well, if you're going, I'll just say good-bye now!" Ramzi shot over his shoulder as he walked through the open gate. I held my breath, imagining motion detectors or another force that would spring to life at Ramzi's invasion. But nothing happened. He continued up the long pebbled driveway and disappeared around a bend.

I'd thought Ramzi was helping me, but what he really wanted was an assistant of his own. Now I wondered if he was about to deface the house, or steal something from it—perhaps the ibex vessel. Ramzi had never answered me straightforwardly about whether he'd seen the piece; and now, because I'd asked about it, maybe he'd gotten an inkling of how important it was, and how its loss could devastate Emi's father.

I had promised Michael that I wouldn't go into the house, but I couldn't let Ramzi get away with the vessel. And that could be done, if there was anther exit from this large property. I picked up the cell phone and called the first number Brenda had given me, then the second. She didn't answer either. Well, so much for support. As I listened to her recorded voice tell me to leave a message, I decided against it. I'd come up with a plan.

I was going to walk onto the property, but I would wait in a hidden position outside the house, to see what Ramzi was up to. And then, if things looked bad, I'd call Michael Hendricks. So with a flutter of excitement overlying fear, I nipped through the opening Ramzi had left me, positioning the gate so it looked closed but still would allow me passage out.

39

I jogged up the wide driveway, which led through a naturalistic garden filled with tall pines and cedars. The Emerald Forest, I thought to myself, because in my girlish frock, I felt a little bit like Judy Garland going up the yellow brick road toward Oz. My expectation that this house would have magical qualities was confirmed when I turned the bend that Ramzi had taken and saw a long, single-story stucco house, elegant in the same East-West style as the Haradas' home at Setagaya. Under a tiled-roof carport, two cars were parked: a black Mercedes and a white Toyota Camry, both with Tokyo plates.

Two cars. I immediately got off the path and went behind a stand of trees. As I stopped and tried to still my breath, I thought frantically about possibilities. Had Mr. Harada received a call from the loyal potter and come here to spirit away the ibex ewer? I hadn't believed that I'd given Kazu Sakurai the impression I was any kind of police officer or agent, but the fact that Harada was probably inside the house had to be connected to my visit. But why two cars, instead of one? And had Ramzi dared to go into the house when it appeared to have people inside?

He probably had, I realized when I heard dogs barking within the house. Kenichi Harada must have brought the guard dogs that had been shut up in his house during the memorial service in Setagaya. And judging from the timbre of their bark, they were not a small breed. Also, Ramzi had said something to me about the dogs. What was it—that they were German shepherds? Perhaps Mr. Harada might not call them off if they attacked an intruder.

I slipped my phone out of my bag and programmed in the digits 110. At the first sound of something ugly, I planned to call Japan's nationwide police emergency number. The prickling feeling I'd had when I'd encountered the fake cop had come back. Something terrible was going to happen; I felt it.

The door slid open with a crash and two huge, furry beasts bounded out. The gate was too far away for me to get back to it. The only way I could go was up, and I'd always been rotten at climbing ropes. Still, I did my best, flailing my way four feet off the ground on the lean cedar. Why hadn't I raced over to one of the large maple or ginkgo trees nearby? I cursed myself because the cedar had no large, sheltering limbs. The dogs surrounded me, barking raucously and jumping. The phone. I still had my lifeline to the outside world, even though I had to deal with it one-handed, because my other hand was hanging onto a limb. It was a fidgety thing to handle, and as I was searching for the "talk" button I lost my grip on it. The phone fell to the ground, and the larger dog took it, then spit it out a few feet away. The other one raced over, made a few circles around it, and then came back to me.

Did they think I was playing? I began feeling around the tree for a furry cedar branch I could snap and throw. If I got them far enough away, I could slide down and get my phone, which lay half-buried in a heap of red maple leaves.

Before I could attempt anything, I heard the crunching sound of leaves and someone walking. Timberland boots came into view before I saw Ramzi. I was getting ready to call to him about the phone, but then realized that he was not alone. He was followed by his uncle Ali Birand and Kenichi Harada.

Harada said a few words and the dogs came to stand behind him, their tails wagging. I was not a dog person, I thought to myself. Never had a dog, never wanted one. But now I wished I had the kind of dog savvy to befriend them, trick them into letting me get away.

"Oh, hello. Thank you. I didn't know if they were playing," I said in Japanese, striving to act normally—as if it could possibly be normal for a thirty-year-old Lolita to be climbing a tree in a locked-up garden.

"Why don't you come down? Please." The tone of Harada's voice was anything but courteous. I also noticed that he'd spoken English—was it because he wanted to make sure the Birands understood?

I slid down faster than I intended, scratching my legs as I went. I smoothed down my short skirt as I landed, unable to stop feeling ridiculously vulnerable. I thought about picking up my phone, then thought better of doing something that seemed so obviously panicky. Instead, I continued in my faux friendly tone. "Well, then! What a coincidence to see Mr. Birand is here with you, Harada-san, when Ramzi and I had come out to the area to—pay our respects."

"I called Birand-san here because I thought I needed to solve a faraway problem. But the problem's right here." Kenichi Harada spoke English and looked straight at me.

"And we found another problem in the house!" Ali Birand cuffed his nephew on the ear. Ramzi flinched but didn't do anything in return. He looked as frightened as I felt.

"What have you explained, so far?" I asked Ramzi. I needed to know the basic framework of what our excuse was going to be.

"I told my uncle that I was here to get what was mine," he said stonily. "I said nothing about you. Why are you even here? You said you were staying outside."

Now both men were staring at me, waiting.

"As I was saying, we traveled to Izu so Ramzi could pay his respects. I came into the garden because I was afraid for his safety," I explained, wishing now that I had worn my usual clothes. It was hard to act convincingly like an adult while dressed like a Polly Pocket doll.

"I doubt that entirely. From my conversations with Birand-san and others around the country, it seems clear that you want to take something from me." Harada watched me as he spoke.

"I'm not sure what you're talking about," I said mildly. "All I've heard about is a gift from Ramzi to Emi that he wants back for his own personal sense of peace."

"My nephew has no right to give away anything from our shops or storage areas," Ali Birand said hotly. "This vessel was a gift my brother made to the ambassador. That's all there is to the matter!"

"Please, that's enough information. She knows too much already," Harada said reprovingly to Birand.

"Who would say such a thing?" I asked, watching him.

"A colleague showing proper respect," he said. "That's all you need to know."

Mr. Watanabe. He had become a mole, when it turned out that the scandal over the ibex vessel could taint a government official. The situation had turned out just as Michael had predicted. But Mr. Harada didn't know that I knew Mr. Watanabe, or he wouldn't have spoken the way he had. He still thought I was clueless. I would have to use that fact to my advantage.

"Which vessel are you talking about?" Ramzi seemed to have regained a bit of confidence. "All I wanted was my watch, which I left here by accident—the last time."

"Really? What kind of watch?" I asked skeptically.

"A Tagheuer. It has my initials engraved on the inside. You know, Uncle—my watch!"

"Yes, yes, he does have a watch of that description—a gift from his father, his last birthday." Ali Birand spoke in a placating way to Mr. Harada, who seemed to bristle a bit less.

Well, maybe. Maybe a Tagheuer was the kind of thing you wanted to take with you, no matter what. Or was it that Ramzi was trying to annoy Emi's father by making it clear that he'd taken off his watch and clothes and slept with Emi in this house?

"The watch is irrelevant. You are not to disturb my household anymore. I know that your father and uncle made that clear." Harada spoke to Ramzi firmly. Then he turned to Ali Birand. "So, this is what we will do. You and your nephew will go into the house and retrieve this watch, and then the two of you may drive back to the city. In the meantime, I will take Shimura-san out to the gate."

Ramzi cast an awkward last look at me and went inside with his uncle. Obviously, Harada trusted the uncle in the house. But he didn't trust me to walk to the gate.

"I can go alone."

"I don't think so." Then he pointed me not toward the driveway at all but toward the woods behind the house.

"That's not the way to the street," I said, and for the first time I felt fear. Ramzi and his uncle wouldn't know what had happened. Even if they came out in five minutes, it would be too late.

"It's—how do you say it in English? A shortway."

"Shortcut," I said, and then switched to Japanese. "And it's not a shorter way. It's the wrong direction."

"Ah, so Shimura-san thinks she knows the boundaries of my property better than I do."

"I know the way out. After all, I just followed Ramzi in." I thought about running down the path toward the gate, but there wasn't enough space between us. And he had a small bulge in his pants pocket, something that couldn't possibly be part of a Mae West joke. It might be a weapon. In Japan, there was gun control, but there were still guns. Gangsters had them, and diplomats who could travel without having their luggage examined might have them too. I knew for sure that this man, not Ali Birand, was the dangerous one.

"If you're sure that I'm a thief, why don't you call one-ten?" I asked. My two goals were delay and distraction. If only I could stay in place until the Birands emerged. Why was it taking so long to find the watch?

He didn't answer, so I tried again.

"Yes, you went to great lengths to try to get rid of me. I almost wonder at times if it was revenge because of Emi. You know, I'm very sorry about that—"

He wrinkled up his nose. "Revenge? Because you desire to take her former fiancé, now that he's free? That's not of interest to me."

So he didn't know about that night. He wasn't out to avenge Emi. But he still felt strongly enough to want to walk me into the woods, away from the Birands, and get rid of me.

Why was he so worried about the vessel? It was more than a gift. Something my aunt had taught me early on came back, all of a sudden; that once you gave someone a present, he was duty-bound to give you one in return, something that was worth the same.

I wondered what the Birands might have received in exchange for an ancient, indescribably gorgeous piece of pottery. A favor, perhaps. What had it been? I tried to recall how long Ali Birand had been living in Tokyo. When was it that Ramzi had said that his uncle was granted a visa?

The visa. I remembered Simone and Richard talking about visas, and my own hassles. It was very difficult for most foreigners except Americans and northern Europeans to get visas to live and work in Japan. Ramzi had used a French passport to get in. Yet Ali Birand, a citizen of Turkey, had gotten a visa and been able to secure a business address in a top-flight section of Tokyo. That was what frightened Kenichi Harada—the threat of exposure of how he'd abused his government privilege for a gift.

"Go," he ordered me, in the imperative form used with inferiors. "If you don't do as I say, I'll set the dogs on you!"

I eyed the dogs, judging my chances against the two of them. If they attacked me and the Birands came out, he'd say it was my fault. And even if they doubted him, they'd be afraid enough of the dogs—and of what might happen to them as foreigners in the Japanese judicial system— to agree with whatever he wanted them to do, or say.

My survival was contingent on the Birands' coming out before I was dragged into the woods. Delay was the only strategy I had left. If I could get Kenichi Harada invested in finding out more about what I knew, I'd live.

In a steady voice, I said, "The Birands were able to give you the ewer because they couldn't possibly sell it. But I feel worried that maybe it was an unfair thing that happened to you—how could you know its origin?"

"Obviously, there's something important about it, if you came all the way here to take it from me. But that is not the point. All I know is that you have invaded my property with the purpose of theft, and I plan to exercise my right to order you to leave." Again, he waved his hand in the direction of the woods.

Keeping my gaze on him, I asked, "As I was trying to explain to you, the history of the vessel is unusual. It was stolen from the National Museum in Iraq."

Kenichi Harada's face flushed deep red. "I never heard that. I'm completely innocent in this situation. As Birand told you himself, it was a simple gift—"

"You must have had some inkling it was stolen property, because you didn't exhibit it in your house in Setagaya with all your other beautiful, legally acquired things." I paused. "I wonder what other treasures are in your house. Was that your game? Gifts of art and antiques in exchange for visas?"

"Whom do you work for?" Harada asked quietly.

"I work for people who know my suspicions about you. If you take me into the woods and shoot me, the first person they'll interview will be you." At least, I hoped so. Mr. Harada would find a way to pin things on the Birands, who had the bad luck of being on the scene in Izu, too. The foreigners, not the government minister, would make the police suspicious.

"I want you to start walking now, quietly. Don't make me angry."

"I won't go," I repeated. "You shouldn't, either. You should call the police and tell them you want to turn over something that you've just discovered is a missing international treasure—"

I'd meant to give him a way out, but I'd gone too far. He reached his hand into his pocket and pulled out something small and hard and wrapped my hand around it.

I opened it up and saw a vial of pills—lots of them, small and red and stacked almost to the top.

"I want you to swallow them. My idea about taking you through the woods was to make it easier. There's a stream there; you could have had water. But now, you'll have to swallow them without. Take them all. I tell you it will make you happy for a short while— or if you'd rather, I'll tell the dogs to do their job."

I did then what I should have done the minute the Birands disappeared into the house. I screamed, yelling the names of Ali and Ramzi, beseeching them to call the police. Then I shouted out again, this time in Japanese, in the unlikely event that anyone in the neighborhood would help.

"You fool. Give it to me—" He came at me, and I turned and hurled the vial as far as I could. I expected that the dogs would go after it, and the pair of them did, joyfully.

My plan was working. With the dogs and Harada diverted, I started my run for the gate. Behind me came Ramzi's voice. "What's going on, Rei?"

"Yes, what did you do?" Ali called out.

I heard the sound of crunching leaves and realized that one of the dogs was heading right for me. Kenichi Harada had made good on his threat, but to my delight I noticed that the dog had, in its jaws, something red. To him, my cell phone was a toy. He dropped it at my feet and stood waiting, as if he wanted me to throw it. I glanced over to see what Harada was doing; he was scuffling around with the other dog in the pile of leaves for the vial. To think that all my terror had ended up in a search for dropped tablets. I was reasonably sure I could get away from this situation.

"Good boy. Just a minute," I said, putting the phone to my ear and pushing through on the 110 exchange I'd set up earlier, in anticipation of trouble.

"No, no!" Ali Birand was shouting suddenly. "Don't do it!"

A competent-sounding Japanese woman's voice came on the line. "Emergency services; do you require the police?"

I was about to answer her when I heard Ali Birand scream.

Something had happened, and I could barely bring myself to turn and see what it was.

40

Kenichi Harada had tossed down his own throat all the tablets in the vial: enough amphetamines to kill two men. Six doctors, a week in the hospital, the attentions of his wife, and an anxious nation would aid in his recovery. Mr. Harada had already offered his resignation from government service for reasons of health. Nobody had to know that he'd been the one who'd lived for years with an on-again, off-again amphetamine habit to cope with the stress of long working hours. It was by raiding her father's well-stocked medicine cabinet that his daughter had become hooked, too.

A quick resignation was prudent; in the eyes of Japanese society, the minister for the environment had gone to the rural area he loved best and, stricken by grief over his daughter's death, attempted to end his own life. This played much better than the reality that was emerging after government intelligence agents interviewed Ali Birand, who maintained that Kenichi Harada had streamlined the approval of twenty visas to Turkish citizens in exchange for the gifts. All the immigrants had paid special fees to the Birands, who personally handed over their passports to Kenichi Harada. As a result, the Birands had made plenty of extra money, and instead of having to share a portion of those fees with Kenichi Harada, they'd been able to unload a dangerous asset on him that they didn't dare sell.

On paper, it looked as if the Birands were the worse villains, but the truth was that they hadn't played any role in trying to track and terrorize me, nor was the vessel even in their custody. It was back in Iraq, in a box that had been mailed from Tokyo in care of the provisional director of the National Museum in Iraq.

We'd done it together: Ali Birand, Ramzi, and me. It was my idea; after the police and ambulance had roared away with Kenichi Harada, I'd suggested that the three of us drive back together to Tokyo and, along the way, figure out our next step.

As I drove, Ali's defenses tumbled down. He was worried enough to tell me all that I needed to know. He'd driven to the house under the direction of Kenichi Harada, who'd asked him to get rid of the ibex vessel. So he had wrapped it in bubble wrap inside a plastic shopping bag; the whole thing was in the trunk of the Camry.

Ali was indeed desperate to get rid of the piece; he'd known that it was stolen, of course, and he understood that sooner or later the police would come calling for it. As we drew closer to Yokohama, he begged me to make a quick stop so that he could throw it away. I refused, telling him I had an idea that would set everything straight.

I drove all the way to Yokohama Station, where I asked the men to stay in the car while I took the bag with me into the station. I retrieved my luggage from the locker, and stopped in at a shop in the station's arcade. There I bought a set of cheap everyday soup bowls because I liked their sturdy wooden packing box, and the larger cardboard carton that the saleswoman gave me, upon request. I retreated to the ladies' room, did some packing, and in the end had made up a secure parcel that contained within it the ibex vessel and its bubble wrap tucked in the Oriental Bazaar box that had once held the police dolls. I also included Kazu Sakurai's cups in their own brown satin-lined box, plus the receipt for them. Then I walked again through the crowded station to its busy postal station, where I addressed the package to the museum and gave as the return address Brenda Martin at the American embassy in Tokyo. On the customs declaration form, I described the contents as contemporary Japanese tea bowls and a rustic pottery pitcher, valued at $5,050. I'd thought there might be some fuss about the high value of the package, which I insured, but the clerk either didn't notice or didn't care about the irregularity. I was just another Lolita in a line of twenty customers, all of them anxious to get their mailings completed before their trains came in.

And that's how my last few days in Japan went. I hustled around, making peace with my aunt and Chika, who were outraged most about my actions with Takeo. Following their advice, I didn't see Takeo in public again, but we talked on the phone several times. Takeo expressed horrified surprise about where Emi's drugs had really come from and told me he was going off women for good. Jokingly, I offered to have Richard bring him to one of the cool gay clubs in Tokyo, but he told me that he'd already been accepted at a Buddhist monastery in India. He'd take a brief break from Tokyo and flower arranging, and then return, if the situation suited him.

The other man in my life wasn't as easy to say good-bye to. I'd called Hugh from Japan to apologize again, and he'd said that he'd already packed up my clothes and sent them to Kendall's house in Potomac. Moving the furniture would be harder, because there were some things we had chosen and bought together. "It's like a common-law marriage, practically," Hugh said, when he started trying to explain the legal ramifications of our furniture. I shook my head, thinking it was so like him to say that—to find a marriage, even when it had never been.

I was back in Washington a week later. It felt colder than before, and winter seemed to be setting in. But there was a bit of a thaw with Hugh. He'd finally agreed to meet, face to face, for a cup of coffee before we started allocating the furniture. He'd suggested going to the Evergreen, a new coffee bar that had opened in Adams-Morgan just after I'd left for Japan. Probably, this was the reason that Hugh had suggested it; we had no shared history here, and the shiny espresso maker and the assortment of inexpensive scones and sandwiches couldn't possibly trick us into thinking we were having a dinner date.

Striving to seem as though I didn't care, and also to show that I was ready to lift furniture, I came in my trusty yoga pants, as good as new after a thorough laundering in Kendall's washing machine.

With them, I wore a trendy argyle sweater that had shrunk and was too small for Kendall but was perfect for me. On my feet were the same trusty Asics that had gotten me away from the phony cop. Hugh disliked the American habit of wearing running shoes everywhere; I thought about that as I put them on. I was going to make it as easy as possible for both of us to say good-bye.

I arrived at five-thirty and found that Hugh had gotten out of work early and was already there, in a black Italian business suit and wing tips. He looked sharp but somber. His only item of color was a red-and-gold Aquascutum tie that I particularly loved.

"Right on time," he said when I joined him at the counter, where he was scrutinizing the assortment of pastries.

"I try my best." I kept looking at the necktie, because I was still too nervous to look into his face.

"Well, it doesn't really matter, I suppose. The crowd's huge here in the mornings. But now . . ." Hugh glanced around. "We could have any table we like."

Hugh ordered Earl Grey tea and two blueberry scones. I settled for hot apple cider. I paid for both of us before he had a chance to get out his wallet. I figured it was the least that I could do with my extravagant payment from the U.S. government.

"You may wonder why I picked this spot instead of a restaurant," Hugh said after we'd sat down.

"Because it has no memories?" I asked.

"They offer no alcohol," Hugh said. "I stopped drinking ten days ago."

This was the length of time that had elapsed since my confession. I asked, "Do you mean that you think you are an alcoholic?"

"I don't know. I ran into bingeing problems before back in Scotland. And with my brother and his mates, the rock-band lifestyle . . . I think I forgot who I was." Hugh smiled without warmth.

"I never thought of your drinking as anything more than—fun. But I guess that at the end, things spun out of control." Just as the typhoon had spun me into Takeo's arms, changing everything over the course of a few horrible hours.

"Even before you left for Japan, I felt as if you'd already checked out of my life." Hugh's words came slowly. "That party—I know it wasn't your thing, but I felt that if I did something really grand—made a statement that hundreds of people saw—you'd understand how much I loved you. But I buggered up so badly that night that you shot off for Tokyo almost immediately. Not wanting me to go with you—well, that was the final blow for me."

I wanted to stretch my hand out to comfort him, but didn't dare. "The irony is that while I was there, I wished I weren't. I never felt like that in Japan before."

"My brother phoned me yesterday to say that apparently the picture was mix-up. The tabloid even printed a retraction, at the behest of Takeo's family—"

"So, the Kayamas intervened and saved everyone's reputation." I sighed. "But I'm not going to make excuses. As I said over the phone, I really did sleep with Takeo."

"I wonder," Hugh said slowly, "if that was some kind of mix-up, too."

"What do you mean?" I eyed him suspiciously. Hugh had made it clear over the phone that he wanted me out of his apartment. This meeting was supposed to be about arranging the logistics of my move. Was he trying to offer forgiveness instead?

"I wonder if you went into the situation with all your faculties intact," Hugh said.

"I wasn't drunk," I said tightly. "But I was—desperate in a way that I hope never to be again."

"I appreciate your honesty."

I stared at the grain of the pine table between us. "I suppose you're being like this because you want to part cordially."

"I do want that," Hugh said. "The truth is, I realize that I've got to separate myself from the situations and people that led me into trouble. I've asked for a transfer, Rei."

"A work transfer?"

"Yes. Right now it might be Europe or Latin America. I was passed over for partner, so I don't really care where I go." He paused. "So the flat . . . the reason I want you to move the furniture is that I'm moving out myself. Very quickly."

"It's a good thing you never bought," I said, feeling hollow. Of course I should have known he'd run. He'd done it before, when we'd both been in Tokyo, and once before that, in Washington. Both times, I'd wound up winning, but not on this occasion.

Hugh's mouth was moving, and belatedly I realized that he was asking about my own plans.

"Well, I'm staying with Kendall till I can't stand it anymore—that'll probably be three days, tops—and then I'll go to Grand's in Baltimore or somewhere like that. It depends on the job I take up next—"

"You're staying here? Rather than decamping to Japan?"

I shrugged. "It depends on the job I take. And as far as Japan goes, my visa status is back to normal again. I'm sure I'll go back, but there are a lot of other places I want to see, too."

"So you'll be in the Washington area, still." Hugh picked up a scone as if he meant to eat it, then put it down.

"I don't know. I stayed here because of you, and now that's changed." I stared at the scones, unable to wipe away the tears welling up in my eyes.

Hugh didn't speak again. And when he left the coffee bar, I stayed resolute, not turning to look after him. Grimly, I remembered what Chika had said about her parents not wanting to know the truth—and realized that maybe my young cousin was the wisest one of all.

Michael Hendricks had known about the package I'd mailed to Iraq before I left Japan, but I wasn't sure what his reaction was until I met him for lunch a few days after my disastrous parting from Hugh. Michael had suggested Zola for lunch; his choice of the restaurant, which sat right over the American Spy Museum, was a gesture that made me smile at a time when smiles were in scarce supply. Even though it was early November, the weather felt like winter. I had on Grand's suit, which I decided looked surprisingly hip when worn with a tight black tank top underneath it, thigh-high black stockings, and the strappy high-heeled Manolos on my feet.

Michael was wearing another fade-into-the-background Brooks Brothers suit, but he looked different somehow. Maybe it was because his ice-blue eyes, as they regarded me, finally looked like those of a friend, rather than an adversary.

"I swear to you that from this day forward I'm never going to talk about the Momoyama vase anymore," he murmured after we'd been seated in one of the best places—a red velvet booth with a porthole window, so you could see who was behind you. In our case, it was Italian tourists lost in an argument only they could understand. I sat down, reassured.

"Did you hear what I said, Rei? About the Momoyama vase?" he raised his voice slightly.

"I did. And it sounds as if you are still talking about it."

"I can call it an ibex ewer now," Michael said. "And it's back where it belongs without so much as a chip, which is fortunate, given how it was sent."

I shrugged. "It must be that the sender was an expert at packing antiquities."

"That's right. The government held a news conference showing the vessel in its glory. Three elementary-school classes came to see it. The public knows that it's back."

"I'm glad." And I was, despite all that had happened.

"The ewer's return precludes any prosecution of the Birand brothers for its theft. Did you know?" Michael asked.

"But they're still in trouble for the passport-brokering, I bet." I laid down my menu to pay full attention.

"They're out of Japan for good, and Turkey doesn't want them back. But I understand they want to resettle in Morocco because of the tourist trade. Ramzi, you may be glad to hear, had not been charged with anything. He's going to finish his studies in France."

I'd kept in touch with Ramzi, so I knew that already. But I was anxious to understand more about the situation for Ali and Osman Birand. "Are you saying that the Birand brothers don't face any criminal prosecution?"

"Did you think things should be otherwise?"

"Well, they didn't do anything to hurt me or anyone I know of. And from what Ali said to me, the vessel was a gift to his brother from one of the people seeking a visa in the first place." I suddenly felt anxious. "I'm sorry there was no exposure of an art theft ring, but the fact is that these gift-giving chains, in the Middle East as well as in Japan, are hard to understand and trace."

"Yes. That reminds me of the way the ewer arrived. Apparently, a set of five tea bowls made by a Living National Treasure had been sent along with it. That was a clever touch, leading the customs inspectors who opened the package to concentrate on the known value of one thing, and completely bypass the other. Over at the museum, they're still trying to decide who gets the tea bowls. Any ideas?"

Of course Michael knew that I'd done it; he was just teasing me. "How about the next seriously wounded Iraqi child? Maybe they could parlay it into a visa to a safer country."

I'd expected Michael to protest my partisan political statement, but instead, he looked at me and said, "What about you?"

Vehemently, I shook my head.

"You lost everything, didn't you? Both the men, your place to live in Washington, and the support of your relatives in Yokohama."

"Oh, nothing's irreplaceable." I amended my hard words. "Well, maybe I don't mean my relatives. But I think they've all decided it was just a matter of crazy Rei being a little crazier than usual. They've forgiven, if not forgotten."

I'd given my cousins a sketchy but honest report of the situation: that Takeo had been racked with anxiety over Emi's death, and I'd comforted him. The fact that I'd left Japan proved I had no real interest in resurrecting our relationship, and by now, the media's attention was long gone from me. The truth had gotten out about the drugs that Emi had taken before her death, and the press furthered the idea that the shame and horror her father had faced because of his daughter's drug overdose had led to his attempted suicide.

On the bright side, Tom had told me, there was a sudden increase in serious media coverage of the dangers of Japan's most popular drug, and the warning signs parents could observe. And it seemed that Takeo was no longer a social pariah; he was seen as a sad, flawed hero who had tried in vain to prevent his fiancée's death.

"But what about Hugh?" Michael was like a dog who wouldn't drop a bone.

"It's over, though I haven't retrieved all my things from his apartment because I'm not sure what I'm doing next."

"In terms of work, you mean?"

"Exactly." I watched him closely, because he'd hinted about having more work for me, and I wondered if the offer still stood.

Michael folded his arms and regarded me. "You know that I'm pleased with the way your first job for us went. My bosses are pleased, too. They hope you'll work for us again."

I felt myself flush. "You mean, join the C-I-"

"No names," Michael said in a low voice. "But you're in the right arena. I'll show you my credentials later on, when we're outside."

"I can't believe you could possibly think the job went smoothly," I said. "My mistake with Takeo led to a chain of events that were nearly disastrous."

"What you did the day and night of the storm—getting to the beach town, and finding a way to stay in the house and discover the fake—verged on the heroic." Michael's gaze was warm. "Hugh understandably has a different reading of it, but rest assured that in our line of work, you aren't the first agent to have done that sort of thing."

"But I wasn't an agent—"

"You could be," Michael said, studying me. "If you were willing to sign a secrecy agreement, we could formalize our relationship."

I laughed shakily. "No, thanks. I'm too liberal, and I'd never pass the physical."

"I disagree with both." Michael grinned. "And I promise you that because you're still remaining something of an independent contractor, the training is minimal. For instance, there would be no paramilitary training, although you probably should take some more *kanji* classes, since your difficulty reading Japanese is really the only weakness I see."

Michael was still watching me, so I was relieved to be interrupted by the waitress. I ordered the corn and mussel soup and the vegetable stack.

"Anything to drink?" she asked.

I hesitated, thinking that this was a business lunch, and also thinking about Hugh's problem, but Michael interjected, "Did you know that they serve wines by the glass? I'm having a glass of Pinot Grigio."

Wines by the glass! A brilliant idea. A tiny bit of golden joy in a glass, not too much, just enough to make the flavors of the food rounder, and my back rest a little more comfortably against the banquette.

"Is this a typical workday lunch for you?" I asked after the exquisite food had arrived and I'd taken a few bites.

"This meal is not on the government's tab," Michael said. "Although my time talking to you will be. Getting back to our conversation, I want you to consider taking on some jobs that I might hear about, dealing with cultural treasures and delicate human situations: situations that could be peacefully solved, to use one of your infamous expressions."

"It sounds like the right idea, philosophically," I said, "But I still don't feel I could do things like that. I wouldn't know where to start."

"Consider how things worked out in your debut operation. The ibex ewer is back in Iraq and relations between Japan and the United States are intact, despite our apprehending one of their citizens."

"But has justice been served? Mr. Harada's probably going to retire without going to jail, and the Birands are free to keep running their dubious business in another country. And what about Mr. Watanabe, that double-dealing bastard?"

"Early next year, apparently, he's rotating out of the embassy and retiring to go into private industry." Michael took a sip of wine. "Obviously, the scandal that he tried to prevent wound up tainting him, too."

"Well, frankly, I'm glad he's not staying in office. I can hardly stand to live in the same city as the man who betrayed me to someone who hired a thug to do away with me—"

"Yes. I made a sorry choice in recruiting him to help, although he probably would have been fine if it had not turned out that our real suspect was one of his colleagues." Michael looked at me. "I'm sorry, Rei."

I shuddered. "Well, you did start warning me to be cautious, pretty early on. And at least it's over."

"Yes. And even though there won't be newspaper clippings this time around telling the truth about what you did over the last few weeks, you must feel satisfied knowing that you've uncovered corruption within immigration circles."

"I was lucky. I guessed the truth at the critical moment." I felt uncomfortable with all the praise.

"I disagree, and I'm writing an analysis of your experience, to be shared agencywide. You're the first person in our employ who's pointed out that governments must be highly vigilant to make sure diplomats don't foster immigration fraud. Just think how terrorists might get into our country, if we had an ambassador who operated the way Harada did."

"You're very kind to make such a big deal about it," I said.

"Rei, I want you to work for us again." Michael was looking straight at me in a way that made me drop my own gaze. It was too intense, too close.

"I promise that I'll think about it," I said. Kendall was sure she could find work for me decorating her friend's new restaurant, and my grandmother had cooked up some kind of an opportunity to catalog a famous netsuke collection in North Baltimore. But I'd keep Michael's offer in mind. It was bound to be the highest-paying, and it had the advantage of travel—something that sounded good to me, now that I no longer had a home.

When I left Zola two hours later, I discovered that the sun had completely vanished, obscured by what looked like snow clouds. Snow in early November in Washington? It could happen, though it was unusual.

Much of my trip back to Bethesda was underground, so when I got out of the station, I was pleased to see a faint dusting of white everywhere. The bus to Potomac was delayed because of the weather, so I decided to walk.

The two miles to Kendall's house went rather slowly because of my impractical shoes. But I didn't mind. As I picked my way along the path, I looked heavenward and let the flakes fall on my cheeks, eyes, lips, and hair.

The snow kept falling. The dull suburban landscape was now

completely frosted in white, except for the black asphalt roads and the tiny holes that my heels were making on the snowy sidewalk. Tomorrow I would teach Jackie and Win how to make snow angels.

I had the time, because it would be a snow day—and because I finally understood that my own winter years were nothing to be afraid of.

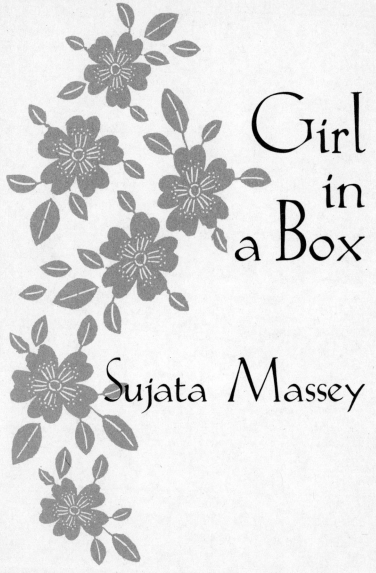

Girl in a Box

Sujata Massey

1

It's taken me almost a whole lifetime to become a decent liar.

I still endure stabs of good-girl guilt about it, even though lying has started a brilliant second career for me. I tell stories easily, rarely missing a step as I switch between English and Japanese. But I often wonder how I ever got to this crazy place in life, and where I will go next.

This day had been like all the others: a cool winter day in Monterey, with eight hours of classes at the Defense Language Institute, followed by my usual routine—a run out to Lover of Jesus Point in Pacific Grove. On days like this one, I felt that the Pacific was my constant friend. The water was the divider between me and Japan, between my old life and the new one. I'd have to cross it to go home.

It was odd that I felt this way, I thought as I ran along the dirt trail that paralleled the coast. California was my birthplace—San Francisco, to be exact, about two hours to the north, where my parents still lived. But Japan, where I'd lived so briefly but happily teaching English and selling antiques, always beckoned. The sensation had been stronger on this day than at any time so far in the two months I'd been studying at DLI, preparing for the kind of career in which you couldn't tell anyone what you did, but that would get me back to Japan.

Good things are worth waiting for. I reminded myself of this truth as I ran, dressed for the winter in a long-sleeved black shirt really meant for bikers, and shorts, because I was too vain to wear sensible running tights. The wind on my legs didn't bother me; but on my way back, my knee started throbbing, and I thought about how much I wanted to replace the Nike Airs. In Monterey, there were a few places to buy running shoes, but nothing with the vast array of choices that a thirty-year-old with fading knees required. Of course, I could go up to San Francisco and easily get my favorite Asics style, but I wasn't in the mood. I'd been there at my family home for Christmas and New Year's, a time when I found myself fending off a combination of unhealthy foods and intrusive questions. As much as I loved my parents, I couldn't tell them about the Organization for Cultural Intelligence—OCI—the super-secret spy agency where I'd been hired as a special informant. I also couldn't explain why Hugh Glendinning, the man to whom I'd once been semi-engaged, had thrown me out of his life and Washington, D.C., apartment forever. But I wouldn't lie to my parents—that would be completely against my internal code. So I chose not to talk.

I actually liked the solitude of the Monterey coast, with its jagged rocks set against the turbulent, frigid Pacific: home of sardines, surfers, seals, and whales. Now I glanced toward the ocean, just to make sure I wasn't going to miss the sunset. Another great blessing of my posting in Monterey was my proximity to sunsets over the Pacific: performance art in vivid shades of red, orange, and purple, each sunset unique, like the kanji characters I was studying.

The sun took its leisurely time slipping down to the horizon, but as closely as I looked, I missed the green flash. I always seemed to miss it, even on the days when I'd been with Hugh, vacationing in beautiful parts of Japan and Thailand, and he took pains to point it out. I never saw the same things he did. Perhaps that had been the problem.

I shifted my gaze forward in the direction I was running, coming close to the Hopkins Marine Station, a research outpost connected to Stanford University. It had a beautiful rocky lookout point, but I'd never gone out because the station had a high wire fence and many signs saying "keep out." I was getting quite used to barriers, fences, and warning signs; usually, the Department of Defense identification card that I carried would get me in most places, but I had no business at the station.

Someone else did, though; a solitary sightseer, who was out on the rocks with field glasses close to his face.

I had noticed the same man half an hour earlier, because of what he was wearing: a business suit, which was a rarity in Monterey. I assumed he had to be some muckety-muck, though in my experience, marine scientists were more likely to wear jeans than gray flannel. Not that I could tell what the suit was made of: I was much too far away to make out those details, let alone the guy's face. I imagined for a minute that he was a spy, watching the coast for his contact to come in. He was probably an out-of-control tourist who just wanted to take pictures—though why he wasn't looking seaward rather than at the recreation trail didn't make sense.

It took me a couple of minutes to pass the rocky outcropping, then the rest of the fenced station, and then its exit. My knee was really bothering me, so I moved to the side and tightened my shoelaces—anything for more support. As I finished tying the knot, I turned around to look for bikers, always a liability on the trail, and I was stunned to see the man in the business suit running out of the marine station's parking lot. Now I knew that what I'd sensed earlier had been correct; the field glasses had been trained on me, not on any form of sea life.

I was fairly breathless because I'd already been running for about half an hour, but I mustered an extra bit of power and began running toward the American Tin Cannery Outlets. The first place I saw was a Reebok outlet, but I ran on, figuring I wouldn't get much sympathy there when I was wearing Nikes. I also passed by Isotoner and Geoffrey Beene, on the assumption that these were not brands that would draw a young, fit crowd ready to aid in my defense. The students at DLI, mostly young enlisted men, were certainly buff enough help me out against an assailant, but I was the last woman they'd want to help. I don't know whether I'd ticked them off by screwing up the academic curve, or because I'd refused any and all romantic propositions. It was impossible to know—and actually of no consequence at a time like this.

Damn, I thought, after glancing backward. He was gaining on me, and the glasses were now hanging around his neck, hitting his chest as he ran. No normal jogger ran in a business suit; he was a lunatic. I broke into a full-throttle sprint. He was still so far away that I couldn't see his face, but from what I'd seen, he had gray hair. This fact—that he was significantly older than I—should have made me calm down, but did not.

There was a little restaurant at the end out the outlet strip brightly painted red, white, and blue, probably in an attempt to cater to both Monterey's military population and foreign tourists. I jogged up the steps and burst inside, finding the place absolutely empty; of course, it was before the dinner hour.

At the far end of the room, a couple of young men in T-shirts and jeans were sitting together conversing in Spanish. They looked at the runner in their restaurant and said nothing. I didn't know if it was because I looked so disheveled, or because there was a language barrier.

"I have a problem. Can you call the police?" I said between heavy breaths.

The two men hesitated a moment, glancing each other. Then they ran back through the kitchen.

"It's a misunderstanding, I didn't mean—" I called out, wishing I had spoken in Spanish the first time. Spanish was the first language of Monterey, I should have thought to speak it right away and not use a trigger word like "police."

A banging sound told me they'd gone out the back door. Now I was all alone. I quickly threaded my way through the restaurant, looking for a telephone. The man had obviously seen me go in; there was no point in hiding. I'd just be on the phone with the cops when my stalker arrived.

I found a phone at last, and as I pressed "talk," I finally got a close-up view of my pursuer through the window. And shakily I put the phone down. I had been right when I'd briefly daydreamed about the figure on the rocks. He was a spy—a spymaster, to be correct. The man I'd run from was the chief of OCI's Japan desk: Michael Hendricks, my boss of the last three months.

"Michael! What a surprise," I said, striving for normality as he stepped through the door.

Michael Hendricks must have become extremely bored with his duties in Washington, because he'd been e-mailing me jokes almost daily, silly lightbulb riddles like *How many spies does it take to screw in a lightbulb? Answer: Twenty. One to do it, and nineteen to develop a distraction.*

However, in Michael's numerous e-mails, he'd never once mentioned that he was planning a cross-country trip to California.

"Why were you running away?" Michael was breathing hard and pulling his tie out of his shirt collar as he spoke. Michael was not a conventionally handsome man; he was too thin, and although his features may have started out

patrician, he looked as if he'd had his nose broken somewhere along the line. But his salt-and-pepper hair was cut
well, in a classic military buzz, and his ice-blue eyes were
so appealing that I often had to look away.

I decided to answer honestly. "I was scared. Wouldn't
you be, if someone watched you with field glasses and
then started running after you?"

"I was looking for you." His breath was gradually
slowing. "When I made the positive ID, I decided to catch
up with you. By the way, did you know that you pronate
when you run?"

"Yes. The shoes make it worse." I flushed, embarrassed
that I'd been seen not only running away, but running
away with bad form.

"You mentioned once that you ran in this area, so
that's why I came, after I found you weren't at your
apartment. I picked that point, on the rocks, just to make
sure I'd see you before you went home, or into town, or
wherever." Michael tugged off his suit jacket. I looked
for huge sweat stains on his oxford shirt, but it was crisp
and dry. Either he was a very cool customer or he wore
an undershirt.

Michael spoke again. "Actually, I've been trying to catch
up with you all day. There's something we have to discuss,
as soon as possible."

"What could it be?" I asked grimly, because I was sure I knew. He had learned the results of my embarrassing polygraph test a few days earlier, and come to tell me that my very short career in government intelligence was over.

"It looks like there's nobody here to take an order, so let's talk about it back at your apartment." Michael reached into his jacket pocket and pulled out a car key with a rental company tag. "There's plenty of room in the Impala they gave me."

A Chevy Impala? "No, thanks. I'd prefer to finish my run. It's barely a half mile back to the apartment. And then I've got to shower."

"Of course," Michael said smoothly. "Hey, I'll get us some take-out food, and meet you over there. That'll give you enough time, I hope."

An Impala was a ridiculous car for a man not yet forty to be driving, I thought as I jogged up Spaghetti Hill to my apartment. I had a feeling that Michael was going to beat me in the car, but I needed the time to clear my head.

But he wasn't there after all. I unlocked the back door to the Spanish-style bungalow on Larkin Street with the key I'd tucked into the inner pocket of my shorts. I went immediately into the small bathroom, took a superfast shower, and dressed, this time in a pair of jeans and a silk kurta I'd bought in one of the little boutiques downtown. I decided against putting on makeup and blow-drying my hair—I rarely bothered with those things these days—but I did attempt to straighten up the apartment a bit before he arrived. The apartment had been converted out of the back end of a modest two-bedroom bungalow built in the twenties. At one time it must have been lovely, but now the stucco walls were crumbling, and the landlord had covered the old terra-cotta tiles with vinyl and had provided only cheap wicker garden furniture. I was rearranging the cushions on the love seat and chairs that made up my living room suite when I heard a knock on the door. I checked the peephole, identified Michael, and opened up.

He was carrying a bag from the Paris Bakery, one of my favorite haunts, and two cups of coffee. But behind him, lying against the small porch railing, were more than a dozen large, flat cardboard boxes—moving boxes, I realized with a start. After handing the food to me, he began hauling the boxes into the room.

"You brought—cookies? What kind of a dinner is that?" I asked as I looked at the enticing mixture of checkerboard cookies and raspberry butter cookies. I was trying to figure out both the meal and the moving boxes.

"There's not enough time for a sit-down meal. But I thought the sugar could carry us both through what we need to do tonight." Michael cleared his throat. "You're probably wondering why I came all the way to see you."

"Yes, I'd say Monterey is a little out of the way from D.C.," I said.

"I took a military hop. Nonstop, on a Learjet. Really a pleasure. "

"So it's urgent." I sipped the coffee and winced. He had added plenty of sugar, but no milk.

"You wanted milk?" Michael's gaze was keen.

"Yes. A latte with just two sugars would have been perfect, but you'll know that for next time." I caught myself. "Actually, I guess there won't be a next time, from the boxes you've brought. Something's wrong, isn't it?"

"I wouldn't say wrong." Michael paused. "And I am sorry to pull you out before the academic course is over. Your instructor told me that you were doing really well, the top of the class."

"Little else to do around here except study." But I was secretly pleased that he'd heard how well I'd done.

"Well, maybe you can come back to Monterey later in the year." He paused. "I need you in D.C. I came out to explain the situation personally, because you have the option to accept or decline."

Obviously he expected me to accept, because he'd brought moving boxes. Carefully I asked, "Do you mean it's an OCI job?"

He nodded. "We have about a month to prepare for the mission. Then, it's back to Tokyo for you."

"Excellent." My spirits rose for the first time in weeks. I didn't mind leaving Monterey if it was for Japan. I knew where I was going to find my replacement running shoes—in Shinjuku!

"I'm going to explain as we pack, because you've got to be out of here, on my flight, tomorrow at ODT."

"What does *that* mean?" I'd noticed that Michael's years in the Navy and then the federal government had resulted in his speaking a language of abbreviations that was as complex as Japanese.

"Oh-dark-thirty. It means very early, before daylight." He paused. "Our flight to Langley leaves at six-thirty. You've got to be packed tonight, and we'll leave everything here for one of our people to move out tomorrow. Your personal shipment will be airmailed space-A after we go."

Another one of his abbreviations, which I'd learned meant "Space available," probably later than sooner. I glanced around my untidy apartment. "How can I possibly . . ."

"I'll help you." Michael was starting to fold and assemble the first box. "I've done this kind of pack-out many times, and yours should be a snap. All you've got are clothes and books, correct?"

"And music. And cooking stuff, and . . ."

"No problem," Michael said, pulling a thick roll of tape from his jacket. "As we pack, I'll tell you everything."

BOOKS BY SUJATA MASSEY

GIRL IN A BOX

ISBN 0-06-076514-3 (hardcover)

Rei Shimura takes on a freelance gig with a Washington, D.C., alphabet agency that might have ties to the CIA. Her mission is to go undercover as a clerk in a big Tokyo department store.

THE TYPHOON LOVER

0-06-076513-5 (trade paperback)

Through her chaotic twenties, antiques dealer Rei Shimura has gone anywhere that fortune and her unruly passions have led her. *The Typhoon Lover* takes her on her biggest adventure yet, a perilous journey that only Rei, with her experience in antiques and her foothold in two countries, can handle.

ZEN ATTITUDE

ISBN 0-06-089921-2 (trade paperback)

When Rei overpays for a beautiful antique chest, she's in for the worst deal of her life. The con man who sold her the *tansu* is found dead, and like it or not Rei's opened a Pandora's box of mystery, theft, and murder.

THE PEARL DIVER

ISBN 0-06-059790-9 (trade paperback)

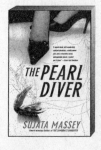

A dazzling engagement ring is an added bonus for antiques dealer and sometime-sleuth Rei Shimura, who is commissioned to furnish a chic Japanese-fusion restaurant, where, in short order, things start to go haywire.

"A riveting story." —*Library Journal*

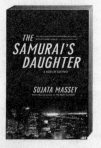

THE SAMURAI'S DAUGHTER

ISBN 0-06-059503-5 (trade paperback)

Antiques dealer Rei Shimura is in San Francisco tracing the story of one hundred years of Japanese decorative arts through her family's history. Before long, Rei uncovers troubling facts about her own family's actions during the war.

"Absorbing cross-cultural puzzle." —*Publishers Weekly*

THE BRIDE'S KIMONO

ISBN 0-06-103115-1 (mass market paperback)

Rei Shimura has managed to snag one of the most lucrative jobs of her career: a renowned museum in Washington, D.C., has invited her to exhibit rare kimonos and give a lecture on them. Within hours one of the kimonos is stolen, and then a body is discovered in a shopping mall Dumpster.

THE FLOATING GIRL

ISBN 0-06-109735-7 (mass market paperback)

During research for a comic-style magazine, Rei stumbles upon a disturbing social milieu of pre–World War II Japan. It evolves into something much darker when one of the comic's young creators is found dead—a murder that takes the tenacious Rei deep into the heart of Japan's youth underground.

THE FLOWER MASTER

ISBN 0-06-109734-9 (mass market paperback)

Life in Japan for a transplanted California girl with a fledgling antiques business and a nonexistent love life isn't always fun, but when the flower-arranging class Rei Shimura's aunt cajoles her into taking turns into a stage for murder, Rei finds plenty of excitement she's been missing.

THE SALARYMAN'S WIFE

ISBN 0-06-104443-1 (mass market paperback)

Rei is the first to find the beautiful wife of a high-powered businessman dead in the snow. Taking charge as usual, Rei searches for clues by crashing a funeral, posing as a bar-girl, and somehow ending up pursued by police and paparazzi alike. In the meantime, she manages to piece together a strange, ever-changing puzzle.